# THE SEAL

*Also by Meg Hutchinson*

ABEL'S DAUGHTER

FOR THE SAKE OF HER CHILD

A HANDFUL OF SILVER

NO PLACE OF ANGELS

A PROMISE GIVEN

BITTER SEED

A LOVE FORBIDDEN

PIT BANK WENCH

CHILD OF SIN

NO PLACE FOR A WOMAN

THE JUDAS TOUCH

PEPPERCORN WOMAN

*Writing as Margaret Astbury*

THE HITCH-HIKER

# THE SEAL

Meg Hutchinson

writing as MARGARET ASTBURY

Hodder & Stoughton

First published in 2002
by Hodder & Stoughton
A division of Hodder Headline



10 9 8 7 6 5 4 3 2 1



A CIP catalogue record for this title
is available from the British Library

ISBN 0 340 79295 7

Typeset by Hewer Text Ltd, Edinburgh
Printed and bound in Great Britain by
Mackays of Chatham PLC, Chatham, Kent

Hodder & Stoughton
A division of Hodder Headline
338 Euston Road
London NW1 3BH

My sincere thanks to Anthony Brooke (BROOKIE) for his help and advice with printing terms. A master printer now, he remembers his days as a 'Joey'.

[illegible] dark-haired figure [illegible]

Do I [illegible]

[illegible] of Sarum [illegible]

# Chapter One

'He is the one, the chosen of the Most High.'

'But we know nothing about him.' Max Gau looked at the tall dark-haired figure standing before a wide stone fireplace.

'Do I have to remind you, Max,' the dark-haired figure glanced across the elegantly furnished sitting room, 'we knew nothing of you when the servant of the Most High brought you into our circle. You were chosen, as were we all, to do his bidding, to do it, Max, without question; but of course should you wish to question him . . .'

Max Gau shifted nervously as a long-fingered hand touched a medallion hanging from a golden chain about his colleague's neck. The Seal of Ashmedai, the talisman of the First Lord of the Dark Throne, Archangel of the Prince of Darkness, Messenger of Satan. To call him was to call death itself.

'No.' He tried to swallow, feeling his throat constrict. 'No of course not, if the Master has chosen then we obey.'

'A wise choice, Max.'

Ebony eyes glittered coldly, sending a shudder along his spine. Max Gau looked away. Julian Crowley was no more to be trusted than the master he served, the master each one of these people served. They had all been chosen, brought one by one under the auspices of Crowley . . . and of Satan.

He had chosen well, the Lord of Darkness. Max only half listened as Julian Crowley continued to speak. Satan had made a bargain with each of them, a bargain he knew they could not break. He had given each of them that which their heart most desired and in return would take their soul.

His bargain had been made gladly. Relieved that at last the meeting was over, Max slid thankfully into his car. He had been glad to exchange his soul for what Crowley had offered. Slipping the car into gear he eased on to the road that would lead through the quiet Worcestershire villages to the M5 motorway.

The choice was his, Crowley had told him that night, the night he had found Christy with another man.

With the warmth of the car and the comfort of its expensive interior soothing the stress of the evening, the memories held deep in his heart slipped into his mind. He had been negotiating a deal intended to supply the motor trade with component parts, and the firm's managing director, Ben Ainsley, suggested he stay with the clients, '*Wine them, dine them, you know the routine, Max.*'

Easing the car around a tight bend, Max Gau smiled grimly to himself. Yes he knew the routine, it was he who practised it whenever a weekend away was called for! This was to be an important deal for the firm, things hadn't been going too well so he had agreed to act as host.

He had suggested Christy go along but Ainsley had laughed off the suggestion; the clients were expecting an all-boys affair, he'd said, grinning as he'd added that Max was a lucky bugger having a beautiful wife who adored him and he should give other poor sods the opportunity to make up what they were missing. But he had said to put the offer to Christy, see what she thought of the idea.

She hadn't wanted to go with him.

Max's foot pressed the accelerator pedal but he was oblivious of the speed sending him shooting along the narrow lanes.

'*You go, darling.*' She had smiled deep into his eyes as she had pulled him down on to her, that lovely body pressing itself into his. '*But don't stay too long . . . I miss you.*' The rest had been lost beneath her kiss, stifled by the passion of their lovemaking.

The business had gone well, finishing before the expected time and he had decided to cut the rest and return home. He hadn't rung Christy, wanting his early return to be a surprise. On the way back he had stopped off at some town to buy a necklace from a local jeweller, sapphires the exact colour of her eyes. His fingers gripped the wheel, memory slashing pain through every part of him. Christy was much younger than he was and so beautiful you wouldn't believe, so he'd bought a necklace he couldn't really afford because he loved seeing the excitement dance in those beautiful eyes, the smiles on her lovely face as she tore a package apart; yes, his wife loved surprises . . . but him? Not any more!

It had been early evening when he had finally reached home.

A trace of perspiration now trickled across his upper lip but Max ignored it.

He had let himself into the house and knowing Christy liked to soak in the bath he had not called out when finding the sitting room and kitchen empty.

Mindless of the danger of driving too fast along lanes barely wide enough to pass without brushing hedges on both sides, he pressed his foot harder on the pedal. The Prince of Darkness would have nothing new for Max Gau, he had already been to hell and back.

He had been halfway up the stairs when he had heard it. He swallowed hard as if trying to wash his mouth free of some vile taste.

Christy's voice. He had heard it. Thick with excitement, it had panted a name over and over again. Then he'd heard a man's voice, deep and husky it had seemed to vibrate off the walls of the staircase, rumbling like cannon fire, the shells smashing into his brain!

He closed his eyes against the pictures in his mind, opening them as the powerful car bounced off a gate set in the hedge, but even then the pictures stayed taunting him as they always did.

He had taken the stairs two at a time but the noise from the bedroom had masked his coming. Sheer impetus should have sent him crashing into that room, yet something had held him back, something stronger than himself, stronger than the rage that had burned in him, and he had stood just beyond the open door . . .

With his slate-coloured eyes fixed on some invisible scene, Max Gau's finely drawn mouth tightened to a non-existent line, a film of perspiration edging greying temples.

It had been open, not ajar but wide open as if whoever was inside that bedroom had been in too much of a hurry to close it. He had moved towards it – his breath came hard with the memory – whatever power had held him had released its grip, and the burning rage had disappeared beneath a douche of cold black hate.

That was the part he had not understood, that he still did not understand. All of the rage that had been in him only seconds before had vanished. He had listened to his wife moaning a name that wasn't his, listened to a man grunting, a man that wasn't him and he had been calm.

Seeing nothing but the shadows in his mind he let the car hurtle on.

He had watched from the doorway, watched his adoring wife. She had lain naked on the bed, legs and arms splayed wide, a man on top of her pushing and grinding while she moaned her pleasure. That was when he had gone into the next room to fetch the gun he kept there.

Christy would not have the gun in their bedroom, she couldn't stand having it anywhere near her; guns killed people, she said.

In the darkness of the car Max smiled. How right she was!

The man had been propped up on both hands when finally he had entered the bedroom – Max stared at the scene playing in his mind – propped up and ramming into her like a stag in full rut. Her legs had still been spread apart but her arms were around him now, long, tapering fingers stretched away from each other, perfectly manicured nails like tiny drops of blood against the bronze of the man's skin. He had watched that bronzed body, watched the tanned backside going up and down and thought how like Ben Ainsley, he liked his tan to cover everything.

*'More . . . oh yes . . . more, more like that . . . please more, that's the way I like it!'*

Christy's words lanced in his brain but now they gave no trace of pain.

Ben Ainsley had stopped pushing then. Max watched the scene play on, saw the glistening moisture film the man's bare back as he'd asked, *'Does Max give it to you like this?'* Christy had laughed at that.

Max felt his innards tighten.

She had laughed then slid her hands down to that brown backside, pulling him deeper into her.

*'Max!'*

He heard the laugh, soft and deprecating, as fresh in his mind as if Christy were in the car with him.

*'Max doesn't know how to screw a woman, not the way you do . . .'*

She had lifted upwards then, quick short movements that slid him in and out of her body.

*'. . . but then it's not his fault, I suppose, the prick he's got wouldn't stuff an olive with any satisfaction . . .'*

Drawing a long breath through widely flaring nostrils, Max smiled again.

That was when he had killed her!

He had walked to the side of the bed, put the gun to Christy's temple and pulled the trigger! Ainsley had leapt from the bed.

Gazing into darkness relieved only by the glare of the car

headlights Max seemed to see the terrified eyes of his managing director stare at him as they had stared then.

He had waved the barrel of the gun towards that still-open door and Ainsley had scrambled for it, his bronzed arse moving quicker than it had ever moved when riding a woman. He had let him reach the door before shooting him.

Satisfaction, rich and warming as hundred-year-old brandy surged through Max Gau.

Three shots . . . Three shots was what he had allowed himself. The first in the shoulder had spun Ainsley around, the look on his face one of sheer terror. The second shot had been aimed carefully, slow and deliberate to give Ainsley time to realise where it was going, but his hand had fallen just too late to protect the organ that had so satisfied Christy.

The third shot! Max laughed softly. That had been the best. Ben Ainsley had watched the gun lift and his eyes showed clearly that they had read the last sentence in the book of life. His mouth had only just opened to scream when the bullet took his throat away.

He would have thought that any man who took the pains Ben Ainsley had taken to get him out of the way so he could sleep with Christy would have taken her to some discreet hotel.

Whipping the car fast down the slip road Max swung on to the M5.

But then – he smiled again – Ben Ainsley never did think a deal through to all possible conclusions!

Nobody would have blamed him for panicking, in fact it was to be expected from a man who had just committed double murder. But he had not panicked.

Max Gau watched the drama unfold, it played across his mind's eye like a film on screen; he watched himself, calm as he might be with any client, pick up the bedside telephone and dial, every move, every thought controlled. The call to their favourite restaurant made, he had stepped over Ainsley's corpse and gone into the bathroom. Showered and dressed in fresh clothes, he had walked back to the bed. He had smiled at Christy, smoothing a strand of hair away from the dark hole at her temple, then he'd turned and left the house.

He had been having coffee when Julian Crowley had asked to speak with him. He had looked at the total stranger dressed smartly in black suit and white shirt, trying to remember if they had some pre-arranged business meeting he had forgotten. It was as the man sat down he had noticed his eyes, blacker than pitch but intensely brilliant, the sort people described as being able to see into your mind.

And what an apt description that was! Max glanced at the huge road sign, not really needing its direction. It had seemed at that moment the devil himself watched him across that table and, as he had found out, that too was an almost perfect description.

*'No, Max, you and I have not met before—'*

The not unattractive face had smiled but the eyes had remained cold and calculating as if reckoning on some degree of failure. But Julian Crowley had not failed!

*'– I know you rather well—'*

The voice had gone on, touching his brain like dark silk.

*'– I know for instance that you have just blown out your wife's brain and emasculated her lover before shooting him through the head. No, Max—'*

A slight movement of the hand had prevented Max's surprise becoming vocal.

*'Don't draw attention we can both do without. Pay the bill and we can leave, there is a lot to be done if you are not to face a charge of murder.'*

In the opposite lanes of the motorway, vehicle headlights shone in a continuous string. Glittering like the necklace he had bought for Christy! The thought curved his mouth in an icy smile. His wife would wear no more jewellery . . . neither would she feel another man between her legs!

The man had not followed him or been to his house. Max remembered the continuing conversation, the answer he had given.

*'So where's the use in hurrying? I have killed my wife and my shit of a partner, it will come to light soon enough.'*

Crowley had looked at him then, black serpentine eyes glinting in the light of the fake candles set in the centre of the table.

*'I fully intend it to come to light, only not in the way you think. Do as I say, Max, and the police will find a woman shot through the heart by a crazed lover.'*

He had laughed at that, attention calling or not he had laughed.

Christ, how bloody gullible did this Crowley fellow think he was? Would any man shoot off his own balls for a woman! So he had made a clean breast of it, the man need try no more clever police tactics, he could just make his arrest now without any more stupid little charades.

Julian Crowley had stood up then but his relentless eyes had held on to Max's. They had returned to the house to find everything just as he had left it, Christy naked on the bed, her legs still wide apart, while Ainsley was slumped in the doorway with his genital organs, or what was left of them, spread over a yard of carpet.

It was only in later years, following many experiences of seeing Crowley in action, that he had at last believed what had happened next.

The man had walked to the bed where Christy lay. The shot had burned an area of flesh around her temple but Crowley had not even flinched. He had spoken quietly, a few words Max had not caught then his voice had risen.

*'Great One, Prince of Darkness, show thy powers that the unbeliever may believe, that he who now walks in blindness may be given sight; Aged of the Ages, Unknown of the Unknown, Thou who was before the world, show now thy greatness.'*

With that he had taken a medallion Max had not noticed hanging beneath his jacket and, holding it over Christy, he had called out.

*'High Lord of Earth, thou who command the Malakhe Khabalah, hear the word of thy servant, let thy will be done.'*

At that the lights in the room had begun slowly to dim. Max remembered the way his pitying smile had faded on realising the room was not fitted with dimmer switches. Yet they had faded like gaslight faded when his grandmother had turned the jet low. Then finally the lamps had gone off completely but the room had remained lit: a clear, pale blue light enhanced the figure on the bed. And the light had come from Crowley!

Easing his foot off the accelerator Max nosed the car up to the motorway junction at West Bromwich, waiting his opportunity to circle the roundabout and join the M6.

The man's whole body had glowed. Max dropped back into memory. Light had emanated from Crowley, shimmering like pale blue torch-light. It was then the truly unbelievable happened, that which would have had Max Gau committed to an institution for the criminally insane had it ever been told.

The hole in Christy's temple, that round black-edged hole that marked her lovely face had closed, leaving not so much as a bruise, her legs had come together and she was no longer naked . . . Crowley hadn't touched her, yet somehow she was suddenly wearing a silk nightgown, a bullet hole directly above her right breast. Then he had turned towards Ainsley, the bastard Max had blown away an hour or so before.

The eyes had still been open. Max blinked perspiration from his eyes. Ainsley was stone dead but he had stood up as Crowley pointed. The pulpy mass at the base of his stomach had begun to solidify into re-formed flesh, genitals once more in pride of place and no mark to tell his pride and joy had once been blasted to hell.

Hell! Max laughed into the warm darkness. That was a good one, all things considered.

He had pumped three bullets into Ainsley, two where they counted most yet the man was on his feet and moving! He'd picked up his clothes, first putting on the G-string he had always said highlighted his manhood. Ainsley had thought that one hell of a good joke but then Ainsley had never been aware of his own coarseness. Next had gone on the cream silk shirt, dead arms sliding into sleeves, dead fingers doing up buttons and shoes until he was entirely dressed.

And all the time he, Max, had stared in dumb unbelieving silence. The man was dead for Christ's sake! The dead didn't get up and walk, but this corpse was walking . . . walking to the dressing-table, picking up Christy's comb, smoothing the hair Christy's fingers had played through. That done he had replaced the comb and walked easily to where the gun had been left on the bedside table. As he picked it up Max had noticed the flashy beige suit was stained with crimson spots where blood had sprayed from the gash that had once been a throat.

Then Crowley had begun to lower his hand and Ainsley's body had followed the motion, lowering like a puppet on invisible strings. He had rested only seconds in a crumpled heap before the legs had suddenly shot straight, the back had stiffened, while what remained of the head lay awkwardly, the neck craned its entire length as if the shot had almost lifted the body from its feet before sending it falling on to its back.

Crowley had spoken to him then.

Max guided the car along the exit road driving it through mostly deserted streets towards home.

Crowley asked him to look at a note now lying where the gun had been. He had made to pick it up but Crowley had prevented that, saying he was to read but not touch. It said Ben could not live without Christy, he had loved her for so long but she despised him. He had come to the house to beg her to leave with him and when she refused he had shot her, he loved her too much to let any other man have her. It was signed with Ben Ainsley's signature, and the writing was unmistakably his. Over the years they had worked together Max had come to recognise it as well as he did his own.

After he had read the note the pale blue light enfolding Crowley had faded and the electric lamps had come back on.

'*Well –*' he'd spoken in that soft tone that Max now knew so well '*– do we leave things as they appear now or do I reverse the process and you stand trial for murder?*'

He had not answered, his mind trying desperately to come to terms with what he had seen, what even in that confused state he *knew* he had seen, but Crowley hadn't touched Christy . . . he hadn't touched either of those bodies.

'*A little more, Max?*' Crowley had smiled. '*Let me show you a little more.*'

Then a series of pictures had floated in the empty space between them. Pictures where Max Gau was shown his future in one of Her Majesty's prisons, followed by another totally different scene where he was living in all the comforts life could give. Which would he choose?

He'd had nothing to lose.

Drawing the car up to a large stone-built house he sat looking at it.

Everything that had mattered in his life was dead. So he had accepted Crowley's offer, he had become a follower of the Left Hand Path, a member of a coven and Worshipper of Satan!

There had been no recourse with the law, a suicide note and the gun in Ainsley's hand had satisfied them, and once it was all over he had resigned his job and taken over the position Crowley had offered as managing director of Darlaston Printing.

So Julian Crowley had gathered in one more disciple for the Lord of Darkness, now it seemed he was bent on gathering in another.

Christmas [illegible]
sound; his body [illegible]
same way it had happened [illegible]
the Birth-in-Hand [illegible]
mind for it. But no one [illegible]
imagined I [illegible]
the wicket raising [illegible]

'Good evening, [illegible]'

Even the [illegible] quite early in the [illegible] words [illegible]

'What are you [illegible]'

The same [illegible]

It is what I [illegible]

Then [illegible] the joker, whether he [illegible]

I assure you I [illegible]

After the [illegible] might almost have [illegible]

I would rather [illegible] voice laughed softly [illegible] time—

# Chapter Two

Christ, not again! Richard Torrey swung around at the first soft sound, his body tensed to face a possible attacker. This was the same way it had happened before, except that night in the yard of the Bird-in-Hand he had expected an attack, prepared body and mind for it. But no one had insulted him this evening, no one had impugned his masculinity or affronted his sensibilities. So why the sudden raising of the short hairs?

'Good evening, Mr Torrey.'

From among shadows cast by a tall hedge to one side and the main body of the Frying Pan public house on the other the words slid quietly to where Torrey waited.

'What do you want?'

The voice seemed to smile at the snapped question.

'It is not what *I* want, Mr Torrey, but more what you want.'

Deep inside, Torrey had a feeling he should move on, leave the joker, whoever he was, to play his games with someone else.

'I assure you I am playing no game, Mr Torrey.'

At his sides Richard Torrey's fingers flexed. Christ, the man might almost have read his thoughts!

'I would rather that had been phrased a little differently,' the voice laughed softly, 'however we can discuss that some other time—'

'Look,' Torrey snapped, 'I don't know who you are or what you are about and furthermore I don't care for conversation with any man who hides himself in the shadows; either show your face or get lost now while you are still in one piece.'

'Ever the commando, but then perhaps that is to be expected. Training of the sort you were given dies hard.'

Who the hell was this? And why the background information?

'The reason is not important—'

Once more the unseen answered the unspoken. Torrey's blood chilled.

'– suffice it to say I am here to welcome you into . . . how shall I put it . . . into our organisation.'

'Organisation?' Torrey snapped again. 'I've joined no organisation and what is more I have no intention of doing so.'

'You need a job, Mr Torrey . . . take the one I offer. You may not get chance of another.'

Was that a threat? Was whoever was doing the talking alone or did he have a bunch of bully boys secreted among the shadows? Somewhere in the darkness a deeper blackness moved. Every painfully learned reaction coming into play, Torrey stepped backwards, bringing his spine against the pub wall. However many there were they would have to come at him from the front!

'I think it's time you left,' he growled, 'better for you to walk away than go in a mortuary wagon!'

Hearing the quiet laugh he peered into the semi-blackness. Christ, where was the bloody moon! Not that it would do much good, this bloke knew how to use cover; apart from the patch of denser shadow he could make out nothing. Torrey forced his breath to come slow and even. This customer knew the value of riding the dark! His arms automatically adopting a loose position, Torrey stared towards the shadowed hedge.

'Back off!' he warned softly. 'Back off unless you fancy leaving this earth by way of a broken neck!'

'I assure you that is the last thing I want.'

'You do a great deal of assuring for a man too afraid for his skin to show his face!'

The area of shadow Torrey guessed to be the man's head moved. To see him the better or position himself with a weapon? Arms deceptively loose at his sides, Torrey waited. Let the enemy make the first move.

'Believe me, Mr Torrey, my only intention is to help you.'

'I need nobody's bloody help,' Torrey spat the words coldly, 'especially not from—'

'I know.' A rustle in the darkness belied movement. 'Especially not from some character too shit-scared to show his face, is that not what you were about to say?'

What was the guy after? A little light blackmail? Pressing his back into the wall, Torrey waited.

'Let us not indulge in further childish argument, you wish to see my face, then you shall.'

Was this it? Torrey tensed, a silent laugh rumbling through his entrails. Let the bastard try and Inspector Bruce Daniels would be investigating another case of grievous bodily harm!

A few yards in front a shadow detached itself from the others, yet still seemed a part of them. With nerves cold as steel Torrey watched it. Christ, this man was good!

'You do not wish my help . . . I accept that, Mr Torrey.'

The words seemed alive, seemed to touch him with hot fingers. Steady! Torrey breathed regularly. Don't let him throw you! Staring at a shadow that seemed to float above the ground he snapped again.

'How come you know my name?'

'I know a great deal about you—'

The patch of shadow moved again but Torrey could make no more of it than the outline of a tall figure.

'– much more than just your name, but this is neither the time nor the place to discuss that. I have offered you assistance and now I am leaving, but we will meet again, Mr Torrey . . . most definitely we will meet again.'

As if on cue the moon sailed from behind deep cloud, etching the tall figure in silver.

Opening his mouth to reply, Torrey felt the words die on his tongue as light erupted, seeming to envelop the figure in flames, dancing silver-tipped flames. And from the centre of them a man's face smiled.

*'Witness my protection!'*

Gulping at the cold air of dawn Torrey sat up, one hand pushing dark hair back from his brow but failing to register the wetness of nervous sweat bathing his fingers, the nightmare still vividly alive. He hadn't thought of that episode in his life for years, yet that dream had shown every action, given every syllable . . . and more!

His nerves still jangling, he listened to the silence of the bed and breakfast he had booked into since returning to Darlaston, but it was a silence that throbbed with the boyish fears of childhood.

*'Deal with your own problems, you'll have to sooner or later.'*

That had been the answer when as a small boy he had gone to his father with some seemingly insurmountable problem; there had never been a hint of 'Let's look at it together, son.' Then after his father had walked out he had done just that, dealt with his own problems, knowing his mother had enough of her own to deal with, asking no help from her.

He had asked for no help with Ronald Webster.

The image printed on his eyelids faded but not the memories. Despite his efforts they played vividly in his mind.

Ron had been tall even at fifteen, six foot with an ego to

match. None of the other lads challenged his authority, supplemented as it was by a squad of the school's heavies seeing to it that the status quo remained static.

Three years younger than they were, Torrey had kept a low profile, somehow managing to pay the gang's 'fines' imposed for imaginary misdemeanours. Then had come the day he had been summoned to Court. This was the name the gang had given to a shed on Ron's father's allotment which they were allowed to use until Mr Webster came to work on his flowers and vegetables, usually around seven in the evening. Here Ron was judge and jury, here trial was conducted and sentence passed.

Passing his tongue over dry lips, Torrey tried to ease the fear that still gripped. He had been a kid, for Christ's sake! Who could blame him for being scared? But he wasn't a kid now, yet that dream had left him sweating!

They had laughed with each other, Ron, Jack Connor and Sam Deeley. He could see them now, faces shining with sweaty expectancy, grimy hands flitting about their flies like bloated bluebottles. He wasn't there because of any crime he'd committed. Ron had grinned when telling him that. The gang had invited him here because they liked him, they wanted him to join them, to become part of their élite.

*'You'll like being with we.'*

Torrey saw again the little eyes glittering among the puffy folds of acne.

*'You'll 'ave power, Ricki, none of the other kids will dare stand up to you.'*

Torrey swallowed hard, the memory of what came next a sickness in his throat.

Ron Webster's fingers had released the buttons of his trousers and pushing them downwards, his two henchmen grabbing Torrey's arms and marching him across the shed to a bench stood against the far wall.

*'An' you'll like the things we do together, Ricki—'*

Ron had stepped out of his trousers. A hand-knitted Fair Isle pullover that must have once belonged to his father reached only to a couple of inches below his waist, adding to the nakedness below.

*'– especially the things we're gonna do now.'*

*'I be next, Webbo.'*

Sam Deeley had leered as Torrey's own clothing had been snatched downwards.

*'Eager to play ain't ya!'*

Across Torrey's inner vision the mouth of Ron Webster split into a flabby grin, displaying teeth no toothbrush had ever seemed to help, while folds of spotty flesh encroached further on to small glittering eyes, almost closing them away.

*'Ya said as I could be next, Webbo!'*

*'An' I meant it—'*

The answer rocked in Torrey's brain now as it had all those years ago.

*'– you'll be next after me an' then Connor after you . . . but it might be a long time . . . I don't know 'ow many goes I might want!'*

Fingers thick as Cumberland sausages had closed around the column of flesh rising from a mound of red hair, all three boys laughing as Torrey had been spun on to his face across the workbench.

Torrey's eyes flicked open. For all the years that had passed since that day he still felt the same relief he had felt the very next moment. An act of God? Maybe, but all he had known was that fire had put an end to their dirty little initiation ceremony.

Had it been the force with which they had thrown him across the bench or had one of them knocked against that shelf?

All he'd known and all he'd cared about was that the gallon demi-john had come crashing to the ground and the next moment half of the shed had been an inferno.

Petrol, he had heard people saying for days after. Ron's father had kept petrol in a glass jar and when it smashed it had only taken a spark from the metal studs hammered into the heels of the boys' shoes to ignite it. The three of them had been badly burned but he hadn't been so much as singed. Why? Maybe he would never find out, but one thing he did know: the rest of that nightmare was no real answer.

He was awake now, the hold that dream had had should be gone, he should be laughing at himself for the fool he was. Only he wasn't laughing!

The fire had put an end to the happenings in that shed, but in the nightmare it had been different.

They had thrown him across the bench but instead of that explosion of flame there had been a silence, a silence broken only by the rapid, excited breathing of boys intent on abusing him. But at that moment the shed had begun to vibrate, shaking as if caught in the throes of an earthquake while wind screamed like a banshee out of hell. Then had come the shadows, creeping out of juddering walls, growing, spreading, filling every corner, and among it all he had seen the faces of those three lads, their fear becoming terror as shadows emanated from wooden walls. Separate at first the shadows had combined, drawing each into the other until the whole stood floor to roof in a nebulous breathing cloud of blackness.

Somewhere to his left, Deeley had whimpered, then bolted for the door, but a thin whiplash of shadow snaked from the central mass, whirling itself about the running boy, smashing him aside before recoiling.

And all the time he, Torrey, once again twelve years old and petrified with fear, had stood and watched.

Webster had stood a few feet away his mouth slack, his eyes screaming his fear.

*'Wha— what is it, Webbo?'*

A flicker of shadow smoked towards the frightened whisper. Ronald Webster made no reply.

*'Where . . . where's it come from?'* Jack Connor screamed as

the shadow flicked again, a quicksilver movement that touched the frightened face, leaving a scorched gash where lips had been.

Throwing an arm across his eyes, Torrey tried to shut out the pictures that were nothing more than the fruits of an overtired mind; but still they came passing across his inner vision with slow relentlessness.

No one in the shed moved. No sound other than the gibbering from that charred mouth disturbed the stillness. Then had come a coldness clawing at bodies sweating with fear. In the deep gloom he had looked at Webster and seen the short white wisps of rapidly drawn breath.

Then the snaking whip of shadow had reached for Webster. A scream as if he had been touched by molten metal opened the boy's mouth as the shadow curled about his semi-naked body, leaving trails of smoking flesh as it withdrew.

Then it had turned to him!

Wide awake now, fully conscious of the fact that part at least had been a dream and had no basis in reality, he felt again the fear he had seemed to feel in his sleep, the horror of waiting for that hand to point to him.

But there had been no whiplash of shadow, no burning of his flesh. The shadows had begun to thin, to split into drifts of grey-black mist that, while he stared, began to recede into the walls of the shed; and as the last of it dissolved the voice had come. Clear and unmistakable as the rest of that dream he had heard the words . . .

*'Witness my protection!'*

The words still playing in his mind, Torrey finished the last of his breakfast. It was strange even for a tired brain, and as for the rest of his nightmare, that had been rubbish, straight out of a kid's comic.

Come in Superman, he chuckled to himself, save the world from the demons of hell!

A dream and nothing more, what was strange about that? Walking from breakfast to tea-time looking for work that was never there then, after the one drink he could afford on dole pay, coming back to his room too tired to sleep was enough to give anybody nightmares.

No, the real strangeness was the reality!

That petrol had burst into flame, that shed had been incinerated, the three lads only just getting out in time, but even then they had suffered multiple burns while he—he had suffered none.

He hadn't run from the shed; although he was terrified it had felt almost like he was being guided out, shielded from the leaping flames. And he had told no one he had been there with the other three nor the reason for it . . . and though he had lived in the same street as them, seeing them every day except for those spent in the Army, they too had never once spoken of it.

How many nights had he lain awake trying to reason with what had seemed impossible? And when he'd closed his eyes it was with the dread of reliving it all again and of course he had, but never with the clarity of that dream . . . and never with the trimmings! Lord, what had it taken to dredge something like that up? Even the business of Anna's ghost had been nothing compared to that.

Anna! Leaving the table he blinked as he walked out into the bright sunshine of early summer. The pain of that affair was at last beginning to fade. He had scoffed at Martha Sim, calling her attempts to free him of that haunting nothing more than hocus pocus but without it – he turned towards the town centre – without it there might well be no Richard Torrey!

Ghosts! Who would have thought he could have believed?

And even now he was not certain he did, his only certainty was that if any of his Army colleagues got wind of it he'd be a laughing stock for years to come.

Torrey, the toughest bloke in the platoon . . . Torrey, a believer in ghosts!

He smiled grimly to himself. It didn't bear thinking of.

# Chapter Three

'C'mon, Scotty, it's only kids playing bogey man, where's the news in that?'

David Anscott, editor of the *Star* glanced up at the young woman facing him across a desk littered with copy held over for the lead story of the evening edition. He had no time for arguing but Kate Mallory always argued.

'Mebbe, mebbe not, Kate,' he answered patiently, 'but you don't know that for sure and neither does Daniels even though kids and vandalism is what he puts it down to.'

'So what do you put it down to, if not kids?'

Slipping a hand into her capacious leather bag, her fingers closing about the pack of Rothmans, Kate let them lie as she caught her editor's glance. Scotty put up with most things but smoking in his inner sanctum? That was a definite no!

'I don't put it down to anything.' David Anscott took a pencil from behind his ear, running a line through a neatly typed sentence as he spoke. ''Cos unlike a Hollingsworth's pig I don't draw my own conclusions, at least not until I've heard the report.'

'Unlike what?'

With his eyes on the paper he was mutilating, the editor shook his head. 'Never mind . . . it was all a bit before your time;

now be a good little reporter and get yourself where you should be before anything that might be there, isn't. It'll do no good you turning up when the last of the harvest has been gleaned.'

'Kids with nothing better to do than play around with cans of spray paint! I'm no alchemist, Scotty, I can't make gold out of lead!'

While he kept his head bent over the next sheet of paper, the hint of a smile touched David Anscott's mouth as Kate continued to grumble. She was a fine reporter; it was a good job she had done on that drugs case, getting into Bartley's supermarket and bringing home first-hand material. The nationals had picked up on that. He ran the pencil through a paragraph. How long before one of them offered Kate something she couldn't refuse?

'Keep practising, Kate.' He kept the smile hidden. 'One day you'll hit gold and then we'll all be able to retire.'

'You retire!' It was Kate's turn to smile. 'It would take a heavy-duty road drill to prise you free of that chair and then I doubt they'd make a clean job of it.'

This was the third time this year! Hitching the bag that held everything from Tippex to Tampax, Kate left the office lighting a much wanted cigarette the moment her wedge heels tapped the footpath.

The first time it had been lights. They had been reported as being seen flickering in the churchyard at Bentley Mill Estate. It had caused a bit of a stir and the usual bevy of explanations from flying saucers to black-magic rituals.

Drawing deeply, Kate blew smoke from a pursed mouth.

The only flying saucers seen in Darlaston were those Maisie Billings threw at her husband when he returned home on a Saturday night having had a drop too much of the hard stuff, and the only black magic came in boxes marked 'chocolate'.

Second time around it had been singing, screeching some had called it, but by the time the police had arrived all the would-be pop artists had disappeared. Both times nearby graves had been daubed with paint. Probably it had been intended as a sort of symbol, a mark of the particular group of kids who were playing their stupid games, but if so it was one she had not seen before. But that didn't mean anything. Looking at the half inch stub of cigarette Kate took a chance on one last puff. Tabs were too damned costly to chuck away before they were smoked so low they scorched the lips.

Then a month ago it had happened a third time. Deep in thought, grinding the last of the cigarette underfoot Kate walked toward, the bus stop.

'It were like the times it 'appened afore.'

A stout woman looking like a post box in her bright red coat was holding forth to all that wished to listen . . . and tough for the ones that didn't! Kate thought as she joined the queue of people.

'I told my 'usband, it be them black magicians I told 'im, they be practisin' their evil up in the churchyard. Well I wasn't 'aving no bobbies tellin' me I 'adn't seen nuthin so I meks my 'usband get up an' come see for 'isself.'

Whether he wanted to or not! Kate smiled to herself.

'I told 'im, I did,' the stout woman continued her oration, 'I said to 'im, if we both sees it then can't nobody say we be imaginin' things.'

'That's right . . . that be right enough.'

Several women murmured assent as the stout woman's challenging look swept the queue.

'An' what was it yoh reckoned yoh seen?'

Thank God for small mercies! Fishing her purse from the depths of her shoulder bag Kate appeared not to look at a short wiry man dressed in baggy jeans. He'd asked the question she wanted answering.

'It were folk, men or women I can't be sayin' for they was covered 'ead to foot in some sort o' dark robes—'

'What time was this?' the little man interrupted again.

' 'Alf past midnight, that were the time I called them bobbies.'

Nodding his head the man smiled. 'Oh ar! So it were 'alf past midnight, at that time it be pitch black yet yoh see a bevy o' folk dressed in dark clothes molin' around a churchyard that be well back from any 'ouses. Yoh got bloody good eyesight, missus!'

'Good enough to see yoh be about to get a lift from a car lessen yoh get yoh're backside on the footpath.'

The blare of a car horn and the two-fingered salute of its irate driver as it whipped past had the man jump back into place among the line of grinning women.

'Might 'ave done a bit of good had it hit 'im, Hil',' one of them laughed. 'It were 'is arse 'e were talkin' through so mebbe that car would 'ave shook 'is brains up a bit for that's where most men 'ave theirn!'

The arrival of the bus cut off the woman's story. Kate watched her heave herself on board and take a seat near to the front, the rest of the women clustering around her, eager for the rest of her story.

Just as you are, Kate Mallory . . . a girl can't get it from the cops so she must needs get it somewhere else. Choosing her own seat Kate held the fare ready in her hand.

'Like I was sayin' afore some smart Herbert put his pennorth in—'

The lady in red . . . nobody argues with the lady in red. Mentally matching words to the tune of the hit song of Chris de Burgh, Kate watched the woman tilt her head to allow her glance to follow the man as he climbed the stairs to the upper deck.

'– we seen 'em, my 'usband and me seen 'em clear as clear. They was in a circle all dancin' round a fire, it lit the place up it did, that be how come I knows they was dressed in them robes, I could see 'em outlined by that firelight.'

'Dancin' round a fire in the churchyard, an' at midnight . . . it meks your flesh crawl to think what they might 'ave bin up to!'

'There ain't no *think* about it.' The heavily built woman replied, stuffing her ticket into her pocket. 'It be black magic they be up to an' no which way about it!'

'Did the bobbies catch 'em?'

'Not them!' The first woman's tone was cynical. 'It be my bet they d'ain't want to for the answer were the same as before, there were nobody in that churchyard. What did they expect? By the time they dragged theirselves up there them folk 'ad disappeared.'

'Now that were a sensible bit o' magic.' Handing Kate her ticket the conductor winked as he slipped the coins she gave him into the leather bag hung from his belt.

Would Scotty want the woman interviewed? Was the Pope Catholic!

Taking pen and notepad from her bag Kate scribbled brief reminders of what had been said, then gave up when she could not read the lines and squiggles that were the result of the jerky ride. She would leave the bus where her lady in red left it and hope she was as forthcoming as she had been so far.

'Yoh'll see for yourself if yoh goes up there, yoh'll see for yourself the paint daubed over them there 'eadstones and the black patch in the grass where they danced around that fire.'

Sat in the neat-as-a-new-pin living room of her informant, Kate accepted the freshly brewed cup of tea. The woman had been willing if not downright eager to give her story to the *Star*. 'Tell folk what them bobbies along of Victoria Road ain't tellin' 'em!' she had answered when Kate approached asking for her account of the happenings in the churchyard.

'There be black magic goin' on.' The woman's eyes sought Kate's over the rim of rarely used Royal Albert china. 'You mark my words, there be a coven somewhere an' they've chose Darlaston as the place to worship the devil . . . that be what me an' my 'usband seen and 'eard last night, the fire and the chantin', it were devil worship and nothing that detective inspector can say will tell me otherwise.'

'Did the police say what they thought had been going on?'

Seeing the glance going to the notepad still balanced on her knee and interpreting the hesitation that followed, Kate slipped pad and pen into her bag.

'I don't want you writin' what was said in that newspaper. Bobbies 'ave long memories and my 'usband as bin 'ad for speedin' a couple o' times as it is.'

'You have my word, but if you would rather not say any more . . .'

Stopping the woman from talking would be the difficult part! Looking down as she lifted the cup to her lips, Kate hid the smile lurking in her hazel eyes.

'They said it was my imagination, no more than the moonlight playin' tricks, that there 'ad bin no fire an' nobody dancin' in that churchyard. But when we went up there this morning me and my 'usband we seen for ourselves, seen the things them bobbies denied, seen the daubings and the scorched earth . . . ar!' She glanced meaningfully at Kate. 'And we seen the looks on the faces o' them young bobbies; scared they was and not only of that inspector neither! They knows there be summat bad goin' on, summat as 'ad their flesh crawling same as mine. I tells yoh, luv, if they don't catch them devil worshippers soon there'll be a lot worse than paint on gravestones next!'

'You say you saw for yourself the paint sprayed everywhere?'

'I seen it all right.' The woman's tightly permed hair bobbed vigorously. 'But it weren't sprayed everywhere, not careless like, it were more methodical as if whoever done it chose each place specific . . . as if to show why it were done.'

She could do with a tab. Kate felt the longing for a cigarette that came whenever she sat with a cup of tea. But she couldn't light up in the house of a stranger. Suffocating the urge beneath a mouthful of liquid she listened as the woman continued.

'It were sprayed on each place a cross was carved in them stones, blottin' it out almost complete and another drawed in its place, drawed upside down, and underneath it were a sort of design.'

'A design?' Kate lifted an eyebrow.

The woman nodded again. 'I be sure of it and so does my 'usband. We both seen it clear as day afore that vicar 'ad it scrubbed off. The mark of kids was what that inspector called it, their badge, the sign of their gang . . . but kids round 'ere ain't never bin ones for desecrating the cemetery, I doubts if any of 'em has the courage to be anywheres near one in the daytime much less play games in one at the dead of night.'

'Can you describe the mark you saw?'

It was of little consequence other than to make Kate appear interested, and she owed the woman that, after all she had agreed to 'talk to the paper'. Laying her cup on the mock silver tray embossed with the royal arms and the words 'The Queen's Silver Jubilee', Kate waited, seeing a frown of concentration play over the plump face.

'I can't rightly say as to what shape it took, it were like nothing I've seen afore, but if you likes I could try drawing it, though mind, you ain't to put it in no paper!'

The same terms as before! Kate nodded agreement. Lord she was dying for that tab! At least Scotty couldn't say she hadn't earned the next one.

Passing pen and notepad she took them back as the woman finished her sketch, glancing at it before slipping them once more into the capacious maw of her bag.

The woman was right. Making her way towards the cemetery Kate flicked through the filling cabinet that was her memory. Of all the signs and slogans she had seen daubed on the walls of buildings, the many works of the town's spray-can artists, she had never come across the like of the one drawn on her notepad. She would just check that nothing had been left for the inquisitive then she would pay a visit to the local library.

* * *

This wasn't going to get her on to any one of the nationals. Having spent an hour in the library Kate walked along Picturedrome Way. Her landlady had often talked of the old fleapit cinema that had once stood here, laughing at the memory of how as children she and her friends jostled for places that would best receive a drenching from the perfume sprayed over the audience by an usherette wielding a hand pump; it wasn't until years later she learned that the so-desired perfume was none other than disinfectant! 'Change,' Mrs Price had mourned, 'everything 'as changed.'

Joining Crescent Road Kate walked towards the park; it was about the only place left where a girl could have herself a cigarette without somebody glaring and muttering about passive smoking! Her landlady was right about things changing, she could hardly remember a time when her father or the rest of the men in Birtley didn't have a tab in their mouth.

*'Everything 'as changed.'*

As she took a seat on one of the benches placed at intervals between the neatly bordered flowerbeds the words echoed in her mind. But not everything had changed, she was still a reporter on a farting little provincial newspaper!

Finding the much-wanted cigarette she lit it, holding it in her mouth while she returned lighter and packet to her bag. They had taken her story of Bartley and his dope-peddling friends, some of them had even run it as their lead with headlines splashed across the front page. But they hadn't taken her! She blew a stream of smoke, watching it drift listlessly across a circular bed filled with scarlet geraniums. Another lady in red! One had given her a story, the other was trying to lift her spirits. Kate smiled ruefully, both had failed. The woman had done all that was asked of her. Kate apologised to her finer feelings. But interesting as it might be to folk hereabout it was hardly a story that would have the nationals beating a path to her door. It wouldn't exactly have her editor salivating! Would Scotty bother with it . . . would he slip it in between the adverts? She wouldn't put it to a vote!

Flicking the stub of cigarette between finger and thumb she watched it arc through the air and descend in a curve into oblivion among the scarlet-headed blossoms. Was that the path her career was taking, the peak having been reached with the heroin bust, leaving her to descend into the oblivion of a poky little newspaper?

Reaching for the copy she had written up while in the reference section of the library she stared at it. Maybe she should be happy with what she had, after all it could have been a job on one of the freebies, those papers pushed through letter boxes and from there straight into dustbins, most of their recipients not even bothering to open them.

*'Be thankful for what you have, hinny . . .'*

Those had been the last of her aunt's words as the family had waved her off from Newcastle-upon-Tyne Central Station. But they were words hard to live by for a girl with ambition; 'any job is better than no job' was the wrong signpost on her path of life. Yet there were those who would be glad of any job, Richard Torrey for example. No, she corrected her thoughts as a picture of a tall, well-muscled, dark-haired man flashed across her inner vision, perhaps not any job.

They had met while she had been following the lead given her by Amos Hodgkin; Torrey had been driver-cum-bodyguard to Philip Bartley, one of the top players in that lucrative drug business. Torrey hadn't known of that side of things until the very end, he had sat on Bartley's tail for a much more personal reason, the feeling that in some way the man was responsible for the murder of Anna.

Anna! She had thought Torrey to be speaking of a woman he was in love with, but when at last he had told her of how she had left him to play whore with Philip Bartley and his friends she knew that love was dead.

Automatically reaching for the half-full packet of Rothmans she paused, then let it lie. Scotty was right, she smoked too many.

Torrey had almost been driven crazy . . . and all for a whore! It was incredible when you knew him, an ex-commando, a man with a 'take no shit from anybody' attitude. That he could fall in love with a trollop was impossible to believe; but then how many men were ruled by their heart? And Torrey was no different.

So was the story of the hitch-hiker impossible to believe? A ghost who had followed each member of that dope syndicate around, haunted them to their deaths then tried to take Torrey the same way. She hadn't believed at first, who the hell believed in ghosts? But on getting to know Torrey better, watching the emotions tear him apart as he spoke of the Anna he had loved and the Anna that had betrayed him, she realised he wasn't a man to invent things. Hitch-hiker, ghost, emissary of the devil – call it what you would – the fact remained something had, and memory of it still sometimes did, haunt Richard Torrey. And now the ex-commando was on the dole and, along with many others, searching for the work the government told them was out there, that all they needed to do was look for it; the only problem was the government hadn't said which direction to go and not all roads led to Rome!

The notepad, forgotten on her lap, slipped to the ground. Retrieving it Kate glanced at her notes then at the crude drawing she herself had made, the same design as her lady in red had drawn earlier. She had finished writing up her report and was ready to leave the library when she had remembered the real reason for her being there. The sketch the woman had made for her. It had been as though she recognised it . . . no, not the sketch exactly but something about it. The thought had plagued her as she had returned to the Bull Stake, staying in her mind as she left the bus to walk the few dozen yards to the library; once inside it had disappeared as she struggled to inject interest into the alleged happenings in that cemetery. But as she had shoved pen and pad into her bag, that paper with its sketch had caught her eye and suddenly she was a teenager again, one of three frightening themselves to death with stories of black magic and the occult. That was where she had seen that design before! They had found a book by Aleister somebody or other, who claimed to be the most famous black magician of all time, and something very similar to that sketch had been in that book, but it wasn't quite the same.

It had been after some coaxing that the librarian had at last come up with a book kept only for the serious student. Christ, what did he think she was going to do with it! Summon the evil one right then and there! The book had been written by a man called Caddiente and the language was ancient but she had found what she was looking for in a chapter called 'The Chosen'. The sketch, it seemed, was of the symbol of this elect few, the sign of their high calling. The Seal of Ashmedai, a triangle enclosed in a double circle and in turn enclosing three interwoven sixes, was claimed by Caddiente to be the most potent of all the forces blessed by the devil and whoever knew its secrets could command that most powerful of all demons to do his bidding.

Had it done that for Caddiente, that self-styled prince of the black arts? And was someone here in this town picking up that man's fallen cloak, following in his footsteps?

Who the hell believed in ghosts? Kate folded the slip of paper, dropping it back into her bag. Who the hell believed in black magic!

If what she had been told by that woman was the truth, and providing the sketch she had drawn really was a representation of something sprayed over those gravestones, then it seemed somebody did . . . and that somebody was at work in Darlaston!

# Chapter Four

That had been one more waste of time! Richard Torrey nodded to a smiling receptionist as he left the offices of the motor component company. They were taking on no more workers, in fact it was a high probability they would be announcing redundancies in the near future. So why the hell had he been told to come here!

Irritation streaking through him, he turned along Pinfold Street. Had somebody in the Job Centre done their job so well they hadn't taken the company off the files? Busy! He snorted. Each time you went in one woman was filing her nails, and the bloke? Less said about that one the better; but one of these days that smarmy smile and condescending 'look here my good man' tone of voice was likely – no, positively – going to get him a knuckle lunch.

So, where to next? Coming to the Bull Stake he stood looking at the town centre his parents had known so well and now wouldn't know at all. Streets that hadn't seen a man other than a shopkeeper during the day now saw them dotted everywhere as they collected their dole and hurried home with their pittance or hung about, too disillusioned to do anything else. The whole place seemed to be in limbo, waiting for the last axe to fall.

He had thought of settling in another part of the country but given what you read or heard via the media, everywhere was in the same straits. But he had to find something soon or go crazy.

His glance following a bus as it pulled to a stop, he watched several passengers alight. Lord, was this to be the be-all and end-all of his days, standing on a street corner counting folk off a bus?

'I thought it was you.'

Turning towards the voice, Torrey gave a half-smile. 'Bold, beautiful and in the flesh!'

Kate Mallory's slightly tilted mouth tilted a little further as she smiled back.

'Would that be you or me?'

'Let's say both.'

'Deal!' Kate hitched her ever-present bag higher on to her shoulder. 'Now for the second compromise, we share the price of a coffee and a sandwich, but –' she raised a finger '– it had better be somewhere I can have a ciggy or I warn you I'll scream.'

'Throw the fags away,' Torrey's half-smile gave way to a positive grin, 'my life could use the excitement right now!'

'For that you can buy me a drink . . . and suddenly I don't feel I want coffee.'

'You'll have what you're given, my girl.'

He had liked this girl with her funny Geordie accent since first meeting her. Torrey fell into step leading the way to the Frying Pan. The place had a new landlord who had changed its face somewhat, serving meals in the lounge, but he had left one corner for customers who liked a smoke. Kate Mallory could have her cigarette there.

Her smile approving as she settled into a corner alcove, Kate swept the room with a glance. Not quite as it had been the last time she had been in this pub, but then changes didn't take time these days.

'Nice.' She nodded to Torrey as he set drinks on the table. 'But what have they done with the rest of the old fixtures and fittings?'

Drinking first from his own pint of Banks's best, Torrey followed her glance. 'Can't say I've noted anything missing, all seems here to me, rearranged but here.'

'Mmm!' Kate brought out the packet of Rothmans, selecting one and putting it between her lips then holding the lighter to it and looking at him through a thin stream of grey. 'Strange that . . . I would have expected you to notice, though Echo Sounder probably won't mind.'

'Sounder . . . that fixture and fitting!' Torrey's grin flashed again. 'Oh, he's still here but says the lounge be a bit too flash for him, he stays put in the bar . . . mind so far I haven't heard the rest of this half of the clientele making any complaint on that score.'

Probably not. Kate sipped the coffee she had changed her mind and asked for as they had entered the pub. Somehow she missed the scruffy little man, and apart from that she preferred to keep traces on him for you never knew when he might prove useful again.

'He was quite a help telling me about Amos Hodgkin . . . I doubt I would have guessed Bartley's game without it.'

'We all have something to thank him for but don't go telling him or the price of information will rocket, and inflation is high enough already.'

'And payment is not all taken in cash.' Kate's hand closed over the cigarette packet and dropped it into her bag. 'Although I'd be willing to trade a few tabs for a lead on something . . . in fact anything right now. Scotty says I spend too much on them as it is but at this moment I reckon I would be getting the best of a bargain.'

'That bad?'

Kate waited while the pretty young waitress placed a sandwich with salad in front of each of them, her smile bestowed on Torrey.

'The underestimation of the year. As me mam would have said, I've seen more activity in a ragman's vest!'

As his teeth sank into a ham sandwich, Torrey nodded. 'Same here,' he said swallowing, 'seems like I'm always in the lezzer when I ought to be in the lane.'

'You're always what?'

'It's an old Black Country saying, it means I never seem to be in the right place at the right time. Like earlier on, I was sent for interview for a job but when I got there the manager said they were firing not hiring.'

Selecting a sandwich of her own, embellishing it with several slices of tomato, Kate took a bite before answering.

'How particular are you about what you do?'

'How particular can I afford to be! Anyway I wasn't too particular to drive Philip Bartley around.'

'From what you told me the job itself didn't seem too bad.'

Taking another drink he shook his head and helped himself to a second sandwich.

'It wasn't. In fact you could say I had an easy number. Bartley spent five days a week above the shop, he liked to keep an eye as well as a finger on everything that came or went in that supermarket, which left me free to come and go as I liked and a Rover to come and go in. I must say not many blokes in Darlaston had a job like that, not to mention a cottage in grounds like some of 'em never even get to see, much less treat as their own.'

'You sound as if you miss it.'

'Kate,' he looked at her across the table, 'I've been many things in my thirty years but never a hypocrite, but I would be one now if I said I didn't miss it; except—'

Kate filled the rest of the sentence for herself: except for the suspicion his employer had had a hand in the murder of Anna.

'If you don't mind another driving job I know of one that's going.'

The hope springing to those dark eyes made up for the scolding she might well get for giving advance knowledge of an advert scheduled for the *Star*'s evening edition. 'It's the printing works along at Kings Hill, they are looking for a driver.'

He had his ordinary road licence plus an HGV licence he'd acquired in the army, that should equip him for driving any vehicle.

'The advert doesn't state any salary,' Kate was still talking, 'it says that is to be agreed. No doubt they mean they will pay the government-stipulated minimum and no more.'

That would do. Torrey pushed away the remainder of his beer. The extra salary he would have liked could be written off as a health benefit: the job, if he got it, might just save him dying from a surfeit of boredom.

'Strike now before the iron goes into the fire.' He was on his feet while Kate was still heaving her bag from the floor. Taking three steps to his every one she struggled to keep pace and was glad when they reached the Bull Stake and she could climb thankfully on to her bus. She would keep her fingers crossed that he get the job . . . but that was not all they would stay crossed for. She liked Richard Torrey . . . liked him enough to hope he stayed in Darlaston . . . at least as long as she did!

'This is all you got?'

Kate winced as David Anscott ran a quick eye down the page it had taken her some time to revise and re-revise. It was all hearsay, nothing first-hand or concrete about it. The story of the lady in red. She held her breath. The piece might as well bear that heading, the words were mostly that woman's.

'Vandalism, kids with nowt better to do, that's what the police say?'

Her breath still tight as the vaults of the Bank of England, Kate made no reply. Talking as he read was only one of her editor's skills and he missed on neither of them.

'You went to that cemetery, you saw for yourself? Then I suppose there can be nothing to add to this piece.'

Kate let the breath free.

'Get the shots taken the last time this thing happened, tell photography to put one alongside this and get it ready for bed.'

Back at her own desk, Kate touched the packet of Rothmans. A tab would help settle her nerves. Better not take the risk! She withdrew her fingers . . . God was in His heaven at the moment and all was right with Scotty's world, best not upset the issue. He had accepted her copy but it had not been the whole of what she had heard that morning. It had no mention of the sketch that woman had made, and she had not shown the diagram to Scotty or told him of the time she had spent in the reference section of the library finding corroboration of it in a book by a man named Caddiente.

That part he would have torn up but not before throwing her out on to the street. Rubbish, he would have called it. Taking the piece of paper from her bag she laid it on the desk. He was probably right; but then again one man's rubbish was another man's treasure.

The Seal of Ashmedai.

She stared at the convoluted numbers enclosed by the circled triangle.

Prince of the Throne, Highest of the Demonic High, First Lord of Satan.

Those had been only some of the titles Caddiente's book afforded the one this seal represented.

First Lord of Satan!

Kate stared at the drawing. What was he doing here in Darlaston?

* * *

'The bobbies think as how these goings on over at Bentley be the first time as 'appened but it ain't.'

'What was that?'

Her mind only half on question and answer, Kate Mallory toyed with the idea of going to her room. She could light up there but this was the time she usually spent with her landlady, sharing with her as much of any day's activity as was feasible; to walk away now might hurt the feelings of the woman who had become almost like a mother to her.

'This 'ere!' Annie Price laid the newspaper flat on a brilliantly polished coffee-table that had never once felt a coffee cup, her fingers tapping the article carrying Kate's name. 'It ain't the first time, I remember the same thing 'appening when I was just a little wench; course there weren't no cans o' spray paint in them days, they had to use a brush, but whatever they used results was the same.'

'Sorry . . . what was that you were saying?'

'This!' Annie tapped the paper harder. 'I be sayin' I've seen this thing afore and not three weeks ago neither.'

Her interest still only vague, Kate glanced to where the older woman's fingers rested on the photograph the *Star* had published, along with the report about several paint-daubed gravestones, showing clearly an upside-down cross.

'I don't care what Daniels and the rest o' them bobbies says, this ain't the first time!'

Thoughts of a cigarette already gone from her mind, Kate glanced from the photograph to her landlady.

'Did you just say you think you might have seen something like this before?'

'I did, wench, and you'd have 'eard had you been listenin', which you ain't. I didn't say I thought I *might* have seen something, I said I '*ad* seen, and not something *like* it but this actual thing.'

With the page half-turned, Annie looked up sharply as Kate's hand came down on it, holding it in place.

'When was this, Mrs Price?'

'It's been some years, I don't remember.'

'Try.' Kate's eyes were suddenly alive.' Please try.'

'It . . . it were during the war, like I says I were only a little wench but I remembers my mother and the neighbours were right upset by it.'

During the war . . . over fifty years ago! Would memory serve after so many years?

'Why were they so upset?' Kate urged gently, but was not surprised by the older woman's sharp retort.

'Why do you think, wench! We were 'aving the living daylights knocked out o' we night after night, never knowin' whether the next bomb had our address on it, then comin' up from the shelters to find that lot daubed over graves, it ain't surprisin' they was upset!'

'What did they think it was?'

Annie looked again at the photograph. 'Well they didn't think it were Hitler droppin' cans o' paint, and they didn't think as it was kids, they said it was . . . eh, wench, you'll think they were a bunch o' loonies but they said . . . they said as 'ow it were black magic.'

Kate's teeth clenched and she hoped the lurch of her stomach didn't reflect in her eyes.

'Ar, wench,' Annie went on, 'that were what folk thought then, they reckoned they was black magicians worshipping the devil in return for him ensuring Germany won the war. I remember my mother saying as 'ow if they was caught they should be stood up afore a firing squad and then see if the devil saved his own.'

'Were they caught?'

Annie shook her head, old-fashioned metal curlers jangling together.

'No, wench, they was never catched. But you couldn't really blame the bobbies, what few men was left behind was run off their feet and none of 'em too young. The war was a tryin' time for everybody but I reckon them folk with the paint brush must have realised they would by lynched afore any bobby could get to help if any of mother's neighbours laid 'ands on 'em first cos it stopped after a while . . . but there ain't no war on now an' I reckons the police should be a bit more concerned than they appears from your report.'

*Full-scale operation mounted to apprehend black magicians.*

Kate could just see Inspector Bruce Daniels's face if a headline like that were propped against his cornflakes. Leaning back in her chair she kept silent as Annie turned the pages of the *Star*'s evening edition. Her landlady spoke of having seen inverted crosses but she had made no mention of any other symbol. Had there been anything else . . . anything resembling the Seal she had seen in that book? If she asked then she would have to admit to having seen a representation of it herself and, as Annie wasn't exactly the soul of discretion, she was likely to mention it to her bingo-playing companions . . . and if she was asked to keep it to herself? Kate dismissed the idea, that would give the whole thing an importance it didn't really have.

Black magicians? She stretched her legs towards the glow of the gas fire. Not in this day and age!

He had followed Kate's tip, gone to the printing works, but the optimism he had felt on leaving the Frying Pan had been as flat as a model girl's bust by the time he had reached the yard.

Richard Torrey picked up the phone, dialling the number of Kate's digs. P'raps they could finish that drink. He couldn't really afford it, but what the hell!

'When are you going to give those things up?' Setting drinks on the table they had chosen in the corner of the Frying Pan,

Torrey frowned at Kate Mallory, her lighter already held to the tip of a cigarette.

Squinting as smoke curled into one eye she grinned. 'As soon as hell freezes over and you take me skating on the devil's furnace.'

'I give up.'

'You give up!' Kate shook her head, her sherry-coloured curls catching the gleam from the overhead lights and reflecting it back with rich amber glints. 'Now hell really would have to freeze over before that happened.'

'Then all I can say is the devil and his demons must be feeling pretty chilly by now.'

'That bad?'

Cradling the tall glass in his hands, Torrey stared into its depths. 'That bad,' he nodded.

'So I take it you had no luck at that printing works?'

'They said the same thing I've heard in a couple of dozen other places,' he laughed cynically. 'It was a case of thanks but no thanks.'

Kate blew a column of smoke towards the ceiling.

'They told you no?'

'Not in as many words.' He leaned back in his chair as he looked at her. 'But I know the drill. Though to be fair to that manager bloke he was more sympathetic than many I've had dealings with, but sympathy doesn't pay the bills.'

He should have listened to the fellow who had spoken to him last night, at least asked what was the job he had been about to offer . . . but he hadn't and now it was too late.

'There'll be other chances.' Kate tried to inject a measure of conviction into her reply but in truth she felt the chance of employment here in Darlaston to be negligible. And if he left . . . decided to try his luck elsewhere? Picking up her glass she sipped her lager and lime, hiding the look that thought brought to her eyes.

'I might have been given a job last night, a bloke was on the verge of offering one.'

Why on earth had he let that cat out of the bag! Torrey swore silently. Now he would have to tell her the whole bloody episode; he wasn't the only one who didn't give up . . . Kate Mallory carried the same bug!

'On the verge?'

Wide brown eyes already alive with curiosity regarded him over the rim of her glass.

*If you gambols in thistles yoh'll get pricked!*

Advice he had often heard given by older men and women returned to him now. It might not have been given in this case but it was applicable none the less. Kate Mallory wouldn't let go until she heard the last syllable!

'So why didn't he go all the way?' Kate set her glass down.

' 'Cos I stopped him.'

'You stopped him! Why?'

Shaking his head Torrey met the puzzled frown. He could ask himself the same question. Why hadn't he heard the man out, at least given him the chance to say what the job was?

'Well!' Kate's slightly tilted mouth set in a determined line. 'So why did you stop him?'

'I don't know.' Deciding a confession might bring remission from the penalty of long explanations, Torrey smiled. But how would she answer that? Nod and say I understand, or answer as he had himself before going to bed.

'You don't know! You turn down an opportunity a thousand men in Darlaston would lick their own balls for and you say you don't know! Christ, Torrey, are you a total bloody fool?'

As it was she didn't nod and she simply glared as she called him a bloody fool.

'Did you always cuss like that or have you only learned how since moving down country?' He tried passing the whole thing off.

'Cut the humour!' Kate answered tartly. 'Just tell me why you refused a job without even knowing what it was.'

'I suppose it was because whoever it was took me by surprise.'

'And that hurt your pride . . . the oh-so-competent commando caught unawares, and you couldn't cope with that!'

The tone was one he had used many times on himself after, as a child, having given in to Ron Webster's bully-boy tactics; it was the same mix of criticism and anger.

But why should Kate Mallory feel any anger . . . and more to the point why should he care?

'You could say that.' He shrugged, pushing the thought away as he answered. 'Certainly I wasn't pleased with myself and the fact that the guy kept to the shadows didn't help. I thought maybe it was another attack by my yobbo friends from the Bird-in-Hand.'

Acknowledging that she would not let the account end there he went on to tell the rest, leaving out the fanciful bit about silver-tipped flames because that had been no more than imagination. Kate Mallory already thought him a fool, tell her that part and she would have him lined up for a psychiatric ward!

'Could it have been an acquaintance of Philip Bartley's, someone who had known you from being his driver and wanted you to go work for him?'

Taking a swallow from his glass, Torrey shook his head.

'I doubt that, men of Bartley's creed don't go looking for men to work for them.'

'And he said you might not get the chance of another job. Do you suppose he could have anything to do with you being refused at the printers?'

Torrey shrugged again. 'Same answer, Kate. I don't know, and it's a red-hot certainty I won't ever find out.'

*Witness my protection.*

With the words heard in that nightmare echoing in his mind, he watched Kate light her second cigarette.

Help of that kind he didn't need, what he did need was a job.

# Chapter Five

Fastening the knot of his silk tie, Max Gau listened to the slow chime of the antique long-case clock stood in the hall of his home. Like everything in this house it was worth thousands but for him it held no value. The only thing he had valued in life had been taken from him with the death of his wife. Would he change things if he could, would he forgo all of this in exchange for a whore? That was what Christy had been, beautiful, but a whore playing him for a fool with his best friend. But they had paid, he had killed them both, then had chosen to live life as a free man; but freedom carried its own price, one that would take all of eternity to pay.

'Your guests have arrived, sir.'

Nodding to his manservant he reached for his jacket. He had been given all the comforts in life . . . but what of death, what did that hold for a follower of the Left Hand Path?

'Julian will not be joining us this evening.'

The two men and one woman Max had served with drinks made no answer but he could almost feel the tension ebb from them. They too were fearful of Crowley, not so much of the man himself but of the powers he held, of the forces he could command. Crowley held their lives in his hand but he also held their death and it was that . . . the sure and certain knowledge of what it held for them . . . that caused the fear that rippled through them whenever he met with them.

'What's this all about, Max?'

'I think perhaps you can guess.'

Taking a chair Max looked at the woman who had spoken. Brunette hair complemented clear ivory skin and eyes rich and clear as amber, while her face and figure were desirable from any point of view. Carol Brent was undoubtedly a very attractive woman, but as with the rest of Crowley's associates she had paid a high price for beauty. Crowley had told him of that price and taken pleasure in the telling, just as he had when telling of the 'arrangements' the other two had made with the advocate of the Prince of Darkness. But Crowley was not the Devil's Advocate, that honour was held by another, one who held far more power than Crowley, and that was the thorn in that man's side. Magus was a high rank in the service of their dark lord, but Ipsissimus was higher. Julian Crowley hoped to obtain that rank no matter the price tag it might carry.

'The business in the cemetery?' Carol Brent spoke for the others. 'It was a mistake.'

Max Gau shook his head. 'Julian does not see it as a mistake, he sees it as carelessness.'

'Nobody paid it much attention.'

'It caught the attention of the newspaper.'

'Pah!' Alex Davion, head of Davion International waved a dismissive hand. 'A tuppenny little provincial . . . who's going to take any notice of that?'

Another of the beautiful people! Max smiled at the man sat opposite. This one had been born handsome yet looks without money meant very little in Davion's book and he hadn't the brains to utilise the one or make the other and so . . . another victory for Crowley and another disciple for Lucifer.

'Who takes any notice of a raindrop, Alex, until it becomes a flood?'

'Talk sense, Max.' Alex Davion answered irritably. 'It won't come to that.'

'No, Alex, it won't come to that, but to make certain we have to ask protection of the All High.'

'What do you mean?'

Why had Crowley given this to him? Max laid his glass aside. Why ask – no not ask, Julian Crowley never asked, he instructed – but why instruct him to tell what was to be done? Surely Crowley would have thoroughly enjoyed the stir the next words would cause.

'Mistakes, carelessness, call what happened by either of those names it still needs to be rectified. The High Coven must be protected and protection paid for.' He spoke quietly, watching each face in turn.

'Tomorrow night payment will be made.'

'Do you really think this is necessary?'

Max Gau shifted uncomfortably beneath the cool gaze that turned to him. With the high rank of Magus of the dark priesthood Julian Crowley did not take kindly to being questioned by subordinates.

'The Prince of Darkness has given without stint,' he answered coldly, 'all we have asked and more. Should we then not show our gratitude for his protection now? Should we refuse the payment he asks for?'

Max dropped his gaze. 'There are payments and payments, Julian.'

'Precisely!' Julian Crowley's dark eyes swept the group assembled at Whitefriars. 'And this is the payment called for. If any of you do not agree it be made then you are at liberty to call upon the master for yourself.'

The members of the High Coven glanced at each other but none looked at Max Gau. He had challenged the decree given by

Crowley, it was a dangerous course and one none of them was ready to follow.

Julian Crowley felt a surge of triumph as Max Gau's glance fell away. They were all nothing . . . they would always be nothing . . . only he was of real use to the Master, only he would receive that ultimate glory that went with true belief and absolute obedience. He turned to a figure whose hands played nervously together, a small spare-framed man dressed in brown, a colour which accentuated his sparse sand-coloured hair; but it was the eyes he really looked at, pale grateful eyes. Stephen Geddes too had signed his soul to the devil.

'You have fulfilled the requirements, Stephen?'

Yes he had fulfilled all the requirements! Stephen Geddes's nod answered himself as well as Crowley, and as the other man shifted his attention he slid further into the depths of memory. He and Lisa had both been children of penniless Hungarian families who had suffered the rigours of war so when trouble flared again in the Balkans they had escaped to England. But even here living had not been easy, the only job he could get had been cleaning toilets in an engineering works. But they had felt safe . . . safe until Lisa had developed cancer! In the early days drugs had kept physical pain at bay, helping his wife go on fairly normally but the pain gnawing his heart would not be soothed. Lisa, the one person he loved and who loved him would soon be dead. Each day he left for work he felt troubled . . . would he still have Lisa when he got home?

Then had come the day.

Eyes fixed on his restless fingers blurred with tears of memory.

She could not bear to see the pain in his eyes any more – the note had read – she could not watch him suffer because of her. The empty bottle of painkillers had still been in her hand.

But he would gladly have suffered all the pain of the world to keep his wife! It had been too much. Life without Lisa was a life he did not want. He had walked out of the damp basement flat that was their home to the bridge that crossed the busy railway line.

*'Why are you doing this, my friend, why choose to end your life?'*

Stephen remembered the laugh he had given to that, a dry, soul-tormented laugh. Why not end something that had been one long punishment!

*'It need be a punishment no longer.'*

It had been as if the figure cloaked in shadow had read his mind.

*'No!'* Stephen had answered. *'So why should the Lord change His mind now? Why when He has ignored my prayers for so long?'*

*'Perhaps you have been asking the wrong Lord.'*

Away up the line a tooter had heralded the approach of an express train and Stephen had stepped nearer the scrolled ironwork railing of the bridge.

*'My Lisa is dead –'* he had set one hand on the railing *'– there is nothing to live for any more.'*

*'Are you sure that Lisa is dead?'*

It had been asked quietly, soft as the shadows that hid the face from view.

*'Of course I am sure, I saw the bottle in her hand, I kissed her poor cold face; my Lisa is gone and now I go too.'*

The train had rounded a curve in the track, its snaking body visible in the moonlight.

*'Wait!'* A hand had touched his arm as he made to pull himself on to the edge of the parapet. *'You might have been wrong, nerves can play many tricks; what can you lose by checking? If you are right then there is always another train.'* Framed in silver moonlight that almost seemed a part of him Julian Crowley had stepped forward. *'Come, my friend, show me your Lisa.'*

She was lying as he had left her, her small body made almost child-like by the wasting tumour. In tears Stephen had dropped beside her, kissing the thin cold hand.

*'Stephen,'* Crowley had asked, *'what would you give for the life of your wife?'*

It was an empty question, a stupid question but Stephen Geddes remembered the answer.

*'Anything!'* he had sobbed, holding the icy hand against his cheek. *'I would give my own life for my Lisa!'*

*'But your own life is of no value to you, is that not so? Why, moments ago you were about to throw it away, how can you now offer something that is of no value in exchange for the life of your wife?'*

He had looked up then.

*'You have said this is the life the Lord you worship has given for your obedience and love, and this,'* Crowley had pointed to the still form, *'is the life He has taken away. Will you exchange that God for mine, Stephen? Will you give him the obedience you have given for so long to an unanswering nothing? Will you take back the life of your wife, a life cured of cancer?'*

*'I don't understand,'* Stephen had stared blankly, *'my Lisa is dead, how can I take back her life?'*

*'By giving yourself.'* Julian Crowley's eyes had begun to glow like burning coals. *'Not just your life, which you have proved is of no value to you, but your soul, will you give your soul in exchange? Will you forsake the God that has given you nothing and follow the One that can give you everything, even the life of your dead wife?'*

*'Yes.'* Stephen had gathered the stiffening corpse into his arms. *'My life . . . my soul . . . what are they without my wife?'*

*'Stand up.'* Crowley's voice had sounded hollow in the musty room, as if coming from a long way off. *'Listen carefully, consider the bargain for there can be no going back; the Prince of Darkness, the Powerful One, the true Lord of the Earth will return the life of your wife if you accept him as your Lord, give your soul to him completely and swear to do all that he asks.'*

*'How?'* Stephen's bemusement had shown through his tears. *'How can the dead live?'*

*'You cannot understand now,'* Crowley's eyes had flamed, *'but in time you will if you choose the Prince of Darkness.'*

Stephen had looked at the still figure of his wife, her face beginning to take on the waxy marbling of death. '*Give Lisa back to me,*' he whispered, '*give me back my wife and I will be a true follower of your God.*'

At that Crowley had raised his arms, palms lifted to the ceiling. '*Siras Etar Besanar,*' he had begun to chant softly, '*Lord of Ten Wisdoms, Thou who holdest eternity, Lucifer greatest of High Angels, Prince of Creation, listen to thy servant. Thou Sammael and Ammon show now thy powers, send forth of thy hand and give this woman life.*'

For several seconds he had remained absolutely motionless, his eyes on Stephen. Then lowering his hands he had placed them on the body of Lisa, one on the head, the other across the heart, and as he had touched the corpse he and the bed had been suddenly enveloped in a burst of brilliant flame.

'*Netsah,*' he had called aloud, '*Keeper of the Flame, in the name of the Most High Lord, Satan, Prince of Darkness, I command thee return that which thou hast taken.*' Within the brilliant circle a spear of light, blue yet at the same time gold, had hovered above the head of the dead woman. Slowly it had lowered, touching the brow where Crowley's hand rested, then it had slid downwards to the chest where it hovered again. Slowly, after several moments Crowley had withdrawn his hands and the flame had faded. On the cramped bed Lisa Geddes had moaned softly then opened her eyes.

'Stephen . . . Stephen . . .'

A gentle shake of his arm dispelling the memories, Stephen Geddes looked at the woman calling his name.

'We are ready, Stephen.' Carol Brent smiled as the still half-dazed man got to his feet. He looked the way she felt, wanting only to see the end of this night.

Situated on the first floor of Whitefriars the room was one Carol Brent had often been in before, but as Stephen Geddes stood aside for her to enter she heard the silent words she always heard . . . will you walk into my parlour, said the spider to the fly

. . . only Crowley was more a scorpion than a spider and his catch was more than flies.

At first glance everything appeared ordinary enough. Heavy brocade drapes hung from high oval windows, expensive carpet covered the floor, in fact the room appeared perfectly in keeping with the rest of the elegantly appointed house; all, that was, except for the walls which were completely devoid of pictures.

The last to enter, Max Gau closed the door. To Carol's tightened nerves the click of the lock held an almost threatening quality, and she could not repress a shiver as she looked to the furthest end of the room to a raised dais, at its centre an altar draped in black velvet with two tall candlesticks, each with a lighted black candle, flanking a huge inverted cross.

With the closing of the door, Max touched a switch and the sibilant swish of closing drapes hummed on the silence. In seconds walls and windows disappeared, shrouded in black cloth which spread like a stain around the entire room.

Barely discernible, the hum of electric motors continued and the carpet began to recede, sliding away, swallowing itself where wall joined floor until the centre of the room lay uncovered. At the same time subdued light was switched on behind the moulded plaster architrave to play eerily over the darkened walls, flickering on a double band of gold set flush in the floor, a circle that held a five-pointed star, each tip touching a rim decorated with symbols.

Carol Brent stared at it. Powerful as Julian Crowley was, even he needed the protection of a pentacle when dealing with the Forces of Darkness.

Taking her place with the others grouped in a half-circle around a table stood at the foot of the dais, she caught her breath as Crowley entered followed by a girl dressed in a simple white dress, her brown hair caught in a circlet of white flowers.

He couldn't be going to do it! Her fingernails driving deep into her palms, Carol watched the obviously drugged girl lie across the table. An involuntary gasp breaking from her lips brought a quick answering glance from Crowley, a warning glittering in his cold obsidian eyes.

'We are all agreed?'

Carol Brent's glance fell away. The question was meant for each but she knew it was addressed to her. Crowley was issuing a challenge, but to accept it would be to follow in the footsteps of the girl lying so still on that altar.

'We are all agreed.'

She had to answer with the others. She had accepted the Prince of Darkness as her master, now she must acknowledge his will.

'Siras Etar Besanar.'

As he stood within the pentacle Julian Crowley's voice pierced the throbbing silence.

'Siras Etar Besanar, I call upon the Powers of Darkness, Zazas, Nasatanada, Zazas, open to me the Gates . . .'

He paused and for a moment Carol thought he had changed his mind, that the whole thing was abandoned, finished. But as she glanced up she saw Crowley's face in the flickering light and knew her hopes were false.

'Hear me, Oh Bornless One, I am the servant of the Lord of Darkness, in his name I conjure thee, Ashmedai, Messenger of the Most High . . .'

In Carol Brent's head the sound swelled, rolling and gathering, ringing like the toll of some great bell, while her gaze was riveted on a cloud of nebulous grey forming above the inverted cross.

'Ashmedai, Sword of Satan,' Crowley went on, 'I summon thee to my will.'

As he spoke a sound, soft and moaning like wind in the trees, rustled about the room, feeling its way like some sightless animal, licking at the gold rim of the pentacle, following the circle as if seeking a way inside.

'In the name of Lucifer, Lord of the Earth, I charge thee to take the offering we make.'

Above the cross the cloud spiralled then spread, stretching out towards Crowley, seeming to touch his head.

'Lord of Darkness—'

Crowley raised one hand, candlelight flickering on the knife clutched in his fingers.

'– Great Prince of the Universe, receive the gift of thy servant.'

In the dimness, Carol Brent whimpered softly as the knife descended, sinking deep into the chest of the sleeping girl.

# Chapter Six

Tell the truth and shame the devil!

Detective Inspector Bruce Daniels thought of the letter he had received a month ago.

. . . the position of Chief Detective Inspector . . . we hope at some future date . . .

They hoped! He kicked savagely at the leg of the desk, all that bloody interview panel hoped was Detective Inspector Bruce Daniels would get lost, pack the job in and go on a lifelong fishing trip! He had passed all the exams . . . had plenty of experience . . . he'd crashed that heroin racket . . . sent Doc Walker and several others down for a ten-year stretch. He should have been given promotion for that but fancy-talking James bloody Connor had took it! And then he'd brought in Bartley . . . well, he would have if the man hadn't thrown himself from a third-storey window; the whole kit and caboodle, he'd brought in the lot and who had got the post Connor's leaving Victoria Road had left vacant? Not bloody Detective Inspector Bruce Daniels!

His face didn't fit . . . it hadn't fit the first time and it didn't fit now!

Anger stirred the bile in his throat surging acid into his mouth.

His face didn't fit and he didn't have a fancy tongue, without that nobody got promotion in this bloody borough! Snatching open a blue and yellow carton he flicked a tablet on to his tongue. Of course he could have gone through the canine act, licked a few arses. He sucked hard on the tablet, seeking to quench the burning in his throat. He could have . . . but he never would, Bruce Daniels was no dog; that promotions board would wait a bloody long time to see him sit up and beg.

'Super wants a word, Bruce.'

Bruce Daniels glanced at the man stood at the partly opened door of the poky little room grandly termed an office. The two of them had served together on the Darlaston force for almost twenty years and it seemed both had reached the zenith of their careers; still, there was one consolation, for himself if not for the sergeant, that being so low on the ladder he didn't get dizzy!

'What does he want now?'

Returning the carton to the pocket of his jacket, a tweed that had seen as many years of service as he had, he watched the other man smile. The condemned man smiled, he thought bitterly. Well at least one of 'em did, though how the hell he could smile at being sentenced to serve the rest of his working life as a bloody desk sergeant . . .

'Didn't say.' The sergeant shrugged as he withdrew leaving the door ajar.

What was it this time, another bloody hare-brained idea, one more of his crackpotical notions of 'how best to address the problem of rising crime'?

Ten minutes later, his fingers touching a pocket that held stomach tablets and car keys, he walked from the station.

There was only one address for anyone who broke the law: Her Majesty's bloody prisons! The gospel according to Chief Detective Inspector Martin Quinto!

* * *

Was there such a thing as a casting couch in journalism? If there was she might be very tempted to try it. Jammed into her seat by an elephant masquerading as a woman, Kate Mallory felt herself smile at the thought.

. . . Kate Mallory offered as willing sacrifice on the altar of ambition . . .

It might be worth making the offer just to see the look on Scotty's face when she did. But it had been sheer luck she had landed this post, get thrown out on her butt and chances of another were dead! Still, the thought had been amusing while it lasted. More amusing than the assignment she was landed with now! She stared disgruntled through a dusty window. Why her . . . why give her this one to cover? 'Because,' as her editor had so tactfully phrased it, 'a sports writer knows bugger all about women's fashions!'

He couldn't be sure of that! Kate grinned at the thought. For all Scotty knew he could be into transvestism . . . now *that* she would enjoy covering! Chuckling at the explosion it would cause if she asked her burly macho colleague 'Are you into women's clothes?' she breathed with relief as the bone-crushing passenger heaved from the seat to shuffle from the Metro.

'I have no idea how,' Scotty had answered when asked how come the *Star* had been invited to view what was to have been a strictly 'no provincial press, affair. Could the House of Jarreaux be feeling the same economic pinch many other businesses were feeling? Did they hope a little free advertising might strengthen the bank balance? They could always hope . . . that sprang eternal. But, given the price tags on some of their creations featured on the pages of the glossy fashion mags, and hopes of selling to the average woman in these parts . . . even eternity wasn't long enough to see that hope realised.

That journey had been no more comfortable than the more usual bus journey! Hopefully the next seat she sat on wouldn't be swamped by an escapee from Dudley Zoo! The salon was bound to be decorated on every side by delicately worded signs denying her smoking a cigarette. Well, she would do a lot for her profession, but going straight to that show before having a tab? That was asking too much!

Settling herself on one of a series of benches set around the pedestrianised shopping centre, she lit her nerve-soothing Rothmans. She had counted on being sent to try finding out more about the desecration at that cemetery but Scotty had thrown the idea straight out of the window, it was dead as the bodies in those graves he had said. But was it? Kate blew a pensive smoke ring through pursed lips. Somehow she had the feeling that Scotty was wrong . . . very, very wrong!

The phone call came just as he entered his dreary digs. Usually not returning until late, today he had forgone the pleasure of yet another hour sat in the park staring at flowers he knew so well they could have been related to him.

'. . . if you are interested, Mr Torrey perhaps you would come and see us . . .'

Was he interested? Lord, if he moved any faster his shoes would catch fire.

The fellow he had spoken to yesterday had as good as told him he had about as much chance of that job as he had of winning the national lottery so why the hell had they changed their minds now?

'You are expected, Mr Torrey, would you go right in?'

He hadn't seen her yesterday. Torrey smiled at the young girl holding a telephone in one hand and a pencil in the other. But then he hadn't got this far yesterday, his questions had been answered with him still in the yard.

'Forgive my asking you to come again, Mr Torrey, I am Max Gau.'

With sunlight glancing off the silvered tips of brown hair,

slate-grey eyes holding a friendly smile, a tall spare-framed man rose from behind a desk, his hand extended in greeting.

'Fred, the man you spoke to yesterday, thought you very suitable but of course he could not offer you employment himself.'

'He's not the manager?'

'No.' The other man smiled as he sat down. 'Fred is our typesetter, at least that is the post he originally held, but with our work force being continually scaled down he has taken on just about everything apart from making the deliveries.'

Lucky for some bloke. Torrey took the chair indicated. With a bit of luck maybe that bloke would be him.

'I recognised your name when Fred spoke of you and on reading what little information was on your card from the Job Centre I think my supposition is correct.'

They hadn't met before or he would have remembered. Torrey looked keenly at the fine-boned, still good-looking face.

'A friend of mine once spoke highly of you, it seems he heard of you through an acquaintance . . . Langford Wyndham.'

Wyndham! Even the name brought a rush of cold anger. The late, and for him unlamented, Foreign Secretary. He had been part of that Monkswell affair, one of Philip Bartley's cronies, one of the five driven to their death by a hitch hiker, a ghost with half a face. If this guy had known Wyndham then he must have known the rest of the men responsible for Anna's murder and as such he wanted no part of Max Gau or his job!

'May I offer you a drink, Mr Torrey, some coffee?'

Biting back the snarl already sliding between his lips, Torrey shook his head. He had never set eyes on this man before so bad mouthing him would bring no true satisfaction, best just to leave.

'Your name was mentioned merely in passing, my friend once had business with the foreign office and whilst there his chauffeur was taken ill and it seemed Wyndham commented he should get one as reliable as the driver Philip Bartley had.'

'The racket Bartley was in . . . I want none of it!'

'Neither do I.' Max Gau shook his head as Torrey got determinedly to his feet. 'I will not pretend I did not know of that man's business connections, we all read newspapers do we not? But for myself, that is as far as it goes and I can say the same for Julian.'

'Julian?' Torrey frowned.

'Julian Crowley, the man who advised that I think of you for the post I have to fill which, let me add, has nothing at all to do with narcotics.'

And murder? The question reared itself in Torrey's mind. Did it have anything to do with that?

'You applied for a position as driver here at the Darlaston Printing Works yesterday?'

Torrey nodded. He could hear the guy out and then leave.

'Fred, as I mentioned before, seemed to think you a suitable candidate for the post and, like him, I too think you are just what we are looking for. But the post calls for more than just a driver, Mr Torrey, it calls for someone who is mentally alert and physically capable of taking care of himself and of any one who attempted to interfere with his cargo.'

Mentally alert. That was a good one! Would this Gau fellow think him mentally alert if he knew how he had been surprised that night on leaving the Frying Pan?

'You see, printing leaflets is not the only thing we do here, some of our work is of a more sensitive nature.'

'Girlie mags?' Torrey frowned. 'Each to his own but that's one more addiction I'm not into.'

'It isn't what you think—'

Max Gau laughed, a quiet sound that Torrey found pleasant. 'But please sit down, taking a seat will not constitute a binding contract I promise you.' Pausing while Torrey re-settled in the chair he then went on. 'We, Darlaston Printing that is, have contracts with several commercial companies. As you will understand we must ensure that literature concerning a client's business does not fall into the hands of their competitors, for that reason we maintain a low profile.'

'So how come you are telling me?'

'There is a quite simple answer to that.' Max Gau's slate-coloured eyes looked directly into Torrey's. 'You must have known a great deal about your late employer, not all of which I suppose was to do with the drugs market, but whatever you might have known you said nothing, you told the police only that you were Philip Bartley's chauffeur. Am I right, Mr Torrey?'

'The man had the same rights as we all do, that of living his private life privately so long as he doesn't harm anybody else.'

But Philip Bartley had harmed others and not just as a result of drug trafficking. He had helped murder Anna; oh, not by pulling the trigger but by doing nothing to prevent it being pulled. Philip Bartley had been as guilty as the others, and he, Torrey, had wanted to make that bastard pay for his complicity, but the ghost of Anna had beaten him to it; Anna, dead for over a year, had taken that satisfaction. There had been nothing to be gained at the end of it all except disbelief on Detective Inspector Bruce Daniels' part and a great deal of ridicule from the media, and there was nothing to be gained by telling of it now to this man.

'Exactly.' Max Gau nodded. 'You know how to keep quiet about the work you do, and given the nature of some of the work we do then that makes you a perfect candidate for the job.'

How long had Darlaston been a place for the security minded?

Torrey suppressed the smile building inside him. He'd never known it be such a place and doubtless not many others had either, especially not Echo Sounder, for that little songbird would whistle the whole tune given a few quid. So what was it that was so close to the chest? If it wasn't your average-type porn magazine, then what?

'This place is not a hot-bed for printing pornography nor a cover for the heroin racket.'

'I'm beginning to think you are psychic.'

'Not one of my skills I'm afraid.'

Max Gau's answering laugh was quiet as before. There was something about the man. Torrey watched the smile settle about the well-formed mouth. Something he liked.

'It was the look on your face that told me what you were thinking. I assure you, we give the work done here privacy only in as much as it is a requirement of our clients, and as you will find, supposing you join us, none of the material we produce is in any way offensive.'

*I assure you.* He'd heard that a few nights ago and then it hadn't rung true. Was it any different this time! The same words, a different man. It was simply coincidence. Torrey watched the other man rise. That fellow waylaying him in the pub yard, taking him off guard was what had put his hackles up, not so much the words he'd used. Max Gau had not approached him that way yet still those three words had set his teeth on edge.

'I would have liked to discuss your proposed employment a little longer, Mr Torrey.' Gau held out his hand. 'But today is a busy one for me, I'm afraid, and as I must fill the position fairly soon I will have to ask for your decision before close of business this evening. I appreciate you probably have something else in mind but do at least think about my offer before taking that of anyone else.'

Somebody else offering a job. Christ, it would have to be on another planet! Torrey shook the extended hand. Van driver-cum-minder to . . . what? A load of top-secret buy-one-get-one-free posters for some supermarket! A highly volatile do-it-yourself catalogue? What the hell, it could be a load of highly controversial cotton wool for all he cared! This guy wanted a virtual one-man security service for a load of pamphlets! Well he'd had worse jobs in his life.

Torrey kept his amusement well under wraps as the other man touched an intercom to summon the young girl from the outer office.

'We might meet again, Mr Torrey, should you choose to take the job and if not then I wish you well in whatever employment you do decide to take.'

It hadn't taken much thinking about. The pay he had been offered was what he would call a damn sight more than moderate, beside which he had liked Max Gau from the beginning; he had come out in the open, not waylaid him like that bod in the yard of the Frying Pan. Who the hell had that man been and what was the job he'd had to offer? Not that it mattered now. Torrey lifted his face to the mid-morning sun, really enjoying its touch for the first time in weeks, feeling the pleasure of at last being among folk who worked for a living. Funny! He smiled openly. The number of times he had heard others say it must be great never having to work, to have the State support you . . . well they could have it, he preferred the old-fashioned way, the way you worked for what you ate!

'Now that's what me mam would say is a right bonny lad. You have the look of a man who lost a five-pence piece and found a fiver in the place you dropped it.'

'As good as.' Richard Torrey grinned at the young woman walking towards him, an outsized bag hanging from one shoulder. 'I've just landed a job! I start on Monday.'

'Great!' Kate Mallory's smile matched his own. 'When, where and how?'

'Today. I had a call asking me back to the printing works . . . the bloke there said the job was mine should I decide to accept it.'

'But you said you had already seen him and his answer had been thanks for calling but nowt doing.'

'Not the same man. The one I spoke to yesterday was the typesetter, where the other one, Max Gau, is the manager. It was he who wanted to see me, judge for himself, I suppose.'

'Judge for himself . . . for a van driving job!'

'A delivery driver, and don't be snobbish, it isn't you!' Torrey smiled as he replied, deliberately leaving out the part of his agreement with Gau to fill in as chauffeur should the need arise. 'It's the same job I applied for. Seems Fred, the typesetter, thought I fit the bill but the top man had to see for himself first.'

'His prerogative, I suppose.' But interviewing a van driver? I wouldn't have expected a managing director to do that. Her thoughts tight in her mind, Kate glanced at her watch.

'Don't let me keep you, you probably have a deadline to meet.'

'I have.' Sherry-coloured hair bounced as she nodded. 'And Scotty will have my innards gilded and hung on the office Christmas tree if I miss it but—'

'But?'

'It's this feeling I have, one that says there's more to that business in the cemetery than kids having a rave up with paint cans. Inspector Daniels has dismissed any investigation, he says there are more pressing things for his officers to attend to. Huh! Such as what, may I ask? There's been nothing worth investigation gone on in this town since Bartley!'

'And you think a few paint-daubed gravestones is . . . worth investigating, I mean?'

'Laugh if you want!' Kate answered truculently. 'I can't sue you for doing so, though I would if I could make a story of it.'

'Which you can't make of our phantom artists?'

Hitching the bag higher on her shoulder Kate turned towards the bus station. 'That would be no problem, getting Scotty to print it would be.'

'Isn't this the wrong bus?' He had walked with her to where several buses were lined up, each bound for separate destinations.

'Not if a girl is going to Bentley, and this one is.' Kate Mallory's tilted mouth spread in a grin. 'I'm going to have another scout around that cemetery.'

'And your deadline?'

'Dead!' She looked up at him. 'At least it will be if I don't get this other bee out of my bonnet first.'

'Your funeral!' Torrey shook his head. 'Just remember jobs are hard to find and not only in Darlaston.'

'I'm allowing myself an hour.' She took a second glance at her watch. 'If you have nothing better to do how about coming with me? You could act as my time-keeper.'

He had said he had nothing better to do but surely he could have found something better than sitting perched on a tombstone watching Kate Mallory flit around the cemetery like a demented bluebottle!

Torrey stared around at the medley of burial places, just the odd few carefully tended and set with fresh flowers. Anna had no grave! He swallowed hard, remembering the pain of that funeral service when he had been the only follower, when he had stood alone in that crematorium watching as Anna slipped quietly from this world. But Anna had been gone long before those crimson curtains had closed behind the coffin, and departure had not been quiet; Anna had been blasted into the next world, sent there with only half a face!

'Help me . . .'

Too late, Anna. He answered the words that had crept into his mind.

'Please . . .'

Torrey gave himself a mental shake.

He must not let those thoughts begin again. Anna's voice had haunted him once before, haunted him until he'd gone almost mad. He mustn't let it happen again.

'Help me . . .'

God Almighty, this place was giving him the creeps! Annoyed

at his inability to control his own thoughts he stood up. Two more minutes and he would prise Kate loose from whatever she was knee-deep in and march her back to the bus stop.

'Help me . . .'

Despite the knowledge that what he heard was no more than the work of his imagination, of thoughts prompted by his surroundings, Torrey threw a quick glance about the deserted grounds. There was no sign of Kate Mallory, there was no sign of anyone.

'Get a hold of yourself, Torrey!' he scorned quietly. 'You're worse than a kid frightened of its own shadow!'

'Help me . . .'

This time it had been no thought, no product of his own mind! Turning swiftly, every sense alert, he scanned the spacious grounds.

'Please . . .'

Coming to a spot marked by a spreading tree, his eyes rested on the figure of a woman. No, not a woman. He focused more intently. More of a girl, no more than sixteen or seventeen. Who was she with? There was no interment taking place, no other mourners, and this girl wasn't dressed in black!

'Sorry!' He realised he was staring. 'I thought you spoke to me but obviously I was wrong.'

He had expected her to smile and say no, but instead she looked back with a kind of helpless gaze.

'Are you lost?'

'Of course I'm not lost, I was just checking a few places to see if our diligent police force might have missed anything.'

'I wasn't asking you, I was asking this young woman, she seems to be lost.'

Coming to stand beside him Kate Mallory shook her head. 'Is that the best you can do . . . really, Torrey, you disappoint me. Nutters talk to trees, more hopeless nutters talk to themselves.'

'I was talking to—' Looking back to where the girl stood, he paused. There was no girl there. In fact he could see no girl anywhere.

'Well, if it was a young woman she's gone now and I must follow suit or Scotty will have my head.'

Kate's tone said she saw his imaginary woman as a sorry attempt at a joke. Falling into step beside her he made no effort to deny it, smiling as he answered, 'I thought you said it was your innards, gilded and used to decorate the Christmas tree.'

'Those too.' Delving into her bag she fished out cigarettes and lighter. 'And he might as well have them for I'll be dead in two minutes unless I have a tab.'

Waiting for the inevitable sigh that said her life had been saved, he glanced through the transparent lavender-grey pool of smoke that spread on the still air of midday to where, moments ago, he had thought a girl had stood. He could have sworn she had been there! He'd spoken to her, but then . . . He shrugged inwardly, he had to be mistaken; the girl would have to have been very adept to hide so quickly, one of the 'now you see me now you don't' acts you saw on television. Probably! He dismissed the episode . . . but she'd been damned good!

A squeak from Kate grabbing his attention he ground a foot on her fallen cigarette then ran after her to where the bus was already drawing to a stop. Settling beside her on the one remaining empty seat he glanced through the window, meeting the gaze of a solitary figure still stood at the bus stop. The figure of a young girl with a desolate, helpless look, a figure who mouthed the words, 'Help me.'

# Chapter Seven

Kate Mallory leaned back in her chair, half-heartedly scanning the monitor in front of her. This wasn't what she wanted to write, she wanted to write what she had heard while covering that business of the cemetery. But hand that in as copy and Scotty would have a dickie fit!

Tripe, he would call it. Bloody invention. It's facts I want, girl, facts!

So he'd got facts. She switched on the printer, watching it greedily swallow several sheets of paper before burping to a stop. Not that he would appreciate them any more than he'd appreciate the niceties of slub-linen trousers teamed cheekily with pure silk shirt, or trendy pink tartan with chiffon top, or anything else gleaned from that fashion show he had given her to cover. Now if Scotty would give her a gossip column, something she could really sink her pearly whites into . . .

What's Cooking . . . Kate's Tasty Titbits!

Why not, a column such as that? It would be quite apt for the roasting some celebrities would get! Smiling inwardly, savouring the impossible, Kate flinched as the well-known shout emanated from the small inner office.

'You roared, master?' The quip a carefully guarded murmur

she gathered her copy. If it met with Scotty's approval she would be finished here and could go . . . where, where would she go? Back to her digs? Be honest, Kate, she told herself, you want to get back to that cemetery, but there's nothing there. Just face it, lass, there's nothing there, it's simply the place itself that's getting to you! It seemed to have got to Torrey too, imagining he saw a girl that wasn't there; he'd even spoken to her!

Kate watched the editor's head nod as he read through the papers she had given him. Were the editors of the nationals as conscientious as Scotty, did they read everything before letting it into print?

'Enjoyable, was it, Kate?'

Looking up quickly he caught her off guard, experience telling him it was no fashion show his budding journalist was thinking of.

'So what else have you caught a whiff of?'

It wasn't a whiff: it was a full-blown stench and she hadn't caught it watching stick-thin women parade along that catwalk; it had been in her nostrils since first visiting Bentley cemetery. But she had better not say so.

'If you are on to something—'

'Now what gives you that idea?' Kate smiled as the youngest member of the office team popped his carroty head in at the door with some message from the print room.

A raised hand halting the young lad in mid-flow, David Anscott ran his other hand through prematurely grey hair, his keen eyes boring into Kate's.

'Knowing you is what gives me that idea,' he answered. 'I've seen that look before and it tells me there's been more under your nose than a cigarette and I want to know what it is.'

'There's nothing. Honestly, Scotty, would I keep anything from you?'

'Honestly . . . yes!' Pushing her report into the hands of the waiting junior he kept his gaze on her face, but his eyes smiled. 'Just let me have the finished copy.'

She had told him part of the truth. Out in the street Kate breathed more easily. Any story she got would be given to the *Star,* but what was that story . . . was there one?

Lighting the last Rothmans she sucked hungrily drawing its relief deep into her throat. Yes there was a story and Kate Mallory was going to find it.

There had been something going on at that fashion house.

Kate walked slowly towards the town centre, the letter she was sending home to Birtley occupying the tiniest corner of her mind, the rest going over the conversation she had heard that afternoon. Bored with tartans and taffetas she had slipped away from the salon, seeking refuge and a tab in the ladies' rest room. Locked in a cubicle, she had been about to light up when those two girls had come in. There had been polite notices all over the place. She grimaced as she thought of them, bloody polite! What they were really saying was either you don't smoke or you pee off! It had galled her but she had complied with the 'requests' and held off lighting her tab, waiting for them to leave.

'Ooh, I'd give anything for a trip like that.'

'You would have to give *everything,*' the second voice had answered, 'and when you returned it would be to find no fashion house would touch you, men with open wallets often have closed minds. They take what they want and you finish up on the heap. They make sure you never talk . . . and I mean *never.*'

They had left the rest room then, the click of high heels the only sound drifting behind them.

What was the trip they had talked about . . . who were the 'they' that ensured a girl *never* talked of her experiences . . . and, what was even more intriguing, how was that accomplished?

Walking into the post office Kate joined the queue. She needed more stamps.

'Can't yoh read?'

As the irate question jerked her back from her thoughts she looked at the woman turned to face her, then followed the finger pointing to the ever-present sign. Lord, there was no let up anywhere! Mumbling what she hoped sounded like an apology she went back outside, abandoning the crushed remnant of her precious cigarette to a waste bin clipped to a lamp post, then rummaged in her purse to find a couple of one-pound coins. She would get stamps from the dispenser embedded in the wall.

What and who had those mannequins been talking about? Much as she regretted it, she resigned herself to the fact that she didn't know, and most likely never would.

'I mustn't.'

Sat in the expensively exclusive restaurant, Isobel Davion shook her head negatively at the assortment of French pastries. 'I put on so much weight while we were in Chamonix.'

'You have a marvellous figure,' Nicole Jarreaux answered in the expected vein. Normally she would not pander to another woman's vanities but Isobel Davion was extraordinary in so much as Alex Davion was her husband.

'Thank you, darling.' Isobel's eyes gleamed satisfied acknowledgement. 'But truly one has to be so careful, I mean I should only have to touch one of those things . . . and Alex does so like me to look good.'

Alex doesn't give a shit how you look! Nicole eyed the face pinched from constant dieting. He hasn't slept with you in years, nor any other woman come to that.

'That's why I need an entire new wardrobe,' Isobel gushed, taking her companion's silence as mute admiration. 'Alex is taking some business clients on a cruise of the Hellenes in a few weeks – combine business with pleasure wherever possible is a maxim of his – and this time I have decided to go along.'

So for business clients read and/or studs. Nicole surveyed the expertly made-up face. Isobel Davion, married to one of the wealthiest men in the country, took her pleasures frequently but never carelessly. To play so near to home must mean a particularly attractive specimen somewhere in Alex's proposed entourage . . . interesting!

'I know it's short notice, darling,' Isobel trilled, 'but do you think you could possibly arrange something?'

'The salon is always open.' Nicole sipped her coffee, watching annoyance flit briefly across the other woman's face.

'Yes, darling, I know.' Isobel smiled; Jarreaux was a bitch but a useful bitch. 'But since Chamonix I need new fittings.'

Gold glints flickered among expensively coloured hair and perfume Nicole recognised as one of her own top range drifted across the table as Isobel reached for the cream leather Gucci bag dropped casually on to an empty chair.

'Guillermo is fully booked for the whole of the next two weeks.'

Nicole watched expertly manicured fingers flip the pages of a small diary. Well at least the wealthy Mrs Alex Davion was not dedicated to the eternal filofax.

'I said *new* fittings, darling –' almond-shaped hazel eyes looked bland '– who else do you have might suit?'

'I have recently appointed several new additions to my team.' Nicole flicked a glance over the cream silk suit bearing the Jarreaux label. It had set Isobel back several thousand but that was a mere item; the lady would willingly pay more should something particular appeal to her taste. 'Yet I must admit their expertise surprised even me.' She didn't miss the pleasurable twitch of a professionally shaped eyebrow. 'It is refreshing to come across young people already so expert at their job, there are so many of the mundane in our business. Jacques—' She sipped her coffee, a little finger delicately poised.

Get on with it, you shit! Isobel extracted a slim gold pen from the Gucci original. I know you're gonna take the hide off me so why piss about?

'Jacques,' Nicole repeated, replacing the porcelain cup in its saucer, 'I confess is no more French than you or I but he is quite innovative.'

'Or?'

'Or there are Michael and Petra, they are more daring, their technique has left some of our clients quite breathless . . .' She could feel the almost physical vibration of carefully masked excitement. Isobel Davion would pay and gladly. 'But I think it's Diego will suit you best. His style is unique, strong but subtle, and his designs are devastating.' She stopped again, knowing the pause was doing more to increase Isobel's desire to see Diego than flattery of his talents would. 'A session with him,' she went on pleased at the white pinch of annoyance around those aristocratic nostrils, 'is more of an invitation than a fitting and needless to say, his work, as that of all my team, is of the very best or he would not be with the House of Jarreaux. A few weeks in Diego's hands should see you suitably equipped for a cruise of the Hellenes.'

Isobel looked up from the perusal of the gilt-bound Moroccan diary. She knew by heart every appointment she had both in and out of that little book and there wasn't one she wouldn't break. 'Shall we say Tuesday the seventeenth?'

'Tuesday the seventeenth.' Nicole beckoned an attentive waiter to order fresh coffee. 'By the way,' she smiled, waiting until pen and diary were dispatched into the cream handbag, 'I have a photo session next month . . . some of Petra's new range.'

'I thought you said Petra was one of your new acquisitions to the salon!'

'So she is.'

'But surely you don't use salon creations in your boutiques?'

Nicole could understand the evident distaste; Isobel and any other Jarreaux client paid enough to expect no cheap copies of their clothes paraded in every high street in the country.

'No,' she answered, 'a Jarreaux exclusive is always that, exclusive. They are never included in catalogues or copied for the public market. This session –' she waited while fresh coffee and china were placed on the table and the used ones removed '– will be for a private collection designed especially for the women of the household of Sheikh Hamed Abdel Khadja. He has all the old ways of his desert ancestors, the women of his house are for his eyes only. They have the very finest that money can buy but it must be chosen within the home.'

'Christ, what a life!' Isobel shuddered an elegant shoulder. 'You mean they never get to go out anywhere?'

'I don't know the Sheikh's family well enough to answer that with any truth.' Nicole added a tiny amount of cream to her coffee, watching pale circles spread on the dark surface. 'In fact I don't know them at all. We – the London Salon that is – are always contacted by an aide, we then compile an entirely exclusive portfolio that must be okayed by the Sheikh. From there it is taken by some of our female staff to the Middle East where selections are made by the women of the household. Once the garments are made up the patterns and original sketches are handed to the Sheikh for destruction.'

'You mean anything the man buys is truly a one-off?' Isobel was impressed. 'You don't use that design again in say . . . a modified context?'

'Never.' Nicole tasted her coffee. 'The Sheikh pays for exclusivity, my dear . . . I mean *really* pays. So I see he gets what he asks.'

'The fittings are all actually carried out over there?'

'Of course, but only our female staff are allowed to do that. We have arranged private viewings from time to time and the Sheikh has sometimes preferred the creations of some of our male designers.'

'But they're out . . . as far as making up the clothes, I mean?'

'Exactly.' Nicole glanced around the restaurant, noting with satisfaction that the Jarreaux label was not thin on the ground. 'They, as I said, are not permitted to carry out the actual fittings. If their creations are accepted then measurements are brought back here and the making of patterns and the finished garments takes place around them rather than around the woman for whom they are intended.'

'But surely you find models whose measurements match up?'

Nicole watched the other woman's glance follow a tall muscled figure, Isobel always was impressed by measurements.

'No garment intended for that family is ever modelled by another person,' she went on as Isobel's attention returned. 'To the Sheikh's way of thinking that gives it the equivalence of second-hand goods and that, my dear Isobel, is another of the man's taboos.'

'Interesting.' Isobel's eyes hovered again on the exit. 'I wouldn't mind meeting that man.'

I've no doubt you'll find a way. Nicole read the real meaning behind the reply, seeing the other woman's reluctance to pull her gaze away from the exit. Isobel Davion had a remarkable talent for that aspect of engineering, the only area of conjecture being which got her legs open first, the tight-arsed figure who just left the restaurant or the Sheikh. Not much of a contest either way!

'So you can,' she said aloud pushing the empty coffee cup aside. 'I told you I have a photo session arranged next month, we're using a place in Worcester, Whitefriars. It's owned by an acquaintance of mine, you might know him . . . Julian Crowley. He's in the printing business among many other things,' she continued as Isobel nodded her head. 'Anyway when he heard I needed somewhere never likely to be used as a location for catalogue shooting he offered his place. See if you can get Alex to come along. He might not care for the photography but the place has the usual shooting and fishing, and meeting Sheikh Hamed might be beneficial commercially.' Not to mention uncommercially, she thought acidly, like him our Arab friend doesn't mind whether his toys have tits or not!

'Mmm.' Isobel reluctantly left off watching for the return of the tight buttocks. 'It does sound rather fun but won't Crowley resent your bringing along uninvited guests?'

Nicole Jarreaux lit one of the three cigarettes she allowed herself a day. 'The invitation was an open one,' she said through a trace of perfumed smoke, 'I intend to use only the very minimum of staff, and in any case Julian knows I would never abuse his hospitality. Apart from the Sheikh, you and Alex are the only guests; if I intend to keep the custom of the Sheikh . . . and believe me I do . . . the whole affair must be strictly private.'

'In that case,' Isobel rose, 'I'll see what I can arrange with Alex. Perhaps I can let you know on the seventeenth?'

Nicole smiled at the supple figure encased in cream silk, the face that money had created. At fifty going on thirty, Isobel Davion wasn't doing badly.

'The seventeenth.' She stubbed the cigarette into an elegantly cut crystal ashtray. 'I'll tell Diego to expect you.'

'*We must address the problem of rising crime.*'

The words he had guessed would be first to slide off that oh-so-cultured tongue rang in his mind. It had rung there all of yesterday afternoon and kept him company most of the night. Detective Inspector Bruce Daniels guided the Ford along Willenhall Street. What was he expected to do? Give him more bobbies and there might be results, but with the manpower he had now the bloody Chief Detective Inspector might as well whistle in the wind!

*'Those upstairs are demanding results.'*

Those upstairs! He twisted angrily on the wheel, setting tyres screeching as he swung the car into the forecourt of the Frying Pan. The man not only talked as if he had a bibble in his mouth, he also talked crap! Why not say the top brass had been on his back? Or was that a bit beneath his level of English!

*'They want results, Daniels . . . and I* want results.'

Climbing from the car he slammed the door, jabbing the key in the lock and turning it viciously. They all wanted results and they all wanted Daniels to bring 'em in; Bruce Daniels was a bloody good detective they said, he could shit miracles and wipe his arse by magic, but where was Daniels when promotion was in the offing? Right at the end of the line, that's where Daniels was!

*'I want results!'*

The phrase with its underlying warning stirred the acid already searing the back of his throat. He could have that operation the doctors had told him he needed for his stomach ulcer, retire on the grounds of ill health as Marjorie urged him to do. Extracting a tablet from a slim carton he placed it on his tongue. But spend all day and every day watching his wife protect her precious furniture and cushions from his touch, brush every imaginary print left on her carpets from slippers ever-ready as he set foot through the door? Christ, he'd rather keep the ulcer!

'Ain't nuthin' goin' on, Mr Daniels.'

Hunched over a week-old copy of the *Sporting Pink,* Echo Sounder didn't look up as he answered the inspector's question.

If the little nark thought his memory was going to be improved by liquid refreshment then he could think again. The new arse in the station wanted results. Sounder could well be the first!

'And here's me thinking you be the best radar-set this side of Brummagem airport.' Inspector Daniels hooked one foot around a chair leg and pulled it beneath him.

'You cleaned that patch good an' proper, ain't been nuthin' outta that stable—'

'Cut the race-track lingo!' Daniels snapped sharply. 'I'm in no mood for jockeys and that means your sort as well. Try running one past me, Sounder, and you'll find yourself on a nice free holiday, all expenses found . . . by the Crown!'

His fingers tightening about the newspaper, the scruffily dressed little man hunched his shoulders tighter together. Daniels had his arse in his hand . . . somebody had rattled his cage!

'It be the truth,' he answered cautiously. One wrong word and his own arse would find a new resting place, one he'd like as not have to make do with for a few years. 'You disinfected Bartley.'

'Didn't I! And I'll bloody well fumigate you unless you open that greasy little mouth and quick! Nobody knows this town's underbelly better than you . . . and nobody knows Winson Green better than me, and I can arrange you be given a room among the select. You wouldn't want to go rubbing shoulders with any down-market little breaking and entering toads, now would you? So seeing as we are friends I should arrange it so you were put to play with the big boys.'

Christ! Folding the newspaper and jamming it in his pocket, Echo Sounder hoped to disguise the nervous twitch of his fingers.

Daniels had never been what you might call of an easy disposition but since the force had appointed some other fella as Chief Detective Inspector he'd acted like a bear with the gripe; but he was a bear could swipe a man out of existence for a five stretch, maybe more!

Reaching the carton of BiSoDol from the pocket of his

jacket, Daniels's fingers closed about it, crushing it with a clearly illustrative move.

That would be his neck! Sounder watched the carton hit the ashtray. Daniels would grip tight and throw away the empty carcass!

'If you tells me what it is you be after—'

'Everything!' Daniels's growl slid across the beer-stained table. 'Anything and everything, and Sounder . . . you're a betting man, what odds would you put on your next visit to the race track being no earlier than, say . . . five years?'

He'd wrung the little runt dry. Daniels sat in the car. Put him through a bloody juice extractor and he'd have spilled no more, and what he had spilt wasn't worth the laundry bill. It would cost more in police and court time mopping up a few kids daubing lamp posts and potting windows of derelict factories than it was worth.

Slipping the cellophane wrap from a fresh carton of antacid tablets he popped one into his mouth. Jesus, he'd suck the bloody box if it would only shift the fire in his gut!

Daubing! Sounder's use of the word had tinkled a bell. That cemetery had been daubed, paint sprayed over gravestones. But Sounder had vowed he knew nothing of that and loath as he was to admit to it, for once in his dealings with the little squealer he believed him.

So given the state of play in Darlaston at this moment where were his almightyness the superintendent's results to come from?

Turning the key in the ignition, Bruce Daniels guided the car his wife had vacuumed at seven o'clock that morning on to St Lawrence Road. Like the station's new boss Marjorie wanted everything spick, span and in its place. They both wanted the same thing and Detective Inspector Daniels was the one they looked to for getting it, Marjorie wanted him to retire, the other one wanting not a slice of bacon but the whole bloody pig!

Well! He pressed the accelerator, knowing the needle passed thirty and not giving a damn.

Marjorie? She could assuage her ambitions by polishing her beloved furniture and plumping her revered cushions, and the Chief Detective Inspector? Let *him* worry about his bloody results!

# Chapter Eight

Stood beneath the shower, Torrey let the hot water play over his face. This was the only good thing to be said about this bed and breakfast, the shower was hot; but the cost on the pocket was the same.

''Lectricity don't come cheap! If yoh don't want to pay the price then go to the public baths . . . but yoh'll find that don't be no cheaper either!'

Turning so the hot stream played over his back, he smiled grimly, remembering the landlady's curt reply when he had questioned the extra daily charge. Not given to fine words was that woman . . . nor to charity . . . you'd have to pay for a kind word . . . supposing she knew how to give one!

It was so different to what he had had at Monkswell. The cottage set in those well-cared-for grounds, the use of a car to go with his free time, and there had been a lot of that, but it was the people he missed most; no not Bartley, that man he would never miss . . . but George and Maggie Barnes, the Harpers, Martha Sim and her daughter, those were the real people, the ones who had accepted him for what he was. They had not judged, on hearing of Anna they had not condemned; and when it at last dawned on him that the spirit of evil wanted him then they had rallied around him like God's little army.

He had thought what he saw was real, that it had been Anna. He had believed his eyes though his mind had told him it was impossible, that Anna was dead. But in each of those moments he had been certain he looked at a living, breathing person. Just as he'd believed the other day.

Kate had laughed at him. With his eyes closed he twisted beneath the spray of water, letting it rinse the lather from his body.

*'hopeless nutters talk to themselves'*

He smiled as he stepped from the shower. Kate Mallory was not the most tactful woman he'd ever met! But she had been right, he had been talking to himself, otherwise where could that girl in the white dress have disappeared to so quickly . . . and how come he had not seen her as he and Kate had run for the bus? The street, as he remembered, had been so deserted even a fly would have had a pronounced presence!

Was it something to do with Anna? He rubbed briskly with the towel he laundered at the washeteria. Was his mind still not free of that business, was a trace of it still lurking somewhere inside him, making him believe? But it had not been Anna! Whatever it was he had imagined he saw in that cemetery it had not been Anna.

Throwing the towel aside he dressed quickly. A young girl in a white dress! He grinned to himself . . . he'd read one too many Stephen King books! Now had he imagined Catherine Zeta-Jones calling to him, that he could understand, any man could fantasise in that direction.

The thought bringing a smile to his lips he picked up the comb from a small dresser. Lifting his hands to his hair he looked into the mirror . . . looked at a young girl who watched over his shoulder, staring at him with hopeless, pleading eyes.

* * *

He had never questioned Julian Crowley's decisions before. Like the other heads of the High Covens he had accepted what they did as the will of the Master, accepted it as the desire of the Lord of Darkness. But this latest offering, the life of a young girl . . . had that been an offering asked by Satan or one demanded by Julian Crowley's own vanity, had the girl died to satisfy his own lust, to prove his own powers? The others, what had they thought as that knife had plunged into the girl's chest? Davion? His face had held almost the same maniacal smile as Crowley's, but Geddes's had shown revulsion and Carol Brent had almost passed out; and himself, what had he felt?

Max Gau stared unseeingly at the papers placed before him on the desk, the noise of machinery from the print room unheard as his mind played over that night at Whitefriars. Like Geddes he too had felt revulsion but, like that man, he had done nothing to prevent it.

Julian Crowley was a Magus, that was the excuse he had given himself; he was far more powerful in the black arts than a Magister Templi, powerful enough to call on the High Angel of the Dark Throne, to have each and every one of them dragged into hell.

But could there be a worse hell than he was in now? Crowley had given him every comfort, every luxury in life but what had he taken in exchange? Self-respect might come cheap to some but every day Max Gau's life was becoming more difficult to live without it!

'Boxes be ready for dispatch.'

Max looked up at the man who entered the office. Fred Baker was the 'Joey', the Jack of all trades here at Darlaston Printing and like the newly appointed van driver he knew how to keep a closed mouth.

'They are all there?'

'All two dozen.' Fred Baker wiped the back of an ink-stained hand across one cheek. 'Seen to 'em meself as always.'

'Labelled?'

'Like you said, Mr Gau. Labelled "House of Jarreaux" and sealed over the label.'

'Good.' Max Gau nodded. 'Those catalogues have been excellently done, the client will be pleased and that will carry a bonus for you, Fred.'

Crowley had chosen well. Max watched the man leave. But then Crowley always chose well, taking those that life had already robbed of all they cherished, returning that which he knew would hold them to the Path.

As he had chosen Davion, a man who pledged his soul in return for money; then Geddes, a man willingly giving his in exchange for the life of the woman he loved, and Carol Brent? Oh yes, Julian Crowley had boasted of how she had been brought into the dark fold; that was Crowley's weakness. Along with too high a sense of his own self-importance he liked to boast!

Carol had run away from home when little more than a child. Crowley had revealed the girl's past one evening at Whitefriars when the business that had brought Max to that beautiful house was done and they sat together over a drink.

*'This is just a little of the powers of a Magus.'*

Max stared again at the papers neatly arranged on his desk, the words of Julian Crowley filling his brain.

It seemed he had merely lifted a hand but with it the room had filled with a pearly evanescent mist that had floated between them before fading to leave pictures, clear, sharply defined pictures that appeared to play over an invisible screen.

There had been a girl in a bed. A girl with wide, pain-filled eyes that watched the door with a fixed look. Then the door had opened and a man had entered.

Max's fingers curled as those same pictures played now in his memory.

The girl had held the blankets close up against her throat, her mouth trembling as the man, older than her by some ten years, had come to the bed, a warning finger touching his own lips as he had snatched the blankets away.

The girl had whimpered. Max pressed his eyelids hard down over his eyes but the pictures refused to be banished. Tears had streamed down her thin face as the man had slapped away hands trying to hold on to the nightgown, then after removing his own clothes he had raped the terrified girl, her own brother had raped her as he had done since she had been given into his care following their mother's death. It was the price she must pay for a home. But one night the price had become too high.

Max saw the knife being slipped beneath the pillow. The girl had held to the blankets as if even now wanting to give him the chance to leave, but it had simply caused him to grin his own warped pleasure. And it had happened as it had so many times before, the warning finger, the stripping of her slight body, his lowering himself on to her. That was when she had struck, sinking the knife between his shoulder blades, and as he had screamed and rolled off her she sank it again into his throat.

For several moments Carol Brent had stared at her hands sprayed scarlet with blood, at the knife still protruding from her brother's throat. With a strange calm she had climbed from the bed and gone to the bathroom, washing herself from head to toe, then dressed in T-shirt, jeans and jacket, she had peeped into her brother's bedroom, the room where his wife still lay sleeping, a wife who had known of a child's torment for years yet never done a thing to end it.

Max had been aware of Crowley's eyes on him, those black serpent-bright eyes that saw every nuance of pity and disgust. But Crowley's vanity had not been satisfied; he, Max, must see it all, see the powers of a Magus.

The girl had closed the door quietly, tiptoeing downstairs to the kitchen. There she had turned the taps of the gas cooker full on. In the garden she had stood in the blackness of night looking up at the window of the room that held the brother she had killed. Then taking a box of matches from her pocket she had struck one, holding it to a corner of a handkerchief. Waiting until the flame licked along the cloth she had opened the letter box, pushing the handkerchief through on the end of a thin branch snapped from an ornamental bush.

The pictures had flashed more rapidly then. Staring at them now flicking across his mental vision Max remembered thinking how they were like the brief clips of forthcoming films he used to see when, as his Saturday afternoon treat, he had sat with eyes glued to the cinema screen; just as he had sat at Whitefriars . . . as he sat now!

Carol Brent had gone the way of many a teenager who had run away from home, falling in with the wrong sort, sinking deeper and deeper. Then had come the drugs and breaking into cars to snatch the radio or mobile phone. The breaking and entering, carrying off anything that would sell, had given way to a new low, had taken on the form of street robbery, mugging the old, robbing anyone likely to have a few pounds or a piece or two of jewellery on them, not caring how much bodily harm she dished out in the process, knowing only she must feed the habit, have the next fix that cost more and more each time . . . until she had done what she had done in her bedroom, she sank a knife into a man's back. But the man had been an undercover agent with the drugs squad and as she bent over him, hands searching his pockets for cash, car sirens had announced the coming of his colleagues.

That had been when Crowley had made his accustomed move, stepping from shadows that seemed somehow to be part of him, a deeper shade of dark etched on dark. There had been no contest for him. She had accepted what was offered without question; she, like himself, had only given what was already damned. Carol Brent had been recruited.

Yes, Julian Crowley always chose well and in return for

services rendered he was given power. But powerful as he was there was one to whom had been given more, an Ipsissimus, master of all magic, enabled to travel in different dimensions, other astral planes. And this was the dagger in Crowley's flesh, a dagger which sooner or later he would attempt to remove.

Somebody somewhere must know something about this! Kate Mallory looked at the sketch the lady in red had made for her then at the one she had drawn herself, copied from a book written by somebody called Caddiente. She had visited the library again since then, spending more time trying to find information about the so-called Seal of Ashmedai but had come up with nothing fresh.

Yet it had to be there! Sat cross-legged on her bed she stared at the two pieces of paper placed side by side on the pillow. She had found the diagram in a chapter called 'The Chosen', nine-tenths of which she couldn't understand and the remaining tenth she couldn't read; but those two words she had managed to decipher, despite the ancient spellings and a language she guessed might be Latin (for her it could have been anything; English had been the only language she had mastered with any efficiency, much to the despair of her language teacher at Birtley's Lord Lawson of Beamish High School). Rummaging in her near-bottomless bag she lit a cigarette, a tab always did help her to think more clearly.

A chapter entitled 'The Chosen'! Pursing her lips she blew a slow stream of smoke, watching it drift towards the slightly opened window. It touched a chord deep in her memory but she just couldn't place it.

Think, Kate! She drew heavily on the cigarette. Think, lass . . . The Chosen! For the writer of that old book it had been a symbol of an angel of the devil, but that was crap, nobody believed in witches and warlocks these days and the devil was old hat.

It had been part of a chapter . . . a symbol . . . that was it!

Kate almost choked on the smoke in her throat. The only mystery was why she hadn't realised this before. Chapter . . . that was the name a little group of Mods and Rockers had given themselves way back in the sixties and seventies and they had each worn their symbol either as a medallion or on a jacket . . . and there was her answer! She smiled, savouring the last of her cigarette. Revivalism . . . wasn't that the modern craze? Had some kids come across the picture she had seen and taken it as the signature of their chapter, daubing it over those gravestones? Or could it be a newly formed band wanting some eye-catching sign to go with a name?

Carefully grinding the stub of her cigarette she flicked the remnant through the window before closing it.

Bands meant gigs . . . gigs meant posters . . . posters were signs.

Clever lass, Kate! After opening the bottle of anti-tobacco air freshener she always sprayed out of regard for her landlady's furnishings she reached her coat from the wardrobe. Posters meant printers . . . and Darlaston had one such establishment.

It would be closed for the night. Would there be a night watchman? Even if there was he probably wouldn't know a heavy-metal band from an elastic band. Turning along Pinfold Street she glanced at the one-time cinema turned bingo parlour. The Regal. Lord, what a mistake of a name that had turned into, it was every bit as squalid-looking as the old Apollo picture house that had once entranced Birtley's population, but like the Apollo it was plastered with posters. She could wait for Mrs Price to come out of that building, ask her if she remembered some band who used a sign similar to that drawing; but that would be near enough ten o'clock and even then the woman might not be able to help.

'But I know a man who can!' Her slightly tilted mouth curling in a satisfied smile as she murmured the slogan heard so often on television, Kate veered left into King Edward Street. This way would lead her straight to the Frying Pan; and Echo Sounder was that pub's most ardent devotee . . . and who had a memory more acute than his?

'I tells you I don't remember no such poster.'

Hunched over a near-empty glass, the scruffily dressed little man ran a tongue over dry cracked lips while his eyes remained fixed to the television set attached to a corner of the wall opposite a dart board.

'P'raps I didn't describe it very well—'

'Don't matter 'ow much you describes . . . I tells you I don't know of no such poster; now bugger off, a bar room ain't no place for a woman!'

'Not worried about my reputation are you, Echo?'

'Not your'n . . . mine!' The tight mouth snapped like a mouse trap.

Kate Mallory smiled as she glanced around at the men in the bar. None of them seemed to have the least interest in Echo Sounder or his unwanted companion but that fact would provide little remedy for the condition of the man's nerves.

'I see.' She lit a cigarette, dropping another beside his hand. 'Your reputation is in the balance . . . the town's best tenor seen singing to a journalist! Not a happy situation; but then it is one that is easily rectified, tell me what I want to know and the weight can be taken off the scales, restore things to a more acceptable balance so to speak.'

'Speakin' be your bloody trouble!' The answer was scratched from between tight lips, bright ferret eyes never leaving the television screen. ''Specially when it be me yer speaks to.'

'Now really, Echo, is that any way to talk to a nice girl?'

'Nice!' Scrabbling up the cigarette he placed it in his mouth. 'All newsperper writers would mek better sculptors for they comes from a long line o' chisellers. Trust me, they says, I won't print a word o' what you tells me and then next day there it is in black an' white . . . an' yoh be no diffrunt!'

'If I promise, it will be a secret between us two.'

Lighting the cigarette from the lighter Kate held to it, Echo Sounder blew a sharp stream of grey smoke. 'Pah! Yoh knows what be said about promises! Yoh be like other folk in this town, yoh can keep a secret, it be the people yoh tells it to that can't!'

Would she ever understand the logic of the Black Country? Kate frowned, trying to unravel the strand of thought tangled as a cat's nest. Maybe . . . if she lived as long as Methuselah! Dropping the lighter into her bag, she picked up the cigarette carton.

'It's a pity you can't help me,' she smiled, 'but maybe one of the others can, I've no doubt they won't mind a fiver for my interrupting their evening.'

'Wait!' Sounder's ferret eyes flicked to the cigarette carton in Kate's hand, then back to the horse race showing on the television. 'I can't remember no poster but maybe—'

He knows a man who can! Kate's smile deepened. That advert was doing more for co-operation than its creators ever dreamed.

'– maybe if you talks to Fred Baker.'

'Fred Baker?' Fingers twisting about the carton she waited.

Holding the almost-empty glass to his lips in an effort to disguise the fact that he was saying anything at all, the little man answered, his words almost lost as he swallowed.

'He be the Joey over at the printers, chief cook and bottle washer for years, what 'e doh know about the job ain't been invented. If there's been a poster such as yoh describes, then Fred Baker'll know of it, whether it were produced by Darlaston Printing or not.'

She could go there tomorrow . . . but how might his

employers take to his giving their time to answering her questions?

'Where can I find this Fred Baker . . . I mean outside of working hours?' she asked, solving her own problem.

'Don't know where 'e lives –' Sounder watched the carton travel towards the bag hoisted on Kate's shoulder. The bitch was worse than the bloke in a story he'd once heard at school: this one would tek her pound o' flesh and be buggered to the blood it spilled, but either he tell 'er or her withdrew the bait. Taking a slow quiet breath he finished the sentence.

'– but 'e teks his pint in the Knot.'

Crushing the carton casually, Kate dropped it into the ashtray before turning to leave. That was one expense she couldn't put on her account.

She could only hope it proved worth the spending!

# Chapter Nine

'I think perhaps Diego . . .'

Soft folds of chartreuse cashmere hinted at the perfect body beneath, complementing immaculately styled red-gold hair and flawless complexion, as Nicole Jarreaux fingered the treble row of fine gold chains about her throat.

'. . . I suggest you view at least some of his new creations.'

Waiting for the affirmative nod from the woman whose elegance matched her own in every detail, she half turned, and immediately a slim, tastefully dressed figure moved to where the two sat.

'Madame will view in the Florentine room, Louise.'

Her reply just a whisper on the perfumed air, the figure glided away and Nicole returned her attention to the woman sat in a throne-like gilded chair. Isobel Davion enjoyed being treated like royalty and Nicole enjoyed making her pay for the privilege.

'It will take some time for the models to prepare.' She stood up, every move poised and confident. 'Perhaps while you are waiting you may care to meet the designer.'

It was said casually, giving no hint to any listening ear that the whole thing was carefully organised.

So this was the new acquisition. Isobel Davion eyed the man who came to join them. Not tall, five feet seven or eight, with shoulders just wide enough to deny the feminine label some might attach to that definite waist, tight hips and flutter of the hand; but feminine or not, he was certainly a looker. She smiled into heavily fringed cinnamon eyes gleaming in a handsome, slightly olive-hued face set to advantage by blue-black hair he had paid some designer a packet to style.

Nice . . . and the rest matched. She ran the eye of the discerning over the man who had just touched her hand to his lips. Full lips, good teeth, cream pants and silk shirt that clung like a lover's arms. If his talents bore any resemblance to his looks and flair for dress she might be well pleased!

'Diego.' Nicole turned to him. 'Mrs Davion has agreed to a viewing of your collection, I trust what you have will please her.'

'I trust so too, madame.'

Cinnamon eyes smiled directly into Isobel's, his heavily contrived accent declaring its own illegitimacy.

'Perhaps, Isobel, I might leave you in Diego's hands. I have the Duchess of Retford in the Venetian room.'

'Barbara,' Isobel smiled acidly, 'a sweet bitch but such a shame about the face, it's one a dog wouldn't lick! Sell her something in red, darling, she looks positively ghastly in red.'

That makes two bitches! One who can't wear red and one who can't keep her legs closed! Nicole buried the words beneath a smile.

'I'll leave you with Diego then. Have Louise let me know when the viewing is over.'

'Madame.' Diego gave a half-bow and Isobel followed. Christ, she hoped the little charmer had something worth the effort!

'Of course it can be made in madame's choice of colour.'

'No, I like the colour –' Isobel had asked to see again an organza evening gown '– white is so . . . so virginal.'

So completely wrong for you then, Diego, alias Frank

Partridge, smiled again, long practice hiding the thoughts behind the smile. 'It can reach perfection only on madame.'

Keep going, Diego. Isobel considered the gown. You're doing fine so far.

'Yes, I like it.' She turned to the woman standing a little to the left of the magnolia-taffeta-covered tongue of catwalk. 'Have it put with the others.' She had chosen several evening gowns along with cocktail dresses, day dresses, play and beach wear; but chosen was all. She caught the satisfaction on Diego's mouth as another several thousand pounds was added to the mounting bill; he was going to have to come up with a whole lot more to keep it there.

'Is that the whole of your collection?' The last pencil-thin model swept the platform with silver mink.

'*Si*, madame,' Diego nodded, 'that ees all of my finished collection, there ees more . . .' he hesitated in well-rehearsed style, 'but they are – how you speak it? – undressed?'

'Unfinished.' Isobel reached for the Gucci bag that matched her designer-label saffron suit. If this little shit came up to scratch, that phoney and incorrect Spanish accent would be the second thing he would drop.

'Ah *si*,' Diego's hands spread expressively, 'unfinished, it is only on paper.'

'Drawings.' Isobel stood up.

'*Si*, drawings . . . my next beautiful gowns zey are just drawings.'

'I'd like to see them.'

'*Muy Bien*, madame.' A well-manicured hand moved in the direction of Louise. 'I will ask zey be brought.'

'Not right now.' Isobel's expensively dressed sherry-coloured hair swished softly as she shook her head. 'I'll get Nicole to bring them along to the house, or who knows she may even get you to bring them.' She turned a dismissive back on Louise who glided away. 'I'm afraid I am going to need new fittings.' She smiled as the taffeta-swathed door closed. 'The measurements the salon has must be hopelessly wrong; it's positively ages since they were checked.'

Diego turned on the mechanical smile. 'If madame will come to ze fitting room I will ask for Petra to . . .'

'Why bother Petra? I'm sure you can manage perfectly well yourself.' Isobel walked to a door almost undetectable among sweeps of taffeta that matched walls to door.

'You've only recently joined Jarreaux?' Isobel slid out of the designer-label, letting it lie like some high-street copy on the pearl-coloured carpet. The rest room, as Nicole liked to call those ultra-private rooms leading off the more select suites where the loaded might view the Jarreaux label in more exclusivity, were every bit as luxurious as the rest of the salon.

'*Si.*'

'But this is not your first personal fitting?'

'It is one will surely give Diego ze most satisfaction.'

Evaded like a pro – which is no doubt what the pseudo little Spaniard was before Nicole found him. Janet Reger underwear followed the designer label, creating an island of blue silk on the pearl carpet.

Facing a floor-to-ceiling mirror Isobel surveyed the body money had kept good. The legs could have been longer but she couldn't have everything, the waist was small, the hips neat, breasts high and taut, that was due to not having kids. Kids might be okay for others but for Isobel Davion . . . breasts and the games they inspired were more desirable. She lifted her hands, cupping the small mounds.

'Don't you think it's time we began?' she said to the man at her back.

'*Hermoso*, beautiful.' He stepped close, holding his hands beneath her wrists, lifting her arms until they stretched sideways from her shoulders then his hands rode back, drawing inwards across her shoulder blades. Isobel watched the dark head bend towards her.

'*Hermoso,*' he breathed, his tongue touching her neck and trailing downwards along her spine. 'Ees *seda.*' His hands dropped slowly over her thighs, down the length of her legs. 'Ees *misimo seda.*' His lips touched a spot at the base of her backbone. '*Muy hermoso.*' His tongue touched again. His hands were on the inside of her legs now, moving upwards then pausing as fingers touched against sherry-coloured pubic hair. Isobel was particular that top and bottom should match even if neither were natural. Pushing up from his haunches he dragged both hands sensuously up over her buttocks and around her waist, fingers spread across her rib cage, closing together as they fastened over her breasts. '*Exquisito,*' he murmured, meeting her gaze in the mirror, '*muy exquisito.*'

How did the sly bastard get his eyes to smoke over like that? He'd obviously been in the seduction business too long for it to be natural! Isobel held the hot cinnamon eyes, just what *had* Nicole's little pseudo Spanish rag merchant been told to play for?

With her arms still stretched he pulled her into him, the slim gold buckle of the snake-skin belt about his waist pressed into her back but Isobel ignored it, she didn't want to put him off just yet. His eyes still holding hers through the long mirror, he curled his tongue about her ear, taking the lobe between white teeth and loosing it to drag his mouth down her neck and across her shoulders.

'*Querida.*' he whispered.

Very good! Isobel dropped her arms as he turned her slowly around. He's matching the voice to the eyes; no matter where he'd received the tutoring he'd learned well . . . better than he had learned Spanish, but then that was always supposing the action shots matched the opening play!

For a moment he roved a hot gaze over her nakedness then quickly bent his head to take one nipple in his mouth, circling it with his tongue while his finger did the same to the other. It was several seconds before he pulled away, stretching her nipple, letting it slide slowly from between his teeth; then with both hands cupping her breasts he sank slowly to his knees, his tongue snaking downwards over her flat stomach and touching the silky vee at its base.

'Hey, *hombre!*' Isobel patted the top of the dark head. 'You've taken the measurements now the lady wants to see the goods.'

He withdrew his tongue lingeringly, darting it back several times to touch the silken triangle as if reluctant to give it up; kissing upwards he was naked when his mouth took her breast.

You've dropped the first thing, Diego, Isobel thought as he kicked free of the pants dropped around his feet; one more to go.

'Nice!' She stepped backwards, her keen glance taking in his amber slimness, the colour was the same all over, she liked that. 'Very nice!' Reaching out she spread her hands over his smooth breast bone, hairy men had never turned her on.

'Come, *querido*.' Taking her hand he kissed the palm and led her to a long low couch covered in palest dove silk. As with the viewing rooms the walls shimmered with costly cloth; the theory behind a mound of blush-pearl luxury was that a bed must be provided should clients wish to rest after fittings.

'Lie down *querido*.' Expertly he lowered her on to the couch. Kneeling at the foot he spread her legs, his fingers sliding over her skin. 'It ees good, no?' He spread a little further. 'You like what Diego ees doing, eh?' He leaned upwards across her belly, mouthing a nipple. '*Si* . . . you like it, *mio bello*?'

Isobel felt the muscles of her stomach jerk. The man might be less than an expert with Spanish language but he knew how to pleasure a woman.

'*Querido* likes it?'

Isobel groaned softly, her legs widening. He was right, the little arsehole was right, she did like it!

'Ees agreeable, *si*?' His tongue flicked her navel. 'Ees nice, but Diego has more.'

'Hold it, Diego!'

'*Si* . . . ees good . . .' He leaned over her, his body pressing her back against the couch and something hard touching between her legs. 'Diego know, *mio bello,* you will like . . .'

'I said hold it, Diego!' Pushing him away Isobel sat up, a kick sending the vibrator skimming across the room. 'I never buy imitations,' she said coldly, 'you either come up with the real thing or it's *adios, amigo,* and talking of imitations let's say you drop the phoney Spanish bit.'

'So you prefer the real thing!' He stood up. 'How about this . . . real enough for ya?'

'Mmm . . . I prefer.' She reached forward, spreading a hand low on each thigh, thumbs beneath hard testicles. 'I much prefer.' Sliding her fingers in a half-circle she fastened around the root of the hardened column of flesh, thumbs stroking. What the man lacked in height he made up for in tackle. She leaned into him, her lips brushing his stomach. 'It looks good,' she looked up at him, 'now let's see how it feels.'

'Whatever the lady wants.' Picking her up he carried her to the silk-robed bed, depositing her in the centre. As he stretched beside her and one leg thrust between hers, his tongue teased her nipples. Isobel twined her arms around his amber shoulders, twisting her stomach to the throbbing promise. He hadn't been the first to plough her field, but he had a certain touch, an ability to arouse a jaded palate.

'Wait.' She held him off as he made to slide over her. Reaching for the Gucci bag she had dropped on to a small pearl-lacquered bedside table she took out a square gold compact, the initials ID worked in yellow diamonds. 'Put it on.' Dropping the compact she held her hand towards him, a painted fingernail trailing a condom.

Ignoring it he rolled on to her, pushing between her legs.

'Put it on, you bastard –' Isobel's shoulders dug into the pearl silk, her body arching to the touch that threatened to bring her to orgasm '– put the bloody thing on!'

'You put it on!' He knelt up abruptly, his knees forcing her legs wider apart, his handsome face smiling cynically. The lady wanted it badly, now they would play his way.

'Why, you—' Isobel stared unbelieving. 'You little shit, I'll have your arse for this!'

'It's not my arse you want.' Cinnamon eyes smouldered as he took her wrist, forcing the hand that held the condom into his groin.

Isobel felt the swollen flesh jerk against her hand. Christ, she wanted that!

'*Bueno*,' he smiled as the condom was smoothed into place.

'Hey Diego, *hombre*!' Lying back on the bed Isobel Davion looked into the handsome face. 'Cut the crap . . . just fuck me!'

There must be money in the frock game! Richard Torrey drew the van to a halt as the traffic signals flicked to red. Business was competitive in any sphere but the precautions taken for those catalogues! The traffic light now green he eased the van forwards, following the road out of Wolverhampton. Gau and Baker had watched each box placed into the van, Max Gau satisfying himself that the seals were unbroken, while the same had happened at the other end. Obviously these catalogues were not the sort that landed unsolicited on your doorstep offering ten per cent off your first order as he could tell by the way that woman had watched him unload!

The House of Jarreaux – pound notish his mother would have called that, pretending to be worth a pound when it wasn't worth tuppence. Well, Mother, he smiled, I bet that place is worth a hell of a lot more than that.

He'd carried each box into that building in Temple Street. It was unremarkable from the outside but the inside had been a different story. Not the goods entrance for that delivery, those boxes had gone through the front foyer straight into a lift to be whisked away somewhere among the plush perfumed depths that was a world away from the dusty crowded streets of Wolverhampton.

The boxes gone he'd been gone, ushered from that deeply carpeted vestibule as if he were a stain on it. Crossing the junction at Mount Pleasant he followed along Oxford Street, nose to tail with traffic. He hadn't been surprised at being removed so speedily, the prices he guessed would be paid by any client of the House of Jarreaux wouldn't include a man in worker's overalls stood inside the front door.

If he would wait in the tradesman's department . . .

As the traffic thinned he picked up speed. Even the goods yard had to be given a pound-note description! The tradesman's department . . . Kate Mallory would love that! That girl sometimes had a tongue that made a lemon seem sweet and no doubt she would use it liberally in describing the svelte, not-a-hair-out-of-place female attendant who had shown him the door. But it had been Kate Mallory with her down-to-earth common sense who had helped him finally rid himself of the spectre of Anna. True, Martha Sim had tried to do the same in that cottage in Monkswell, tried to banish the evil that Anna had become, but it was Kate who had really got him to see sense, to realise it was no ghostly hand had prised his fingers from Philip Bartley's jacket; Kate Mallory's common sense had made him acknowledge that in truth the man had simply slipped from his grasp.

*'There are no such things as ghoulies and ghosties.'*

Kate had laughed when she had said that, teasing him about checking beneath his bed before going to sleep.

Driving past Katherine's Cross he glanced at the shuttered and deserted building that had been the Bird-in-Hand; the building where the nightmare had begun.

'No such things as ghosts, eh Kate?' he murmured. 'Then what would you call the girl in white, the girl who spoke to me in that cemetery, the same one who watched me in the bathroom mirror yet when I turned around was no longer there!'

# Chapter Ten

'Who told you?'

'Look, Kate,' Richard Torrey looked across the table littered with the remnants of a pub meal, 'I may be the new lad and, unbelievable as you seem to think it, Fred Baker does talk to me. As he said it, "this wench were asking about some old poster, thought it might have advertised a rock band at one time or another" and from his description I guessed that wench was you.'

'What else did he tell you?'

Smiling at the woman who came to collect the dishes, Torrey waited until she was gone.

'Not here!' Reaching across the table he grabbed the carton of Rothmans Kate fished from her bag, dropping them into his pocket.

'Smoking is allowed in this corner!' Kate Mallory's brown eyes flashed.

'It's also allowed outside and out there I don't breathe the smoke.'

Her stare warning of storms ahead Kate rose from her chair. 'Where's your badge?'

'Badge?'

Nodding to the landlord as she led the way to the street she turned angrily. 'They do give you one don't they? The do-gooders 'let's see what we can interfere with next brigade!'

Torrey gave way to the smile rising inside him. He was right. Compared to her a lemon would taste sweet.

'I wonder if Shakespeare knew a Kate like you?' He grinned amiably. 'It's my guess he must have to have written his *Taming of the Shrew*.'

'Sod William Shakespeare and sod your do-gooders!' Kate flashed. 'Just give me my tabs or you won't have to guess what's going to happen next, you'll feel it . . . and it's likely to leave a few nasty marks on your marriage furniture!'

'Ouch!' His grin widening he handed over the cigarettes, watching as she lit one.

'I know, I know,' she muttered between puffs, 'so you've told me . . . these things will kill me, but at least I won't have to account to my maker for spoiling other folks' pleasure!' She dropped the carton into the wide mouth of her bag, glaring defensively at him.

'Sorry.' He held up both hands. 'Truce?'

With a laugh bubbling in her throat Kate turned away. 'You didn't answer my question. What else did Fred Baker tell you?'

'It wasn't so much what he said as what the words he didn't use said.'

Lord that convoluted way of speaking! It was enough to drive a girl to drink, only this evening she hadn't been given the chance to have even one let alone enough to do that trick!

'Torrey,' I know that having digs at Annie's house should leave me with an eminent knowledge and understanding of the local dialect but that last sentence, as my teacher of religious education would say, – 'passeth all understanding'.

'It means you would do yourself a lot of good to drop it, to forget what it was you were looking for.'

'Then he did recognise that sketch!'

'What sketch?'

Delving once more into the cavernous regions of the bag, Kate held out the sketch her lady in red had given her. 'That sketch!'

'What the hell is it?'

'It's what was daubed on those headstones in Bentley cemetery.'

'But there was nothing like this. You said yourself there was nothing apart from a few smears of paint when you first went there, and there was certainly no trace of any design that day we visited the scene together.'

'Not then there wasn't, but how do we know it hadn't been there? How do we know it wasn't washed off before anybody had the chance of seeing it?'

Torrey glanced at the animated face, seeing the light in those dark amber eyes. Whatever this queer-looking sketch was of, Kate Mallory saw it as interesting.

'Well if it wasn't there – and it wasn't! – how come you think this was part of that paint job?'

'I didn't, my woman from the bus did.'

Words coming between puffs on her cigarette, Kate repeated the whole story, following it up with the sketch she had copied from the book in the library.

'The Seal of Ashmedai.' He handed back both pieces of paper, watching them disappear into the bottomless regions of the bag. 'Could have been a rock band though like Fred Baker says it rings no bells.'

If that's all that symbol was, the flashy sign of some forgotten group of would-be pop stars, why should Fred Baker imply it would be best left that way? But she had no intention of forgetting it. Kate crushed the minute stub of her cigarette, dropping it into an ornate waste bin stood outside the town hall. There was more to it than a poster and she intended knowing what it was!

* * *

'He has settled into the job?'

'Quite well. Fred tells me he is punctual, that he makes no complaint if a job takes him past his finishing time and he knows the local area like the back of his hand; all in all I would say he is the perfect candidate.'

'Good.' Julian Crowley turned from a window that overlooked a small yard at the rear of Darlaston Printing. 'Just as he will make the perfect candidate for the rest of what I have in mind.'

'Really, Julian, I don't think—'

'That's good, Max!' Julian Crowley's black eyes glittered. 'You should not think; somehow I feel the Master would not like that: he wants followers who accept . . . accept what he ordains without asking for whys or wherefores. If you can't do that then I fear for your future, my friend.'

'I do not question the Master—'

'No!' Crowley smiled coldly. 'No it is not the Master you question, even Max Gau is not rash enough to do that; but you do question me . . . am I not correct?'

'It's just that I don't see it as necessary, surely once was enough.'

'Enough, Max?' Cold, reptilian eyes rested unblinking on Gau's face. 'You set yourself up as judge? Saying what the Master should and should not have . . . again, my friend, I advise that you take care.'

He was twisting the words to suit himself. Max Gau looked at the man he had come to detest. Crowley had always liked power, enjoyed domination, now he was developing a taste for murder.

'I just think it's too risky.' Max knew he was backing down but couldn't help it; Crowley didn't hold just the aces, he held the whole bloody pack. 'Richard Torrey is more widely known here than the girl was, to have him suddenly disappear would be bound to raise questions.'

Across the small room that served as Max Gau's private office his visitor waved a dismissive hand.

'Penny Smith! A nonentity . . . a nothing! An unimportant little clerk who came from nowhere!'

'Even unimportant clerks have relatives and they sometimes wonder where theirs might be.'

'Not the Smith girl, you know I have ways of ensuring there can be no comeback from that or any other quarter.'

'But she didn't have to die!'

'Penny Smith was given to the Master,' Crowley's voice rose. 'She was the sacrifice he demanded for the atonement of the mistakes made in that cemetery, her life was the price that had to be paid for the protection of the Covens, and against that she was nothing!'

'And Richard Torrey . . . what will his life purchase? What end do you propose the sacrificing of him to achieve?'

Turning back towards the window Julian Crowley watched the white van with its bronze copperplate lettering pull into the yard, his stare sweeping over the figure slipping lithely from the cab.

'In a few weeks,' he said quietly, 'it will be the Great Sabbat, the most holy night in the Satanic calendar. On that night will sacrifice be made, on that night Richard Torrey will be the gift we make to the Prince of Darkness . . . the supreme gift of our love.'

And the reward given! Max Gau could almost feel the desire he knew shone at that moment on the other man's face. Julian Crowley would send a man to his death and in return . . . the power of Ipsissimus? Would Crowley ask the supreme reward for the giving of the supreme gift, would he dare ask so much?

Yes, he would dare. Max glanced down at his desk, his hands straightening already neat papers.

'Until then we must get to know your new employee a little better.'

Crowley swung round, his face once more bland, giving away none of the desires hot in his heart. 'Have the next delivery sent to Whitefriars . . . and Max, make sure there are no slip-ups . . . on anybody's part!'

Echo Sounder had vowed he knew nothing of that job at the cemetery and she believed him. Kate stared intently at the design sketched on a sheet of her notepad. Had that paint been sprayed by local kids getting their kicks he would have known about it and been more than ready to sell that knowledge on. A fiver was like a quick snort to the man, impossible to resist; he was as addicted to gambling as a junkie to heroin. It was safe to cross him off her list. But what of Fred Baker? He had been talkative enough when she introduced herself in the Staffordshire Knot even when she told him she worked on the news desk of the *Star*; that was the point most people usually stopped talking, but not Fred Baker.

Yes he had printed a lot of show-business stuff, for venues such as the Birmingham Hippodrome, the Wolverhampton Grand, he'd even done stuff for the Shakespeare at Stratford-on-Avon.

He had been proud of the work he had produced, running off a list of groups and singers when she had asked about pop bands, mentioning names that were now top liners and others she had never heard of.

She had let him ramble on, buying him a drink, sharing her precious Rothmans, waiting for a mention of Ashmedai. But he had not spoken that name, made no reference however vague to a group using it as a stage name, no club act no theatre performer. If he had ever printed posters or advertising literature of any sort bearing that name then it seemed it was so far in the past he had completely forgotten it.

That was how it had seemed! Sat cross-legged on her bed,

Kate studied the sketch, a thin weaving mist of cigarette smoke giving it the illusion of movement. But then she had shown him the paper, spread it on the table in front of him and when she had asked could he recall printing anything like that he had closed up like a clam.

Why? She blew a steady stream of smoke towards the ceiling, watching it become caught by air from the partly opened window and, inveigled by some unseen force, waft into the dark oblivion of night. Why had Fred Baker so suddenly lost the taste for conversation? He had been voluble enough up to that point but sight of that circle with its symbols and triangle had his mouth closed tighter than a miser's purse. He had no knowledge of it at all, not what it might be nor who it could represent; but if that were so why had he told Torrey what he had? Maybe he hadn't said so in as many words . . . when did any Black Country person speak in language that the rest of the country could understand! But he had intimated she should drop it, let the whole thing go.

She drew the last puff from the stub of cigarette letting the smoke slide from her mouth in a slow luxurious stream that followed its predecessor out of the window.

From a man who knew nothing, that was a strange piece of advice! But whether he did or didn't recognise it, he was saying nothing and that meant she could cross off number two from her list of likely informants.

Which left Detective Inspector Bruce Daniels. In the bathroom Kate gave her teeth their nightly scrub.

Had he seen that symbol painted across the stones? Had the vicar caused it to be washed off before the police had been sent for . . . had it even been there at all?

Returning to her room she climbed into bed. Snapping off the gaudy pink-shaded bedside lamp she lay with eyes open, staring into the swamp of shadows.

There were so many questions and so few answers. Torrey had laughed it off, implying that this time her journalistic instinct was way off line, but at the same time she had got the distinct impression he too wanted some answers. But who to get them from? He and Fred Baker seemed to like each other so, assuming the man did know more than he had confided to her, would he open up to Torrey? But if there was no more to be got from there . . . where to next? Re-enter Inspector Bruce Daniels.

She could ask to see him. She could try insisting she see him. Kate smiled in the darkness. She almost *could* see him; he would reach for the tablet that would hopefully counteract the acid in his stomach, cursing as he told one of his constables to 'chuck the bloody nuisance out!' Then he would rant on awhile about 'bloody journalists, they never do get anything right, you tell 'em one thing and they prints another . . . well you keep 'em outta my hair!'

But the inspector was much like Echo Sounder. They both had a habit they couldn't kick and neither could resist temptation. Sounder couldn't say no to the promise of a fiver that would give him an hour or two at the race track and Bruce Daniels could not say no to the promise of a clue that might lead him to a haul such as the Bartley one.

But to get a fish to bite you had to bait the hook. But with what . . . and where to get it? What she needed was a worm, the worm of evidence to dangle under Daniels's nose; and that brought her full circle, she was back at the beginning and the first question was . . . evidence of what?

*'I've seen this thing afore'*

The words floated in her mind, a sword edge against sleep.

*'folks reckoned they was black magicians'*

Could whoever desecrated those stones in Bentley cemetery be practising black magic? Was that the answer?

The Seal of Ashmedai, High Prince of the Black Throne, First Angel of Lucifer . . .

Kate felt her pulses quicken. Perhaps the question was not so much could the practising of black magic be the answer as could it be anything else but the answer!

*'No slip-ups!'*

He knew what lay behind those words, the warning they masked! Max Gau swirled the brandy in his glass. Crowley was telling him he would brook no interference with his plans, tolerate no deviation from the Way of the Path.

But whose path was Crowley following, that of the Lord of Darkness or his own? Was it he who wanted that ritual, he who wanted the offering made, his the desire for sacrifice? There had been other Walpurgis nights and each had honoured the Dark Lord with sacrifice, but always it had been the blood of a cockerel that had drained into the dish and always it had been enough.

But now, suddenly, it was not enough. Lucifer must be honoured not with the gift of a cockerel but with the gift of human life; human blood must flow into the dish.

So why had Lucifer demanded change? To safeguard the covens, to protect them against discovery following that episode in the cemetery? No, the All Powerful would do that without taking life . . . and if it should be that the Master must be appeased in that way why not ask the life of one of the people who had taken part in that stupid little affair? That more than taking the life of Richard Torrey, a man they might never have met, would drive the lesson home the hardest!

But Crowley had decreed what was to be done and whether it was the choice of the Master or the servant then that was the choice each of them would follow.

But it didn't have to be like that. Like Davion, Geddes and the rest, Crowley was no more than a puppet, an instrument to be used for a purpose, something that could be discarded or destroyed should that instrument fail to please.

No one had ever challenged Crowley! Max continued to swirl the brandy, watching the light dance in the golden amber liquid, seeing it brighten and fade . . . reflect and change; much as the will of the High Lord might change . . . as Crowley's bright star might be caused to fade.

# Chapter Eleven

'Help me.'

Locking the door of the van, Richard Torrey's fingers froze on the key. It was the voice he had heard in that cemetery, a voice he had heard several times since, the voice of a young girl who disappeared whenever he tried to reach her.

*'There are no such things as ghoulies and ghosties.'*

Kate Mallory's laugh echoed in his mind but it was not enough to drown the words that came again, the pitiful pleading words of a frightened girl.

'Help me, Mr Torrey.'

God Almighty, it had his name now! His fingers still holding the key in the lock, he stood perfectly still. *It* . . . *it* had his name. But what exactly was *it*? Anna? Was it the spirit of Anna returned? But the girl he had seen looked nothing like Anna, nothing like Anna had ever looked, yet if the dead could return to haunt the living what was to say they could not take on a new appearance?

'Please . . .'

The whispered plea raising the small hairs on the back of his neck Torrey swallowed hard. All of his years in the Army, all of his commando training hadn't equipped him to deal with this! So how did you deal with it . . . with something you didn't know and couldn't touch? Yet deal he had to.

Withdrawing the key, he dropped it into the palm of his hand. Something solid to hold on to, something real? He hadn't needed comfort of that kind since the days of Ron Webster and his bully-boy mates . . . but there was always a next time, he smiled grimly to himself, and this, Torrey, is a next time!

With the key gripped in his hand he turned. The yard was empty, there was no one there, it had been his imagination all along! Snapping out a breath that was nothing if not relief, he laughed quietly. 'Get a grip, Torrey,' he murmured, 'or you'll be sharing digs with the psychos!'

It was then he saw it. A movement at the corner of his eye, something white.

Staring towards a window overlooking the yard, he watched the partly lowered blind roll upwards and a face lean towards the glass to look down at him. A young face with eyes wide with fear and a mouth that shaped the same words: Help me.

'How?'

Despite himself, despite all he had told himself regarding imagination Torrey called out.

'How can I help you . . . what do you want?'

Above him, framed by the window a figure raised a hand, a hand that beckoned.

'You can talk.' Torrey took a step forward with each word. 'Leastways you make me hear what you want me to hear so tell me, what is it you want?'

'Eh up, Torrey lad! Where be you going in such a 'urry?' Coming out from the print shop, coat and cap in place, Fred Baker turned questioningly to the man already halfway up the steps that provided a fire escape for the offices of the upper floor of Darlaston Printing.

'Be no use you going up there whatever your reason be, ain't nobody there. That there cleanin' woman be finished an' gone 'alf an hour an' more . . . you an' me be the only two left.'

'What about the receptionist?'

'Left at 'alf four, young 'uns don't 'ang about these days, most on 'em don't want to work at all.'

'Then who is that?' Torrey pointed towards the window.

'Who be who?'

Nerves stretched tight a moment ago made Torrey's answer sharper than intended.

'Don't be vague, Fred, you know who I mean, the girl in the window . . . who is she?'

Pushing his cap back from his forehead Fred Baker squinted at the window.

'Ain't no wench as I can see.'

'There!' Torrey's head jerked backwards, his glance riding to the upper window. 'A girl in a white dress, a girl who—'

The rest dying on his lips he stared at the window, its blind half-lowered.

'Christ, am I going mad!' he muttered. 'First Anna and now—'

'It be the sun, it plays over that winder just about this time and the reflections on the glass makes you believe you sees all sorts o' shapes an' figures.'

Stood at the foot of the steps Fred Baker set his cap back over his forehead as he watched Torrey descend.

The sun might play tricks on the mind but from the look on that man's face it had been no reflection of the sun he had seen. There had been something else at that window, something that had rattled the new van driver.

'Not very flattering to a lass.'

'Hmm?'

'I said it isn't flattering to a woman to be invited for a meal then have her escort sitting with his mind on another planet!'

'Sorry, Kate.' Torrey smiled.

'Sorry don't butter no parsnips! Lord, this town has me talking in riddles now!'

'Go on . . . you know you love Darlaston.'

'I don't love being ignored!' Kate's retort was flammable. 'Your mind has been somewhere else the whole evening so how about bringing it back just long enough to pay the bill, I'll take myself to the bus!'

The teasing glint that had just about made it to his eyes faded, leaving them clouded.

'I'm sorry,' he said again, 'I didn't mean to ignore you, it's just that I've got something on my mind.'

'Is it something a lass from Birtley could help with . . . or would you rather I mind my own business?'

Glancing at the tables nearest to them Torrey shook his head. They were all engrossed in their own conversations but he didn't relish his chances. Kate Mallory already thought him crazy, he didn't want it to become popular opinion.

'Can we carry on with this somewhere less crowded?'

This wasn't the Torrey she knew. Free of the restaurant Kate fell into step beside him. Usually the last thing that bothered him was people; she might go so far as to say she knew of nothing that had ever bothered him . . . except for Anna!

The bus ride from Wolverhampton back to Darlaston passed in virtual silence. Kate's own mind was now operating in some dimension accessible only to her. Torrey was becoming more and more tense, it was obvious each time they met . . . could it be the shade of Anna, was the memory of lost love plaguing him all over again?

'It's okay.' She smiled as they left the bus at the Bull Stake. 'No need to walk me home, I'm a big girl now.'

'Are big girls allowed a drink?'

'Hmmm!' Kate's slightly tilted mouth twisted as she gave the question thought. 'Only if she's allowed a tab with it.'

'Frying Pan?'

'Why not!' Kate nodded. 'It's the only place a girl can smoke without feeling big brother is watching . . . and before you say anything I reserve the right to kill myself in my own way, *capiche*?'

'Whatever that meant, I agree.'

'This place is no less crowded.' She glanced about the pub as Torrey placed drinks on the table. 'But short of the park, I can't think of anywhere that might be. This is the night Annie has her bosom friends round, so my digs are out and our going to the park at this time of night could be misconstrued.'

His hands about his glass he allowed the quip to pass. 'Kate . . .' he paused. 'I don't know how to explain—'

'Ghoulies and ghosties . . . is that it?' Lighting a cigarette she drew in deeply, waiting for his answer, and when it failed to come she asked quietly, 'Was it Anna?'

'No!' He looked up quickly. 'At least I don't think it was.'

'But it was some form of apparition?'

He could always trust Kate Mallory to hit the nail on the head.

'I don't know what else to call it.'

'But you only saw it once at that cemetery?'

'No . . . no, Kate. Not only once and not only in that cemetery; I've seen it since . . . in several places. I'm not imagining things, Kate, not unless I imagined everything that happened in Monkswell too and if I imagined that . . . that ghost, then so did Martha Sim.'

'The mind plays tricks . . .'

'And we all have nightmares! Sorry, Kate, but I'm all out of listening to that. I *do* see and I *do* hear, what I want to know is why . . . why me? I'm no psychic, Lord knows I've never had any time for those who believe the dead can return!'

'Yet you believed it was Anna who talked to you, Anna who you saw, and you believed it was the ghost of Anna drove Bartley and the others to their deaths. You can't have it both ways . . . believing one day and not the next. If it was a ghost then why not now?'

'I thought you were the one said there were no such things as ghoulies and ghosties.'

'We are not talking about me!' Kate blew a peremptory stream of smoke over her shoulder. 'I'm not the one having hallucinations.'

'Now who wants it both ways.' He smiled, cradling the tall glass. 'First you say it's a definite ghost now suddenly it's an hallucination.'

As she tapped ash into the freshly cleaned ashtray, a retort sharp on her tongue, Kate caught the bleak look in those hitherto keen dark eyes. Torrey was doing his utmost to pass off what it was that played on his mind, but passing things off never solved anything.

'Torrey.' She extinguished the cigarette. 'You said you had something on your mind, you asked could we go somewhere other than that perfectly acceptable restaurant in order to discuss it, now . . . do we discuss or do we play ring-a-ring-of-roses for the rest of the evening?'

Staring into his glass he seemed to read his own thoughts in the gleaming depths.

'The first time was at that cemetery. I thought a young girl spoke to me, a girl with short brown hair and wearing a white dress, but then I looked again and she was no longer there. I thought it was a kid acting the fool who legged it when she saw you coming, but as the bus pulled away she was there again, standing at the bus stop. I dismissed the whole thing but that night I saw the same figure again, this time standing across the street from my digs; I'd opened the curtains as I always do before getting into bed and there she was, staring up at my window. The next morning I gave the whole episode the same description you did, imagination . . . maybe an after-effect of Monkswell. Anyway it didn't bother me over much, then in the bathroom I saw it again, the same thin face, the same helpless eyes watching me in the mirror; now this evening at the printers, the same figure . . . the same girl staring down from an upstairs office window. I tell you, Kate, I'm beginning to wonder whether I'm a candidate for the funny farm!'

'Forget the cheap get-out, the NHS is stretched to capacity.' Kate tried to sound unconcerned.

'Then what is the get-out?' He let the attempt at humour pass.

'Have you thought of asking Martha Sim? Could be she knows a way of tackling this . . . whatever it is!'

'That's out . . . that is definitely out!' He shook his head. 'Martha is an old woman, I won't have her drawn into another of my problems, this one I work out for myself!'

'Then start working it out.' Setting her drink to one side Kate produced notepad and pen.

'Don't you ever go anywhere without those?'

'A girl must always be prepared.' She grinned.

Leaning across the table he caught the hand that held the pen, his dark eyes serious. 'No newspaper, Kate!'

Meeting his look with one equally serious she answered quietly, 'This one isn't for the *Star*.'

Starting with the visit to the cemetery they went over the whole thing again itemising each point, noting any and every explanation until an hour later Kate put down the pen.

Watching him set fresh drinks on the table, she lit what she promised herself was definitely her last cigarette before morning, dropping her lighter into her bag before asking, 'You are sure that's it, Torrey . . . that is everything as it happened?'

He had not told her everything. He took a long swallow from his glass, using the moment to decide. Did he want to tell her the rest . . . would it do any good? P'raps not, but would it do any better keeping it to himself?

'No.' He replaced his glass on the table. 'It's not quite everything. Fred Baker said what I thought I had seen at that window was a reflection of the sunlight, but when I asked was he sure the receptionist had left he said she wasn't like the one they had had before. "A nice little wench that one 'ad been," he said, "thin and gauky like, timid as a rabbit; seemed almost as if the world were new to 'er. But ask an' 'er would do anythin' for yer, weren't nuthin' too much trouble, 'er would look at yer with them big 'elpless lookin' eyes an' smile: course I will, Mr Baker, 'er would say, I'll do it right away. 'Er were a real nice wench . . . not like that snotty-nosed bugger Gau's got in 'er place. I tells you, Torrey lad, it fair surprised me when the gaffer says as 'er 'ad left. Just gone 'ome one night an' never come back." Then he showed me a photograph that had been taken at some fete held in the park.'

Kate waited while he took another drink, seeing his knuckles white against the glass as he set it down.

'It was a photograph of Fred and a young girl . . . the same girl who spoke to me in the cemetery!'

'Thanks, you've been a great help.'

Folding the print-out the grey-haired woman handed to her, Kate pushed it into her bag. It had not taken as long as she had thought. Just checking a few details, she had told Scotty when he'd asked why she needed to go to head office. Stepping into the street she fished for a cigarette. She had expected her editor to bombard her with questions but he'd simply nodded and carried on with editing the next edition.

Mrs James, keeper of the archive section of the *Star* had quickly narrowed the avenue of search.

'If it were a fête held in the park then it was most likely to have taken place during one of the summer months.'

The woman had tapped the keyboard of a computer at her elbow.

'Recently you think –' tap . . . tap . . . '– most probably a year or two ago –' tap . . . tap . . .

Kate had watched the fingers fly over the keys, the woman's eyes not once looking at them. How was it some people seemed to be gifted with a multiplicity of skills? Scotty now, he could take a phone call, edit a piece of copy and hold a conversation with one of the newspaper staff at the same time; or the woman she had just seen, her fingers had danced over that keyboard like greased lightening while at the same time giving all kinds of instructions on how to find relevant information on equipment Kate had no idea how to use and was scared to try . . . if anybody could cock a machine up Kate Mallory could, she could have got a Ph.D. in it! Just tell the computer what it is you want and it will bring it up. Bring it up! Kate's insides had rolled as if she were about to bring her dinner up! Lord, all those instructions! Press this key, type in that word . . . the woman had tripped them out one after the other like bullets from a machine gun and Kate had forgotten them just as quickly.

Thank heaven there had been someone else in that archive room, a smiling lad who had set the machine up for her, telling her to sing out if she needed further help. Sing out! She had sung a whole bloody aria!

But she had found what she was looking for. A small piece on page four of a Saturday evening edition. July of last year: *Fête held in Victoria Park at Darlaston, Proceeds given to a Local Hospice.*

She had read the report through but it was the accompanying photograph that had really held her attention. A shot showing a man handing the cuddly toy he'd won at a sideshow to a young girl smiling beside him.

The man in that photograph was Fred Baker and the girl? She was Penny Smith . . . receptionist at Darlaston Printing!

It must be the girl Fred Baker had spoken of. But where had she gone after leaving her job? With a name like Smith! Kate sighed. Even a computer search would take time with that one and still not come up with the right girl. So what other way? An ad in the missing persons column? Somehow that didn't sit right.

An enquiry at the local blues department? And have Detective Inspector Bruce Daniels breathing down her neck? No thank you!

Climbing the metal stairs to the upper deck of the bus ready to pull out of the bus station, she mentally ticked off each idea. This was going to take a little more thought.

# Chapter Twelve

Had he been asked, he would have said places like this didn't exist so close to the industrial Midlands. As he brought the van to a halt, Torrey glanced at the old Tudor manor house, its ornate brick chimneys rising high above gabled roofs. True, there were a few grand places that had once belonged to influential families, places such as Aston Hall, Moseley Old Hall or Wigmore House but for the most part these were now held by the National Trust or local authorities; still, with the lottery creating so many new millionaires he supposed there had to be someone who could afford a place like this, set in so much ground it needed an ordnance survey map to find it.

Resisting some left-over urge of youth to rub his toecaps on his trouser leg, he rang the bell. Glancing out over wide green fields dotted with trees he listened to it echo in the rear of the house; the place must be almost as big inside as it was out!

What would Kate Mallory have to say about this? But then she might be used to grand buildings on her doorstep, she had talked a little of one . . . what had she called it? Lumley! Yes, Lumley Castle.

'Delivery for—'

Torrey began to speak as the door opened.

'Mr Torrey?'

Christ, was this guy an original too . . . one of the original fixtures and fittings! The words still in his mouth Torrey nodded as the dark-suited man stood aside.

'I'll bring the boxes in . . . if you say where you want them put, Mr Crowley.'

'Mr Crowley is in the small sitting room, I am Ellis, Mr Crowley's manservant. I will inform him you are here.'

You'd make a better bogeyman! Torrey watched the sharply thin figure move across the spacious kitchen. You'd frighten the life out of kids, Lord, you even give me the creeps!

As the door closed behind the other man, Torrey grinned. There you are, closed softly as a butterfly's arse on a poppy; the man is a must for Hammer House of Horror! He and Christopher Lee together . . . what other deterrent could the world possibly need? They'd frighten the proverbial crap out of any budding gangster!

Finding it difficult to keep the grin hidden as the man returned, Torrey followed through a house filled with softly gleaming furniture and paintings that just couldn't be fakes.

'Mr Torrey, sir.'

Jesus! Torrey breathed slowly. If this was the small sitting room then how big was the big one!

'Mr Torrey, I'm Julian Crowley.'

Reaching for the extended hand, Richard Torrey felt every sinew of his body tauten, every nerve twang like a bowstring.

He'd heard that voice before . . . ice on black velvet!

*'we will meet again . . . most definitely we will meet again'*

Those were the words he had heard that night . . . words every instinct told him had been spoken by that same voice.

'It was good of Alex to have you deliver to Whitefriars.'

Just *what* had been delivered . . . those boxes or Richard Torrey?

Small hairs rising, Torrey looked into a face he had seen

before, a face that had smiled at him from the centre of silver-tipped flames.

'I 'eard 'em, I 'eard what they said.'

'What was that then, Fred?' Echo Sounder's bat-like ears trained automatically on to the mumblings of the man he had sought out. Like he'd told that Mallory wench, Fred Baker took his pint in the Staffordshire Knot and tonight he'd had a few more than several.

'I 'eard 'em . . .'

The words were slurred, slow products of a mind dulled by alcohol, but patience was one virtue Echo Sounder did have and he practised it now.

'Talked a lot did they, Fred?'

Fred Baker's head nodded tipsily. 'More'n they should . . . they d'ain't know, the bastards d'ain't know!'

Sounder glanced at the two men playing bar billiards, one stretched almost full length across the table, the other intent on the cue ball. They 'adn't 'eard and the blokes playin' darts? If they'd 'eard the sudden rise of anger in Baker's mumblings then they showed no interest.

Who were the bastards Fred Baker was going on about . . . and what was it they d'ain't know? P'raps another pint might oil the wheels a little! Half rising from his chair Sounder sat down again. Another drink might see Baker out for the count and when he sobered up then whatever 'e might 'ave said could be given a soldier's farewell; another thing, paying for a beer could be money wasted. Besides, Sounder smiled greedily to himself, a man d'ain't buy a cow if 'e could get its milk for free!

'Done the dirty on yer 'ave they, Fred?' he urged again.

'They done the dirty all right, but not on Fred Baker, they done it on 'er.'

'Er! Sounder watched the head weave on its neck. Baker 'ad no wife . . . 'e 'ad no kin at all so who was it 'e were talking of?

'Poor little bugger!' Fred mourned into his glass. 'Why 'er . . . they d'ain't 'ave to do that . . . 'er was a nice little wench, why did they 'ave to go an' do that?'

If anything was going to come of talking to Baker it would 'ave to come quick; booze had raised his voice once already, raise it again and the whole room would 'ear what it was some 'bastards' 'ad done that upset 'im.

'They shouldn't 'ave,' he murmured, 'they was wrong.'

'Wrong!' Fred Baker laughed, a trickle of beer oozing from a corner of his mouth. 'They don't know 'ow bloody wrong. That wench were a good girl . . . a friend to me—'

'Who was, Fred?' Echo Sounder's voice was low to keep his question free from wandering ears.

'– a good little wench,' the other man mumbled on, oblivious of the asking, 'a friend to Fred Baker an' 'e be goin' to see to it . . . 'e be goin' to mek 'em pay.'

Feeling his nerves begin to jump as Fred paused to drink again, Sounder wanted to snatch the glass away. Baker was well known to others who used this place and any minute now one of them might just tek it into their 'ead to come an' join 'im! That was the last thing Sounder wanted. He glanced again at the billiards players, they were on the final set of the game, chance was they wouldn't play another. It was now or lose it. He returned his ferret stare to Fred Baker maudling over his beer. This one he mustn't lose! Every drop of his gambler's blood told him, this he mustn't lose!

'*You* can't mek 'em pay, Fred.'

He'd put all he had on the nose. Sounder watched for a reaction. If it brought in a winner 'e could be quids in!

'That be what they thinks but I knows better.' Eyes bleary with drink blinked across the table. 'I knows what they done, they took 'er . . . they took little Penny . . . said 'er 'ad chucked 'er job, chucked it of 'er own free will . . . but 'er wouldn't do that, 'er liked 'er job at the printers.'

Sat at the table Echo Sounder felt his mouth go suddenly dry. It only ever did that when he was on to an outsider! What should he do now, let Baker ramble on hoping it would all come out or give him a touch of the whip?

'You allus said young Penny liked 'er job.' He decided a gentle flick of the whip was best if he was to get a winner.

''Er did.' Bleary eyes spilled their tears. 'And 'er were nice to folk, not stuck up like the one they got now, wouldn't give yer the time o' day would that one, thinks 'er be better than the rest but 'er don't 'old a candle to young Penny.'

'Nice kid,' Sounder agreed taking a sip from his glass, his hooded eyes glancing around the bar. So far so good, but how far would far stretch . . . how long before one or the other game folded and the players came to sit at tables too closely packed for privacy?

'Nicer than that stuck-up bitch,' Fred muttered on. 'Why couldn't they 'ave took that one, why not sacrifice 'er 'stead o' Penny.'

Sacrifice! Echo Sounder's whole body tingled. What did that mean? 'Ad that wench's job been taken simply to give to another woman, and 'er thrown on the redundancy heap? Was that the sacrifice Fred Baker was speaking of? That was all it could be . . . but somehow he felt it wasn't.

'Gau, 'e said there were no need for 'er to die—'

This was no bloody redundancy Fred Baker were maudlin' on about! Sounder's pulses throbbed. It sounded like the Smith wench 'ad bin done for in a damn sight more definite way than that. As his ears strained to catch a voice now mumbling into a glass he listened avidly.

'– but Crowley, that one said it 'ad to be done . . . never liked Crowley, 'e be a sly bastard . . . said 'er were given to the Master, 'er life to pay for somebody's mistakes . . . said 'er was nuthin'

. . . little Penny were nuthin' . . . but Fred Baker'll mek 'em both pay. I 'eard 'em, I 'eard it all . . . about Penny an' about Torrey.'

Torrey! Echo Sounder glanced at the several darts players as a loud whoop of victory swept over the bar room. He had to get the rest before it was too late; if Baker were overheard by them then the information was useless so far as making money from it was concerned.

'Come on, Fred.' He helped the other man to his feet. 'Let's get yer 'ome.'

''Nother drink . . . we'll 'ave another drink . . . Fred Baker'll do fer them bastards!'

Steadying the man on his feet, Sounder caught the surprised look on several watching faces. They knew it was unusual for Baker to have too much to drink . . . if one of them should volunteer to drive him home . . .

'C'mon, Fred,' he said pointedly, 'a walk 'ome in the fresh air'll drive the cobwebs away.'

''Nother drink.'

'Tomorrer, Fred, we'll 'ave another drink tomorrer.'

Taking the banknote Baker had shuffled from his pocket, Echo held it in his hand, tomorrow the man would have forgotten even handing it to him. But that note was only a down-payment on the asking price . . . and he intended the closing one to be high, very high! Smiling to himself he helped the stumbling Baker out into the night. After all . . . what price murder?

What had made him agree?

Torrey guided the large car between hedges that almost brushed it on either side.

What in the world had caused him to agree not only to drive Max Gau to Whitefriars but to stay at the place overnight? It wasn't the house he didn't like, what he'd seen of that made it a dream in anybody's book . . . no, it was the owner of the house he was averse to. There was something about Julian Crowley, something he couldn't put a finger to but it was there crawling up his spine whenever he saw the man. He was polite enough, in fact his manners were impeccable but still there was that air about him, like a coiled serpent about to strike.

Kate had scorned at the misgivings he held about the coming couple of days. 'It's the butler,' she had laughed, 'you think he's so like Frankenstein it's got you jumpy.'

Well Kate had the Frankenstein bit right. Edging the car into a space cleared from the verge, Torrey hugged the hedge whilst a car squeezed slowly past. Ellis was enough to give anyone the jitters, but it wasn't Ellis had him not wanting to go back to that house, it was his boss, and not because Crowley gave him the jitters but because the urge to smack him in the mouth had got stronger by the minute that day he had delivered the order from the printers.

He had been about to question Crowley as to that episode in the pub yard, to face him with the fact that he had been the man in the shadows, but then he had decided against it. Why? Torrey shrugged mentally, he didn't know why.

Perfect as the man's manners had been, still Crowley had riled him. The car safely past Torrey pulled back on to the road. Behind the suave, cultured approach was something threatening . . . sinister.

Lord! He almost laughed himself at that, heaven knows what Kate might do if he let that out!

*'Normally I would drive myself but tonight I can do with the extra time to finish off going through some papers—'*

Gau had indicated a pile of documents half as high as a mountain as he said it.

*'– but if you have plans for the weekend then I can contact one of the professional services, it is very short notice but they may have a driver free.'*

He didn't have plans for the weekend and he wasn't about to

start making excuses; after all he liked Gau and if he could do the man a good turn then he would . . . it was just to be hoped that Crowley kept his distance.

*'I'll try to keep things as brief as I can,'* Gau's smile had been apologetic, *'and you must take time off in lieu of your weekend.'*

How genuine that offer was would remain to be seen, but it didn't really matter if it were just talk for he had agreed to the odd stint of chauffeuring when he accepted the job at the printing works; had it not been that Crowley irritated him the weekend might have been enjoyable.

Torrey turned off the narrow road to take the long drive to the house. In the rear of the car Max Gau slipped papers into a leather briefcase.

'Thank you for doing this, Richard,' he said, 'I would have cried off but the House of Jarreaux is a most important client. A photo shoot isn't my cup of tea but the only way I could get them to discuss new business was to combine it with this damned shoot.'

'No problem,' Torrey answered, then broke off as Ellis came down the steps of the house.

'I know what you are thinking.' Max Gau's lips never moved as he climbed from the car. 'The fellow has all the attributes of Dracula . . . watch out for his fangs!'

The smile only in his eyes, Torrey reached overnight cases from the boot.

'Glad you could make it . . . Ellis will take those.'

Nodding to Crowley now stood on the steps, Torrey felt the smile fade. What was it about the man that made his hackles rise!

Introductions made, he looked at the group assembled in the beautifully furnished drawing room. A fashion shoot seemed apt for this lot, each one of them looked as if they had stepped from the pages of some high-class magazine.

'Forgive my leaving so soon, Max, but Domino tells me the light is perfect for some of the shots he's aiming for and if I help

Jay with the dresses we can probably get through much of the shoot this afternoon. Mr Torrey . . . Richard,' Nicole Jarreaux turned a dazzling smile on Torrey, 'perhaps we might persuade you to take part.'

'No thanks!' He smiled, appreciating the woman's quick friendliness. 'Cameras and I don't agree.'

'Domino would likely have a different opinion,' the smile flashed again, 'but I promise I will not allow him to pressure you if you would like to come and watch.'

He would rather be outside, that way there was less chance of being cornered by Crowley.

'Julian and I have things to discuss so we will not be among the spectators.'

'Coward!' Nicole Jarreaux laughed across at Max before turning a look on Davion. 'Does that include you too, Alex?'

'Not me.' His film-star smile showing perfect dental work Alex Davion shook his head. 'Point me where the interesting action is.'

'Isobel?'

Elegant in a black shantung suit slashed with deep-cut white reveres, Isobel Davion shuddered theatrically.

'After that drive I need a shower and a rest. Why on earth does this country spend millions building motorways and then restrict their speed to seventy? It's positively ludicrous!'

'I said to come down in the helicopter.' Alex Davion frowned at his wife. 'You have things your own way and still you're not satisfied!'

Champagne glass in one hand, Isobel Davion raised a perfectly plucked eyebrow. 'Let's say there are some things other than a husband leave me wanting, darling.'

'Do what the hell pleases you; me, I'm for another drink.'

'Help yourself.' Julian Crowley swept a hand towards a well-stocked bar. 'Ellis will show you upstairs, Isobel, and Mrs Ellis will be there to help you unpack.'

Mrs Ellis! Lord, he hadn't guessed the bloke to be married. Torrey followed to the room allotted to him. But never judge a book by its cover, the man might not be a Davion to look at but then again there might be more to him than looks.

In her own room Isobel Davion barely glanced at the small neat woman transferring clothes to wardrobe and drawers, looking instead at a door she suspected connected to a separate bedroom. Alex's bedroom? How thoughtful, but there wasn't much danger of her beloved husband joining her in here. However, she preferred to play a definite hand.

'Mrs Ellis,' she called as the housekeeper turned to leave. 'Is there a key to that door?'

'That door leads only to Mr Davion's room, madam.'

'Nevertheless I would like a key . . . and I would like it now!'

And I knows why you want it. Suppressing the thought, Sarah Ellis opened a drawer of a petite Chippendale escritoire. Fancy clothes and a lah-di-dah accent made no impression on her, she knew a whore when she saw one and she was looking at one right now.

'The key, madam.'

Placing it in the keyhole she left the room. Photographic! She'd heard dirty weekends called a few things in her time but this was the best so far.

Turning the key in the lock and finding it fit, Isobel left it *in situ*. Then walking to a floor-length mirror she unbuttoned her jacket and spread it wide, surveying breasts only the finest plastic surgery could provide.

'Diego,' she smiled voluptuously at her own reflection, 'you and I are going to have ourselves one hell of a weekend.'

# Chapter Thirteen

'Abdel Khadja?' Alex Davion swallowed whisky, why the hell had he let Isobel talk him into this, a weekend of photography and Crowley . . . Christ, he'd go mad!

'That's the one,' Crowley refilled his guest's glass. 'According to Nicole he likes everything he's involved with to be strictly private, hence her bringing him here.'

'It's certainly out of the way.' Davion sent a second swallow the way of the first. 'Speaking of which, has he arrived yet?'

'Yes, a couple of hours ago. I thought it some sort of advance invasion, the man doesn't exactly travel alone; three cars bristling with men.'

'I believe Abdel Khadja prefers his own form of security,' Max Gau put in.

'He'll have that and plenty,' Davion answered. 'If any of the villagers catch sight of that lot swanning around in flowing robes you won't cop their arse ends for dust.'

'Sorry to butt in, I'm Paul Whiteman, lighting technician. I was told I would find Sheikh what's-his-name here.'

Alex Davion rested his glass on his knee as a man stepped in through the long French windows, young, twenty-five-ish, height around five ten . . . interesting!

'Obviously I was wrong.' The newcomer smiled, one corner of his mouth lifting crookedly.

'I'm sure we can find him for you.' Davion brightened visibly.

'Thanks.' Paul Whiteman ran a hand through hair the colour of polished bronze, his grey eyes laughing. 'I've never known so many twists and turns, I could vanish from the eyes of mankind for ever in this place.'

'Now that would be a waste.' Davion appraised the chocolate-box looks.

'It could be the better way out,' Whiteman smiled again, 'you don't know Nicole when we're on a shoot, everything is allowed to go just one way – the right way – and the lady takes no prisoners, so either I find the Sheikh and get him to location in two minutes or she'll have my balls.'

Not if I can help it. Davion took a more leisurely swallow from his well-filled glass; no, most definitely not if I can help it.

'I'll tell him you're here myself.' Julian Crowley stood up. 'Mrs Ellis doesn't like the guards outside his room, they frighten her; can't blame her really, they are formidable to say the least.'

'A drink while you're waiting?' Davion smiled at the newcomer.

'No thanks, that's something else Nicole won't allow while we're shooting.'

'And when you're not? We must find some way of releasing you from the dragon lady's talons.'

Crowley caught the soft exchange as he left the room; that was Davion's style, he must see if he couldn't clear the path in the man's direction.

'Was the shooting successful?' Crowley held a light to Nicole's cigarette.

'Domino seemed pleased,' Nicole Jarreaux blew smoke from her nostrils, 'that usually means we have a wrap.'

Domino? Richard Torrey glanced across the room to Nicole's cameraman, why the choice of name?

''Cos it suits him,' the lovely red-haired woman answered as if he'd spoken the thought aloud. 'Domino is black and he likes his lovers white and often in numbers.'

'A wrap.' Crowley returned his attention to Nicole, that shade of pale coral suited her. It had been some time since he'd had a woman, tonight might just bring the period to an end. 'I think that means you're finished, right?'

'Partly,' Nicole pulled on the cigarette. 'We've finished the shots Domino wanted the softer afternoon light for but there are still more to take, he intends to try for those tomorrow, supposing the weather holds.'

'The sheikh was impressed enough to buy the collection, I hope?'

'This one isn't intended for His Excellency though future patronage of the House of Jarreaux depends a great deal on what I've brought down here.' Nicole stubbed out the cigarette, a sideways glance assuring her that the sheikh seemed more than interested in her collection. Petra and the three models she had chosen to show her designs knew their job well. 'This weekend is a way of showing the work of Diego and Petra, if it pleases then they get to design an entire exclusive wardrobe for each of the ladies in his household.'

'And you scoop the pool?' Alex Davion laughed coarsely.

'Financially, yes.'

High-pitched laughter catching Torrey's attention he turned to glance at the quartet of lovely women sitting with Abdel Khadja. Was haute couture the only thing the Sheikh was buying this weekend?

Following the glance Nicole smiled derisively to herself. Give the girls a chance and they could earn more from a couple of hours spent in the company of their Arab friend than they could in a year on the modelling platform; besides, she let her cool glance wander over the rest of her group, there was enough talent here to tickle both Davion's and his wife's jaded palate, the weekend would by no means be written off as a loss by any of them, and that included Richard Torrey if he wanted to play, or was that to be a no-go area, Julian Crowley's private space?

Nicole's green eyes regarded Crowley steadily. She had known him for several years, ever since he had brought her from that house. It had been his idea to set up the House of Jarreaux. He'd paid well, given her everything she could want and since then had often used her less exclusive salons to launch special drives, but it wasn't Jarreaux he was interested in, she was just a ticket to wider horizons.

'Julian –' she stood up, folds of soft coral silk jersey swishing against her calves '– much as I love you I really have to say goodnight, I have work to do. Tomorrow's schedule isn't sorted yet.'

'Are you ready to check the gowns, Miss Jarreaux?' Jay Williams appeared at the precise moment Nicole rose.

She had really rather nice eyes, more gold than green, Nicole thought as she always did when she looked at the youngest of her dressers; the girl could be something if she got rid of the mousy look and she'd take the project in hand herself when they got back to London.

'That's all right, Jay,' she gave one of her rare genuine smiles, 'I'll do them myself, you get yourself an early night.'

'Thank you, Miss Jarreaux,' the girl's eyes lit up, 'I . . . I'll say goodnight then.'

To me you will. Nicole watched the slim form skip from the drawing room where they had all gathered after dinner, but it will be hello to Richard Torrey unless I'm very wide of the mark. The two had made their choice immediately upon Jay's arrival, she hadn't missed the look the two had given each other, and why not? Provided the girl's work was not affected it was okay by her.

'Surely you don't need to go yet, Nicole.' Isobel Davion's eyes belied her words. The sooner Jarreaux went the sooner Diego would go and she would follow to find him already in that darling four-poster bed. 'There can't be all that much to do. Relax a little, this isn't a major showing after all.'

'Sorry to spoil the fun,' Nicole smiled, 'but major or minor all showings count. Uneasy lies the head that wears the business crown – not quite Shakespeare but near enough wouldn't you say, Alex?'

'I would indeed.' Alex Davion came to stand beside his wife. 'It would do Isobel a power of good to have to earn instead of just spend.'

'But I have all the good I need,' Isobel purred, 'I have you, darling.'

'There can be no argument against the logic of a woman, my friend.' Hamed Abdel Khadja left his audience, coming to take Isobel's hand and raising it to his lips.

'Especially when that woman is his wife, eh?' Davion's smile was empty.

'We are agreed.' Hamed shook his head in mock grief then turned, taking Nicole's hand. 'Allah in his wisdom gave logic to women.' He raised her hand to his mouth, toast-brown eyes looking straight into hers. 'But I have no quarrel with him when he also gave them beauty such as yours. Sleep in the hand of Allah, Miss Jarreaux.'

Now wouldn't that put the cat among the pigeons; if she slept at all it certainly wouldn't be there! Nicole hid the thought behind a smile. 'I hope what we showed today met with your Excellency's approval.'

'Wholeheartedly.' He held her hand just that much longer, brown eyes stroking her face.

Power to the man's elbow, he knew how to play the game. 'Then I will wish your Excellency goodnight.'

Why did Crowley want Richard Torrey here at Whitefriars? Nicole walked up the wide mellowed-oak staircase, a drift of muted voices following her. Whatever he had in mind would be to the benefit of none but Crowley himself.

'No doubt you have motive and method well paired, Mr Crowley,' she murmured as a swell of laughter followed into her room. 'But take care, Julian . . . method and madness often go together.'

Torrey flipped off the light beside his bed, settling pillows comfortably beneath his head. He had excused himself early, the pretty Jay following suit. He had seen in the way she had looked at him during the evening that she had designs that didn't much cater for sleep and to be honest he'd felt the same, that was until they had reached the door of her room and he'd found himself looking not at her face but at the tilted mouth and gold-flecked cinnamon eyes that belonged to the face of Kate Mallory.

With hands beneath his head he stared into the moon-painted shadow. Was that a win for Kate or was it something else had made him wish that pretty girl goodnight and leave her at her door? Might it be that even now he was not fully over Anna . . . or could it be the evil that had stalked him at Monkswell was not fully banished?

True, he had not seen a hitch-hiker since Anna, but then he'd had no car to drive since Philip Bartley's death so he was hardly likely to have seen a hitch-hiker. But the ghost of Anna was well and truly laid . . . there had been no more hint of spice-scented perfume, no touch of unseen hands on his body, no more whispering of his name.

But there had! Suddenly alert his mind whipped back over the events of the last weeks. No perfume, no sensuous touch of hands . . . but the whispering of his name, that he could not deny. Nor could he deny his own eyes! He *had* seen a girl in a white dress, the same girl Fred Baker claimed had worked as receptionist for Max Gau, the girl he had seen framed in that office window. But when he had pointed, Fred had said he saw nothing . . . and that time in Bentley cemetery, Kate had seen nothing when he said he had spoken to a girl in white. He could see what they did not . . . he heard when they did not . . . and he wasn't imagining, and he wasn't out of his head! But what right-minded man believed in ghouls and ghosts?

Beyond the window a shy moon hid behind a drape of clouds leaving the room deep in shadow.

After what he had been through he could ask that! Torrey's mind turned like a treadmill. After that thing from hell had taken the life of that priest, as well as killing the others before trying to claim him, he could ask were there really such things!

Yes, there were. He watched the shadows silver as the moon gathered courage enough to leave the clouds. His only question now was if that girl in white was a ghost why was she haunting him? He didn't know her, he had never met her . . . unless – he felt his nerves jar – unless evil could take on any shape, unless it could assume any form. Was the girl in white really Anna in another guise . . . was this another attempt to draw him into hell?

Disturbed by the thought he got out of bed, going to stand at the window overlooking the tranquil, silent gardens. It couldn't happen again . . . it couldn't!

'I tell you it has to be done—'

Quiet though the words were they reached up to the open window. That was Crowley's voice! Instinctively stepping out of line of the moonlight so that his body was masked by shadow, Torrey listened.

'– without it we might all be finished. The Master revealed the whole thing to me, the old man overheard us talking, heard our plans for the girl and now is broadcasting it to others, let him live and the entire coven stands to be discovered. That, my dear Max, I will not allow. The man will be dealt with as was the girl.'

'I still say it is too risky,' Max Gau's worried tone answered. 'There has to be some other way.'

'We have gone over this before!'

That was a definite snap! Torrey edged his nose past heavy velvet curtains to peer into the garden.

'I have told you it is what is required . . . nothing else will do . . . nothing!'

'Couldn't we at least try?'

'I will not prevent that, Max; you, Davion and the others do what you feel you must. Call upon the Messenger, but remember that by doing that you place yourselves in grave danger. You are a Magister Templi and though as such you are further along the Path than the others that rank will not guarantee defence. And be certain of this: you will not witness my protection. As I have said once before, Max, you would be better advised to play with me rather than against me, and definitely so in the matter of sacrifice for the Great Sabbat, and that sacrifice will be Richard Torrey.'

*Witness my protection*

His palms moist, Torrey drew a deep breath. Crowley had spoken the same words he had heard in his nightmare . . . but this time he was not asleep, those two men stood on that lawn were as real as he was and one was threatening to take his life.

'I will not go against the will of the Master.'

The words were quieter, almost indistinct as the two turned away from the house and faced into the night-shrouded garden.

Moving the velvet a little to one side, the clearer to see the two figures, Torrey felt the old tingle along his spine. To one side of the house, caught by the shadowed darkness, a third figure moved.

Which of them was this?

He stared into the gloom trying to catch a glimpse of the face. It was probably one of the staff Nicole Jarreaux had brought and that one a woman. Whichever it was must be a really quiet mover, for neither Gau nor Crowley seemed aware that they were about to have a companion. Perhaps it had been arranged, but which man preferred his jollies in the garden . . . or was it to be a threesome?

Each to his own. The tingle faded and Torrey relaxed. Gau didn't strike him as that type, but then he had only known the guy a few weeks, and Crowley? He didn't know that guy at all!

He watched the figure move closer. For somebody who had been invited, the woman wasn't being exactly welcomed, both men were turned face towards her but neither acknowledged her. Nicole Jarreaux, Isobel Davion? He couldn't be sure which but given the men's attitude she surely wasn't going to be pleased, maybe neither man would get what he hoped for!

His interest gone, he made to turn back to bed, but at that instant the garden was bathed in brilliant moonlight, moonlight that silvered a white dress, touched a pale face and reflected on helpless frightened eyes that looked straight up at him!

# Chapter Fourteen

Gau had admitted defeat and retired for the night. Crowley smiled the sweet smile of success. The Dark Lord would have his tribute. Max Gau had not the moral strength to reach for what he wanted, and as for Davion and the others they already had what they wanted.

'– a little more this way . . . let's have the face, lovey—'

The photographer who came with the Jarreaux retinue clicked his camera like a rapid-fire machine gun.

'– lift the chin a fraction . . . I said a fraction, lovey, not a dirty great mountain . . . that's it, that's great—'

Standing just inside the room doubling as a photographic studio, Crowley watched the proceedings. He would face no opposition from any one of the servants of the Master.

'– can we move the right hand, it's blocking the face and we don't want that do we, darling?'

Domino danced about the set angling his camera, searching for the best shot.

'Arch the back . . . up . . . more—'

Crowley's mouth remained in a curve which might have been carved from ice. The major players in this little game had accepted the gifts of the Lord of Darkness, taken his bounty and they would pay him what was required. They would give him the life of Richard Torrey, and if Max Gau objected then he too would make a perfect gift . . . the Master would not refuse a third sacrifice!

'– open your mouth, dearie, that's a favourite dessert of yours so let's see you eat it.'

Aiming the camera the photographer smiled at the scene in the lens. Naked, kneeling with legs slightly apart, arc lights glistening on bronzed skin, Alex Davion breathed in short excited gasps as he arched his body backwards' taking the weight of it on his hands.

'I said *up*, Alex . . . push your botty *up*—'

Tiny twin circles, each perfectly white, marked an oblique line across an ebony brow glinting in the brilliance of a bank of photography lights.

White on black. Crowley watched. Domino . . . the man was well named.

'– UP . . . Oh, for heaven's sake . . .!'

The man was on his feet, his huge organ slapping against bare legs as he jigged across the set. Placing a palm in the small of Davion's back he pushed until it formed an almost perfectly arched bow.

'Hold it!' He flashed a pert smile at Whiteman already bending over Davion. 'I meant his back, lovey.' Back on his knees he turned the camera several times. 'Let the head fall back a trifle more, Alex, that's it . . . now lips parted like you were waiting for a treat . . . that's it.'

Positioning the camera again he focused then glanced over the top of it to Davion's companion.

'Bend closer . . . good, good, lovey . . . now, mouth open ready to take your goodies . . . dreamy lover . . . dreamy . . .'

Twisting and turning Domino trained his shots from every angle, his lithe black body glistening with each move.

'Christ, Dommo, that'll have to do, I can't hold on to this

much longer.' Davion's flesh jerked as Whiteman's tongue flicked it.

'Stay still . . . just a couple more . . .'

Clicking like some trapped beetle Domino moved rapidly around the two men.

'Hold on to it, Alex sweetie.' He clicked again, a short rapid volley of sound. 'You'll get your treat later . . . Paul, let the camera see what it's all about, super, lovey . . . super.'

Davion and Co. were having fun. Crowley closed the door softly behind him. But it was fun they would be called upon to pay for. He needed no stick to beat any of them to his will but it was always useful to have one to hand and any threat of releasing those photographs to the news media would be a stick they would not risk feeling!

His feet making no sound on thick Bokhara carpet he moved along the corridor that served several bedrooms. The talented Domino thought the film he shot tonight would buy him a place in the sun. Crowley smiled inwardly. They would earn him a really warm home, *but it wouldn't be in the sun!*

He had meant to go back to bed but his brain was alive with questions. Richard Torrey put on his shirt and trousers. What was it that Crowley was so adamant must be done . . . who was the Master he had talked of?

The words that had drifted up to his window had intrigued him but none so much as those three. Slipping his feet into his shoes he stared at the moon-washed window, a tall column of silver set among dark velvet drapes.

'*Witness my protection*'

Even now it curled the short hairs! And while thinking of short hairs, imagining the girl there in the garden with Gau and Crowley hadn't exactly had them lying flat. They hadn't seen her . . . she had stood right beside them but they had not looked at nor spoken to her, that could only prove they hadn't seen her. But she had been there, she had looked up as if knowing he was watching from that window, then the figure had faded until it became one with the moonlight.

He needed a drink! Ring for Ellis? No use, he and his wife did not live in. What the hell! He'd find his own way to that drawing room, all that could happen was he might get shot by one of Khadja's bodyguards. Yes, he knew what they carried under those nightgowns they wore, AK 47s, and their faces said they knew how to use them.

Leaving the bedroom he moved quietly, pausing as a shadow flicked across his path, a pale shadow that waited at the head of the stairs. The girl, was she here in this house . . . or was it something else waiting beyond the shadows?

Army training clicking in, his body went instantly into defence mode, arms relaxed, breathing steady; but a moment later he laughed to himself. What was he defending himself against . . . a shadow! Lord, he did need that drink!

Moving on down the stairs he made for the drawing room, followed silently by a young girl who watched him with wide, unhappy eyes.

'Ah, Mr Torrey . . . another of us not ready for sleep.'

Julian Crowley rose from a deep-seated Georgian armchair.

'May I offer you a drink?'

This was the last man he wanted to share a drink with but politeness, as his mother had taught, must always be shown. Nodding agreement, Torrey took the glass Crowley half-filled with whisky.

'I'm glad you came down, Richard – I hope I might call you Richard?'

He didn't want this man calling him anything! Resisting the urge to spit refusal Torrey nodded again.

'I was hoping for the chance to speak with you alone, please . . . sit down.'

From the moment of handing him the glass Crowley seemed to dominate the room. In his late forties or early fifties he was, as Torrey guessed that night in the yard of the Frying Pan, several inches over six feet, his hair touched with grey was designer-styled as was the dark grey suit and pearl-toned silk shirt. He'd heard of Savile Row styling, now he guessed he was seeing it. This man wasn't short of the readies. But it was the eyes that really grabbed attention. A mix between slate grey and the silver blue of fresh-rolled steel they missed nothing.

He glanced at the man who moved to stand with his back to a carved fireplace Torrey could only guess was probably as old and valuable as the rest of the furnishings in this room. What was it he wanted to talk about?

'You must be wondering what it is I wish to discuss with you.'

'That's only one of the things I'm wondering!' Torrey's answer held all the friendliness of a sharp knife. 'The first being where the hell did you spring from that night as I left that pub . . . and don't say it wasn't you 'cos we both know otherwise; and next how come you know my name?'

'Where I sprang from, as you put it, doesn't really matter.' Rolled-steel eyes fastened on Torrey's. 'As for knowing your name . . . I told you on the evening you speak of there are many things I know about you . . . involving a certain Ronald Webster, for instance.'

His muscles like coiled springs, Torrey kept them in check, disbelief hidden behind a lazy blink. There had to be a perfectly logical explanation for this man's knowing what he did, all he had to do was wait for it.

'You'll have to do better than that,' he snapped, 'and don't make the mistake of treating me like an idiot. You don't amuse me, Crowley, and I'm not easily scared so why don't we just move to first base? You risked your neck coming at me from the shadows as you did, and I think you are behind Max bringing me to this house, so spit it out . . . what is it you want from me?'

'You are perfectly correct, of course—'

The voice was velvet, the control masterly. Torrey felt a tinge of admiration. He might as well save his breath, this guy didn't throw easily.

'– there is a purpose in my having you brought here . . . as for our meeting of a few weeks ago, there was no risk involved and, believe me, I have not the least intention of treating you like an idiot.'

'Then tell me how you know what you seem to know.'

Crowley settled himself back into the deep armchair, smiling over his glass.

'You mean the Webster incident? One among many I know about you, Richard.'

His anger rising, Torrey gripped his own glass. 'That's a lie, Crowley, and you know it!'

'Really? Then perhaps I know nothing of this!'

Held fast in the chair by a force the strength of gravity, Torrey gasped. Crowley was changing . . . Jesus, the man was changing right before his eyes, his body dissolving and reforming at one and the same time, half-mist half-solid like a bloody genie emerging from a bottle! Then it was no longer Crowley sat across from him. Shaped into the neck, greying hair had lengthened to collar-touching blonde, curling softly over a clear brow; cold steel eyes softened to the colour of hyacinths; the mouth that smiled at him fuller and wider than the taut line of seconds ago.

'Anna!' Torrey stared, disbelieving the evidence of his own eyes. 'Oh Christ . . . Anna!'

'Ritchie—'

Torrey's throat closed. Even the voice was the same, husky dark and hitting straight between the legs.

'– thank you for the meal at the Flamingo, Ritchie—'

'Cut it out, you bastard!' Torrey made it to his feet but as his hands reached for the throat reason told him was Crowley's he was spun like a top and flung back into his chair.

'And what about this, Richard, is this a lie?'

The voice was once more Crowley's while, seductive as pure silk, the full-lipped mouth smiled, but only for the merest fraction of a second; then the face became half a face, half a charred hole, scars ripping across from its blackened edges.

'Or this?'

The figure Torrey was no longer sure was Crowley became instantly another, one clothed in the brown and green of Army combat uniform while on each side of him, heaped on the floor like so much dung, were two more men both identically attired. Torrey swallowed hard, recognising himself as the man standing, the fallen ones men of his patrol beaten senseless. They had been ambushed during a routine patrol of the border; it was these two kids' first tour of duty since landing in Northern Ireland and all they knew of the Army was playing bloody cops-and-robbers manoeuvres on Salisbury Plain and writing home to Mom to cadge a little extra pocket money. Torrey felt the same gall rising as had risen then, kids . . . nothing but kids and that's all their lives meant in Whitehall . . . nothing!

The men who had taken them had had their fun, to call it revenge was raising it above the realms of barbarism; revenge he could understand, even condone if it involved a quick, clean death, but what did you call beating men mindless before putting a bullet in their brain? He had known they were for execution, it had needed no discussion, they were the enemy and as such the right to kill them existed. The one designated to carry out the sentence moved away from his companions, taking up position a little to the right. Torrey could see the cold shine of his eyes behind the compulsory black balaclava; the man raised his Russian-made Kalashnikov delicately like a ballerina raising her complimentary bouquet.

From his chair Torrey watched his own face, watched his eyebrows fall together in concentration. There seemed to follow the merest pause, a fractional time warp when everything took on the qualities of slow motion.

Through the narrow slits in his balaclava the gunman's eyes caught the rays of the sun as slivers of light ricocheted languidly like slow-moving darts. Torrey saw his own eyes fixed on his executioner, watched them narrow in one eternal second before the rifle in the other man's hand backfired and he dropped, his brains already arranged around his feet.

'Well, Richard, do you still question my knowledge of you? And before you claim you have been the subject of hypnotism we both know you were complete master of your own mind.'

The very softness of Crowley's voice acted like a file on Torrey's nerves and for a split second he was tempted to break him in two, but if the force that held him was anything to go by he knew he would never reach the man.

'Who the devil are you?' he grated.

From the chair opposite slate-coloured eyes cut deep into his own, seeming to lance his brain, dissect his mind, plucking out the last tiny remnants of personal knowledge, stripping him of memories known only to himself, and he was powerless to ward off the intrusion.

'Who am I?' Crowley smiled. 'Simply a man who wishes to be your friend.'

What could Echo Sounder want with her? Kate Mallory checked the large shoulder bag for essentials . . . tabs and lighter, they were both there.

*'At the greyhound track . . . no, not the boozer, you comes to the track at Wolverhampton or else I don't meets you at all!'*

The line had gone dead then. Kate heaved the bag on to her shoulder. She was surprised the weasel-faced little man knew how to use one.

Glancing towards the holy of holies she saw Scotty's head

bent over his desk. If he spotted her he would want to know where she was going and why and, true to form, would sail across the roof when she had to admit she didn't know. Keeping a wary eye on the glass-partitioned office she headed quickly for the door.

Sounder had to be on to something. Aboard the bus, she relaxed. He had never volunteered information . . . well never to her anyway . . . so why ring her now, and why insist on meeting at the greyhound stadium? If this was a ruse to get money he was liable to have to run faster than any greyhound to escape her.

Stood to one side of the entrance he folded his *Sporting Pink* newspaper, stuffing it into his jacket pocket as he spotted her. How could he think nobody would notice such a scruffy little man? Kate followed, noticing the distance deliberately left between them.

At the rail he took out the paper, spending several minutes appearing to study it until Kate had had enough. If he wanted to play the James Bond role he could find himself another supporting actress.

Lighting a cigarette she breathed smoke angrily from her nostrils . . . her imitation of a dragon, Torrey would say. Well, she felt like one right now; though not addicted to the office she could have spent her time better there than watching a few dogs hurl themselves after a stuffed rabbit!

'Right,' she frowned, 'you have one minute before I make a useless journey worthwhile!'

'Flighty Lad.' Sounder held the paper towards her pointing to a spot on the page. 'He's had some good results . . .' Then as Kate opened her mouth to bark said in an undertone, 'Look like you be wanting to back a dog . . . that way keeps the attention off.'

You'll be a flighty lad if this is no more than a joke! Kate breathed her irritation in a veil of grey smoke but aloud she said, 'Flighty Lad . . . what are the odds on him?'

Top marks to the wench. Sounder kept his eyes on the paper. Her answer couldn't 'ave bin better 'ad 'e rehearsed 'er.

'Eight to one, but I reckons 'e be a safe bet.'

It was said just loud enough for passing ears but the next words reached only Kate. 'Ask me to place your bet for you and hand me a tenner.'

'A tenner! Do you think I'm completely out of my mind.'

'I ain't gonna rob yer if that be what you'm thinkin',' Sounder mumbled. 'If you wants what I got then this be the only way I be prepared to give it! Now hand me a tenner or I be off.'

How far could he go on ten pounds? Kate extracted the money from her purse. She would trust him . . . but only once.

'Five pounds on the nose . . . righto, miss.'

The money held openly in his grubby hand he scuttled away to the tote, returning with a betting slip.

'There yer goes, miss, a fiver on Flighty Lad, and there be yer change.' Pressing a banknote into her hand he mumbled again, 'Put that away and don't fetch it out 'til yer be on yer own.'

'Sounder—'

'No questions,' he muttered, 'just listen and while yer does yer watches the racin' like yer be interested. That banknote was gied to me the other night along with a piece of information yer might find interestin'.'

And what is bound to cost half of a week's salary! Kate made the effort to cheer as dogs flashed past. Going hell for leather after something they can't eat, she thought sardonically, just like Sounder if he thought he was going to make a killing.

'And what might your little titbit cost?' She looked again at the paper he held as if sharing it with her.

'Depends.' He ran a finger over the paper.

'On how tightly you think you can squeeze?'

'Bloke 'as to mek a livin'.'

'So does a woman, and this one doesn't intend to work all the hours God sends just to hand a great deal over for what might prove to be of no use to her at all; so unless you want us both to have wasted a good afternoon you had better tell me . . . why have you had me come to a dog track?'

Running a hand halfway down the folded sheet of newspaper he tapped a finger against it as if pointing out another selection of runners then said quietly, 'To give yer that banknote. I d'ain't want the risk of it bein' seen by anybody in Darlaston, that be the reason for not meetin' yer in the Fryin' Pan; and besides, folk stand out less in a crowd.'

Logical! Kate nodded as she pretended to study the fixture list he pointed to.

Glancing at the fresh line up of greyhounds being trotted to the starting traps then back to the newspaper, he went on, 'If yer be interested to know what that information were then it'll cost . . . but as I sees it it'll be money well spent.'

Seen from his side of the bargaining table a deal was never any different. But so far he hadn't cheated. She looked at the betting slip he had handed to her. Five pounds on Flighty Lad as he had said and a five-pound note change. But why all the cloak and dagger stuff? Echo Sounder was normally a shifty character but today more so than ever. She glanced sideways. He was speaking but his lips were absolutely still . . . the man had missed his vocation, he should have been a ventriloquist!

'Any more than your usual "fee" and I would have to ask my editor but I can tell you his answer right now: no talk, no money on the table.'

A shout from the crowd heralding the opening of the traps, Echo Sounder's gaze followed the racing animals as they hurtled around the track.

She had called his bluff. Beside him Kate watched what for her was a boring repetition of dog chasing rabbit. He had nothing to tell her, it had simply been a try on. Vexation tightening her mouth, she turned to leave.

'Tek yer ticket to the window there, miss.'

Once more clearly audible, Sounder's voice halted her.

'I said as Flighty Lad were a safe bet.'

'You mean I won?' Kate stared at the betting slip she had crumpled in anger.

'Eight to one, miss, just 'and yer slip to the clerk an' 'e'll pay yer.' One hand pointing to the tote and his voice lowering he added, 'If yer wants the jackpot then yer knows where I be found . . . an' p'raps yer can tell yer editor it be to do with a young wench left 'er job at a certain printers an' never come back . . .'

'What if my editor says you haven't told me enough to warrant a cheque?'

Taking a stub of pencil from his pocket, Sounder circled the name of a greyhound then held the newspaper for her to see.

White Lady! Kate felt her blood chill. The girl in the photograph had worn a white dress . . . she had also worked at the printers!

# Chapter Fifteen

Sat in the rear of the luxurious car Max Gau looked down at the papers on his lap with uncomprehending eyes, Crowley's words tethering his mind. '*You would be better advised to play with me rather than against me.*'

Safer yes, Crowley could see him damned into hell, but that would only mean his arrival there being brought forward. Being a resident could not be made worse by his refusal to assist in offering Richard Torrey's life in sacrifice!

Richard Torrey glanced at his passenger. Max Gau had been silent since they left that house, immersed as he had been on the outward journey in a whole heap of papers.

There had been more than a hint of threat behind Crowley's words to him in that drawing room. Torrey's thoughts returned to the previous night and despite himself his fingers tightened. Christ, it should be the man's neck in his hands instead of this steering wheel!

How had he known about Webster . . . about Anna? Did he really have the power to look into a man's mind?

Pull yourself together, Torrey! He noticed headlights in his mirror and pulled into the middle lane, allowing a would-be Michael Schumacher to overtake then watching him race away as if doing a trial lap at Silverstone.

No matter how much Crowley denied using hypnotism that was what it had to have been. Hypnotism had caused his mind to reveal its own memories, to hallucinate . . . it was a well-known stage trick, to believe more than that would be playing into Crowley's hands. But what about the pressure that had held him in that chair, that had released him only to spin him like a top before throwing him back into it? He had felt a force like that once before . . . in the church at Monkswell when he had tried to go to the assistance of that priest! Had last night been a demonstration of that same evil . . . an evil returned?

But for what purpose? If Crowley had used hypnotism on him, and it was no more than that, what was behind it all? It was a bit of a drastic way of persuading a man to come to work for you, especially when there were dole queues the length of the land and nine out of every ten men were ready to jump into such a job. No. He stared at the dark ribbon of motorway sequinned with overhead lamps. There had to be more to Crowley's trying to recruit him than simply a chauffeur's job . . . the trick in the puzzle was finding out what that more could be.

In the rear seat Max Gau slipped the papers he had been reading into a briefcase then passed a hand over his eyes. Seeing the movement in the mirror, Torrey felt a brief sympathy. His boss had seemingly enjoyed the weekend about as much as himself . . . that much being not at all!

'Straight home, Mr Gau?'

'No.' The other man shook his head. 'There are a few things I still have to go over before morning. Drop me at the works and then go home, I will drive myself once I've finished.'

'I don't mind waiting.'

'I appreciate that, and I appreciate your giving up your weekend, I know how welcome a break they are after a week of work.'

He was the one who looked like he could do with a break. Torrey glanced at the face that even in the gloom of the car he could see was drawn. Gau seemed very near the end of his tether . . . but who jerked the rope at the other end?

'It was a change.' Torrey kept up the conversation. 'Whitefriars is a beautiful place, quite a difference between that and Darlaston.'

There was a moment's silence, Gau resting his head on the back of his seat with his eyes closed.

'Yes,' he said quietly, 'quite a difference.'

He didn't sound overwhelmingly enthusiastic! Overhead signs indicating he was now joining the route of the M6, Torrey kept his speed to the prescribed seventy.

'Richard—'

Through the mirror he saw Max Gau's eyes were open.

'– did Julian Crowley offer you a job with him?'

'Yes, as a matter of fact he did.'

'Might I ask . . . did you accept?'

Torrey gave a quick shake of the head. 'No, I didn't take his offer.'

'I see.' Another few moments of silence then Gau added, 'If you refused out of regard for me . . . no, no, not that! That was a poor way of putting it. What I mean is if you feel you want to leave your position with Darlaston Printing then do not let a false sense of loyalty influence any decision you might make. If you wish to take the job Crowley has offered then you must take it.'

'Crowley is the last man I would want to work for!' The words spat themselves out, each one thick with dislike. 'I told him where he could stick his job and I hope he finds the operation painful! Sorry to sound so scathing about a friend of yours but there is something about the man that makes it impossible for me to like him.' He could have said, 'makes my blood creep'.

'A colleague.' Eyes wide and steady now caught Torrey's in the driving mirror. 'Julian Crowley is a colleague of mine but I would not call him a friend. Be wary of that man's offers, Richard, remember grass is not always as green as it appears on the other side. There was once a time I believed it was, I accepted Julian Crowley's offer only to regret it bitterly.'

Indicating his intention to leave the motorway Torrey manoeuvred the car on to the slip road, taking Junction 9 for Wednesbury.

'Then end whatever business you have with Crowley, tell him to get lost.'

Turning his face to the window Max Gau watched the church of St Paul slip past in the darkness. It was too late for that, it had been too late the night Christy died.

'That isn't possible for me, Richard,' he said. 'I made an agreement that cannot be broken.'

'There's no such—'

'Believe me, there is.' Max shook his head at the interruption. 'Some contracts are totally binding and they are the only sort Julian Crowley deals with; so I say again, be wary of that man.'

'Well he's had his answer from me, I won't be hearing from him again.'

Veiled by the dim interior of the car Max Gau's face wore a troubled look. Like any other who did not know the real Julian Crowley, Richard Torrey was too dismissive of him.

'I wouldn't be absolutely sure of that, Richard.' He drew a long breath that quivered in his chest. 'Crowley is a man who gets what he wants by whatever means it takes.'

'You make him sound like a Mafia godfather.'

Max gathered his briefcase as the car turned off King's Hill Road and nosed into the yard of the printing works. Stepping from the vehicle he glanced at Torrey, shadows masking the worry in his eyes.

'It is not the Mafia the man is connected with,' he said closing the car door quietly, 'and the word god does not feature in his title, nor I fear in his life. Watch out for him, Richard . . .

watch very carefully, he is prepared to make more than one sacrifice for what he believes.'

'You let him take you for a fiver!' Torrey laughed for the third time. 'You let Sounder con you out of a fiver . . . I'm surprised at you, Kate, I would have given you credit for having more sense than to fall for that old trick.'

'You can give me credit for a kick on the shins for that's what you'll be getting, me bonny lad, if you laugh just once more.'

'Don't get your Geordie elastic in a knot!' Torrey's smile refused to die. 'I'm just surprised that's all.'

'Well show your surprise some other way, the one you are using fails to amuse.'

'So you knew her too?'

'Knew who?' Kate Mallory's toffee-coloured eyes flashed a warning. Very soon now Richard Torrey would get the promised kick to the shins and very likely a follow up . . . in a much more painful area of his anatomy!

Catching the gleam, aware of all it stood for, he got up from his seat and was already a few steps safely away before saying over his shoulder, 'Queen Victoria . . . she was not amused.'

Smart arse! Kate swore softly under her breath as she lit a cigarette. It had been bad enough finding the banknote was not a fiver at all, in fact it wasn't even sterling but some foreign note probably left over from somebody's holiday abroad and swung on to the unsuspecting public. But to describe Echo Sounder as unsuspecting was like putting a fried fish in water and expecting it to swim.

Setting two glasses on their usual table in the corner of the lounge bar of the Frying Pan, Torrey saw the threatening scowl. Not a Nicole Jarreaux or an Isobel Davion, not even a pretty Jay . . . but even in this mutinous mood Kate Mallory was much more to his taste.

'Don't!' She scowled deeper still as he glanced at the cigarette in her hand. 'Don't tell me I'm shaping my own coffin, in fact don't tell me anything at all!'

'Fair enough.' He shrugged but in his eyes the smile still lurked. 'You can do the telling instead. You had a phone call from our friend Sounder, you met up with him at the greyhound stadium, he placed a bet for you then ri—'

'Careful!' A long stream of smoke issued slowly from Kate's nostrils. 'Smarter types than you sleep on a water bed, the river Tyne is thick with 'em!'

'Remind me not to accept your kind invitation to visit the North East.' He grinned. 'Maybe Sounder?'

'Now him I would not hesitate to invite, the little rat could do with a nice long swim, preferably with a grindstone tied to his neck.'

'Now, Kate, remember Sunday School: faith, hope and charity.'

'Huh!' Kate drew heavily on her cigarette. 'Faith in Sounder? I never had any. Hope? Forget it, and as for charity what I said he should get *was* charitable compared to what I would really like to see happen to him.'

'That's a bit hard, after all it was only a fiver he ripped you off for.'

Stubbing the cigarette end viciously into a large, green-lacquered metal ashtray set in the middle of the small round table she glared.

'It's not the money . . . it's the fact I almost lost my job! It seems while I was away playing Sounder's daft game there was a hold-up at the post office and this time it wasn't kids out for kicks, it was a man . . . a man with a mask over his face and a gun in his hands. Don't you understand? A real live hold-up and yours truly was watching dogs chase after a stuffed rabbit. Scotty was furious. I can't blame him for threatening to take my hide, everything was over by the time

I reached the office. But to be fair, Sounder's tip did pay off, my dog won the race.'

'What about Daniels? He could have given you the low down.'

'Oh he could!' Kate's smile was instantly unadulterated acid. 'But he wouldn't. I could read it all in the evening papers was what he *did* tell me; but credit where it's due, our detective inspector did smile as he said it.'

No wonder she had a face like a fourpenny hock! Lifting his glass to his lips, Torrey hid the smile brought on by the words his mother would have used. Like for himself, having a job meant release for Kate from soul-crushing visits to the dole or the offices of Social Security, more than that it meant self-respect, something that didn't come as part of a social handout.

'But Scotty didn't take your hide?'

Sherry-brown hair glinted as Kate shook her head. 'No, but in a way it might have been better if he had. The one decent story in God knows how long and what happens? I put a bloody fiver on a greyhound!'

'God does know.'

Her exasperation mingling with irritation, Kate snapped, 'Torrey, what the devil are you on about?'

'Now don't go mixing the deities.' He grinned again. 'I was saying God does know how long it's been since you got a real headliner and so do I.'

'Moving with the upper set!' She smiled sarcastically. 'Told you did He, well p'raps your high-placed friend told you when I might get another, or is that confidential?'

'Not at all, God hasn't shared any secret with me but Sounder will . . . after I've squeezed him a little.'

'I don't like being threatened.' Echo Sounder glanced nervously about him, his fingers weaving agitatedly in and out of each other. He didn't like being in the lounge of the Frying Pan either, the bar was more his turf; here he felt like a tiddler in a goldfish bowl.

'I'll do more than threaten unless you tell me what that fiasco at the greyhound stadium was all in aid of, apart that is from conning Kate out of a fiver. And while we are on the subject, wasn't five quid lowering your sights? You might not have got more, but you never even tried.'

'I d'ain't ask for more cos I weren't out to rob yer,' the little man looked at Kate with frightened eyes, 'an' I d'ain't rob yer, I put five pounds on Flighty Lad an' I give yer a note in change.'

'Yes you gave her a note she couldn't spend!'

'More importantly to him it was one he couldn't spend himself,' Kate spat. 'Had it been sterling I probably wouldn't have had sight of it.'

''Ave yer looked at it?'

'What do you think?' Kate's irritability was evident in her snapped reply.

'But you ain't burned it nor nuthin'?'

First he told her to keep the money out of sight now he was worried she might have destroyed it . . . why?

'It is still safe.'

'And so is he,' Torrey chipped in as she answered, 'but if you want to stay that way, Echo mate, you'll tell what this is all about. And Sounder, forget payment . . . at least of the kind you can spend on the track!'

'Be that *your* answer an' all?' Shifty eyes squinted at Kate. ''Cos if I ain't gettin' paid then I might as well tek what I 'ave to Daniels, maybe he'll be more appreciative.'

Torrey's smile spread across his mouth but his eyes remained hard. 'Why don't we all go see the blues, I'm sure they'll be more than interested in a certain banknote passed at the greyhound stadium . . .'

'I give her that note in good faith . . . I could just as easy 'ave took it to the blues meself.'

'And as easily explained what you were doing passing a dud?'

'A dud!' Echo Sounder's grubby fingers tightened about his glass. 'That ain't right, Torrey; that note were a foreigner but it don't be no dud an' you knows it!'

Leaning back in his chair Torrey watched Kate fumble in her bag. She was reaching for her precious Rothmans but Sounder could not be sure of that so p'raps now was the time to play his reserve.

'I didn't know it when Kate gave it to me,' he smiled again, 'but I did after a mate of mine looked at it, he works for Barclays in Wolverhampton and his job is identifying counterfeit currency, English and otherwise, and yours, my little chum, is forged . . . now, do you still want to talk to Daniels?'

'I knows nuthin' about any dud money.'

Ignoring Kate's puzzled glance and keeping his own on the flustered Sounder, Torrey answered smoothly, 'Then you won't mind your next drink being luke-warm tea in a station mug.'

'Wait a minute!' Sounder swallowed, the noise of it rattling in his throat. 'That note . . . it were give to me a few nights back—'

Pausing only because it was breathe or choke, Echo Sounder repeated what had passed between himself and Fred Baker, finishing with, 'Baker said young Penny was given to some Master, 'er life to pay for somebody's mistakes and then he said your name . . . said 'e 'eard all about Penny an' about Torrey, but that were all, 'e was too drunk to say any more an' I knowed it be no use to ask once 'e were sober.'

'Do you think—'

'I don't think anything, Kate!' Torrey cut her off quickly. The more that was said in front of Sounder the more could be echoed to another buyer. Placing a ten-pound note on the table he glanced at the disappointed face as it was grabbed.

'That's on account,' he said, 'there'll be more if what you have said proves to be interesting.'

'Is that note counterfeit?' Kate asked as the scruffy jacket disappeared through the door.

'I've no idea.'

'You've frightened the life out of Sounder, and for no reason.'

'No, I scared our scruffy friend for the best of reasons, to make sure he doesn't sing this particular song to anybody else before I have a chance to talk with Fred Baker.'

'You think Fred might know who this mysterious Master is?'

Picking up his drink, Torrey held it thoughtfully.

'Again, Kate, I've no idea. But I'm certainly going to find out.'

# Chapter Sixteen

'What can you tell me about this?'

Taking the note from his pocket, Torrey held it so Fred Baker could see.

'Christ, Torrey,' the man's face paled, 'where did you get that?'

'From the man you gave it to, the same man who gave it to a friend of mine. Now I want to know where you got it but don't bother saying it's left over from a holiday abroad 'cos we both know that's not true.'

'This friend o' your'n, he be tellin' you a lie.'

'Is that so?' Torrey returned the note to his pocket. 'Then why are your hands shaking? Look, Fred, I want the truth, and I also want the truth about the girl who disappeared from her job and if you don't tell me then you'll tell Bruce Daniels.'

'No!' Fear showing on his lined face, Fred Baker darted a glance towards the window of the office of Darlaston Printing. 'Not the bobbies, Crowley'll know it were me who shopped 'em.'

The man was clearly afraid, but of what? with the van loaded, Torrey closed the rear doors. 'What has Crowley got to do with it?'

'I ain't sure, but I gets the feelin' Max Gau be scared of 'im, leastways 'e allus seems to look that way whenever Crowley be around.'

Can't say I blame him, Torrey thought. The man gives me the creeps!

'So why does he come around . . . does he do much business here?'

'They be partners, 'im and Gau; bought this place together so I believes, but I ain't sayin' no more . . . not 'ere, it seems even the walls be listenin'.'

'Fred—'

'No more!' Glancing again at the upper window Fred shoved a clipboard into Torrey's hands, at the same time handing him a pen with which to sign an invoice.

'It ain't safe to talk 'ere,' he murmured, 'meet me tonight, we'll 'ave a drink an' I'll tell yer all I know. Meantime, lad, tek care nobody sees that banknote . . . and Torrey –' he took back clipboard and pen '– keep clear o' Crowley and keep that girl friend o' your'n clear of 'im an' all, that one don't be all 'e seems!'

*'don't be all 'e seems'*

The words rang in Torrey's mind as he drove. He had already had proof of that. The man was a pretty good hypnotist despite his denials, so what else was he . . . and what was the hold he had that caused Max Gau to be scared of him?

*''er life to pay for somebody's mistakes'*

Was Max Gau the 'somebody' Echo said Fred Baker had talked of? The thought hit like a brick. Drawing the van to a sharp stop Torrey leaned over the wheel, his breath tight in his throat.

Sacrifice . . . Sounder said Baker had talked of a sacrifice! Did that mean murder . . . had Max Gau murdered that young girl? Was that the hold Crowley had over him?

It seemed unbelievable. He straightened, breathing deeply. But then so did a lot of other things. Gau looked like anything but a murderer . . . so had Crippen!

A man who knew his past . . . another who could be guilty of taking a young girl's life . . . a foreign banknote . . . somehow they were all tied in together.

He slipped from the van and locked it. He needed to think!

'Lord, Torrey! You almost had me dead in my shoes, you scared the life out of me!'

He hadn't realised he'd stopped the van here and that the place he sat was Bentley cemetery.

'Did you have to sit perched on a gravestone like that? You could give a lass a heart attack.'

'A lass would have to have a heart for that to happen.'

'Funnny!' Kate Mallory walked from the shelter of the church porch. 'What are you doing here anyway, shouldn't you be at work?'

'Shouldn't you!'

'Okay . . . okay!' Kate lifted both hands in an attitude of surrender. 'We are both playing hookey, but why here?'

Torrey perched again on the wide slab of some Victorian sepulchre. 'I didn't know I was here, I certainly had no intention of coming; that leaves you.'

'I guess I just can't get it out of my mind. I keep thinking about what happened here, wondering if it had anything to do with that girl's disappearance.'

Suddenly the warning Fred Baker had left with him seemed very relevant. If Crowley and Gau were mixed up in one girl's murder then another one wouldn't make a great deal of difference to them.

'Forget it, Kate!' he said sharply. 'The girl decided to go home, there's no more to it than that.'

'You don't know that . . . does anybody know that, has anybody even bothered to find out?'

'Why would they? If she had been reported missing we would have known about it.'

'Oh, how?' Kate Mallory's brown eyes were challenging. 'Inspector Daniels would have had her picture blazed across the front page of the nationals would he . . . had a report put out on television's *Midlands Today*? Not with a dozen kids a year quitting this town for the bright lights. No, his idea of a missing person's report is sticking a photo on the noticeboard of the nick . . . and how many times a week do you go in there?'

Kate had a point, but to admit that would have her digging even deeper among the rubbish.

'All right I admit it, we don't know what happened to the girl . . . if anything happened at all, but you don't have to go tying that up with the paint job done on this cemetery.'

Kate delved into her bag, coming up with a six-by-ten photograph. 'Don't I? You might change your mind when you take a look at this.'

'This is just a copy of the photograph taken at the fete, it's the same one Fred showed me.'

'The same girl . . . not the same photograph. Look at it carefully.'

'Penny and Fred.' Torrey frowned as he looked at Kate. 'Like I said . . . the same photograph.'

'No, it's not the same!' The answer was snapped irately. 'A press photographer never takes just one shot, he takes several. That is one taken the same day at the same fete but it wasn't published.'

'So if a press photographer takes several yet only uses one that makes it usual procedure, Kate . . . you've lost me.'

'Then let me give you a hand.' She touched a finger to the print. 'It's my guess this photo was passed over in favour of the one printed in the *Star* because in this one the girl has her face turned slightly away from the camera.'

'But you can still see her fairly clearly.'

'You can also see something else fairly clearly. Look there –' she touched the photograph again '– where the breeze has lifted the cap sleeve of her dress; I thought at first it was a blip on the film or even the mark of a not-too-well-done vaccination. Then I had it blown up and looked at it under a magnifying glass, see for yourself.'

What else did that Aladdin's cave of a bag hold?

Torrey could not resist a smile as he took the small magnifying glass, but the smile faded as he trained it on the dark spot peeping beneath the sleeve of the white dress.

'God Almighty!' He whistled softly.

'God . . . or the devil? Which one has his followers marked with the Seal of Ashmedai?'

It was that seal! Torrey handed glass and photograph back to Kate who slipped them into her bag. That meant the 'sweet little wench' Fred Baker spoke of might be mixed up in something unpleasant and if, as Kate obviously thought, that something was dabbling in black magic then she probably deserved whatever had happened to her and he wanted no more to do with it.

'The blues said it was no more than kids arsing about with paint cans, that cemetery photo proves it.'

'Not for me.' Kate fell into step as he moved towards the road. 'There's a story in this, I know there is, and I'm going to find it.'

Waiting for several cars to pass he crossed to where the van was parked. 'That's up to you but count me out, I've got better things to do than play hide and seek with a bunch of kids.'

She didn't have to voice her displeasure, Torrey felt it as she slammed the door after being helped into the van. She didn't have to say anything, but knowing Kate Mallory that wouldn't stop her. As for himself he meant those words of a minute ago, he would see Fred Baker as arranged and that would be the end of it!

'Mr Torrey.'

The driver's door of the van already half-open he looked quickly over his shoulder. The street was empty and the grounds of that cemetery had been deserted except for Kate, and that voice was not hers. He had imagined . . .

'Please . . . help me.'

Every syllable crystal clear, the words drifted to him across the quiet road. Words he had heard before!

'Help me . . . please.'

Torrey whipped round. Just inside the cemetery grounds a fine mist seemed to rise from the ground. Heat mist, a hot day and damp earth always resulted in mist, there was nothing strange in that and mist certainly didn't talk! Dismissing it he made to climb into the van.

'Mr Torrey . . . please . . .'

Mist didn't talk . . . it was impossible! But the words he heard came directly from it, and he looked around to see it form into a single column which circled a foot or so above the ground.

His eyes fastened to it; unable to blink, he watched the circling slow, then begin to take on shape. With breath held in his throat he stared. Legs, torso, arms, a mist-formed figure gradually grew until finally there was the head and face . . . the pale unhappy face of Penny Smith!

The lift halted as it had travelled, soundlessly. Waiting until the doors were fully parted Julian Crowley stepped out. Facing him along the peacock-blue-carpeted corridor of Davion International head office were two tall figures dressed in the flowing white robes of the Middle East, their faces, or what little could be seen of them beneath their headcloths, almost hidden behind short black beards and heavy moustaches. They guarded Hamed Abdel Khadja, the man through whom the Master's will would be accomplished.

Brady, the man Crowley always used to travel with him to London, brushed a hand along the line of the Beretta he carried beneath an expertly fitted jacket. The move was slight enough but was seen and echoed by the watching Arabs. No one was giving anything away, but each relayed their own warning to the other.

'Will I come in with you, Mr Crowley?'

'No need.' Crowley had almost reached the door marked Managing Director.

'I'll wait here then. I trust these bastards about as far as I could throw a ten-ton weight.'

'No afternoon of pleasure?' Julian Crowley raised an enquiring eyebrow.

'There's nothing as won't be there next week so with your say-so I'll stay right here.'

'If you wish.' Crowley nodded. 'But remember, we don't want any breakdown in East–West relations.'

'Judging by this pair, any sort of relations would be a bloody miracle!' Brady positioned himself square on to the Arab guards. 'By what bit can be seen they might have been poured from a concrete mixer.'

'Good afternoon, Julian.'

Inside the lavishly appointed office, Crowley replied as Max Gau moved towards him. The man still had all the attributes of the small-time salesman! Switching his glance to a figure seated in a white leather armchair he smiled.

'*Salaam Alaykum*, Excellency. Thank you for coming, it is kind of you to do so; I fear it is us should have come to you.'

'*Alaykum-as-Salaam*.' Sheikh Hamed Abdel Khadja touched the fingertips of his right hand to heart, lips and brow. 'The place of our meeting is of no consequence, the fact that we meet is what gives my heart joy.'

Crowley smiled into eyes that glittered. They were sharp as a desert hawk's and so was this man's brain. He had come here only for what he could get . . . but that would be as much as he could pay for and no more.

'May we offer you coffee?' He turned to Gau as he spoke. Arabs considered it bad manners to wade straight into business matters, social proprieties must first be observed.

'There is no need.' Abdel Khadja resumed his seat. 'While here in the West we will follow the ways of the West, the drinking of coffee can come later.'

'As your Excellency wishes.'

Ignoring the massive walnut desk that squatted on four-inch-deep white Axminster carpet Crowley chose another of the white leather armchairs. The whole room was white . . . except for the Degas originals that punctuated its walls. White for a follower of the Lord of Darkness! Davion had a sense of humour.

'I believe your Excellency is in the market for armaments.'

Abdel Khadja didn't blink an eyelid. 'Not just armaments, my friend, the best the world has to offer.'

'That being?'

Khadja's hand rested on white leather. 'That being the Emissary!'

'That is a very new weapon.' Max Gau looked nervous. 'Your Excellency should understand it has not yet been offered for sale.'

'Precisely why we want it, Mr Gau, because no other nation has it. It is being one step ahead that keeps you alive, is that not so, my friend? Especially in a climate of – let us say, take-over bids – our Emir has no intention his country be annexed by his neighbour, be it East . . . or West.'

'Understandable,' Gau was apprehensive, 'but there are other planes available.'

'Not with the speed and strike power of the Emissary.' Khadja's bird-bright eyes never blinked. 'We know its Milton-Paige engine can outstrip the speed of the American F14s, F15s and even the F18 and F117 Stealth Fighter Bomber; we know also the range and accuracy of its Epee air-to-air missiles and that it shows no trace on radar.'

'You are well-informed, Excellency.'

'We try to be, Mr Crowley.' Sheikh Hamed Abdel Khadja leaned both hands on the arms of his chair, the movement rustling the sleeves of his robes against leather. 'But I am here to talk business not to discuss our information or its source, however reliable. I am instructed by my Emir to transact the sale of twenty of your Emissary strike fighters along with an undefined supply of its accompanying missiles, also the same number of Merlin helicopters. We also intend to purchase a bevy of other armaments that we hope will be supplied by Davion International, otherwise,' he shrugged, 'we must turn to other suppliers.'

'Has Milton-Paige that number of engines ready for use?' Crowley looked across to Alex Davion.

'Seventeen crated for shipment to Davaston Engineering –' Davion's eyes were on the Sheikh '– another half dozen within a day or so of completion.'

Alex Davion, international arms dealer, director of Mercury Airlines, smiled through tinted contact lenses, their vivid electric blue highlighting his bronzed skin. Handsome he certainly was, and aware of the fact. Watching him now, Crowley smiled to himself. Just as the man was aware of who it was pulled the strings.

'And how long for the bodies to be built?' the sheikh asked.

'We could have them ready within two months,' Davion answered, 'but that kind of effort doesn't come cheap.'

'Money is of no consequence,' Khadja's eyes were contemptuous. 'Once we are agreed the money will be paid.'

'It is usual procedure for payment to be made fifty per cent in advance, the rest on taking delivery of the goods.'

'That may be the procedure in the West—'

Listening, Crowley was sure the sheikh wanted to add 'little man'.

'– but in my world once a bargain has been struck payment is given in full. You see, Mr Davion, the word of an Arab is not merely his bond it is his life; if one becomes broken, the other is forfeit.'

'You mentioned other armaments,' Max Gau broke in diplomatically, 'if your Excellency can specify.'

'To put it bluntly, Mr Gau –' vibrant desert-hawk eyes swept each face '– my country finds itself in a delicate and precarious position. On our Eastern frontier we find our neighbours massing instruments of war, that particular president has flexed his muscles before, he has dreams we think, dreams of enlarging his territory at the expense of ours, dreams that will not come true, Mr Gau, yet dreams that will be dreamt nevertheless; we intend to be ready for the dreamer.'

'But the rest of the Arab nations, would they sanction any invasion of that kind?'

'Who knows, Mr Gau,' the sheikh smiled, 'who knows where the sparrow will fly when the eagle sweeps; it is better that one should be the eagle do you not agree?'

'Indeed, Excellency,' Max Gau ran a hand across greying hair, 'I hope Davion International may give strength to the eagle.'

On both sides, thought Davion; this is one bloody eagle which could do with his wing feathers clipped!

'We can take it that our subsidiary companies can supply all that you need,' Crowley once more took the lead, 'but might I be forgiven for asking if your Excellency has taken other methods of attack into consideration?'

'Such as what?' the sand-dry voice rustled.

'Such as chemical or biological warfare . . . there is a possibility of these weapons being brought into play should an open conflict break out.'

'You are of course correct, Mr Crowley, such a possibility does exist and His Majesty the Emir is aware of it, that too must be prepared for.'

'Then might I make a suggestion?'

'We listen always to the tongue of a wise man.'

'Coton Pharmaceuticals have developed a new strain of virus, used in connection with nerve gas it proves deadly. If your Excellency wishes I will have Mr Geddes, Coton's director, get in touch with your Embassy.'

'Not the Embassy,' Khadja's right hand lifted from the arm of the chair then lowered again. 'The government of my country is not involved in the purchasing of weapons of any kind. You understand, Mr Crowley? However what is discussed between friends . . .'

'Then perhaps your Excellency will honour his friends by accepting an invitation to the races, your Excellency is famed for his own bloodstock.'

'A pleasant prospect, Mr Crowley –' Hamed Abdel Khadja stood up, his white robes whispering into the carpet '– and I hope a profitable one for both of us. Until then, *way alaykum as salaam wa rahmat Allah wa barakatu,* on you peace, and the mercy of Allah and his blessings.'

You part with prayers easily. Crowley acknowledged the slight bow. As easily as you are going to part with your money.

# Chapter Seventeen

Sheikh Hamed Abdel Khadja stepped from the gleaming Rolls Royce that had brought him to Whitefriars, one glance checking it was set well back amid parkland. Privacy was important to him and Crowley had chosen wisely the venue of his entertainment.

'We thought your Excellency would prefer a less public evening.'

'Most considerate, but was that not expensive, my friend, to hire a race track for the pleasure of just one man?'

Max Gau smiled as he led the way into the house, two robed bodyguards, who bothered to make little secret of the fact they were armed, as close to the sheikh as feathers on a goose.

'Davion International does not count the cost of its hospitality, especially when its guest is your Excellency.'

The enforced wait at the hotel; Khadja suddenly deciding that this time he would observe the custom of the East rather than the West so having coffee served before leaving for Whitefriars, had irked and the irritation still rubbed; but Max knew he must control it, Crowley would not take kindly to things being messed up now.

'The race track is privately owned,' he began, then as the other man halted abruptly, a question glaring from bright, hawk eyes, he added, 'that is, it is owned by Davion International. The company uses it solely for guests.'

Above a well-trimmed beard that showed not a single trace of grey the black eyes glittered. This man could make a dangerous enemy . . . for any man other than a Magus of the Left Hand Path. The thought reassuring him, Max led the way across the large, flagged entrance hall.

'This race,' Khadja asked again, 'it is only for one man?'

Max felt reassurance turn to thin ice beneath his feet. Crowley needed time to institute his protection, the guns beneath those robes needed none.

'We—' He cleared his throat. 'We have taken the liberty of inviting one or two others, Your Excellency, all of whom you have met before.'

Not a hand, not even an eyelash appeared to move as the sheikh listened but like a pale shadow one of his bodyguards now stood between him and the door Max had reached for.

'Who, who are these guests I have met before?'

The question was quiet yet it sang across the silent hall like a whip. Max Gau knew he must make his answer a wise one.

'Mr Crowley extended the invitation to Miss Jarreaux and several of her employees, all of whom your Excellency may remember from your last visit to this house.'

'Ah!' Between moustache and beard, white teeth gleamed. 'That is acceptable, Mr Gau, the company of such charming people turns dull hours into a delight.'

Not to mention the company of a woman, or two, or three! His contempt hidden, Max Gau opened the door ushering the sheikh into a softly lit room.

'Which ones did you bring?'

Max Gau accepted the glass Nicole Jarreaux held out to him. She was a beautiful woman. Auburn hair caught into a chignon, shapely body enhanced by exquisitely contoured eau-de-nil silk gown, her face, already lovely, complemented by just the right amount of make-up. Yes, the woman was beautiful, but she was also cold as arctic ice. Several men he knew had tried to make a play for her since her coming into the coven, Davion included, though his true preferences lay on the other side of the fence; but Nicole had refused them all . . . or could it be she was Julian Crowley's private reserve? Doubtful. He sipped the whisky, feeling it bite against his throat. Julian Crowley had only one interest and that was no woman.

'I told you Crowley would want the best.'

'Relax.' Nicole turned sea-green eyes on Alex Davion. 'You go on worrying like that and Davion International is going to need a new director.'

'Not to mention the House of Jarreaux, should tonight prove to be a non-starter!' Davion's apprehension showed in the snap of his answer.

'The House of Jarreaux is on safe ground,' she smiled cynically, 'let us all hope you can claim as much for Davion International.'

'So who did you bring?' Max stepped in as peace maker.

'Petra, Yvette and Lisanne.' Nicole returned her attention to Max. 'The sheikh enjoyed much more of them than just their company while he was at Whitefriars. Then there is Carina, and a few others to provide the supporting cast.'

'And the men?'

Her smile devastating in its icy contempt she turned again to Davion.

'I would have expected no other question from you, Alex. Thinking to have yourself a sporting evening of a different kind? Well for your choice I brought Paul Whiteman, Caspar, Pierre, Marcus, Domino and Diego.'

She watched Davion's handsome face. Had he any idea Diego was his wife's latest stud?

'A good selection, Nicole.'

'I thought so.' She answered Max, but her eyes were on Davion.

Julian Crowley sat in the tapestried dining room of Whitefriars. Built during the reign of the Tudors it had been altered little apart from the encircling moat being drained and grassed over, the rest stood as it always had among several hundred acres. It was those acres with their scant habitation, a couple of farms and a tiny hamlet, which had prompted him to buy the place, its privacy served well for occasions such as tonight.

Across the table Max Gau watched critically. It was against all ethics of the Followers that any put their personal desire before the work of the Master, yet Julian Crowley was doing just that. How long would the Lord of Darkness accept that, how long would he allow it to go unpunished? Crowley was a Magus, well-advanced along the Left Hand Path, a man skilled in the Black Art, a master of magic . . . but even masters of magic were not above being chastised.

'Perhaps your Excellency would like coffee in the drawing room.'

Max watched as Crowley pushed back his chair. Nicely done; that gave the specially brought in caterers time to clear away and leave before the evening entertainment began, and as always on such occasions the Ellises were away enjoying the benefits of a short holiday . . . courtesy of their employer.

They had eaten well, dining on moules gratinée followed by lain-el-Maroc and finishing with petits pot-de-creme au café. Glancing down the long refectory table Max smiled inwardly. A man's last meal should be a good one . . . he could remember it in hell!

An hour later, coffee finished, he followed through low doorways to a graceful long gallery that overlooked the rear gardens. Apple logs burned in huge twin fireplaces, their light flickering on tapestry wall hangings to give an eerie semblance of movement to fleeing animals chased by galloping horses, their riders aiming bows and spears. At the north end a long, intricately carved wood screen closed off the solar, the original bedroom of the old house. Most of the furniture had been removed from the gallery, leaving it virtually clear except for the huge hand-woven Flemish carpet around which a double row of silk cords roped off a horse-shoe-shaped avenue some four feet wide. Facing the Solar several stools padded in various colours of silk were set out in a straight line.

'What is this?' Sheikh Abdel Khadja glanced about the room then back to Crowley. 'I thought I was invited to the races?'

'And so you were, your Excellency,' Crowley smiled, 'but I am certain your Excellency will enjoy the evening none the less. If not, then perhaps he will have the goodness of heart to forgive our flimsy offering of amusement and accept the gift of any racehorse from a stable of his own choosing.'

Abdel Khadja smiled, instant interest grabbing chocolate-drop eyes. One hand stroked his dark beard. 'A hefty bet, Mr Crowley.'

'No bet, your Excellency, more a consolation . . . should one be needed!'

'And one I shall take!' Khadja chose a glass of fruit juice from a silver tray; he must be seen to observe the custom of his country, no matter that the juice was heavily laced with vodka.

'Would your Excellency accept a list of the field?'

Alex Davion's designer-styled hair glistened as a series of overhead lamps suddenly flooded the centre of the ancient room.

'Thank you.' Khadja ran an eye over the hand-engraved card. 'I do not recognise any of these runners.'

'Then perhaps, your Excellency, you may have the pleasure of seeing something a little less usual. May I suggest that here would be a good point from which to follow the race?'

Leading the sheikh to a chair placed strategically opposite the line of silk-topped stools Davion glanced across at a man stood with a dark-haired companion. Joining them, Mitchell Walters, head of Walters Engineering, smiled as he was introduced.

'Fancy a little bet, your Excellency?' Walters dropped his heavy frame on to a chair beside Abdel Khadja.

'Why not.' The sheikh read the pale card more slowly. 'What is your fancy, Mr Walters?'

'What about having a book?' Davion called across the roped-off enclosure. 'Let's get some odds on the runners, what do you say, Julian?'

'As you wish,' Crowley answered. 'If you gentlemen will give me a moment I will arrange it. Alex, perhaps you will help.'

Five minutes later they returned with a list of runners, their odds written in large black lettering. Davion pinned the sheet of paper to a tapestry hanging beside the fireplace to the right of the solar.

'A list of this evening's field,' he announced. 'Any bet you care to make, gentlemen, will be accepted by Davion International.' He turned to the sheikh. 'If your Excellency has no objection I will ask Miss Jarreaux to hand you all a betting slip.'

'How could a man object to such a delightful work of Allah?' Khadja's eyes glinted at Nicole. 'It is my hope the Almighty will reward me a second time tonight and smile with grace upon my endeavour to select a winning horse.'

From a table at the furthest end of the room Nicole collected a handful of slim gold pens and several slips of paper. Starting with the sheikh she handed one of each to the assembled group before leaving the room.

'Gentlemen!' Alex Davion positioned himself at the left side of the entrance to the roped-off venue. 'The runners are about to proceed to the starting gate.'

A rustle of excitement greeted the announcement and every eye fastened on a door now opening beside the solar screen.

'Wearing the yellow and sage of Davion International Stable we have Carina. Carina is ridden this evening by Diego.'

Sat on his chair the Sheikh leaned forward, his interest well and truly kindled as naked, except for a narrow strip of sage-and-yellow silk fastened bridle-fashion about her face, a girl of little over twenty, slim and pretty, the true hallmark of the House of Jarreaux, stepped from behind the solar screen, her tight breasts bobbing, a dark thatch at the top of her legs glinting in the overhead light. Behind her, the end of the bridle in his right hand, was Diego, equally naked except for a yellow jockey cap and a sage-and-yellow silk band cupped beneath his testicles, crossing his hips to circle his waist. He smiled, saluting his audience with a thin whip held in one hand.

From the opposite end of the 'track' Crowley watched the sheikh. He would need to present him with no other racehorse.

'In the slashed blue of Aroil we have Lisanne, a mettlesome filly this, but capably handled by Paul.'

Colours of silk the only difference, the second pair emerged and followed along the roped-off 'course'.

'And in the familiar red and white of Coton,' Alex Davion continued his commentary, 'we see Yvette. Yvette's rider this evening is Casper.'

A long breath of admiration tinged with expectancy rifled the tense atmosphere.

With scarlet-and-white bridle set around her dusky face and looping into tight-cropped hair, breasts hard and pointed above an hour-glass waist, a dark thatch topping never-ending legs, another girl sauntered on to the track. Arrogance cohabiting with contempt, her glance swept the faces grouped around the silken cordon. Behind her Casper, his dark skin gleaming, flicked the red-and-white rein.

Yvette remained still.

'Hup!' Caspar flicked the silk.

'Hup!' This time it was loud and the thin whip snaked out its tip, kissing the girl's glistening bottom.

Yvette threw back her head, a screech gurgling in her throat.

Without turning she kicked out, checking the force inches from Caspar's crutch, then she stretched slowly until the sole of her foot touched against his body.

Walters drew in a harsh breath, wiping a hand across flabby lips. The girl looked towards the sound and smiled then, wiggling her long toes, began to fondle Caspar's already hardened flesh.

'Can the jockey bring his mount under control?' Davion laughed. 'We must observe the rules, no one begins before starter's orders.'

Yvette dropped her foot as Caspar flicked the silken whip harmlessly to one side. Hips rolling, black breasts thrust forwards, she strolled around the horse-shoe-shaped enclosure, Caspar's muscles rippling with every step of his long legs. Proud in their red-and-white bands, rock-hard testicles swung rhythmically.

'That one might need more than a touch of the whip to bring her into submission.' Alex grinned, watching the girl swagger forwards. The onlookers laughed agreement, all except Walters who wiped another unsteady hand across his sweating upper lip.

'Pink and maroon,' Alex announced, 'Satel Aeronautic colours, gentlemen, and they are worn this evening by Joanne and her rider, Marcus.'

From his place at the side of the gallery Crowley watched. The girl was young, perhaps not yet twenty; tall, at least five-ten; a mane of reddish-blonde hair spilling into the hollows of her shoulder; large pale eyes lifting almond-fashion at the corners. She wore little make-up, the maroon bridle band held loosely in her mouth contrasting sharply against clear pale skin. She was sleek and beautiful and matched top and bottom, unusual in most blondes, more so in the strawberry variety! His stare swept the girl moving towards them. Khadja would like that.

The couple had drawn level now with Davion, whose eyes were for the jockey. He was a couple of inches taller than the girl;

pale yellow hair curled softly into the curve of his bronzed neck, eyes brightly blue stared wide, full lips opening into a smile.

Davion swallowed hard. This one was quite a looker. Mitchell watched too. Watched the slap of genitals against bronzed legs, the seductive roll of bottom as the young man passed. Nice arse, he thought, and knows the extras it can bring judging by those eyes . . . Marcus. He made a mental note.

'Now I think Mercury.' Davion returned his attention to the job in hand, wishing it were something else he had in hand. 'Yes, gentlemen, turquoise with pink chevrons, the colours of the Mercury Stable, and their runners are the lovely filly Tamsin and her jockey tonight, Pierre.'

The girl was as beautiful as the others. Huge sloe eyes dreamed out beneath dark, winged brows complementing high cheekbones and soft moist lips, her hair a blue-black cloud.

Mitchell Walters was sweating openly now. Beside him his young companion twisted a large square-cut diamond nestling on the third finger of the left hand. The sheikh sat motionless.

'Tamsin is new to the Mercury Stable.' Alex Davion continued, 'this is the first time out for her. Her trainer reports she prefers a hard ride, let's hope she's not disappointed. Pierre, however,' he paused, waiting until the pair drew level, 'is an experienced jockey, he's ridden many times and can be trusted to get the best out of his mount.'

The man jerked on the pink-and-turquoise band pulling the silk into the corners of the girl's mouth so her head came back sharply on her neck, at the same time snaking the whip over her shoulder. The girl gasped, nostrils flaring.

Crowley nodded to himself. The girl was putting on a good show.

Without amendments [illegible]

The [illegible] that [illegible] [illegible]

[illegible]

[illegible]

Miners [illegible]

and [illegible]

that [illegible]

[illegible]

on the [illegible]

served.

[illegible]

period [illegible]

the [illegible]

[illegible]

[illegible]

[illegible]

[illegible]

[illegible]

[illegible]

[illegible]

[illegible]

# Chapter Eighteen

'We have one more entry for tonight's race.'

The sheikh who had been ticking off names on his race card looked up as Alex Davion announced a sixth runner.

'Running in the black and white of Cardine Banking we have Petra, a filly used to the track, and in the saddle we have Domino.'

Memory stirred in the depths of Abdel Khadja's hawk eyes and his long fingers tightened about the slim gold pen but other than this he displayed no recognition of the name.

For several seconds no one appeared. A tense hush descended on the room, eyes turning to the low doorway beside the carved screen.

Seconds drew into minutes. No one spoke. Then, almost as if spirited there by unseen powers, Petra stood at the entrance to the cordoned 'track'.

'Christ!' Mitchell Walters leaned forwards his race card fluttering to the floor. 'Christ!'

Davion dragged his gaze from Marcus's swaying hips, suddenly aware of the shattered silence.

'Jesus!' Mitchell breathed hard, a fresh tremor rattling the zip of his trousers. 'I don't know who is producing this little show but he can arrange a production for me any time. Where the hell do you suppose he finds such lookers?'

'That is an untold story,' Davion answered. 'I for one don't care so long as action speaks as loudly as presentation.'

'I doubt you will have grounds for complaint,' Max Gau said quietly. 'Julian Crowley's efforts usually meet with approval.'

At least they've always met the Messenger's approval, he thought, watching the dark-suited Crowley. Was he truly the favoured of the Lord of Darkness? Or was Satan merely playing with them all? Inwardly trembling, he flicked away from the compelling eyes watching him from the other side of the horse-shoe, eyes that seemed to read his soul.

'Mr Crowley!' Abdel Khadja's low tone drifted across the room. 'Is this a selling plate?'

'The winning runner will be auctioned after the race, your Excellency,' Crowley answered, 'and of course the jockey will ride for the stable which offers the highest fee.'

'What sort of fee do you think he might require?'

'Fillies such as these command a high price,' Crowley replied.

'True,' Mitchell joined in, 'but then there's always the jockey, if one can't get Bollinger one must accept Heidsieck.'

'Do you think our friend Khadja might buy the field, Max?' Davion murmured, coming to stand beside Gau. 'He has, so I hear, rather a liking for horse flesh and he has enough oil to grease anyone's palm.'

'He might buy them all,' Max answered, glancing across at the undoubted interest of the sheikh. 'But then as the man would no doubt say, Allah is Merciful.'

Davion laughed. 'As of this moment, Max, I've changed my religion.'

'You mean you had one to start with?' Max returned drily.

'Petra, gentlemen, is good on any ground.' Alex Davion resumed his patter, ignoring the ironical reply. 'She has run several times in the Cardine colours, which you see are black and white.'

Petra moved further on to the track beneath the centre lights.

'Holy Christ!' Mitchell Walters spoke to no one in particular. 'What do you reckon to this one?'

Pure-white ribbon circled Petra's brow and cheeks then twisted into ash-blonde hair dusted with pearl powder. High breasts jutted out above a twenty-inch waist, slim legs rode upwards to a vee plucked free of public hair. With toe and fingernails painted with pearl lacquer and her entire body covered with pearly body sheen, she gleamed, angelic pure, a newly created Eve rising fresh from the dust of Eden.

Mitchell Walters released a long, trembling breath. Beside him his companion's attractive mouth drooped in a pout, the square-cut diamond reflecting spears of light as it was twisted around a slim finger.

The end of the white rein looped over the fingers of his right hand, head held at an arrogant angle, Domino followed as Petra began the walk around the horse-shoe-shaped track, the rhythm and pace of their steps a perfect match.

A black jockey cap set straight hid most of Domino's thick tight hair. Black silk straps, hardly discernible against the glistening blackness of his skin, scooped his testicles, crossing the root of a flagrantly erect penis before disappearing into an ebony bush from which they caressed flat hips, wrapping his waist in a circle. He walked placing bare feet ball first on the ground before dropping softly on to the heel, the cat-like movement rippling the length of his long legs. Sleek and muscular, two tiny white circles marking his brow, his oiled skin gleaming like black satin, he was a stallion in every sense of the word.

'He's carrying a cargo worth a fortune,' Mitchell glanced across to the list Alex Davion had pinned up. 'No wonder he's odds-on favourite.'

Two to one to win. Davion placed a tick on his race card. What else was expected? You could hang a flag on a pole like that.

'Bit thick for my money.' Max Gau put a line through the Cardine entry.

'Not for mine,' Davion grinned, following the rippling backside with an appreciative look, 'but I'll lay you even money Khadja takes it, he likes pricks the way he likes his oil wells, strong and gushing.'

'He has to win first,' Gau ticked off a choice higher up the list, 'the favourite isn't always first past the post.'

'Will the jockeys bring their mounts to the starting gate?' Alex Davion resumed his role. 'Gentlemen, if you wish to make a bet Max will collect your slips now.'

Collecting the various slips of paper, Max Gau made a swift calculation of what Davion International stood to lose: the amount would ruin Ladbroke! When Crowley had told him to set up this little entertainment he had guessed approximately what the cost would be, but Julian Crowley was good for the money should the need arise.

With the last slip of paper collected he placed them on a table at the rear of the room, returning to stand directly opposite Crowley. He looked across for the signal to begin but Crowley wasn't looking at him; eyebrows drawn together in a frown, one thumb stroking his wrist beneath the cuff of his shirt, he was staring at Mitchell Walters's companion.

Gau waited but Crowley's unblinking gaze never left that taut face. The buzz of conversation began to lull. Taking the initiative he nodded to Alex.

'Gentlemen,' Davion's response was immediate, 'they are under starter's orders.'

Touching the whip to the girls' naked bottoms the jockeys guided them to the silk-topped stools, choosing that which matched the colours of their cross-bands. Bending forwards, each girl placed her hands on the stool, gripping the sides tightly.

The jockeys stepped forward.

Max glanced again at Crowley, he was still staring at Mitchell and the attractive creature beside him. Max raised his right hand. The jockeys manoeuvred.

'Christ!' Mitchell Walters whispered hoarsely, 'I never expected anything like this.'

The diamond-fingered hand came down demanding attention, Walters shook it off.

'Mitch . . . I want—'

A mild explosion shook Mitchell Walters. 'Either keep quiet or piss off!'

The pout on the attractive mouth became suddenly sullen. Across the track Crowley stared.

'Ready –' Davion watched Max's hand.

The jockeys raised their whips.

'Quite a line up!' the sheikh murmured.

'Up being the operative word.' Mitchell's eyes seemed glued to the line of men, their hard flesh brushing the jutting bottoms of their partners.

Max dropped his hand and the jockeys lunged.

'– and they're off!' Davion shouted.

'I'd say they were in,' Mitchell drawled, 'right up to the bollocks.' He passed a tongue over his flabby lips, a moustache of sweat gleaming in the light as he strained forward.

As Max's hand had dropped each girl began to sway backwards and forwards, smoothly riding the flesh between her legs.

'They're going well,' Davion began a running commentary, 'seems to be neck and neck . . .'

Max looked across to Crowley. Those eyes hadn't blinked once.

'. . . Joanne is straining at the lead but Marcus is holding her . . .'

Light gleamed on swaying buttocks, breasts swung like soundless bells.

'. . . oh and Aroil is beginning to flag . . . yes . . . yes, Paul is down at the first fence.'

Paul shuddered, pressing harder into Lisanne as he came.

'The runners seem to have found their stride . . . no, I spoke too soon, Caspar is in trouble . . . Yvette has got her head . . . she's running away with him, yes! . . . Yes!'

Caspar's whip swung downwards.

'Ohh!' Davion moaned theatrically. 'And he's down.'

'Ohh,' Mitchell Walters's gasp was for real. At his side an angry hand pushed through raven-dark hair, the gleam of a diamond dimmed by the flash of temper in green eyes.

'I think we are past the halfway line and they're still neck and neck! Which of them will make it to the post? It's anyone's guess at this stage.'

'We'll be lucky if we make it to the bloody post,' Mitchell grunted.

'Watch the Mercury runner, gentlemen,' Davion raised his voice excitedly. 'She's stopped . . . she's refusing—' he paused. Blue-black hair floated like tropical storm clouds as Tamsin threw up her head and hard breasts stabbed forwards. With her sloe eyes dreaming into the distance she resembled some lovely figure-head.

'Pierre is losing his seat . . . she's too strong for him . . .'

Tamsin's stomach clenched, the cheeks of her bottom dimpled, Pierre gasped, a film of sweat wrapping his brows like cellophane.

'. . . Tamsin is loose . . .' Davion pretended to hold his breath.

Tamsin clenched again, squeezing, relaxing, squeezing, smiling as Pierre's breathing became louder, then twisted her bottom in a rolling motion. Pierre gasped, dropping the whip; grabbing her hip bones he pulled her further on to him, ramming several hard jerks before pulling off.

'. . . he's down!' Davion acted his surprise well. 'But the race isn't over yet, we still have Joanne, Carina and Petra . . . which one is your choice for the winner?'

'I wouldn't refuse any!' Davion's eyes devoured the sweating men.

'What do you think, Mr Mitchell?' Abdel Khadja's voice betrayed no emotion. 'Joanne . . . Carina, or maybe Petra, the so lovely pearl? Come, Mr Mitchell, which is your preference?'

'They're all my preference,' Mitchell croaked again, 'I'd ride any one of 'em, win or lose.'

'Mitchie . . . you promised—'

'Shut up, you moaning bitch!' Walters flashed. 'If you don't like it then bugger off out of it, I don't see nobody holding you.'

Across the room Crowley's dark eyes watched.

The diamond flamed downwards, resting against cream silk, mascarared lashes half closed over green eyes.

'Is he—' Davion ignored Walters's outburst. 'Yes Marcus is falling behind and Joanne knows it . . . she's breaking her stride.'

Reddish-blonde hair spilled like a shawl over the girl's pale shoulders, tightly pointed breasts bobbing with each rapidly drawn breath as smooth, regular rocking gave way to fast, dragging jerks.

'Marcus is failing . . .' Davion paused. 'He's using the whip . . . yes, the whip has gone down, Marcus is out of the race . . .'

Taking control of his own finish Marcus pushed violently, slapping against the girl's soft flesh.

'. . . a valiant try,' Davion chuckled as the man slumped across the girl's back, 'but the going got a little too rough. However we have two runners still on the field, Carina and Diego in the yellow and sage of Davion International, and the favourite Petra and Domino in the black and white of Cardine Banking, but will the favourite last the finish? They are entering the home stretch and I think Carina has the edge!'

Abdel Khadja's hand tightened on the edge of his white robe as Petra changed her steady rhythm to a series of short rapid jerks. Above her pearl-powdered hair the black silk whip cracked and she dropped once more into a long slow rock.

'I think this will be a photo finish . . . wait . . . wait . . .'

Khadja's hand relaxed.

'. . . Diego isn't going to make it!' Davion's voice squeaked with excitement.

Slashing the narrow whip to the floor Diego wrenched the sage-and-yellow rein, snatching Carina's dark head back on her shoulders, his hips welded to her tight bottom as he lost the race.

'Tough luck, Davion International, but that leaves Petra and Domino clear winners . . .'

Two tiny, obliquely placed circles gleamed white against Domino's black skin, his teeth gleaming in a victor's smile.

Davion looked across at Crowley. How much longer did he want Domino to perform? But Crowley's attention was still fastened on the podgy Walters and his elegant companion.

He couldn't call him, that would only highlight the fact he had been oblivious to the entire proceedings. Davion hesitated. Just what was Crowley up to?

He tapped the race card against his mouth.

'. . . Domino is coming in to a stunning finish . . .' He caught the signal to wind up. '. . . watch him go over the line.'

Without loosening the silk rein Domino leaned forwards, his left arm sliding beneath Petra and lifting her rear on to his flat stomach. Slowly twisting her pearl-covered legs around shining black ones she pressed back against his chest, her hair covering one black shoulder in a film of pearl. With a cry Domino brought down the whip.

'And another hundred!' Mitchell Walters waved the race card he had retrieved from the floor. The sheikh had bought the services of Petra, Yvette and Joanne, and he was determined to get one of the remaining three.

'Two hundred!' The sheikh topped his bid. Watching the petulant face beside Mitchell cloud with anger, Crowley smiled.

'And two!' Mitchell Walters's face was florid.

'The lady is yours!' Khadja inclined his head, tapping the race card against his palm.

'Mitch!' The cry was high, angry. 'Mitch you promised!'

'Here!' Snatching a handful of notes from his wallet Mitchell Walters flung them at his companion. 'Buy yourself a jockey, with your talents you might just get him in the saddle before morning.'

'Mitch!' It was almost a scream.

'Bugger off!'

Walters had already claimed the lovely Carina, a podgy arm marring her delightful waist as he walked her away from the silk-roped enclosure.

'Mitch, you're not going to play being a jockey.'

Walters stopped. His arm falling away from Carina he turned.

'You said there would be no more girls!' The voice was high-pitched with tears. 'You bastard, you promised . . . you said there wouldn't be anybody but me ever again . . .' A thin black line of mascara trickled wetly, glistening like a black worm over the expertly made-up face.

'Well you ain't gonna ride, Mitch, not tonight . . . not any night.'

The square-cut diamond glittered as the left hand came up, squashing the trailing worm, spreading its black guts.

'In fact, Mitch, you ain't never gonna ride again.'

Crowley's frown deepened, his stare becoming even more intense.

Across the room the gun went off.

Alex Davion retched as Walters's chest exploded, spraying the cream silk suit with crimson.

'The stupid shit! The bloody stupid shit . . . he's . . . he's killed Walters!'

# Chapter Nineteen

Sat on the edge of his bed, Richard Torrey stared at the wall.

Kate Mallory had seen nothing unusual in that cemetery, she had not seen the figure form out of mist, the figure of the girl in white. Why did it come to him? It wasn't as if he had known the girl. With the ghost of Anna it had been different, he had loved Anna until . . . but he wouldn't think of that, it was over . . . finished; and what was happening now? That also could be finished: if he ignored it long enough it would stop.

But how did you stop a dream? When awake he could consciously direct his mind, but when asleep . . . ? And the girl he had seen today, had heard call from that cemetery, often troubled his sleep. Getting up from the bed he crossed to the window, drawing back the thin cotton curtains. Tomorrow he would start looking for another place, new digs, new start.

With one hand resting on the frame of the window he looked out over houses that lined each side of the narrow street, houses that had been built to serve factories such as Rubery and Owen, Garringtons, Guest Keen and Nettlefold . . . factories that had been the lifeblood of Darlaston but now stood empty and lifeless if they stood at all. The town had its houses and its people,

people like Fred who clung to a job not knowing from one day to the next when it would be snatched away.

Fred had told him the printers might soon be for the chop. It had come out when they had talked of that banknote. Fred had heard Crowley say something about this consignment being the last, that the work would soon be finished, but it wasn't just the worry of that had the man's hand shaking when Torrey asked again about that banknote.

He didn't know why he had taken it, never in all the years of his life had he stolen anything before.

But what good was it to him, he couldn't spend it, the only thing would have been to take it to a bank and change it for sterling.

Fred had agreed when Torrey had put that to him, but had been totally against taking it to a bank.

*'That would be like jumpin' into the fire, Torrey lad.'*

The look that had crossed his face seconds after the words slipped out had said it all. Fred Baker was scared . . . really scared.

Torrey watched the headlights of a car sweep the road as it drove past, disappearing as the vehicle turned the corner.

It was just a matter of weeks after the printing works had been bought from its previous owner that Crowley had called on one of his visits and asked to see Fred.

*''E laid it on the line, lad.'*

Fred Baker's trembling voice echoed in Torrey's mind.

*'I were a master printer and 'e was pleased with the work I done but there were summat special as needed printin' an' I only got to keep me job if'n I took that one. It were not 'til after when I realised what was wanted an' that were when I told 'im what 'e could do wi' his job. At that 'e sent Max Gau out on some pretence, tellin' 'im to tek young Penny along wi' 'im.'*

'Then what?' Torrey had needed to urge him to go on.

Fred had looked at him across the glass that shook in his

hands. *'You'll either laugh or call me a ravin' loonatic,'* the man had shaken his head, *'but I swears to you lad, I swears on all that be 'oly, what I be goin' to tell you now be the God's 'onest truth. Crowley waited 'til we 'eard Penny and Max Gau talking in the yard then 'e said I'd told 'im what 'e could do with that job an' now 'e was goin' to show me what 'e could do should I refuse it. It were then he pointed to a spot on the floor between the two o' we and soon as I glanced at it it were like as if my eyes was welded to it, I couldn't look away.'*

Fred had taken a drink then, his shaking hand spilling as much of his beer as he swallowed.

*'It be unbelievable I knows that, even now I tells meself it d'ain't never 'appen yet I knows it did. It come up out of that floor, right there in front o' my eyes. First off it seemed like a mist, the sort rises wi' a summer dawn, all milky an' vaporous like, but it d'ain't drift nor fade like you'd expect mist to do, it seemed to come together forming one bit on another 'til it 'overed just above the carpet. It seemed to hang there just doin' nuthin; then—'*

Torrey remembered the look in the other man's eyes, a look that was absolute fear.

*'– then,'* Fred's voice continued in his mind, *'it began to sprout arms an' legs, then a 'ead but it were a 'ead like no other I've ever seen.'*

Sweat had run quickly down the old man's face, sweat that glistened like the tears in his eyes.

*'It weren't human, where it come from I don't know but I knows what I looked at there weren't human an' it 'ad nuthin' to do wi' God. It were evil, pure evil, its eyes glowed like fire though I could see as they was black an' the mouth that opened an' closed 'ad a tongue like that of a snake, and its chest . . . on its chest, flames edging it all about were that mark, the design I told you I knowed nuthin' about, the same design that were painted on young Penny's arm the day of the fete, the transfer given 'er by Crowley. It were then 'e spoke. "See the powers I can call upon," were 'is words to me. "See the Messenger of the Master, the one I can call to take you into hell and one I will summon should you refuse to do as I say." He moved a finger then . . . I swears 'e no more than moved a finger an' that . . . that thing floated towards me, its arms reachin' an' its forked*

*tongue flickin'. I must 'ave gone out of my mind for all I remember after that was seein' the sleeves of my jacket spurt into flame an' Crowley smilin'. Then he said, "You have seen my vengeance, now witness my protection", an' he moved 'is finger again an' the thing were gone.'*

*Witness my protection!*

Torrey drew a long breath. The words he had heard in that nightmare, the words he had heard Crowley use in the garden at Whitefriars. Was their connection one of black magic? The apparition and the Seal both seemed to point in that direction; and Fred Baker hadn't lied . . . a man as scared as he was didn't lie. He had been threatened with the same evil that had once threatened Torrey himself, and that girl was part of it; she had stuck that transfer on her arm, she had worn the Seal of Ashmedai, Archangel of Lucifer, like Crowley she was a disciple of the devil!

No. The word whispered softly, a reflection of what he wanted to hear, what his own mind wanted to tell him. Torrey remained still, his hand clenched against the frame of the window. He didn't want to believe that girl was the essence of evil, but that Seal was undeniable. Crowley had offered Fred Baker the chance to keep his job and paid him a wage that even now the man could not believe, but what was the carrot he'd dangled under Penny Smith's nose, and having taken it why had she finished up dead?

'You played the game and you paid the price, it's nobody's fault but your own!'

He struck the clenched fist against the window frame as the words burst from him.

'No . . . not my fault . . .'

Soft as before the words whispered. But they were no projection of his thoughts! They had been spoken by someone . . . and that someone was in this room with him.

'Not my fault . . .'

Torrey turned slowly, the hairs on his neck rising. Stood just inside the door the girl in white looked at him as she pointed to a mark high on one arm.

'Crowley . . .'

The pretty mouth shaped the word while helpless, frightened eyes watched him.

'Crowley made you wear that?'

Across the room the figure floated. Intangible as the air it rested upon, yet at the same time real, the short brown hair moved gently as the head nodded.

'You didn't know what it was?'

'Fred . . .'

The figure began to waver and from where he stood Torrey saw the helpless look change to one of desperation.

'Fred . . .'

'Wait!' He reached for the figure that was mist in his fingers.

'Fred –' the voice seemed a breath on the silence '– help me . . . please.'

'I can't believe it.'

Kate Mallory watched the man sat with his head in his hands.

'Neither can I.' Richard Torrey laughed scornfully. 'First I see a girl no one else sees, I hear a voice no one else hears, now I'm talking to a girl who isn't there and you say *you* can't believe it! Christ, Kate, what the hell do you think *I* believe!'

'Well you might not be out of your tree,' she grinned, 'but the branch you're swinging on now is a bit thin.'

'Thanks, Kate.' He sat up. 'That's just what a chap needs to boost his sanity . . . a few reassuring words from an understanding friend.'

'Sorry, I didn't mean that the way it sounded.' The words were repentant but a hint of the grin remained. 'But you must admit it does sound a bit far-fetched. You seeing ghosts, Fred Baker threatened with a ghoul dredged up from hell by a black magician . . . you sure you aren't reading Brian Lumley?'

He couldn't blame her for thinking him ripe for a holiday on the funny farm, he was thinking much along the same lines himself.

'Were you looking for some easy bedtime reading when you went searching the library after seeing a sketch some woman drew for you?' He couldn't resist the jibe. 'Forgive me for forgetting but which one of us was ready to believe in black magicians then?'

He was right, of course, she had thought that affair of the cemetery might have been a black-magic rite, now with Torrey's account of what Fred had overheard Crowley and Gau talking about she was almost convinced of it.

'So I take it we are both on the same wavelength?'

'If you mean do I think Crowley is a playmate of the devil, then yes.' Torrey nodded.

'And Max Gau?' Rummaging in her bag for the pack of Rothmans she had bought earlier she reluctantly dropped them back.

'Giving up?'

Kate caught his smile. 'You wish! I don't have one except in my bedroom. I respect Annie's home too much.'

'She seems nice.'

'None better.' Kate remembered how the woman had smiled as she had consented to Torrey's visit. Annie was a landlady in a million.

'So, I asked about your thoughts on Max Gau . . . do you think he is the same – a black magician?'

'Fred said he heard words sounding like magistrate and something about being more powerful than the others, of Gau being further along the Path, and then Crowley said Penny Smith was given to the Master, she was the sacrifice and that he went on to say if Gau didn't go with the game then Crowley wouldn't protect him.'

'That's no answer!'

How could he explain what he really felt? That if Max Gau was involved then it must be that Crowley had some sort of hold over him.

'It's a mercy you're not in Daniels's house.' Kate smiled. 'Marjorie would have your hide for twiddling with her cushion, and while we are talking of Daniels . . .'

'Were we?' Torrey dropped the tassel from between his fingers.

'We are now,' she answered pertly. 'What about taking all of this to him?'

'All of what? A sketch of some ancient seal, an old man's half-heard conversation of human sacrifice, a ghost! C'mon, Kate, he'd have us chucked out of the station, and who could blame him, bizarre isn't the word.'

'There's the banknote, we have that.'

'And Daniels would have the answer; it was dropped on Fred, some fresh-back-from-holiday tyke slipped it to a barmaid who slipped it into the first change she gave before her boss found out she'd been conned.'

'So what do *you* suggest?'

'I'll talk to Fred again tomorrow. He was pretty riled up at the possibility that the girl has been murdered, maybe I can get him to let me have a look around that office after Gau leaves.'

Tucking her feet beneath her on the comfortable chair Kate watched the man sat opposite. Why did she have the feeling he had not told her the all of it . . . and why the suspicion he wished Max Gau had not been part of that conversation with Julian Crowley?

'I could ask for an interview with Gau or Crowley. You know, old established firm holding its own in the market place, that sort of thing.'

*'keep clear o' Crowley and keep that girl friend o' your'n clear of 'im an' all'*

The words leapt into Torrey's mind, screeching like the siren on a racing fire engine.

'No, Kate!' There was no half and half in his answer. 'You stay clear of that place and you stay clear of Crowley!'

'Then what *do* I do? You can't expect me to wait for any scraps you throw me, or are you trying to freeze me out!'

'I know it must seem like that,' Torrey's tone softened, 'but honestly, Kate, I'm not, it's simply that given what we know so far I think it best to give Crowley a wide berth.'

Again he had not included Max Gau. Mentally filing that under 'to be investigated', Kate nodded.

'In the meantime what do we tell our friend, Echo?'

'Sounder! Lord, I'd forgotten about him.'

Uncurling her legs she already had the carton of cigarettes in her hand before realising it. Letting them drop into her bag, she answered drily, 'Most of the time I would say that would be just what the man would want, but not when he is expecting to be paid. He will have to be given a little on account or he might just stick to his word and spill everything to Daniels.'

'And tell him what? That he had a talk with a drunk who gave him a foreign banknote he can't produce? No way. Besides I hear Mr Sounder doesn't much care for visiting a dentist and he knows he will need a good one if he whistles a particular tune too loudly.'

She could believe that if nothing else. Richard Torrey had changed a great deal in the time she had known him, his feelings were not so raw, his attitude much less volatile, but that did not mean all of the old Torrey was dead, somewhere in the depths the commando still lurked.

'So then, we could—'

His shake of the head halted her as the returning Annie called from the hall. 'Leave Sounder to me, and whatever you do, hold on to that note.'

An hour later, Annie's 'little bit o' supper' inside him Kate saw Torrey to the door. She would hold on to that note . . . but that didn't mean she wouldn't wave it under somebody's nose.

# Chapter Twenty

'No . . . no, I'll ring again tomorrow, thanks for your help.'

Kate Mallory replaced the telephone, a touch of a smile painting her quirky mouth. It was today or maybe never. But how? Annie's steel curlers and scarf were not how. Running back upstairs to Annie's spare room she threw open the door of the old-fashioned wardrobe. Use anything you want, her landlady had told her, I never uses 'em any more. There had to be something she could wear.

It took an hour before she was satisfied. Is that Kate Mallory? She grinned at the reflection in the mirror. Thank heaven for the seventies! Sherry-brown hair covered by a dark wig and caught at the nape of her neck with a slide, heavy-framed spectacles that seemed to swamp her face, the peep of a white blouse between the reveres of a battleship-grey trouser suit, the whole finished off with sensible low-heeled black leather shoes. The last she had needed to borrow from her landlady, seventies winkle-pickers she really could not cope with. She was always telling herself to buy a couple of pairs of flat, sensible walking shoes yet had never once taken any notice. Fortunately Annie believed the tale she had spun about covering the opening of a new supermarket and the standing about that would entail.

It hadn't really been a lie, well not a whole one. She grimaced at the eyes that seemed to accuse. She would go to that place later and talk to a few of the staff, she could waffle the rest. It had better be good, the reflection grimaced back, Scotty wasn't fooled easily. Would he be fooled by this? She stared again at the sombre-suited image looking back at her and her aunt's voice seemed to echo the answer, 'Eeh, lass, gerra look at you . . . your own mother would never 'ave tell't ya!'

Neither might Annie recognise her in this get-up. The clothes and shoes yes, but the wig! How did she explain the need for that? Hearing the click of the downstairs door she moved to the window. The Fates were on her side. Annie was off on her weekly jaunt to Birmingham Rag Market, that meant she would be gone all day; but would the Fates that smiled now remain faithful that long? Well, my girl, the longer you hang about asking yourself questions the longer you give them to change their minds. Glancing at her bag, stuffed as usual to the hilt, she paused, it did not exactly add to the image of terribly efficient secretary. But what the hell, she scooped it to her shoulder. Nine out of ten wasn't bad.

'Mr Gau did not tell me you would be returning today.'

'That's because he didn't know.' Kate Mallory smiled at the girl sat at the reception desk of Darlaston Printing. Phoning for an interview for the *Star* she had learned that he would be out all day on business and Richard Torrey had told her he had several deliveries that would keep him well clear of Darlaston until late afternoon, that left Fred Baker and the temporary secretary. Fingers crossed Fred wouldn't need to come up to the office.

'I'm not due back for a few days, as you know, but I went down with a severe case of hill sickness.'

'Hill sickness?' Expertly plucked eyebrows closed in a frown that was immediately smoothed by a mind ever-conscious of wrinkles.

'Mmm.' Kate nodded. 'The Lake District is as beautiful as the brochure said it would be but after a week looking at nothing but hills . . . it felt a bit like sea sickness only green. Anyway enough was as good as a feast, as the saying goes, next year it'll be the beaches of sunny Spain for Penny Smith.'

Had saying that name been a step too far? Kate held her breath. Her tongue had a habit of running ahead of her brain.

'My choice too. Nature has to be at least six feet tall with muscles like Sylvester Stallone before it has my interest.'

'Sounds more like heaven than a holiday, you must give me the name of your travel agent.' Kate loosed the pent-up breath.

'Well I'd better leave now you are back.'

'Hey, I might have given up the green hills but I'm not giving up the rest of my holiday. I just nipped in to get a file. In the excitement of going on holiday I forgot to order some special inks and Max will kill me if they don't arrive in time for printing the Grand posters.'

'Grand posters?' The tiny frown tried for an encore but was whisked off.

'Sorry, I'm always doing that.' Kate forced a grin, trying hard to quieten nerves growing more restless by the second. 'They're for the Grand Theatre in Wolverhampton. They are going to stage *Swan Lake* and asked for posters that would glitter, you know . . . moonlight on the water . . . well Fred said that would need a special type of ink and like a fool I've forgotten to order it. Do you mind? It won't take a moment.'

'Be my guest.' Padded shoulders shrugged. 'I would help but I wouldn't have a clue what it was I was looking for.'

Thank God for that! Kate crossed to a filing cabinet and pulled open the first drawer. Catalogues! She pushed it closed. Lord, what was she looking for, what did she hope to get by pretending to be Max Gau's secretary? It would be a sentence for breaking and entering if she were caught. Well entering anyway, she hadn't broken in but Daniels wouldn't let that stand between her and prison . . . not if he could help it.

'It must be in Max's office.' She closed the last of the cabinet drawers. 'Keep your fingers crossed he hasn't looked at it yet.'

Blessing the phone that rang at that precise moment, Kate slipped into Gau's office, careful to close the door behind her. There had to be something that would point to that girl's death.

'Found what you were looking for?' The girl looked up as Kate emerged from the private office.

'Yes thanks.' Kate held a sheet of paper in her hand. 'I can fill this out and send it off from home, Max won't know the difference and it won't matter so long as those inks arrive.'

'Look, this is a cheek I know, but would you man the desk for just five minutes, I need to go to the chemist. The curse and all that! I thought I had some Tampax in my bag but the box is empty . . . who wouldn't share a flat with another girl?'

Was this where the Fates took their leave? Kate felt her heart sink. She had everything in her bag including her own empty Tampax box!

'No problem.' She eased her bag to the floor. Just five minutes, she prayed as the girl left. Let her luck hold for just five more minutes.

Clothed once more in her usual garb Kate waited for the arrival of the *Star* photographer. Scotty wanted photographs to go with her copy. It wouldn't take long, she could write this stuff in her sleep. Watching a red Hyundai Coupe pull into the kerb, Kate Mallory smiled ruefully as a youngish man climbed out, a camera swinging from his neck. Maybe she should have taken a course in photography instead of journalism, it seemed one paid much better than the other.

'Nice new car, shame about the same old face.'

'Now, now, Kate, flattery isn't going to get you a ride.'

'Good!' She grinned good-naturedly. 'That's one wish granted.'

'How many more left to go?'

Kate watched him check spare film and built-in flash. 'Two,' she answered.

His pleasant face creasing into a broad smile he settled the camera on his chest then looked at her. 'Can I grant them?'

'Hmm!' Kate's mouth twisted in contemplation. 'You don't look much like a fairy—'

'Well thank God for that!' His laugh boomed over the street.

'– however,' Kate continued, 'you can grant one, you can get those blessed pictures and get me out of there.'

Following the direction of her glance towards the group of people milling on the forecourt of the new supermarket, he shook his head. 'Photos *and* get you out of there, that's two flicks of the magic wand.'

'Maths was never my strong point.' Kate grinned again. 'You do the counting and I'll buy the sandwich.'

'And the drinks?'

Hitching her bag higher on her shoulder Kate led the way to where the mayoress was receiving a large bouquet. 'Don't push your luck, bonny lad,' she said fishing pen and notebook from the depths, 'by my count I've still got one wish left and you never know what I might do with that!'

She could go back to the office. That would mean being under Scotty's eye, at his call for any other little job that might crop up.

'No thanks.' She refused the offer of a lift. 'I'll hang around a little longer, see if I can find something to put a little life into a dreary script.'

'Right, then I'll be off.'

Having finished the coffee he had chosen to go with the sandwich Kate had bought, the photographer made his way out of the attractive little restaurant that was part of the new building.

She could go back to her digs but that didn't feel right either. She sipped at her own coffee wishing she could light a cigarette to go with it.

So where, where should she go? Writing up the copy for today's little shindig would take no more than an hour, but it wasn't the notes she had taken at that opening she wanted to go over, it was those papers shoved at the bottom of her bag.

It had been something of a blessing that girl at the printers asking her to cover for a few minutes. It had given her time to photocopy several likely looking documents and get the originals back in Gau's office before she returned. They might prove of no use at all, but then again they might prove the opposite.

But prove what? She sipped the luke-warm coffee. What had made her do such a crazy thing as going to that office, pretending to be Penny Smith; what could she hope to gain from it? Her family was right, she did go crazy every time there was a full moon!

At least that temp had appeared to believe she was who she claimed to be and what was more had promised not to mention to Gau that she was back from holiday. Kate had smiled as she had asked the girl to keep the fact secret, saying once it was known she had returned from holiday she might be asked to report back to work and holidays were few enough without giving half of one up.

Lord, she had taken a risk. Not only that but she was now a thief! Wouldn't Daniels just love that! But it wasn't the thought of the detective inspector that brought a sudden jolt to her nerves. He needed concrete evidence that it was Kate Mallory who had visited that office, but did Max Gau need the same? If the man truly was a black magician might that mean he had the ability to see what Daniels could not? Would he know who it was had entered his office, taken documents from his desk and photocopied them . . . would he know it was Kate Mallory?

It was too late now. She set her cup on the tray, nodding her thanks to the woman who swept it away on to a trolley filled with used dishes. She still didn't know why she had gone to that printers, but since she had she might as well make of it what she could.

Once more in the street she lit the much-wanted cigarette, inhaling deeply. She could go to the park but then she needed somewhere to spread the photocopied sheets and a park bench was hardly the best of choices.

That left only one place. Hoisting the bag firmly, holding it close against her side, she turned in the direction of the town.

Taking the several photocopied sheets from her bag Kate spread them on the wide table. She had chosen the best place to look at them. The reference library was not exactly the favourite venue for the local youth so there was a good chance she would not be disturbed.

She had been about to leave that office when she thought she heard the girl returning. Nerves had caused her to drop the paper she was holding and on retrieving it she had tripped in those unaccustomed shoes and stumbled against a corner of Max Gau's desk. She must have touched against some mechanism or other for the bevelled side of the desk had swung open, revealing several files. She should have pushed the thing closed. Kate's fingers shook as she held a sheet of paper to the light streaming from the wide sweep of the library window. But she hadn't. Curiosity ever her failing, she had drawn a paper from the top file and as she lifted it out the watermark had shown against daylight: the Seal of Ashmedai! The same mark she had found in a book here at this library, the same one peeping beneath the sleeve of Penny Smith's dress. That, together with a host of questions, had beat at her brain . . . why the paperwork, why wasn't all of this firm's business on computer?

So why wasn't it? She asked the same question again. Was it because of hackers . . . were Crowley and Gau involved in something so sensitive they were afraid to trust it to a computer?

Laying the paper back down in front of her she smoothed it with the edge of her palm, her eyes following the movement. Catching her breath sharply she closed her eyes, pressing the lids hard over her eyeballs. Sensitive! She breathed out slowly . . . try electric, that might be more the word.

Caught in the fever of her own racing brain she drew book after book from neatly stacked shelves, checking what she knew, looking up that which she was not sure of, working steadily until with the last of the papers her suspicions were verified.

Max Gau and Julian Crowley were into more than the printing industry . . . much, much more!

She couldn't take this to Scotty, he would want to know the hows and whys of her having it and somehow she didn't think he would swallow being told she had found it in the bushes. But she wasn't going to destroy them and she certainly couldn't forget them. Fred Baker believed those two had murdered Penny Smith even though no body had been found, and she could not bring herself to disbelieve it. They were hand in glove, the evidence of that was here before her eyes, and if they were hand in glove in this business then why not in another?

Gathering the papers together she pushed them deep into her bag. Whatever she decided to do with the information she now had, it needed to be done quickly. Perhaps that girl might not keep her word to say nothing of her visit to Max Gau, perhaps even now she had told him his receptionist-cum-secretary had returned from holiday and collected a file from his office. If so how long would it take for him to find out who the pseudo Penny Smith was . . . and where she could be found!

Swinging her bag on to her shoulder she walked quickly downstairs to the main body of the recently built library, nodding to the pleasant woman assistant as she made for the exit.

Standing just outside the door she drew several long breaths, trying to calm tingling nerves. She couldn't just stand here, she had to do something! She could phone Torrey, ask him if he could get away for a few minutes. No! She dropped the mobile phone back into the bag. Do that and it wouldn't take a P A system to advertise what was happening. If Gau had been told of his office having been entered and most likely searched by a woman he might know no longer existed, then saw Richard Torrey haring off somewhere it wouldn't take a great deal of mental energy to put the next bit together. No, telling Torrey was out . . . at least for now.

'Bin yoh a comin' or bin you a gooin'? Yoh mightn't be as big as a bonk 'oss but yoh gives a good impression o' one stood theer so a body cort get in nor out o' that door!'

'What?' Kate blinked.

'I be askin' if yoh'm goin' to stand theer all day, be them inside payin' ya to keep folk out?'

'Sorry.' Kate moved aside, allowing the still-grumbling woman to pass. Lord, the house she lived in needed no Rottweiler!

Walking away rapidly she turned the corner into Victoria Road. Perhaps she ought to have accepted that offer of a lift after all, gone back to the office. But she needed to think, to sort out her next step, and there would be fat chance of doing that there with phones ringing constantly and Scotty shouting that this and that needed to be done if they were ever going to 'get this bloody paper to bed'.

Not Scotty and not Torrey. So who could she tell about what was in her bag. She hadn't felt so horribly alone since climbing aboard that train at Newcastle Central. Apart from Annie there was nobody else and she would die rather than involve her with Crowley!

Face it, Kate, she told herself, you are on your own with this one. You got your own little arse into this mess and there's only you can drag it out again!

Crossing the quiet street she entered the deserted Victoria

Park and chose a seat that looked on to the road. This needed all her concentration.

There were several avenues open to her. She could post those photocopies to relevant government departments. The Ministry of Defence would surely be interested in the business dealings of Satel Aeronautics, together with that of Davion International; and Coton Pharmaceuticals might catch the eye of Trade and Industry. They would probably investigate even if they did nothing else, but given what she had read in that library she couldn't really see the government doing nothing. So giving it to them would mean MI6, or whatever government investigators were called, getting involved; or failing that then most likely those papers would be quietly shuffled across to Scotland Yard. Either way the *Star* would have lost the chance of a scoop, it would only get what the big nationals got and what benefit was that to Scotty . . . or to Kate Mallory?

She let her glance play over a squat red-brick building across the street.

One place she would not be sending those papers to was the House of Commons.

# Chapter Twenty-One

Detective Inspector Bruce Daniels glanced to his right, waiting for several high-sided vans and a lorry to clear the St Lawrence traffic roundabout.

'Getting to be more bloody traffic through this town every day!' He swore softly, bile acid in his mouth, his continuing thoughts sour. And for what? It brought no work to the place; a couple of dozen employed by that new supermarket . . . call that an upward trend in employment? He called it a salve for the public arse after it had been kicked! Promises, huh! He drew the car to a halt, the signal turning red as he came up to the Bull Stake. Politicians were a dab hand at making them but they were even smarter when it come to breaking them.

Fishing in his pocket for the carton of BiSoDol Marjorie had placed beside his keys that morning he popped a tablet on his tongue, glaring through his driving mirror at a car behind, the driver blasting his horn the instant the lights changed to green.

Daniels let the clutch out, allowing the car to move slowly as it cleared the lights, almost smiling as another irate blast of a car horn followed him. 'Right, my little smart-arsed friend,' he murmured, 'let's see you blow your horn at this!'

That had made the little speed freak feel sick!

Daniels watched the other car drive away. He signalled for

the driver to pull over, waiting while the man swaggered from his car, then he flashed his warrant card. That one would be up before the Bench for harassment and use of abusive language on the Queen's highway. Being a copper sometimes had its rewards.

But there had been no reward an hour ago. Echo Sounder knew nothing, either that or he'd been taking a course of amateur dramatics. He hadn't given so much as a flicker of the eyelids when mention had been made of a note, he hadn't even asked who the note was from nor what it might have said. That was what had given the scruffy little toerag away.

Echo Sounder had more information than the *Guardian* and carried more dirt than a well-known Sunday newspaper. Why vary the act? Normally there was no way he would have sat quiet, making no attempt to ferret out the reason for a visit from the blues. So why not today? Pulling into the station yard he switched off the engine. Sounder was speaking no evil . . . but no doubt he'd seen and heard plenty!

Sergeant Dave Farnell looked up as Daniels walked into the station and immediately assessed the results of the inspector's visit to the Frying Pan . . . no results! Picking up a fawn-coloured file he followed Daniels to the tiny office, its desk already cluttered with files and papers.

'No luck?' he asked, closing the door.

'Waste of bloody time! An atheist says more in his night-time prayer than Sounder said today, but he'll need more than words, prayer or otherwise, if I find he's mixed up in anything.' Daniels grimaced as a fresh burst of acid bled into his throat. 'He knows something, I'm as certain of that as—' He might say he was as certain as the fact he had killed his own father. For a moment a picture of a slimy worm-riddled face rose in his mind, the face that had tormented him during the hitch hiker case, the face of Jack Daniels, the father he had murdered.

'Do you think our town canary is keeping more than dirt under that scruffy hat of his?'

'You could safely lay a thousand on it.' Daniels sat down. The sergeant's question had dispelled the picture in his mind, but it would return . . . it always returned.

'You'd have to loan it to me first, I haven't had a spare thousand to spend on anything since signing on the force.'

'You and me both, would it do any good calling in at the Job Centre do you reckon?'

'Already been.' Dave Farnell grinned. 'British Gas are looking for a new managing director, Manson Aggregates want a vice president, I might accept one of those.'

'Not worth making the move for.' Daniels flicked a dismissive hand. 'The pay isn't worth putting in a packet, and besides that you don't want to start at the bottom of the ladder again.'

'We should have such a pay packet, I'd *hold* the ladder for a quarter of the salary those lads take home.'

Balancing his chair on its two back legs, Bruce Daniels looked up at the smiling face. 'I thought you liked working in a shit of a job.'

Dave Farnell's clear eyes glowed warmly. 'I said last week it wasn't often you made mistakes but now you've just made another one . . . must be old age creeping up.'

'You mean you *do* like working in a shit of a job?'

'No . . . it's the shitty people I work with that I like. Now how about me leaving you this file . . . some of us have work to do and mine is backing up out there.'

'Did you come up with anything?'

With the door already open the sergeant looked back. 'It's all in the file; read it, Bruce, you'll get more out of that than Sounder gets from his *Sporting Pink*.'

It didn't look good. There were questions being asked. It placed him in a very awkward position. What answers could he give? The words of the new Chief Detective Inspector rang in Daniels's ears. They should try asking him, he could give them a few answers to their bloody questions! Bristling from the latest of the man's complaints Daniels threw a tablet into his mouth. This bloody stomach was giving him gyp! Crumpling the empty carton he aimed it at the wastepaper bin, swearing again when it missed. Connor had been bad enough. He had harped on regularly, always wanting results, but this bugger, he wanted bloody miracles . . . and for why? Why was he so determined to have their quota of arrests go up every month? To safeguard the town, to ensure the safety and wellbeing of the citizens of Darlaston? Like bloody hell!

Chief Detective Inspector Martin Quinto couldn't give a rat's arse for Darlaston, but the more arrests made, the brighter his halo gleamed. Statistics! Christ, you'd think the man had invented the word!

Sucking hard on the tablet he swallowed minty-flavoured bismuth, feeling no effect on the fire that ravaged from his stomach to his throat.

What the hell was he expected to do? Darlaston was no bloody metropolis, there wasn't a criminal under every stone you kicked over. Maybe he should import some, get Echo Sounder to bring in a few shady characters, the little nark knew plenty.

'Be a woman asking for you, Inspector.'

Daniels glanced at the fresh-faced young constable. Six months on the force . . . wait 'til he'd done twenty years, he wouldn't look so bloody eager then.

'Let the desk deal with it,' he scowled, irascibility in every word.

'Woman wouldn't have that, sir, said it had to be you or nobody.'

'Then it's bloody nobody!'

'All right, lad. Leave this with me.'

The voice at the young constable's back was quiet but the relief shooting across his face shouted like a town crier.

'I think you might want to see the woman.'

Sergeant David Farnell looked at the man he had worked alongside for so long. Bruce Daniels was a good detective but the acid burning away at him wasn't all due to the stomach ulcer he wouldn't see a doctor about. He had reason to be resentful, being passed over for promotion was bad enough when it was deserved but Daniels had earned that step up the ladder.

'It ain't often you make a mistake, Dave,' Daniels growled.

'I'm not making one now.'

'Want to bet!'

'Can't afford it on my pay.'

'Remind me to introduce you to Sounder, he can teach you how to lay odds without parting with a penny.'

'Interesting company you keep.' The sergeant smiled. 'Now how about giving five minutes of your company to this woman.'

'If I must.' Daniels sighed, swallowing the last trace of indigestion tablet. 'Who is it?'

'Name's Mallory . . . Kate Mallory.'

'Christ, Dave, I told you, I told the lot of you, keep that woman out of my hair!' The front legs of Daniels's chair hit the floor with a crash.

'The public have a right to ask.'

'Yeah . . . and the bloody copper has to suffer them. Look, Dave, just tell her I'm busy . . . tell her anything you like but get rid of her!'

'As you like, Bruce, but you might just want to look at this before I do.'

'What is it?'

Sergeant Farnell smiled again. 'Don't know, Bruce, but I reckon your friend Sounder might be on to a winner if he bet it wasn't a love letter.'

'Shock you if it was!' Daniels came dangerously near a smile, averting it at the last second.

'True,' the sergeant agreed. 'But it would kill *you*.'

'Hang on!' Looking up from the paper, Daniels held it out.

Returning the few steps from the door the sergeant took it, scanning the one sentence written in pencil.

'I'll send her in,' was all he said.

'What's this all about?' Daniels tapped the sheet of paper with one finger, glaring at Kate as his office door closed behind her.

'Good morning to you too, Inspector.' Kate helped herself to a chair, the look on Daniels's face saying an invitation to sit down could be a long time coming.

The trite retort doing nothing to ease either his throat or his temper, he waved the paper before slamming it on to the desk snapping, 'What does this mean?'

'Exactly what it says,' Kate answered coolly.

' "This could be bigger than Bartley",' he read the words aloud.

'Correct. Do you mind, Inspector?' Cigarette packet in hand, Kate raised an enquiring eyebrow.

The new chief detective inspector frowned on smoking inside the station. So, Quinto could add a few more lines to the ones already decorating his forehead! Daniels nodded, offering Kate a lighted match before holding it to the cigarette he accepted himself.

'So what is it could be bigger than Bartley? More drugs? Heroin . . . ecstasy, which shit is it this time?'

Watching the tiny cloud of smoke accompanying each word, Kate Mallory smiled to herself. He looked like Puff the Magic Dragon.

'Nothing you will find wrapped with gizzards and livers and stuffed inside frozen chickens.'

'Then what?'

The free tab hadn't improved his humour any. Kate drew on her own, feeling the smoke bite at her lungs. The health warning printed on every packet wasn't there simply to embellish, smoking was definitely not good for a girl . . . nor for detective inspectors, judging by the one she looked at now.

'You must promise me something.'

Was the look he gave her due to her question or had his ulcer finally burst? She listened to the rattle in his chest as he choked.

'Promise!'

It wasn't his ulcer. She breathed relief. It was simply his uncertain temper and he'd get over that.

'You'll get no offers here! What do you think this is, a bloody bargain basement!'

Blowing a stream of smoke towards the ceiling she watched the irate face through the pearl-grey haze. She had taken the first step, she might as well go all the way.

'Echo Sounder's payment is of the spending kind . . .'

'And you want the same?'

'Did I ask for money when I told you about the special deliveries being made to a certain supermarket?' Kate's tone was brittle, as disparaging as his. 'If you think that then I feel sorry for you, you are not the intelligent man I thought you to be!'

She had nerve, not many of the local yobs would talk to Bruce Daniels that way, let alone a woman.

'So what's the promise you be wanting?'

'Forget it!' Kate snapped, grinding her cigarette into an overful ashtray. 'I might as well go to Sounder. He'll want a damned sight more than a promise from you, Inspector, and if he takes my advice he'll double his price . . . whatever it is!'

She could use that bag as a tent if ever she found herself out of a home! Daniels watched her scoop the strap to her shoulder.

'Miss Mallory,' he said, 'do you realise I can have you done for withholding information?'

That was only one of the repertoire of dirty tricks she was sure Bruce Daniels was familiar with.

'Wasting police time, now withholding information,' she

smiled sweetly, 'really, if I didn't know you better I would say you are hungry for my company, Inspector. As for that note . . . I never wrote any note, that was dropped through the letter box of the *Star*, I am merely passing it to the police.'

This wench deserved promotion every bit as much as he did, she knew the game and wasn't afraid to play it, and if it was that she did have a whiff of something big going down then it wouldn't be Echo Sounder she would give it to . . . a letter to Quinto? That bugger's gold braid already glinted bright enough!

The thought of the new Chief Detective Inspector getting one over on him brought fresh acid surging up from his stomach. Feeling in the pocket of his jacket he brought out a fresh carton of BiSoDol. Marjorie was right when she said he should get this bloody ulcer seen to!

'Wherever this note came from I'd like to know more about it so let's hear what this promise is you want in exchange.'

He had capitulated. Kate experienced a tinge of satisfaction but at the same time there was no feeling of revenge in it.

'I want your word that the *Star* will be the first newspaper to get any story that might come out of what I tell you.'

She hadn't steered him wrong the last time. Daniels sucked on the tablet. And he had no other case that would suffer harm by being quietly slipped down the line to somebody else. Results! He swallowed hard. Was he kow-towing . . . taking to heart what Quinto had said about numbers of arrests, was he grabbing any straw because of it?

Crumpling the sheet of paper with its one sentence, he threw it into the bin. Was he hell! And that was where Quinto could go an' all!

# Chapter Twenty-Two

'Kate Mallory and me had a nice little chat this morning.'

Disbelief dark in his eyes, Richard Torrey stared at the man watching him across a table in the tap room of the Staffordshire Knot. He had come looking for Fred Baker and found Bruce Daniels doing the same.

'She called in at the station, said as she had something I might find interesting.'

'How nice for the pair of you, I hope you enjoyed it.'

Torrey could almost feel the knife behind the gaze. Had Detective Inspector Daniels been a surgeon he would have needed no scalpel, he could cut through a man with no more than a look. That had been the downfall of many a would-be criminal in Darlaston, they had been taken in by the threepence-short-of-a-shilling look that said Daniels hadn't quite stepped up to the ockey, that he hadn't reached the starting point after they were streets ahead. Lifting his glass Torrey took a drink. Who said appearances didn't deceive?

'I enjoyed it.' Daniels watched the glass go back to the table. 'Her visit proved most enlightening.'

'I'm glad the whole of your day didn't prove a complete waste of time.' Friendly it wasn't. But the last thing Torrey wanted right now was a roll in the hay with the blues.

Daniels's gaze showed the sarcasm had gone over his head. 'My day ain't over yet.'

'You've been in the force too long.' Torrey smiled coldly. 'You are beginning to believe your own crap, "a copper don't sleep" not even when he's in bed all by himself . . . you'll have to try a different line.'

'Then how about this one: Kate Mallory asked to see me, she gave me a note.'

A note! Torrey's pulses quickened. Kate had handed over the note Fred Baker had warned them to keep out of sight. Why? Simply to get a story? No, Kate Mallory wasn't fool enough to risk losing a race by taking the jumps too soon. But she didn't know the risk she was taking, she didn't know the all of Crowley's evil and maybe that was his fault; he had told her almost all of what he had heard in that garden at Whitefriars . . . but not quite all. He had not told her who Crowley had in mind for his next presentation to the Master. Rattle the man's cage and he might strike before the great Sabbat.

'What did the note say?' he asked, deciding to play ignorant until he was sure it was that banknote Kate had handed over and nothing else.

Another one knew how to play his cards! Daniels took a swallow of beer, knowing he would suffer for it later. Bloody stomach . . . it was ruining any pleasure in his life.

'It said as there was something might be bigger than the Bartley racket.'

'Bigger than heroin . . . wonder what that could be?'

The glass of beer he had only half drunk took effect more quickly than he thought and Daniels caught his breath at the rapid surge of fire into his throat.

'Stop buggering about, Torrey!' he snapped. 'You know it were no drugs that wench told me about.'

Let's hope it wasn't black magicians either or we might both find ourselves sharing the same hospitality suite. Torrey watched the other man fumble a white tablet into his mouth.

'She gave me this as well, said as how Fred Baker thought there might be more to the girl's leaving than simply wanting a change of job.'

He was going to strangle Kate Mallory! Torrey took the copy of the newspaper photograph.

'Before my time.' He handed back the photograph. 'I was working for Philip Bartley at the time that was taken and that fella wasn't into town fêtes, as for the girl I never met her.'

'So Kate Mallory told me.'

'You know journalists.' Torrey shrugged. 'If they don't have a story they make one up; anything to keep the presses turning.'

'I know journalists, same as I know when a man is hedging.' Daniels swallowed but there was no quenching of the flame ripping his gut. 'You never met the girl in this photo but that don't go to say you don't know what happened to her.'

If Kate had told about that figure in the cemetery then he would cheerfully strangle her!

'I know only what Fred has told me,' he answered blandly. 'The girl's name is Penny Smith. She worked for some eighteen months as receptionist at Darlaston Printing. She was a nice kid and old Fred took to her like she was his daughter. What else can I say?'

'You can say what you know about the kind of work Fred Baker does along Kings Hill.'

'He's a master printer!' Torrey laughed scathingly. 'He takes care of the printing.'

'What exactly does he print?'

'Pamphlets, posters . . . look, how the hell should I know? I'm just the blokes who makes the deliveries.'

'To where?'

Torrey's patience began to fray. 'That's company business . . . I suggest you ask Max Gau anything you feel you should know about that.'

Reaching for his glass, Daniels changed his mind. If the fire in his throat got any worse he might cut the bugger and get it all over with.

'I shall be talking to Mr Gau,' he said, pushing the glass away, 'and also to Fred Baker, but right now I'm talking to you and you can answer me here or down at the station, it's all one to me.'

Fred Baker wasn't the only master of his trade, Daniels was a fair hand at what he did too, he could come up with enough trumped-up charges to hold him at Victoria Road for a week. Torrey watched the face screw with discomfort. He would even take pleasure in doing it.

'I've delivered to a number of places, shops, bingo parlours, cinemas you name it.'

'Do you see any of the stuff you deliver?'

'No.' Torrey shook his head. 'It's always wrapped. The inside of a van gets pretty dirty being climbed in and out of every day, and I suppose customers don't like paying for stuff that's marked so everything is wrapped before I get it.'

Probably true enough. Daniels nodded. But not what he wanted.

'You never wonder what it is you're handling, never take a look . . . p'raps take a sample?'

Careful, Torrey, the sly bastard's trying to get you to loosen your hold! The warning in his mind becoming a smile on his mouth Torrey held the other man's eyes.

'I'm not into collecting, Inspector, posters or otherwise, I wouldn't know a valuable item if you hit me with it.'

And you wouldn't tell me if you did. Keeping the thought silent Daniels pushed to his feet, one hand brushing the pocket that held tablets and car keys.

'Don't be taking any unexpected holiday,' he said quietly, 'I'll be wanting to talk to you again.'

Several customers suddenly found the view at the other end of the tap room more interesting and turned their heads as the inspector passed their tables. Daniels almost smiled, the fog of cigarette smoke parting as he walked to the door. Word would spread. Daniels was looking for something. Tomorrow he would have a quiet little tête-à-tête with Sounder, just a friendly chat. If there *was* anything going down, that little canary would know the song by heart come that time.

'He ain't 'eard nuthin' from me.' Echo Sounder's ferret-bright eyes were anxious beneath their heavy hoods. Richard Torrey were no man to fool around with when he felt threatened, them three blokes he'd laid out in the yard of the Bird-in-Hand a year or so back were proof of that, a couple of 'em still couldn't walk wi'out sticks an' the other 'adn't worked for months, an' all that cos they'd called his woman a whore. But weren't that just what 'er 'ad been, a tart who'd buggered off and left 'im when a bigger pay packet 'ad showed itself?

He probably hadn't told Daniels anything. Torrey watched the scruffy jacket squirm. Sounder had put the squeeze on Kate Mallory, he was hoping for a handout from the *Star*, a nice little extra before peddling the goods to Daniels, milking the cow from all four teats at once, so to speak, but even so he wouldn't go to one man before telling the other . . . not unless he'd already booked his hospital bed.

'I be tellin' yer the truth, Mr Torrey, on me oath I be, I ain't never said a word to Daniels.'

'Then how come he's taking such a sudden interest in the printers?'

'You said you wouldn't . . . you said as I'd get a 'andful afore sayin' anythin' to the blues!' Removed momentarily from a group of horses racing across a television screen, Echo Sounder's close-set ferret eyes were suddenly vicious.

Calmly taking a drink, Torrey's brain moved quickly. Seeing his profits drift away Sounder could play dirty. If he knew it was

Kate had gone to Daniels then she could be in for a surprise and it wouldn't come wrapped in pretty paper. He must be made to believe Daniels had got his information from some other source. Replacing his glass he stared evenly at the scruffy little man. 'Then there has to be somebody else knows about that note.'

'Baker?' Echo Sounder's hooded eyes narrowed.

'No!' The snap of Torrey's answer left no room for argument. 'Fred Baker is no fool. He knows whoever is behind that dud money will play only one game when it's discovered the blues have had their noses tickled, that game will include a back alley, a dark night and a sharp knife, and knowing that he will have kept his mouth shut; and as for the banknote, Kate Mallory handed that over to me an hour after you gave it to her –' already incisor sharp his voice became laser sharp '– so that rules *her* out of taking it to Daniels.'

'It must be summat choice for Daniels to 'ave moved so rapid like, 'e 'as reached fer it quicker'n 'e reaches fer them stomach tablets 'e be so fond o' suckin'. But I can't rightly reckon it,' Sounder squinted again, ''ain't nuthin' goin' down in Darlaston, choice or otherwise, I'd 'ave 'eard on it if there 'ad.'

This was the chance! Torrey grabbed it with both hands. Cold, hard and definitely poisonous his eyes bore into the other man. 'That brings us back to you, Sounder; you say it wasn't you spoke to Daniels but you don't always tell the whole truth and nothing but the truth, do you? You have been known to mislay that virtue from time to time. Well the arm of the law is long but remember, mine moves faster and its action is always lethal so any chances you take from now on best be solely on the horses!'

'You 'as my word, Mr Torrey, I ain't sayin' nuthin' to nobody.'

'Keep it that way.' Torrey pushed to his feet. 'The canal locks are deep in these parts and life jackets are not a feature.'

Outside he watched two cars race each other along St Lawrence Way. Bloody kids risking their necks for kicks!

And what was he doing? He turned towards his lodging. He was risking his neck and no kicks in it. Why hadn't he insisted that banknote be handed to Daniels in the first place for it was almost certain that where there was one there might be others; why give Kate the opportunity of holding on to it until today?

But Daniels hadn't said it was a banknote Kate had taken in to Victoria Road, so it could be feasible to assume she hadn't and that Detective Inspector Bruce Daniels did not yet know of its existence.

*'bigger than the Bartley racket'*

Those had been Daniels's words. But why tell him yet? That was easy, the little news-hound smelled a story. It wasn't just Richard Torrey suspected there might be more to that banknote than merely left-over holiday cash, Kate Mallory suspected the same; and so did Fred Baker or he wouldn't have been so adamant it be kept out of sight. To be as jumpy as that man was could only point to there being a project going on. Money! Torrey's nerves jarred. Money had to be printed and if it should be of the duff variety then it would have to be done somewhere out of sight and in a place you might think of as being the last on earth a racket like that would go on. Darlaston might fit that description . . . and Fred Baker was a master printer!

Torrey stared at the shadows teasing the streets as clouds played tag with the moon. He had lied when telling Sounder that note was counterfeit, but had that lie somehow been the truth? Crowley had threatened Fred Baker, terrified him into doing something he hadn't wanted to do . . . was that something printing funny money . . . and if so why foreign currency, why not sterling? Fred Baker had bought himself more than a pint of Banks's best when he'd handed over that money to Sounder, he had bought a whole load of trouble and it wasn't all for him alone. If that printing works was a cover for counterfeiting then both Gau and Crowley had to know about it, it had to be their game . . . and Crowley wasn't the man to balk at murder.

As he turned into his digs Torrey made a mental note. Tomorrow he would talk to Fred again, the old man had questions to answer!

'You were at Darlaston Printing. Kate, what the hell do you think you are doing? Crowley is no pet puppy, touch him and he'll bite!'

'There was no other way.' Kate Mallory's slightly irregular mouth set in a mutinous line.

'Of doing what?' Torrey snapped back. 'What is it you are trying to prove?'

'That Crowley is what we both suspect he is . . . a murderer!'

'Well you won't do it by snooping around that office, all you are likely to do is land yourself in goal for breaking and entering.'

'I entered,' Kate grinned, her anger melting, 'but I didn't break anything . . . well not on purpose, that desk swung open, I swear it did.'

'You just happened to find some secret catch, I suppose.'

Extracting a cigarette Kate lit it, blowing a stream of smoke into the evening air before answering.

'Much as you don't want to believe it, that is exactly what happened, though it might be more pertinent to say the catch found me rather than me finding it.'

'The plot thickens, it'll soon be strong enough to stand on!'

'Good, I'll just give it a moment to set and it will be as hard as your sarcasm.' Halting in mid-step Kate felt her anger make a sudden comeback. 'Look, Torrey . . . I don't ask you to look out for me, I can do that for myself.'

'And get yourself very dead in the process. I've told you, Crowley is no man to play footsie with.'

And Gau, is he any less dangerous, is it that you think him less of a threat just because he is pleasant-mannered? Kate noticed the omission yet again of the name Max Gau.

'Which is exactly why I needed more than a photograph from a newspaper and the not-easily-believed story told by Fred Baker!' she flashed. 'Daniels wouldn't even have listened to that much less act on it.'

'So you decided to go looking for clues.'

Sherry-coloured hair swinging as her head came up, Kate met the hard grey stare. 'Yes, I decided to go to look for clues and I found them.'

'You found proof of Penny Smith's murder?'

Her angry stare dropping away, Kate was silent for a moment. She hadn't found what she had gone to that place to look for and having to admit as much would have him bawl her out again.

'I found something as bad as that.'

'But not that . . . you didn't find any clue at all; be honest, Kate, you have no more on Crowley now than before you went nosying around that office.'

Drawing deeply on her cigarette she let smoke dribble slowly from her nostrils for the moment curbing her anger but not her irritability.

'I think I have a great deal on Mr Crowley,' she snapped, 'just as I have a great deal on Mr Max Gau. I may not have found proof of one murder but I believe I may have found proof of intended mass murder, in fact –' she drew again on the cigarette, letting out a long breath before finishing '– I believe Julian Crowley is planning nothing less than genocide and that Max Gau is his accomplice!'

Richard Torrey's brow pulled together in a frown, then he laughed. 'Are you sure that's not marijuana you're smoking?'

Dropping the stub of tobacco to the pavement and stabbing it with her foot, she then picked it up and walked with it several yards to a waste bin attached to a lamp post before answering.

'I'm glad you find what you say amusing, but then little things . . . little minds, you know the saying.'

'Okay, okay I'm sorry!' He raised a hand, the gesture apologetic. 'It's just that I get the horrors every time I think of you in that place . . . of what could have happened had Crowley caught you there.'

'You mean you care!' She had laced it heavily with sarcasm but underneath it she wanted to hear that he did.

Coming to stand beside her he took both of her hands in his, the smile soft on his mouth, his eyes gentle.

'Yes, Kate, I care. You are a good friend and I don't want to see you get hurt.'

A friend! Kate swallowed the feeling that followed his words. How did she feel about that? She looked at the hands holding hers. She would rather he thought of her as a friend than not think of her at all.

'Do you really want to see that film?' She drew her hands away, using the pretext of hitching her bag more comfortably on her shoulder, avoiding eye contact. She couldn't cope with that, not right now.

Torrey smiled, glad the anger between them was gone. 'I'd rather go for a drink.'

'Say where.'

'Somewhere that doesn't allow smoking?'

'There you go again!' Indignation swept through her, leaving a trail of relief at being able to meet those grey eyes without his reading the tell-tale evidence in her own. 'Remember, lad, fingers that are poked in other people's pies often get baked in the next one!'

'Now *that* is rich!' His laugh rang out. 'Coming from Kate Mallory *that* is very rich.'

'Which is more than Richard Torrey will be . . . after he's paid for supper!' Her slightly off-line mouth curving in a satisfied grin, Kate turned in the direction of the town, leaving her reply to float behind.

# Chapter Twenty-Three

'What are these clues you spoke of?'

Torrey's question was out before he set glasses on the table.

Well at least something about her interested the man. Kate took her time lighting her cigarette, blowing a little cloud of smoke sideways over one shoulder. Not the most glamorous place for a date but at least she could smoke here 'legally' and as the local watering holes went the Frying Pan was the best. But could this evening really be classed as a date . . . true Torrey had invited her to the cinema but was the underlying reason for his doing so simply to bawl her out over her escapade? She could have told him to get lost. She dropped the packet of Rothmans into her bag and watched him settle into a seat. She had told him she could look out for herself so why hadn't she followed it up, told him not to bother calling her in future? But she had said nothing of the sort. She dropped her glance to the drink set in front of her. Her life would no longer be the same without Richard Torrey, even as just a friend!

'Kate.' He broke into her thoughts, his voice quiet beneath the surrounding throb of conversation. 'I know why you went to that works but how the hell you got away with it I don't think I'll ever know, imagine what would have happened had you been recognised.'

'But I wasn't.'

'Recognised or not, it wouldn't have mattered had Max Gau returned while you were there, you would be a guest of Daniels right now.'

'But I'm not.'

'Kate! I'm warning you, one more answer like that and you are going to be given a short, sharp dose of medicine and it won't be of the liquid kind!'

The explosion was mild for Torrey. Kate sipped her lemon and lime. It might be interesting to see his idea of administering medication . . . then again it could leave a person with more than a bruised ego!

'Fred Baker was the only one who might have recognised me.' She gave in gracefully. 'That was why I borrowed some of Annie's clothes from way back, teamed with heavily framed spectacles and a black wig—'

'A black what?'

Watching him wipe spluttered beer from his lips she answered cheekily, 'I often suspected yoh wuz gooin' deaf but I d'ain't think yoh wuz mutton yedded an' all.'

With his handkerchief half-returned to his pocket, Torrey gaped.

'Where did you learn to speak like that? And don't tell me it was at your mother's knee.'

'There are more things than dialect to be learned in Darlaston . . . the first being having enough sense to listen carefully to what is said to you.' Having made her point again, this time in her more usual style, Kate picked up from where he had interrupted. 'Put all together with some of Annie's flat-heeled shoes I would have challenged my own family to say who it was they were looking at.'

'You keep practising that Black Country dialect and that family of yours won't even recognise your tongue. Seems you have a flair for something—'

Kate watched the strong mouth twist in thought.

'– only what that something is I don't quite know . . . p'raps a few more years of rehearsing, then . . . mmm! Maybe.'

Her smile lost in the pucker of her mouth as she blew a stream of cigarette smoke, she answered condescendingly, 'You know, Torrey, for a bright guy you don't have much sense, do you? I mean given anything near a brain you would realise even a one-time commando stands no chance against a woman whose talents have been scorned.'

'Less of the "one time",' Torrey grinned, 'or you could find yourself in a precarious position.'

Stubbing out the cigarette, she met the grin. 'Pie crusts again? It's a good thing I prefer a drink!'

'Aah!' Clapping a hand dramatically to his chest, his face contorted with mock pain, he gasped, 'You actresses . . . you really know how to hurt a guy!'

'Stop clowning, you fool, you have the whole room looking at us!'

'Is that how I get you to give up smoking . . . it's so easy, why didn't I see it before!'

'One more daft remark and you won't see anything but stars for a week! Now do you want to hear what I found in Gau's office or do I go back to Annie's now?'

The blush of embarrassment suited her, or was it anger causing the red flag to fly? Anger, Torrey decided, at the sametime deciding not to push his luck any further, Kate Mallory could be hellish stubborn when the mood took her.

'So you visited the printing works and you got away without being recognised,' he dropped the banter, 'so what did you come up with?'

Going quickly over the events of the morning, Kate finished with, 'I believe this could be bigger than the Bartley affair.'

'So you told Daniels, but why go to him?'

'Because given what those papers contained Crowley

wouldn't hesitate to kill to keep it secret. You yourself heard him talk of a master and as far as I am concerned that watermark tells who that master is, and commando expertise or not you can't fight something like that on your own.'

'And Daniels can?'

'Daniels has the back-up!' Kate answered exasperatedly. 'If need be he can call in Scotland Yard and who knows what MI numbers . . . who can we call on? Each other!'

What she said was logical but still it didn't help. Torrey's fingers closed into fists. He wanted to take Crowley himself, squeeze the man's throat 'til his eyeballs looked down his back!

'We are both certain he murdered that girl, Fred said she was killed in some sort of ritual . . .'

A sacrifice offered to the devil . . . and he was to be the next! He wouldn't be human for that to have no effect, but Torrey hid the effect it had on him by reaching for his glass.

'I don't like the idea of parting with a story 'til the last T is crossed and the last I dotted, but this is out of our league, Torrey, in fact I think it's out of Daniels's league.'

'Then why give it to him? Honestly this time.'

'He agreed to give me first bite of the fruit,' she answered resignedly. 'I couldn't hope to be given any such had I sent it to one of the others I mentioned, and once the nationals get a sniff then Kate Mallory can kiss goodbye to a taste of the peach, that lot leave nothing . . . not even the stone.'

And Crowley would leave nothing . . . not even a man's life.

The thought should have counted for something, maybe it would later . . . if he lived that long; but right now it weighed nothing in the balance of Torrey's mind. That man had a view to death, Richard Torrey's death, and Torrey had a profound feeling it would take more than the police and more than any arm of the government to prevent him enjoying the view.

'I looked up each and every one of those firms named in the files,' Kate rolled on. 'They are big names in business, Davion

International manufacture arms, weapons of every kind; Satel Aeronautics build planes, helicopters, jet engines; Mercury Airlines don't only ferry tourists, they deliver anything anywhere; then there is Coton Pharmaceuticals, they deal in the less obvious weapon, their laboratories developed the nerve gas that was meant for use in the Falklands spat. Think of it . . . put that lot to bed together and what do you breed?'

War! Torrey's glass hit the table with a thud. They were the ingredients of war and Crowley stirred the pudding! A pudding the whole bloody world might get a portion of!

All the time she had talked he had only half listened, too intent on his own tree to notice the wood growing up all around. Well he was listening now.

'Can you remember details of sales, where arms went, who it was ordered them?'

'There was something about an Emissary and –' Kate's brow furrowed as she tried to recall what she had read '– yes, Epee.'

Fighter planes and air-to-air missiles! Christ, they could tear a country apart on their own!

'Anything else?' he urged. 'Think, Kate, is there anything else you remember?'

'Helicopters, armoured something or other that had numbers instead of names, long-range guns, ground-to-ground missiles, you name it, but none of those worried me like the Coton file. They had supplied enough toxic products to render the use of any other weapons unnecessary. I never paid much attention to science or biology when I was at school but I learned enough to know no human body could survive breathing that stuff.'

It had been bad enough in Belfast. Torrey's teeth clenched on the memory of mutilated bodies, people ripped apart by bomb blasts, others maimed and blinded by flying glass and debris as buildings were blown sky high. That should be enough to satisfy *any* maniac . . . but Crowley wasn't any maniac and the cause he served wasn't the freeing of a country. War! The thought chilled every blood vessel. Was that what Crowley was about? Did human life mean so little he would furnish a country with the means of destroying another?

Watching the nuances of thought play over his face, Kate Mallory felt a stronger twitch of apprehension than she had when searching Max Gau's office. Whatever was going through his mind was not pleasant.

'Torrey,' she said quietly, 'all of those armaments, those poisons, who would want them, who could pay for them? The amount involved must be colossal.'

Who would want them . . . who could pay for them? It needed less than a moment for answers to begin to click in. That weekend he had accompanied Max Gau to Whitefriars. The Arab ringed around by henchmen! The near East was a hot-bed of unrest, if one country had decided the next was expendable . . . Crowley was selling arms . . . the Arab was at Crowley's home, it wasn't impossible the two were linked by more than an invitation to a pleasant weekend in the country!

'Could be our Arab friend, Khadja,' he answered. 'The country has oil and in the world we live in oil is money.'

'Which brings us back to that banknote. Where does that fit in? It can't be part of Khadja's business, especially if it proves to be counterfeit.'

'Is Daniels getting that checked?'

'No.' Kate shook her head. 'Daniels doesn't have it. I kept it, I didn't want Fred Baker to get into hot water . . . somehow I don't think he's a part of all this.'

'Would you let me have that note, I'd like to face Fred with it again, give him a chance to explain before I ask Crowley where it fits with him.'

Keeping the note hidden in her hand she passed it under the table. 'Torrey,' she asked as he took it, 'are you having the same nightmare I am?'

Torrey nodded. He was having the same nightmare . . . but he was beginning to wake up.

'What have you done with them, Fred?'

Half-asleep in front of his television Fred Baker peered at the screen. 'It is not a television programme and you are not listening to some actor, it is me you are hearing, Fred, and I am here in this room with you.'

'Eh . . . who—'

'Who? Do you really need to ask that, Fred? Well then I must tell you, it is Julian Crowley.'

'What the . . .' Fred Baker leaned forward in his chair, bringing his face to peer more closely at the picture playing across the television screen.

'I said it was not a television production you were hearing!'

With the last softly spoken word the screen shattered, sending shards of broken glass ripping into the old man's face, hurling him back into the chair while the smoke of the burning set rose in a dense black column.

His mouth wide, Fred Baker watched the dark spindrift separate then draw together, each smoky tendril curling into another, drifting, combining, building itself slowly until the figure of a man floated before him. Surprise turning to fear, he stared. 'Crowley!'

'As I said—'

The smoke-formed mouth smiled, its words clear and distinct.

'– now tell me, Fred, where have you put them?'

'I . . . I . . .' Fred Baker trembled, his own words incoherent.

'Where, Fred . . . where have you hidden what you stole from the works?'

'You . . . you killed young Penny.'

'It was necessary.' The image smiled. 'However, I am not here to talk of the girl but to take back that which you have stolen, and you will give it to me, the consequences of refusal will, I assure you, be most painful.'

Whatever this thing was, Crowley or a being from hell, it 'adn't denied killing Penny, it 'ad brushed that aside as if it were of no consequence, the life of a young wench were nothing, compared to banknotes. The thought miraculously reaching through his fear, Fred stared at the smiling face. Crowley wouldn't find out from 'im where them things was!

'Were are they, Fred?'

'You go to bloody 'ell!'

'I will . . . eventually . . . but you will be there in one minute unless I get what I came for.'

Fred knew his courage could not last much longer but while it did he would fight, young Penny deserved that much. Rising to his feet he looked into eyes that gleamed like jet.

'I told yer, go to bloody 'ell!'

His words dropped away into stillness. Where the shattered television had stood the spectral smile faded while the smoke-formed arms lifted over the head. Above it a pool of light, though dark as the figure itself, began to glow. Not spreading or dilating, not reaching over the room as an electric light would have done, it lowered to enclose the figure within itself, a figure that spoke again.

'You have one last chance . . . give me what you have stolen.'

Stiff with returning fear, Fred tried desperately to hold on to his flagging courage. He'd broken the law by going along with Crowley, but he wouldn't give in to the man again. Breathing hard, he answered, 'I 'eard yer talk of yer master, go ask 'im wheer them things be for you'll not 'ear it from me. You killed that little wench an' I be going to see to it that you pays. I'll see you put away for life for what you done!'

Across from him the unreal face twisted in a snarl, and the light that encased the figure changed to an intense glowing orange speared with darts of white-tipped purple, darts that flicked and receded, almost touching yet not touching, playing fingers of flame about Fred's body. Then as if on some unspoken command they rushed together in a whirl, becoming a hideous bloated body, its glowing legs short and stunted, arms thick and ending in clawed hands, its grinning head waving on a long serpentine neck.

Throat locked with terror, Fred stared at the clawed hands, at the odious mouth opened wide.

'The Master has sent his accountant,' Crowley's voice slithered across the room. 'Payment must be made. He cannot return to the Dark Regions without settlement, the settlement of a life . . . your life, Fred, but tell me what I ask and I can direct his collecting elsewhere.'

Had Penny Smith suffered terror such as this? Incredibly, Fred's thoughts held on to the memory of the girl. Had Crowley frightened her witless before killing her?

Fred trembled as the snake-like neck lunged forwards but somehow his mind was suddenly filled with a different voice.

'There is forgiveness, Fred.'

The hideous mouth still gaped but the words were not coming from there.

'You have done wrong but you have not worshipped the devil . . . be brave, Fred . . . it is not too late.'

'I ain't feared o' your master.' The gentle voice in his head could not clear the terror in his heart yet somehow Fred found the courage to defy the thing that leered at him. 'Nor I ain't a'feared o' you, whatever sink hole spawned ya, and I won't never tell no matter what—'

The words died, swallowed in a fiendish howl as the ghastly misshapen form swooped forwards, its repulsive mouth grinning back with long, pointed fangs while slivers of white-hot flame wrapped themselves around the old man's body, the fire of its breath burning strips of flesh on his face.

Fred Baker's eyes were not on the horror that reached for him though, but on a spot beyond the glowing orange mass, on a small white patch that floated in the shadows, on a thin little face that smiled at him.

'Penny,' was all he said as life left his body.

# Chapter Twenty-Four

So the little man was dead. Nicole Jarreaux smoothed the expensive jade-green silk suit over her slender hips. A threat to the covens Julian had called him and as such, of course, he had to die but then Julian Crowley enjoyed killing, that for him was the thrill more ordinary mortals got from sex. But Julian was no ordinary mortal, he was an Ipsissimus, first of the Chosen and all powerful, yet even the all powerful could make mistakes; Crowley's mistake was in thinking of himself as the Son of the Master, as his equal. How long would Lucifer tolerate that, how long before he struck Crowley down? It would come. She glanced at the elegant creation clinging to her shapely body. She had known for some time that Crowley's arrogance would be his downfall, that the coven would require a new leader and when it happened that leader would be Nicole Jarreaux.

First the girl and then the old man, both so soon after that fiasco in the churchyard at Bentley, it was simply asking for the police to come snooping. That had been Julian's second mistake, the Prince of Darkness would not take kindly to such. Smiling, she picked up a perfectly matched coat then, bag in hand, she left the house.

She had laid her plans well. Headlights of the powerful Mercedes pushed back the darkness. The destitute she had taken from the streets of Wolverhampton had been a perfect match for herself in size and colouring, and the knife of a plastic surgeon would certainly match the rest, as it would provide herself with a new face. She smiled at the thought. The covens chose their members well, ensuring the skills of many professions were included.

The face of the House of Jarreaux. That was what she had promised the woman and that was what she would have, except it would be a dead face. The police would find a suicide note written in her hand beside a body that to all intents and purposes would be the owner of the exclusive fashion house.

There were no mirrors in that safe house. Slowing the car she turned into a long drive that led to a three-storey house set well back in its own grounds. Tonight she and the woman would drink to the success of their joint venture . . . only tonight the joint would be broken. Turning off the engine Nicole slid her slender legs from the car. Poison was such a sweet ally!

There was no telling when Crowley would visit the works, when he would see him; but see him he would, and before the blues could whisk him away. It was easy enough to think of, but how to put thought into practice?

'You've become very quiet, not planning anything stupid, I hope.'

'Not planning anything, Kate, just thinking.'

Even if she hadn't been full after the meal they had shared, Kate Mallory couldn't have swallowed that. There was something going on in Richard Torrey's mind, she needed no gold-edged guarantee to assure her of that, but surely he didn't intend to tackle those men alone.

'Thinking of what?' She glanced at the figure walking beside her, moonlight seeming to make him look even taller than he was.

'Nothing in particular, just thinking.'

'You're also just lying!' Kate halted abruptly and as he looked at her she went on sharply, 'I know you better than you give me credit for and I know when you are fobbing me off.'

'*Fobbing* you off!'

Glints of silver light caught by his eyes had them twinkling like jewels. They look like Grandmother's jet beads! Kate swallowed. She needed that taste of sarcasm, she needed something to hold her emotions in place, to stop her making a fool of herself by throwing her arms about him. Torrey had no feelings of that sort, hadn't he said only this evening he looked on her as a friend . . . throw her arms around him and even that relationship would be blown to the four winds.

'Fobbing!' Her answer was firm, though how she managed to make it so was a mystery to her. 'Darlaston is not the only town in the country which has a dialect! But since you have such a fine ear I'll put it more plainly: you are foisting me off.'

He laughed at that, a quiet deep-throated laugh. Something pulled inside Kate, did she want to laugh or cry or both together? what the hell was going on!

'I'm not foisting you off,' he chuckled, 'now why would I want to do that?'

Kate continued to walk. It was the only way to hold on. 'I could give you any of a dozen reasons,' she flashed, 'but we'll try this one first. You are thinking of tackling those men on your own, of getting there before the police make their move and you don't want me getting in your way!'

He could deny it but Kate Mallory was like the bull terriers those friends of his father used to set against each other, get her teeth in and nothing would shake her loose.

'Five out of ten.' He laughed; keeping things light might just see the unexpected happen. 'You would not be getting in my way for the simple reason I'm not about to do anything.'

'Torrey,' she said, her tone quieter, the ring of impatience gone, 'if you change your mind then be careful, remember what Fred Baker said happened to that girl.'

'Crowley won't—'

'Not just Crowley!' she cut in quickly. 'Max Gau too. I know you think he's a nice guy, and maybe he is, but he is no less dangerous than Crowley. Whatever this thing proves to be, they are in it together and if one is dabbling in the occult then you can be damn sure the other is doing the same . . . and don't laugh that off the way you laugh off anybody's offer of help, have the sense to remember Monkswell . . . that almost took your life. Julian Crowley and Max Gau might just finish the job.'

'Kate, I've told you . . . I'm not about to do anything, I'll just ask Fred what else he knows about this banknote and leave the rest to Daniels.'

And which onion boat do you think I came on! Her thoughts caustic, she turned her face away. That was the way he wanted to go, well that was fine with her; Kate Mallory knew a few tricks of her own and Richard Torrey hadn't seen the half of them. Coming to the gate of the trim little semi-detached in Michael Road she paused, glancing at the lighted window.

'Annie is back from her bingo, she'll want you to come in for a chat.'

'And a "bite o' supper". Really, Kate,' he touched his midriff, 'after what we have eaten I really couldn't take that right now and I wouldn't hurt Annie for the world, so best say goodnight now.'

Watching from the doorway of the house as the tall figure walked quickly away, Kate's slightly tilted lips curved ruefully. You don't know it, Mrs Price, but you have just provided our mutual friend with the perfect get-out.

He had told Kate he wasn't about to do anything. That had been a lie and the look that had flashed across her eyes said she had recognised it, but thankfully she'd asked no more questions. But was she correct in saying Max Gau was part of all that Crowley did? They were partners in the printing business, Fred had told him that, and whether it was through business or friendship Gau had spent that weekend at Whitefriars . . . but did that make Max a black magician? It couldn't. Couldn't . . . or was it that he didn't want to face the prospect?

As he turned the corner into Wolverhampton Road, a sudden breeze ruffled the head-high branches of an overhanging tree, the leaves brushing his face.

'Torrey . . .'

'Kate?' He swung round. 'You should have phoned . . .'

There was no Kate. His eyes swept the empty road. There was nobody. Damned leaves! He swiped a low-hanging branch. The rustle of them had sounded like someone calling his name.

'Remember . . .'

The whisper came again, soft as breath on a summer afternoon.

'Kate,' he snapped, 'if that's you then I advise you to pack it in right now, I'm in no mood for party games!'

It cracked away into the darkness, bouncing off the walls of houses, but there was no other sound, no sign of movement, until . . .

'Remember . . .'

Gentle as velvet on his skin the sound touched against his ears.

' . . remember Monkswell . . .'

Kate had said that a few minutes ago, she had said to remember Monkswell. Irritated, he swept the road behind him with another searching look but, as before, nothing moved.

'Play your childish games if you must,' he said irately, 'me, I'm going home!'

Swinging around he caught a slight movement to his right. There! He dropped immediately into the old preparedness, hands loose at his sides, back to a wall, every sense alert. There was somebody there, just inside George Rose Park! It couldn't be Kate, there was no way she could have reached here before him. But there was someone stood hidden in the shadows, someone who must have followed or been close enough to hear what Kate had said . . . and that someone was about to be given a little more information, some he would carry not just in his head!

'Eavesdropping should carry a government warning,' he said quietly, 'it can prove dangerous to health.'

His eyes laser keen, he probed the tenebrous entrance to the park, watching for the least movement. Crowley? Torrey's fingers curled, then relaxed. That man liked the shadows, he'd used them before, only this time they held no advantage.

'Don't hide, Crowley.' His voice was low but edged like a sheathed razor. 'Surprises don't work a second time.'

That had flushed the snake out! Every tingle he had ever felt when tracking ambushers in Ireland pulsed through him now as, across from where he stood, the shadows appeared to move. A torch? No, Crowley wouldn't use a torch but there was a light, a small white patch of light. Not moonlight. He shot a brief glance skywards. The clouds that had been gathering as he'd walked Kate home were thick now and evenly spread . . . the light he saw was definitely not from the moon.

Watching it draw nearer, a luminescence that seemed to shimmer as it moved, Torrey felt the small hairs lift. Even the best he had come up against hadn't moved as silently as this, making absolutely no sound, and neither had they disclosed their whereabouts by carrying a light that glimmered like a Christmas tree. So why was this character doing just that, advertising his coming? It didn't make sense.

Don't rush it, he told himself as the light glided towards him. Make your move now and the guy has time to drop the torch and leg it into the shadows before you get to him. It wasn't Crowley, he was sure of that, so who . . . Max Gau? That didn't fit either. That left only those three yobs who had hoped to give him a hiding in the yard of the Bird-in-Hand . . . so come on, fellas!

He smiled into the night. Try it again and welcome, but this time no doctor will see you back on your feet again!

A few more seconds! With every breath regulated, he watched the small glowing patch. It was well clear of the park, still moving towards him . . . wait . . . wait . . .

Torrey felt the wall at his back. There was still no sound and behind that luminous spotlight the shadows enveloped the figure that carried it; figure or figures . . . had one followed him or all three?

Two more seconds and he would know . . . two more seconds and however many might have come for him the bastards would never see the sun rise!

Now! Action keeping pace with thought, one hand reached for a body, the other raised for a chop to the throat, but his hands made no contact. Staggering a few steps as both hands sliced empty space he recovered quickly, defence mode re-assumed even as he whirled around.

Christ, that was quick! The man had out-thought him, had side-stepped at that last critical second . . . he should be a commando instructor! Composure regained, Torrey looked steadily at the patch of darkness behind the light hovering a few feet from him. Why hadn't they made their move? That second of disorientation where his hands met empty air had provided their opportunity . . . why hadn't at least one taken it?

'Don't be shy,' he taunted, hoping to bring whatever threatened him into the open, 'or is it your face looks so like a punch bag you are afraid to show it?'

The light hovered, not advancing not retreating and still the gleam of it blinded his search of the shadows at its back.

Surely it must be the three who had slated Anna that night; if they hadn't learned their lesson then . . . well, by God they would learn it now!

Laughing quietly he faced the shadows. 'The Three Ugly Sisters . . . that was what folk in the Bird called you; but that was before Richard Torrey laid hands on you, so what do they call you now? Not that it matters for you'll each need a new name for your headstone . . . if anybody can be bothered to provide you with one.'

Frustration, that was the name of their game. They thought by keeping silent they would get him mad enough to throw his hand. Torrey smiled again. He'd learned how to play like that years ago.

'It won't work, ladies,' he sneered, 'one or all three, I can take you and you know it, but one word of advice: slip off your high heels before you make your try!'

Across from him the light moved, widening the space between them. Torrey felt the surge of ice-cold anger surf every vein at the thought of a possible attacker slipping from his grasp. He could make a first move, whip around the rear of that light, take whoever held it before they realised what had happened, but that would leave his back undefended, open to any fist or weapon smashed across it. That would be the action of a fool . . . and fools didn't survive the life he had.

Contempt glaringly obvious in every syllable he called jeeringly, 'Wait, you're not leaving yet, are you? I was hoping to get more closely acquainted . . . much more closely!'

Somewhere in the distance a car hooted, the sound thinned to a mournful sigh as it drifted over the silent street, while overhead clouds blanketed an already grey-black sky.

'Torrey . . .'

With the whisper the light moved, widening and lengthening, spreading a diaphanous veil of silver. Unblinking, ready as ever for the unforeseen, Torrey waited, watching the silver mist; now translucent pearl, now opalescent alabaster, it changed and changed again, each time taking on new shape until finally a figure floated on the darkness, a figure whose radiance gleamed like frost spangles on newly fallen snow.

The girl! He held the breath that caught in his throat. The

girl he had seen at that cemetery, the same face that had stared at him from the bathroom mirror and again from the window of the office of Darlaston Printing.

'Help.'

The small mouth made no move but the pleading in those frightened eyes was stark and clear.

'How?' His own question was loud in comparison to that whisper. 'How . . . how can I help you . . . what is it you want?'

'Remember Monkswell . . .'

The radiance began to fade, the figure to shimmer and lose its form.

'Wait –' Torrey reached for it '– you haven't told me . . .'

'Remember . . .'

The word whispered for a moment on the night air then, like the light, it was gone.

Reaching his lodging Torrey went quickly to his room. Three other guests, all men and all company reps out on the road, were sociable enough but tonight the only company he wanted was his own.

He had seen it again, spoken to it, that girl in white, a girl visible enough but when you touched her . . .

Dropping to the bed he stared at the floor, hands hanging loose between his knees.

His hands had passed right through her, it had been like trying to hold mist. Yet she had spoken to him, it was impossible but – trick of the mind, moon mist or ghost – it had spoken!

But why hadn't it answered his questions? Why not say what that help was it asked for? With each appearance it had said almost the same thing. Help me . . . help Fred . . . and now, remember Monkswell; but what did it all mean?

Undressing slowly he reached for the pyjamas folded beneath his pillow. Halfway to the door, he changed his mind. Those reps would be making their way to their rooms just about now and he was in no mood for conversation. He would brush his teeth twice in the morning.

Turning back to bed he switched off the one lamp the room boasted. He always thought more clearly in the dark.

Help me . . . That thin little face had looked so terrified . . . but the figure wasn't real . . . Lord, he would help if he could but how did you help something that didn't exist! A phantom that melted away as you tried to touch it? And what about the plea to help Fred? If that referred to Fred Baker, he wasn't in need of help unless there was trouble about the stolen banknote, and he could give that to the man tomorrow to return it to where he stole it from . . . so that was all right. It had to be the banknote that apparition had referred to; 'help Fred' meant just that, help the old man return it before he could be found out and prosecuted.

He had thought things through, provided himself with an answer to each question. So why had he deliberately not asked the last one, why was he avoiding facing that? Suddenly he was that schoolboy again, closing his mind to the issue as he had closed it to Ron Webster's bullying. Once more he couldn't look truth in the eyes.

Beyond the window a car passed along the street sending a play of light around the walls of his room, the sound of its engine fading slowly into nothingness. Just as that figure had faded. But the nightmare of his childhood was not completely gone and neither would the ghost of that girl go for good until he took the business of it full on, skirting halfway around the problem wouldn't solve it; and that was what he was doing now, he was only acknowledging that part of what had happened for which he could find acceptable answers.

But were they acceptable, did they solve anything? Such as why would a ghost haunt a man it had never met in life?

His eyes wide, he stared at shadows moving on his ceiling as clouds began to break, freeing shafts of yellow moonlight that fled as quickly as they came as if afraid of being caught and locked away again.

A ghost! In the dimness his mouth curved ruefully. At least he was accepting that much, that the figure that materialised from nothing and came to him from nowhere was a ghost, the shade of a dead girl. A girl killed by Julian Crowley! The smile shot away. Penny Smith had been given as some sort of sacrifice, that much old Fred had heard Crowley admit, and Crowley spoke of a master and for a black magician that could only mean the devil, and where Crowley went Max Gau went also. At last he had admitted what he had suppressed, had kept from entering into his thoughts. Max Gau too was involved in the occult, he must be in agreement with all the other one did . . . and that would include the sacrifice of Richard Torrey!

That thought should have him worried. But Torrey hadn't done the expected since that shed had burned down around Ron Webster and his dirty little gang, just as he hadn't done the expected with Bartley and that hitch hiker, but the figure that had haunted him then had been known to him, loved by him, had . . .

Clenching his teeth he followed the darting beams of moonlight. He wouldn't go down that path.

They must have been as different as chalk and cheese, Anna and that terrified, helpless girl that had called to him. One had been rotten from the start and he had refused to see the obvious; but young Penny Smith, to listen to Fred Baker was to know she had been no whore.

Drawing a deep breath he let it out slowly. He was looking for similarities, a connecting tie that would link the hauntings, but there was none, unless – he breathed again, deeper and more slowly as the realisation canoned in his mind – unless the tie was black magic! When he had refused what was asked, the spirit of Anna had changed from the attractive, smiling woman he had known to a howling demon from hell; Crowley had given Penny a transfer, the Seal of Ashmedai, High Angel of the devil, marking her as one of his own. There was the real answer. Penny had been *given* to the devil whereas Anna had gone to him of her own accord. Penny Smith was asking Richard Torrey's help . . . but was it to save her own soul or the soul of Fred Baker?

But how did you fight the minions of hell?

Across the room, filling the space left by undrawn curtains, a blaze of moonlight turned glass panes to shimmering gold crystal, and from its heart a light gleamed silver white.

Remember . . .

The word sighed across the silence.

Remember Monkswell . . .

# Chapter Twenty-Five

'What time did you finish work last night?'

Detective Inspector Bruce Daniels looked at the man he had had brought in to the station an hour before.

'The usual time, five o'clock.'

'What deliveries did you make?'

'The Grand Theatre in Wolverhampton, the National Exhibition Centre in Birmingham . . . look what's this all about?'

'First things first, and today my questions take priority.'

Daniels flicked a tablet into his mouth. This bloody acid had started the minute he'd woken up. Take an hour off, Marjorie had told him, go see the doctor. He'd half made up his mind to do just that when she had whisked the plate of unwanted breakfast from beneath his nose, washing and whisking it into the cupboard with a speed undreamed of by the makers of daft outer-space movies that kids raved over these days. Sick leave! His stomach churned at the thought; acid might be eating his gut but a month or two at home would eat his brain!

'Did you load the van?' He waited until Torrey nodded then added, 'Fred Baker, did he carry any boxes, lift anything heavy?'

'No. I do the carrying, I load and unload, there's no call for Fred to do any of that. He just keeps an eye on things as far as that goes, watches the stuff loaded, gives me the delivery notes and that's it.'

'Has he given you any delivery note this morning?' Daniels sucked hard on the tablet.

'No, Gau did that.' Torrey glanced across the table of the interview room, a small frown nestling between his dark brows. 'It's the first time that's happened, I've never known Fred be late before, must have had one pint too many last night.'

'That would be in the Staffordshire Knot, would it?'

He could tell Daniels to shove it, to stick his questions where the sun don't shine; then again who wanted to spend the rest of the day in the company of the blues? The choice was his.

'It's the only place I know that Fred takes a drink.'

The choice made he glanced at the young constable stood with his back to the door.

'Speaking of which, do your guests get offered a cup of tea?'

'Did Baker often get well-oiled?' Daniels resumed his interrogation as the constable left on his errand.

'He could be a good man around the barrel, though I've never seen him drunk or known him to have a hangover, but then the Knot is a place I rarely drink in, you should ask the landlord. He'd know the answer to that one if anybody does.'

He could tell Torrey that he had already done that, but he was telling nothing until he was ready. Waiting while the returning constable set two steaming mugs on the table, he went on.

'Could he have gone somewhere other than the Knot, p'raps had a drop more than usual some place else?'

Taking his time swallowing several mouthfuls of tea, Torrey nursed the mug between his hands. 'Look, Daniels,' he said firmly, 'we can dance the tango all morning or for as long as you can get a ticket to hold me here, but I've told you all I know of Fred Baker, we work at the same place, he takes his tipple in the Staffordshire Knot and that's it! Except I won't advise you talk to your pet canary 'cos I know you'll have done that already.'

He had talked to Echo Sounder. Inspector Daniels swallowed hot tea; his gullet was already burned with acid, the tea couldn't top that.

'When Gau oversaw this morning's loading of the van, did he say why Baker was not at work, that he had rung in sick, gone off to see a relative, did he speak of any reason?'

'Ask Gau!' Above the rim of the mug Torrey's eyes were hard. 'Or better than that, wait until Fred comes in to work and I'll have him ring you, I might even run him down here in the works van.'

Clever bugger! Daniels swallowed again, trying to ease the irritation that burned the length of his gut. Flicking open a carton of BiSodol he extracted a slim white tablet. Holding it an inch from his tongue he met the cold, hard eyes that watched him. 'That might be a bit more awkward than you think. Fred Baker is in the mortuary. He was found dead this morning.'

'Be a parcel for you, luv.'

'Me . . . I wasn't expecting anything.'

Reaching for the coat draped carefully across a chair Annie Price smiled at her lodger.

'It be summat from your auntie, I expects, seein' as 'ow it be your birthday soon, only I 'opes as it don't be no cake, no disrespect to the woman . . . God forbid . . . it just be that the postman says it near give 'im 'ernia carrying it up the path; mind you, wench, carryin' two postcards together would give that one a 'ernia!'

The parcel wasn't from home. Kate Mallory looked at the postmark. Nor did she recognise the handwriting, it had that lovely old-fashioned flourish to the letters, a style reminiscent of yesterday rather than the word-processed productions of today. Why was it anything hand-done seemed of no value in the modern world?

'I'll be off then, luv.' Annie had fastened her coat and picked up her second best bag. 'I can't rightly say when I'll be 'ome, once Lil Pagett gets to look for a new frock it can get to be termorrer afore it be yesterday. I keep tellin' 'er, don't expect to look like Sophia Loren if you keeps eatin' like a tunky pig; her's been tryin' to lose three stone ever since 'er left school,' Annie grinned, 'mind, 'er did do it once . . . when 'er lost the engagement ring 'er Joe bought from Woolworths.'

'Don't let her hear you say that.' Kate tried not to giggle. She hadn't understood half of what her landlady had said but guessed it was not exactly flattering to Lil Pagett.

'You be right, Kate me wench, it ain't right to joke about other people,' Annie dropped her voice conspiratorially, 'but what I said about Lil bein' fat as a tunky pig . . . it's goin' to take more'n 'er mother's whalebone stays to get 'er into the kind o' frock 'er chooses.'

Hearing the click of the front door closing, Kate turned her attention back to the parcel. Annie might have been joking when talking of her friend but not about this. It was fairly heavy and it felt solid. Books, perhaps? But who would be sending her books . . . in fact who would be sending her anything?

Fetching scissors from the kitchen she cut through string and several bands of sticky tape. Whoever had wrapped her mysterious gift had no intention of it breaking open in transit.

'Lord!'

The wrapping finally off she sat staring at the contents.

'Why?'

Max Gau stared at the tall figure stood in his office.

'Why!' Julian Crowley laughed scathingly. 'You can ask that when the work of the Master is threatened?'

'Did the Master ask for the old man's life, did he tell you to murder him, or is it you, you who has developed a taste for murder? Fred Baker could not possibly have known the real reason behind the work done here.'

'Then why steal the things he did?' Crowley's eyes glittered like polished jet. 'Did you know he had taken those things, Max; could it be you helped him, hoping that by doing so you could discredit me in the eyes of the Master?'

'Huh!' Max Gau shook his head. 'Discrediting you to advance myself is the last thing I would do. I've gone as far as I want to go, God knows I wish I'd never met you.'

'Which god would that be? The one who gave you a soul or the one you have sold it to? Either way it's too late for you, Max, your agreement was made long ago.'

'Made yes, but it won't be signed as yours is signed in another man's blood! I've followed the way of the Left Hand Path, taken part in many rituals but I will not be part of murder. You killed Penny Smith, not for any threat to the Master nor to the coven but because you enjoyed doing it, the same as you enjoyed the killing of Walter Mitchell; I watched you at that fiasco of a horse race, I saw you bend his partner to your will, controlling his mind until he shot Mitchell and I saw the look on your face when the bullet hit home. It was sheer satisfaction Crowley, the sort any other man gets from sex.'

'Like your partner got with Christy?'

It was meant to stab but Max Gau's eyes showed no pain, that was as dead as his soul.

'Yes,' he answered quietly. 'The same as Ben got with Christy.'

'Oh it was more than that.' Crowley smiled but his eyes were as deadly as a poised cobra. 'It was more than just pleasure, Max, it was an exultation, one I mean to repeat many times.'

'As you did with Fred Baker? That is why he has not shown up for work today, isn't it? Because you've killed him!'

'He was a stupid old man!' Crowley's façade of pleasantry shattered.

'Stupid . . . or stubborn? Was that the real reason for murdering him, because he stood up to the great Julian Crowley, Magus of the High Coven, because regardless of whatever terror you threatened him with he would not tell you what it was you wanted to know? Was that why you killed a man almost twice your age—'

'Enough!' Crowley's fist crashed hard down on a delicate Hepplewhite table. 'The girl . . . the old man . . . what do they matter!'

Max Gau faced the man he knew could destroy him body and soul, and suddenly it didn't matter any more. Death and the torment it would bring would be simply a continuation of the torment that had been with him since finding Christy in bed with another man, since hearing the gasps of passion she had never given when with him. Crowley had saved him from life inside a prison cell but in doing so had condemned him to a life in a different sort of prison, one from which there was no reprieve. Hell and its inmates could be no worse than what he had now, and for a time at least he would not be sharing it with Crowley.

With the calmness of resolution shining from his eyes he answered, 'What do they matter? To you, Julian, they mattered nothing at all, but to me . . . yes they mattered and so does Richard Torrey. I won't stand by and see you do to him what you did to Penny. I will take part in no sacrifice.'

'Be careful what you say, Max.'

It was low, sibilant, the hiss of an angry snake, the hard obsidian stare cold as black ice.

'The Master will not refuse the gift of a life, though that life belongs to one of his own followers . . . even a Magister Templi!'

'Your threats don't frighten me any more.' Max smiled. 'I understood what it entailed when I made my bargain, now you understand this: I will not be a part of murder for the buzz it gives you, nor for any other reason. The devil has claim to my soul, when or how he takes delivery is no longer of any consequence, but this is . . . I will do all in my power to prevent you taking the life of Richard Torrey.'

'Your power!'

From the other side of the room, Crowley's eyes seemed to suddenly erupt into pools of fire.

'What is your power compared to that of an Ipsissimus?'

'Not yet, Julian,' Max answered quietly, 'you are not yet Ipsissimus, true you have the knowledge, you have mastered the ten Sephirath, the Forty-Two Paths of Wisdom and attained the Sanctum Reghum, that ancient knowledge and power of the Magi, but without the blessing of the Great Lord of Darkness all of that is nothing. To gain that blessing you need the whole of the High Coven to sacrifice with you.'

'They are all agreed, Davion, Geddes, all of them.'

'But not me. I will not participate in murder.'

For a few long seconds silence vibrated between them then Crowley spoke, every word venomous, malicious, his evil eyes filled with black threat.

'In a few weeks we celebrate the Great Sabbat of Samhain, the day of the Power of Darkness. On that day the Spirit of Satan is poured out over his followers, enriching their strength, rewarding the faithful; but it also destroys those who are not wholly of the Truth. On that night, Max, you will submit, you will accept the Lord of All Things, give yourself totally to his Will and his work—'

'*His* will . . . *his* work,' Max interrupted, 'but the murder of Richard Torrey is not, I believe, his will but yours and as such I say I will not take part.'

'You forget what happened before I brought you here! Gave you this house—'

'I have forgotten nothing,' Max answered the threat spitting at him like gunfire.

'Then think of this, refuse me and see the power of my hand.'

Stood beside the Regency fireplace Max Gau sighed.

'You have threatened so often, Julian, why not do what you long to do. Show the greatness of your powers, call the Messenger, believe me you will be doing me a service.'

'As you wish.' Crowley's face twisted, his eyes became slits and he breathed heavily. He was not used to being refused, his word was law with the High Coven, he could not allow it to be seen to be denied. Raising his hands above his head he began to intone, softly, quietly, words swishing like the slither of a serpent's tail.

'Hear me, Bringer of Death. Hear me, Messenger of the Dark Regions. Hear me, Ashmedai, Destroyer of life. I conjure thee to my will.'

Beneath the silk of his expensive shirt, Max Gau felt his heart leap. The die he had toyed with so long was cast, the Messenger had been called . . . there was no going back.

Across the room Julian Crowley's head lifted, his eyes closed. 'Ashmedai, Keeper of the Seal, High Prince of the Dark Throne I conjure thee, appear and do my will.'

Bringing his hands slowly downwards he opened his eyes, then pointed to a spot between himself and Max. Almost at once the colours of the beautiful Bokhara carpet rolled and fused together, sliding out of the fabric of the carpet, giving birth to a huge, shining reptilian body.

'In the Name of the Great Lord—'

Free of the carpet the great body half rose, twisting its serpentine coils, its refulgent eyes seeking the slow intoning voice.

'– he to whom Belial, Ashtaroth and all the Angels of Hades must kneel I command thee take that which you were summoned to take, that without which you may not return, the life of a man.'

The long reptilian body reared higher, the flat head swaying inches from the face of Julian Crowley and for a few seconds fear showed in his cold, dark eyes.

'Ashmedai—'

His voice trembling, he watched the swaying head, the forked tongue that flicked less than a hair's breadth from his face. One wrong move, one mistaken syllable was all it would take to bring the evil that watched down on his own head.

'Ashmedai, Messenger of Satan, take the gift I bring to the Prince of Darkness, take the life of Max Gau.'

Dancing to some terrible rhythm the huge head swayed, the great scarlet body writhing as it turned, the flame-filled eyes fastening on Max. Then it began to move, a tortile undulatory gliding that made no sound. Across the space of the sitting room of Max Gau's home, Julian Crowley saw the fear the other man could no longer hide and jubilation replaced his own.

'Servant of the Dark One,' he called again, 'take the life I offer.'

Swallowing hard to free the tongue cleaving to the roof of his dry mouth, Max forced the words filling his heart.

'I reject thee, Lord of Evil; in the name of the true God I renounce thee . . . dear Lord Jesus Christ, forgive me—'

There were no more words to break the silence as black fangs sank into his throat.

Looking at the [illegible] table, Kate [illegible] teeth. Maybe [illegible] in' there [illegible] though [illegible] Near and [illegible] for years [illegible] protect [illegible] bours [illegible] here [illegible]

She read [illegible]

'It [illegible] what to do?'

Why [illegible] come [illegible]

Kate stared at [illegible] Fred Baker's name.

Whatever was going [illegible] send this to the police [illegible] Fred was [illegible] balloon [illegible]

Pulling [illegible]

# Chapter Twenty-Six

Looking at the unwrapped parcel lying on Annie's kitchen table, Kate Mallory caught her bottom lip between her teeth. Maybe the arms and armaments she had read about in that file she had photocopied she could understand, though not the secrecy involved in hiding it away. The Near and Middle East was volatile as every news broadcast for years had testified and each country was determined to protect itself against possible attack from any of its neighbours; but that did not explain Fred Baker's foreign banknote . . . or this.

She read the accompanying note through again.

*'It is too risky to send these to Torrey, but tell him of them, he will know what to do.'*

Why too risky to post this parcel to Richard Torrey . . . how come he would know what to do?

Kate stared at the graceful old-fashioned script signed with Fred Baker's name.

Whatever was going on it was seemingly illegal, or why not send this to the police? Was it because Torrey was involved and Fred was providing him with a chance to get out before the balloon went up?

Pulling hard on her lip she dragged it painfully between her teeth but the sting of it did nothing to solve the problem that parcel had landed in her lap.

Scotty! she thought. She could show it to Scotty . . . but he would immediately call in the police. Kate's mind immediately rejected the idea. Fred Baker had trusted her, so to hand this to Daniels before speaking to Richard Torrey would be nothing short of throwing that trust back in the old man's face. No, she would do what was asked of her and go to Torrey first.

With the parcel re-wrapped she was halfway up the stairs when her mobile phone shrilled. Racing the last half-dozen steps she ran into her room; that might be Torrey now.

It wasn't! Half of her mind on her editor's quickly spoken instructions, and half on the parcel she had dropped on to the bed her eyes searched for a suitable place to put it. Not hiding it from Annie, she told herself guiltily, then as she dropped the phone into her bag asked herself: but if not Annie, then who?

'Nobody!' Cross with herself, Scotty and the world she grabbed the parcel, placing it on the floor of the wardrobe and closing the door. 'I'm not hiding it from anybody!'

But as she left the house she knew that she was.

Taking the plastic shopping bag from a girl who smiled hopefully at him, Torrey left the small corner shop.

Cardiac arrest was the police surgeon's summary report. Daniels had told him. Seeing yesterday's milk still on the doorstep and a copy of last evening's *Star* still stuck halfway through the letter box the local milkman had called the police. They had found Fred Baker dead on his living-room floor. There had been no evidence of breaking and entering, no physical violence to the body, in fact no signs of anything untoward apart from a shattered television set.

*'Must have blown itself up and the shock of it brought on a heart attack.'*

*'Is that what you think?'* Putting the carrier bag on the passenger

seat of the works van, Richard Torrey remembered the look his own question had brought to the inspector's face.

*'I don't think anything,'* Daniels had answered, *'least not before I get the results of the Coroner's report, but this much I will say; I've seen a few stiffs in my time, dead of all sorts, but that one . . . the look on his face, it was like he'd seen a vision from hell, a look only the devil himself could inspire.'*

Torrey slipped the gears home, guiding the van towards the Bull Stake. The devil himself? Or the devil's disciple!

No physical violence. That was no guarantee it hadn't been death by murder, and who stood to gain by the old man's death? That banknote had been stolen from Darlaston Printing, an action that had Fred scared, and the owners of those works were Max Gau and Julian Crowley . . . both disciples of the devil! Fred Baker's so-called heart attack had their signature all over it! But try telling Daniels that, try telling the blues any of it . . . they'd have him in a strait jacket and certified! That was how Crowley and Co. thought to get away with it, this being a new millennium, the world being a thousand years past the belief of black magic, people assuming that that art belonged to ignorance and the Middle Ages. But he had seen proof of its existence, seen the evil it could do and, yes, he believed that power still survived, that it lived beneath the veneer of modern sophistication and that it could be used – used to kill!

Ahead the traffic slowed in deference to a funeral cortege which turned along Whitton Street. Parking on the opposite side, Torrey climbed from the van. One more mourner would raise no eyebrows.

There was no one in the office, not Gau and no temporary secretary. That was all to the good.

Carrier bag in hand, Torrey made his way quickly into the print shop. Checking each machine, he frowned. If that banknote had been printed here then where was the press, the plates? He knew nothing of the art of printing but even a fool would know there had to be machinery of some kind; yet there was nothing that even vaguely matched any conception of currency plates. There had to be. He stared at each large press in turn, it couldn't be a hoax, Fred Baker had been too shit-scared for it to be a wind up. Walking the length of the workshop, his foot caught against an uneven board in the dusty floor. Cursing he kicked at it then stopped. Was it? Dropping to his haunches he smiled. This particular board was part of a trap door and where a trap door was there could also be a cellar!

They would come. Leaving the trap lifted he cleared the few stone steps in one jump. Max Gau and Crowley would come and when they did they would find him waiting. Emptying the contents of the shopping bag on to a workbench he glanced at the items he had purchased. He had wracked his brain, trying hard to remember all that Martha Sim had used that night she had fought the spectre of Anna, but he hadn't the knowledge that went with their use.

But knowledge or not he wouldn't give in without making the attempt, he could well die as Fred and that girl had died but it wouldn't be with a look of sheer terror on his face . . . and Crowley wouldn't find it all going his way.

His hand touching the objects he had brought with him, he paused. Overhead, a sound! The shuffle of quiet footsteps! His breath tight in his lungs, he listened. Had he imagined it? Above him the steps sounded again, quiet . . . hesitant.

Christ, he was too late!

With breath stinging his lungs he glanced to the head of the shallow flight of steps.

'Kate!' Relief was laced with concern as he shouted the words, 'What the hell are you doing here?'

'Well you sure know how to make a girl feel welcome!' She tripped quickly down the steps. 'I came to show you this.'

'Couldn't it have waited!' He glared, anger beginning to burn in him. Kate Mallory could do the most thoughtless things and to do one of her star turns now . . .

Catching the razor edge to his tone, Kate felt her own easily aroused irritation move edgily into her veins.

'Until when?' she snapped. 'Tomorrow, the next day or whenever the busy Mr Torrey deigns to find the time? Sorry, lad, I'm not into your egocentrism and I'm not here for you . . . I'm here for Fred.'

'Fred Baker is—'

'I know,' she answered as he stopped in mid-sentence. 'I had a call from Scotty, some neighbour of Fred's spoke to a young policeman who answered a milkman's phone call, then she phoned the *Star*. I've just come from an interview with her, seems Fred died of a heart attack.'

'If you knew that why come looking for him here?'

Her eyes glinting, Kate glared. 'If you listened as well while in the Army I wonder you ever lived long enough to come home! I did not say I came here to *find* Fred, I said I was here *for* Fred. Read that and you might see why.'

Taking the note she shoved at him, Torrey read the few brief words then opened the parcel.

Plates! Plates for printing currency . . . the banknote Fred had mistakenly handed to Echo Sounder had to be forged!

'They came in the morning post –' she parried the question leaping from his eyes '– and no, I haven't shown them to anyone else, but why should Fred want them brought to you?'

'It's a long story.'

'So start soon and it'll end soon.'

He couldn't let her stay, Crowley and Gau were bound to show soon. Gathering up the plates he turned to her.

'Not now, Kate . . .'

'It won't work, Torrey.' She smiled, a quiet defiance in her reply. 'Fred knew about Penny Smith and it's my guess he knew a whole lot more besides, about both Max Gau and Crowley, just as you do and that is why you want rid of me.'

'You don't understand, it's not a game those two are playing . . . they killed Penny Smith without giving it a single thought.'

'They killed Fred too, didn't they?'

'I don't know.'

'But you think they did?'

'Yes,' he breathed impatiently, 'Yes, I think they did, now go before—'

'Before they come to kill you!'

Glancing at the patch of light that was at the head of the steps he took her arm, pushing her towards them, but she shook it off.

'I'm not leaving,' she declared flatly, 'I liked Fred Baker as much as you did and I intend seeing his death is paid for.'

'Then go fetch Daniels. Tell him what was in the parcel and where you have taken them, tell him they are the plates on which the note I gave him this morning was printed. Go, Kate, please!'

'I'm not sure he'll come.'

'He'll come.' Torrey pushed her again towards the steps. 'Tell him the plates match and he'll come.'

Millions of pounds of arms and armaments and now this.

Detective Inspector Bruce Daniels watched the representative of the local bank Foreign Currency department. He had examined every detail of the banknote which earlier on Torrey had handed to the desk sergeant, telling him to get it checked for forgery and dashing off before a chance had been given for questions.

'Of course one cannot say with absolute certainty.' The dapper little man looked up. 'There are so many things one must check . . . type of paper, ink, calligraphy . . . you understand, Inspector. To do that thoroughly one must have the necessary utensils, chemicals et cetera.'

'But what would *you* say?'

His smoothly brushed greying head shaking slightly the little man pursed his lips giving the question enough thought to set Daniels's hand clenching. Why was it some men had to think half an hour before deciding to wipe their arse?

'What *I* might say could not be used as evidence on its own, this is not UK currency I have been asked to evaluate—'

'I know it's no bloody fiver!' Daniels's patience snapped. 'I know the government will want their own blokes as well as experts from the country that money is supposed to be for to examine that note, but we have to move now if more of it isn't to find its way abroad . . . until it's cleared.'

'I understand your predicament, Inspector, but you must understand mine. Should I pronounce that note counterfeit and it proves not to be—'

Irritation rose in hot waves of acid searing Daniels's throat. They could play bloody pat-a-cake all day! Tossing a BiSoDol tablet into his mouth he shoved the carton into his coat pocket.

'I understand! Nobody likes it to be his arse on the line, thanks for coming into the station.'

'Inspector –' the little man removed the white cotton gloves he had worn while assessing the banknote, folding each finger meticulously into place before laying them carefully in his leather briefcase '– allow me to say this. I would not relish going through that country's Customs with a pocketful of those notes.'

A nod was as good as a wink. Watching the young constable remove the banknote, Daniels thanked the bank representative and accompanied him from the small room set aside for interviews.

'Any luck?'

'Depends on how you look at it.' Bruce Daniels turned to the man who spoke. 'But you know the saying, Dave, acting after the event be like giving a dead man medicine, it don't work!'

'So it's all on then?'

Swallowing the residue of the tablet, Daniels nodded. 'Like your mother used to tell you, Dave, empty sacks never stand upright, and if I wants this one to stand I've got to go find summat to put in it.'

And if you don't then the brass will stick you in it! Keeping the thought to himself but knowing Daniels was thinking along much the same lines Sergeant David Farnell nodded.

'I've got an unmarked car at the corner of Pinfold Street and Walsall Road, and another at the corner of Bright Street so nobody gets out that way, and I've laid on a fast response vehicle should you need it.'

'Thanks.' Daniels touched a pocket, feeling for his car keys. 'I'll sit mine bang in the middle of that works entrance and if any bloody smart arse bangs his way through it then he'll have Marjorie to deal with . . . and Marjorie wouldn't stop at taking just his balls!'

'Bruce—'

Daniels half turned as the sergeant called.

'– the warrant . . . it isn't through yet.'

Despite the acid flaming in his throat Daniels almost smiled. 'So . . . I forgot it! But we'll let Quinto worry about that.'

'Don't stand there, Kate . . . go fetch Daniels.'

Richard Torrey glanced anxiously at the woman stubbornly refusing to leave. He could carry her up those steps, dump her in the yard and lock the print-room door . . . but he knew Kate Mallory, she would sit there, a prize rabbit for Crowley and Gau to collect on their way in, and with Kate in their grasp Crowley at least would guess the fight was over before it began.

Kate read the anxiety in those dark eyes and her heart twitched. Torrey was not afraid for himself, that wasn't his style, the worry was all for her!

'I don't need to go fetch Daniels,' she said quietly. 'I rang him before coming here, he knows what is in that parcel, where I brought it and why.'

'Christ, I wish I did!'

'I lay no claim to being who you called upon.' She grinned impishly. 'But I can answer your prayer; without finding those plates actually on the premises then our friend the inspector would have a hard job proving that counterfeiting currency was taking place here. Really, Torrey, I would have thought you to sus that out for yourself.'

'We can't all be members of Mensa!' Torrey scowled. 'And there's no need for us all to be dead, but we will be if you don't leave now.'

'Forget it!' Her grin at once stone dead, Kate glared, resolute defiance in the slight tip-tilt of her mouth. 'We are in this together and that's the way it's going to remain, so quit the macho bit and tell me how I can help?'

Seeing her glance at the articles laid out on the workbench he hesitated. She would think him ten pence short of a shilling if he told her what it was he'd had in mind; how could he say he expected to be visited by an acolyte of the devil, much less fight it with a packet of salt and a candle!

*Remember Monkswell.*

Those words had plagued him well past the dawn hours. They had been telling him what to do, how to fight, but telling Kate as much . . . she'd think him crazy!

'Don't!' Kate's eyes glinted as she caught his look. 'Don't tell me I can best help by leaving; if I guess right then we don't have the time for argument so what do I do with this?'

'This first.'

Removing the stone Martha Sim had placed around his neck on that terrifying night he touched a finger to his tongue and erased his own name. Then, with a pencil, scratched in hers.

'Put that on . . . and leave it on.'

Taking the stone with its peculiar eye-shaped hole she read the words printed on it: *From all harm Kate Mallory protect.*

'Don't talk, just listen.' Speaking rapidly, Torrey went over the events of the night in Martha Sim's cottage, the night the devil had sent the evil that was Anna to take his life.

'And you think that is what we should do now?'

'We can't follow exactly,' he answered the question that followed on his brief résumé, 'I don't have everything Martha used and I certainly don't have her knowledge.'

'Then we will use what we have.' Dropping her bag on to the workbench she broke open the packet of salt she had picked up prior to his explanation and began to sprinkle it in a circle. Help me . . . The exhortation silent in her heart, she exchanged the pack of salt for the small bottle of water Torrey had also brought.

'That might not work,' Torrey glanced at the bottle in her hand, 'it is holy water but seeing as I invited myself to a funeral in order to nick it from the church then it could have lost any power to help.'

'You stole this?' Kate met the dark eyes with a tilted smile. 'Well done, Torrey, there's hope for you yet. Now all we have to do is remember the formula.'

*'Let your heart speak . . . the words will come'.*

What Martha Sim had said to him seemed to be spoken again now as if to tell him it didn't matter what the words were so long as each was spoken in faith of the Lord's assistance and with trust in His presence.

Taking the bottle from Kate he was suddenly a child again, afraid of being caught in something he ought not to be doing, afraid of meeting what was to come as he had been of meeting Ron Webster and his bullies.

Forgive me. The silent words seemed to reach up from his soul. I meant no desecration. Take Kate Mallory into thy hands, Lord; keep her from the evil to come. Then, using the water sparingly, he touched a few drops to each of two white candles; these were not stolen, not church candles, but perhaps the drops of holy water might replace the blessing of a priest. That done he traced the circle of salt, his quiet intonation natural as his prayer had been.

'Water, blood of the earth, cleanse all evil from thee; Salt, the pure body of the earth, surround and protect thee; Light of the holy candle show thy way; Together they keep thee, let no spirit of darkness approach thee, Permit no evil to assail thee.'

From the gloomy shadowed corners of the room a rustling, like the stirring of dry leaves, came quietly, then began to grow in volume, filling the air with a malevolent swish, like the body of a great serpent being dragged across the floor.

'Don't move!' Torrey met the scared brown eyes that swung to him. 'Whatever happens, whatever you think you see, for God's sake, Kate, don't step outside the circle!'

[illegible]

Sat in the [illegible] hands clutched [illegible] [illegible] that was the [illegible] his quota [illegible]

[illegible]

# Chapter Twenty-Seven

Sat in the driving seat of his stationary blue Ford, Bruce Daniels's hands clutched the steering wheel. Twenty years! Twenty years he had served on the force and where had it got him, bloody nowhere! He had all it took to make Chief Detective Inspector, come to that he had enough behind him to make Chief bloody Constable and like as not do a better job; one thing above all was certain, he couldn't do a worse one! But he couldn't lick arses, that was the trouble behind his being repeatedly passed over for promotion. He'd brought in the goods over the years, more than his quota: scum like Carter who had murdered a seven-year-old girl while banging her mother; he'd busted that paedophile ring that pretended to be church social workers, and a dozen other characters so crooked they couldn't lie straight in bed; then there was Bartley and his little heroin-peddling mates . . . how many on the force could match that record, and how many that couldn't now had their arse cushioned by a Chief Superintendent or Deputy Commissioner's chair!

It would be no different if he brought this off. He stared moodily at the grey Jaguar parked in the yard of Darlaston Printing. Should it prove what he felt in his water, a counterfeiting operation, then who would get the glory for bringing it in? Not you, he thought sourly, not Detective

Inspector Bruce Daniels; a pat on the back would be his share of the spoils.

So why put up with it? That had been Marjorie's question from the early days. Because he hadn't had the backbone was why; he had never told Marjorie the cause of his father's death, never breathed a word of what a sixteen-year-old lad had done, and he couldn't face the prospect of it ever coming into the open. The higher you climbed the ladder the more people you had waiting to push you off and a charge of murder wouldn't just topple Bruce Daniels, it would bury him.

Then if he was so worried about his past why hanker after promotion?

'Something moving, sir.'

Daniels allowed his glance to follow the direction of the plain-clothes man sat beside him, glad of the diversion that meant he need not answer that self-asked question.

'Should we move in?'

'No!' he answered sharply. 'And no one else better move afore my say-so or they'll find more than Gabriel's Hounds snapping at their balls!'

Silent once more he watched the tall dark-suited figure of a man come to the window of what he guessed to be an office and stand gazing down into the yard. The owner, a buyer for fake money or a genuine customer? There was no telling. Move in now and it could blow the whole thing. Christ, it was like a visit to the dentist, the wait was more nerve-wracking than the treatment! Automatically reaching into his pocket for the ever-present tablets he leaned towards the windscreen. The figure had moved from the window. The tablet forgotten, he watched the door at the top of a flight of steps begin to open.

'Cover!' he muttered, raising a newspaper to shield his face at the same moment his colleague ducked.

* * *

'What is it?' Her earlier bravado deserting her, Kate Mallory stared around the cellar as the swishing sound grew, heaving towards them like some great body.

'It's them, Gau and Crowley, they're here.' Torrey swallowed hard. If only he could have remembered that other stuff Martha Sim had used, oil of something or other and a couple of twigs. But he couldn't; candles, salt and water! He laughed silently. What good was that against Crowley?

Touching a little of the water remaining in the bottle to his fingers, Torrey turned to the woman stood beside him. It didn't matter what happened to him but Kate deserved none of it. Flicking the cool shining drops over her head he recited quickly: 'From the heart comes the love; from the water comes the cleansing, from the stone comes protection.'

'Torrey,' Kate's voice sounded scared, 'what do you think will happen?'

Overhead, footsteps sounded; firm and confident they crossed the floor, pausing at the trap door.

'I don't know, Kate.' Torrey's answer was low as he stared towards the opening. 'I honestly don't know, but for Heaven's sake don't step out of the circle.'

If only Crowley were an ordinary man! Torrey's hand clenched. But he was far from ordinary as he had shown at Whitefriars; he and Gau, neither of them was ordinary, they both had the devil at their backs.

'I had hoped it would not be this way—'

Soft as dark velvet the voice slid from the hatchway.

'– I had planned to make my gift at the celebration of Samhain.'

Fluid as water the words bathed each step.

'You were to be the offering made at the Grand Sabbat, but even the plans of a Magus must sometimes be adjusted. Though fear not, my friend, the Master will not refuse you and I have time enough to find another to offer on that great day.'

'Is it—'

A quick shake of Torrey's head cutting off the query, Kate stared to the opening through which slithered a soft menacing laugh.

'A second gift –' the voice changed instantly, becoming vicious then thickening like mucilage '– your generosity amazes me, Torrey, as it will please the Master.'

'Stay away, Crowley, you too Gau, your little game is finished. We know what you were hatching here and I tell you it's over.'

'No, Torrey, it is not over, the work of the Lord of the Earth must go on, that is why you and your friend must die.'

'You're too late!' Torrey whipped back. 'The police know all about your scam.'

'Scam!' Smiling, the tall figure stepped slowly down the few steps and walked to the centre of the room. 'I would hardly call what the Lord of Darkness plans for the world a scam.'

'The police know all about the arms and armaments sold by your companies.'

'And I know all about you!' Crowley snarled. 'Kate Mallory, insignificant little journalist who inveigled her way into Max Gau's office, but let's not worry about that, I know how to deal with a thief just as I know how to deal with the police.'

'Where is Gau?'

Eyes glittering like polished obsidian swung to Torrey. 'Max –' the velvet laugh reached sensuously across the dimly lit space '– I regret he will not be joining us, he proved . . . how can I phrase it . . . expendable.'

'You mean you killed him!'

'Regrettably . . . but yes, I speeded his departure.'

'And Fred Baker, that was no heart attack was it? That was your handiwork!'

'As you say . . . my handiwork.'

'You bastard! I'll do the same for you!'

Lunging forwards Torrey pulled himself back as he saw the black eyes flick to the edge of the salt circle.

'Why?' he breathed. 'Why did you kill Gau?'

From the edges of the room the rustling increased impatiently then fell silent as Crowley raised a hand.

'It was necessary,' the urbane softness went on, 'Gau was a fool, he balked at the thought of offering sacrifice.'

'You mean he refused to take part in murder . . . my murder.'

'Precisely, Torrey. But let us not call it murder, I much prefer the word gift.'

'Call it what you will, you insane bastard—'

'I said it was regrettable, Torrey.' Smooth as cream the words eased from a smiling mouth. 'But the work of my Master must take preference over all else.'

'Not to mention the desires of his minion!' Torrey's words spat out, bouncing back from the shadowed walls.

'Some leeway is allowed,' Crowley answered, 'but no follower of the Dark Lord can satisfy every personal wish; desirable as they may be they cannot be allowed to come before the interests of the One we serve.'

Cannot be allowed. Torrey felt the cold heat of anger drive through his veins. Were Crowley other than a servant of the devil with the devil's own powers he would take those words and shove 'em up the man's arse a syllable at a time. Now he knew that for Kate's sake he couldn't risk stepping beyond that ring of salt.

'By whose authority did Max Gau have to die, yours or the devil's?'

'Enough!' Crowley dismissed further argument. Eyes razor-sharp raked the figures standing across from him. 'You know why I am here, give those plates to me.'

'They are—'

'No, Kate!' Torrey spoke quickly. 'Don't let's spoil the show, let Crowley find them . . . after all he has the devil's help.'

'Then we must not refuse it.'

Crowley's eyes slitted and as he raised both hands above his head his breathing thickened.

'Retribution is taken for the Master, what is done by the servant is for his greater glory and his satisfaction.'

Shadows that hugged the walls moved slowly, drawing together into one vaporous cloud to envelop the figure that stood with arms raised.

Lowering his arms Crowley fastened his brilliant gaze on Torrey.

'Once the Bringer of Death is called he cannot return empty-handed.'

Grabbing Kate by the arm and pushing her behind him, Torrey took the laser stare full on.

'So call him,' he sneered, 'bogeymen don't frighten me any more, mine showed itself a year ago when it blew away half of a woman's face, you are going to have to go some to top that, Crowley.'

Perhaps if he could rile the man enough, get him to make a mistake, maybe drop his guard. But as the enveloping mist of shadow lifted, Torrey saw the venomous eyes flicker and darken. Crowley would not be distracted.

'Siras Etar Besanar—'

Crowley's hands lifted to chest height, the palms upturned in supplication.

'– Siras Etar Besanar, I call upon the Powers of Darkness, Zazas, Nasatanada, Zazas, open to me the Gates.'

What was the man doing? In the short space following the words Kate felt the silence quiver, then Crowley was speaking again.

'I conjure thee, Sammael and Ammon; I conjure thee, Egyn and Gmaymon, Keepers of the Hokmah Nistarah, the Hidden Wisdom; I conjure thee, the Benei Elohim to do my will.'

With the incantation, the breath seemed to gag in Torrey's

throat while a fierce current of energy dragged at his will, pulling him with it into some bottomless darkness until the bite of Kate's fingernails into the flesh of his arm brought him back.

'Hear me, thou Bornless One,' the slow monotone went on, 'for I am the servant of the Dark One, Lord of the Regions of Hell. Pass through the Gates, answer my summons.'

In Torrey's head the sound swelled, rolling his brain in spasms first of delight then of torture, his eyes riveted to the cloud now reforming in a dark nebulous mass. Behind him the candle flames lowered like a turned-down gas jet while the sound in his head grew, heaving itself out of that charcoal mist hurling around the room, the scream of its force spiralling into a great crescendo, reverberating off the walls with convulsive fury, each sound crashing back upon the other, scream weaving with scream to become one long frenzied ribbon. Behind him Kate Mallory whimpered in fear, her hand clutching tightly to his arm as the dark mass floating above Crowley's head began to take on form, moving, spreading, swirling tendrils of grey feathering into a figure from whose huge bestial head a great pair of eyes gleamed in the darkness like brilliant red lamps.

'See that which is done by the Lord of Darkness.'

Above Crowley's head the monstrous figure became more distinct, the huge eyes were flame-filled chasms.

'Torrey . . . Torrey, what is it?'

'Steady, Kate.' His hand closed tightly over hers. 'It's only a projection, Crowley has the power of hypnotism.'

It was a lie but at the moment he could think of nothing better. Kate had to stay on top of her fear.

Caught in the soft gleam of candle light the massive head began to sway. It can't take the light! Torrey felt the pulsing in his head fade, his brain clear as the dark amorphous shape withdrew, coiling into itself. Perhaps the light of the candles . . . perhaps the thing was beaten . . . but only yards away Crowley's eyes gleamed their black message . . . the message of death!

For a split second Torrey felt a stab of panic. Kate Mallory, would she die too? There was no doubt of it, Crowley had tasted the power of life and death, and the bastard liked it. The thought washed his brain, leaving it crystal clear. Across from him Crowley had seen that moment of weakness and laughed.

Torrey breathed hard. That was just the thing he needed; all the hate, all the rejection and all the loss that had been a part of his living surged and congealed into an all-fear-effacing need, the need to be respected.

'Great Lord of Darkness—'

Crowley began again, his suffocating gaze on the couple stood behind the barrier of salt.

'– before whom Ashtaroth, Belial and all Princes of the Throne of Hell must kneel, hear thy servant, send forth the Keeper of the Great Seal, send forth Ashmedai, Archangel of Vengeance that he may do thy will.'

Icy calm now, Torrey pushed Kate back from him, keeping his body in front of hers again. Crowley and his demon friends would have to go through him to get to her and Richard Torrey wasn't down yet.

For a long moment nothing moved in the room, Kate Mallory's rapid, frightened breaths the only sound until . . .

'Ashmedai, Messenger of the Most High, answer him who summons, deliver the Word of him whom you serve.'

Before the circle the vaporous cloud began to form anew, its dark presence widening, contracting, spreading itself on the air then coming slowly together, its outline shimmering yet definable, real but at the same time unreal . . . a man that was no man.

Handsome as the devil . . . appropriate! Torrey felt his own cold smile inside as Kate Mallory gasped.

Floating just clear of the ground a figure with an incredibly handsome face watched them, eyes of golden amber enticing, a full-lipped sensuous mouth smiling.

Barring Kate as she made to move towards the vision Torrey stared defiantly back at the beautiful face. It might have the looks of an angel but it was a demon of hell with all the power that went with the office, and it was there for him and for Kate, to take their lives. Just yards away the figure, beautiful in its nakedness, waited. Torrey knew it waited for him, waited to destroy him, but if death was coming for him it would find him looking nowhere but straight at it, ready to kick it in the teeth, not choke on its arse!

'You called me forth,' the handsome mouth moved, a voice like black music filling the room with dark sweetness, 'ask what you will, answer will be given.'

'People who play with fire often get their fingers burned,' Torrey heard himself laugh, 'you lit that one, Crowley, now let's see you put it out.'

Amorphic tendrils broke from the darkly beautiful form and drifted menacingly towards the roughly drawn circle, testing, searching, reaching for a way inside, only to recoil as its opalescent coils touched the salt.

'You should hurry, Crowley, your friend seems to be getting restless.'

Taunts could only buy him moments. Torrey stared resolutely at those wonderful, compelling eyes. But moments, no matter how small, were valuable. Think! he told himself. What would Martha Sim do?

*'Listen to your heart . . . the words will come.'*

The words the old woman had used seemed suddenly to fill his mind, blanking out all else.

*'the words will come'*

Behind him Kate tried to push her way past, drawn irresistibly towards that floating figure. Holding her, he saw it draw sharply back as the soft glow of the candle light she had blocked fell across it.

'Light of the holy candle show thy way.'

It was almost as if Martha herself spoke the words pushing their way into his mind.

'Ashmedai, fulfil the Word!' The call was sharp. Crowley had seen the dim flicker of realisation cross Torrey's face.

He had no time to reason with Kate, it would likely do no good if he tried, she was straining to get to that thing, too absorbed by its seduction to listen to anything else.

With his eyes still fastened to those that gleamed golden he dragged her backwards until his spine touched the workbench. One hand reaching behind him he snatched up a candle, thrusting it towards the spectre. What was good for the goose was likewise for the gander. Opposites attract. He laughed again, this time to himself. Maybe they could also destroy!

His fingers clenched hard about the slim candle as he thrust it a little further forwards. That thing, whatever it was, drew back, retreating from the glow like flames from water.

Flames from water! Inside the barrier of salt the drops of water he had sprinkled had not yet dried in the damp atmosphere of the cellar and now they caught the gleam of candle light, sparkling together with crystals of salt like a myriad tiny stars.

*'From the water comes the cleansing.'*

The line of the ritual he had remembered and had spoken earlier returned, throbbing in his brain, ordering, demanding, exacting its will upon his. Was this it . . . was this the way? Flames from water! Not really aware of the action that followed the thought he thrust Kate from him, unmindful of the cry of pain as she stumbled awkwardly then fell, hitting her head against the workbench.

But the evil, watchful as before, saw the hand that fell outside the circle scattering the salt, breaking its protection. A smile spreading across its magnificent features, it raised a hand, the fingers stretching like dusky gold snakes, slithering towards the half-conscious Kate.

*'From the water comes the cleansing.'*

The insistent tattoo beat like a drum in his brain. Water . . . he had taken water from the font in that church, water blessed for baptism . . . holy water! His hand at one with the thought he grabbed the bottle, flinging the remnants of its contents full at the slithering fingers.

A scream like that of something scalded echoed about the dimly lit room, sliding its pain around the shadowed walls, spinning it over machines and benches as the serpent tendrils withdrew, being absorbed once more into the shimmering figure, the smile gone from the handsome face, leaving the eyes glistening, amber evil . . . an evil that stared at Torrey.

It had only partly worked. The water had repelled but not defeated, that thing would try again. It had only to wait them out. He glanced at Kate, drawing her away from the salt, closing the gap her hand had made. They couldn't sit here indefinitely, she was already under its influence, given a smile and that being from hell would have her safe in its pocket. He had to get her out . . . somehow or other he must get Kate Mallory away from this cellar.

His eyes on that dark, golden phantom he called to a smiling Crowley. 'I'll make a bargain with you. Let the woman go, swear on the name of the God you follow that no harm will come to her and once she is clear of the building I'll step outside this circle.'

'Bargain!' The answering laugh was hard. 'Dead men are in no position to bargain and you, Torrey, are a dead man.'

Frustration welled high in Torrey's throat. Christ, if only he could get his hands on that bastard then the devil and all his demons wouldn't save him!

'Why take her?' He tried again. 'You don't need her, let her go and I'll step out . . . no more trouble.'

Shadowed by the figure lambent as burnished gold, Crowley's dark eyes gleamed their victory.

'You are correct, Richard, I do not need her, but a good

servant is ever mindful of his master. Kate Mallory is a mere triviality but the Prince of Darkness appreciates any gift his follower offers, no matter how insignificant; as for you . . . you are not giving trouble, merely enjoyment, but I must not indulge my pleasures any longer.' Raising both hands he called loudly.

'Hear me, Messenger of the Dark One, fulfil that which has been proclaimed, take the sacrifice.'

For fully a minute nothing happened, only the shadows leaping from the touch of pale candle flame danced about the walls.

Then the beautiful shimmering figure began to move, its great luminescent eyes fixed unblinkingly on Torrey. Spears of golden darkness sheared to right and left of its graceful body as it floated towards him, leaving trails of iridescent mist swirling behind like transparent snakes. Around and behind they drifted and with their coming was the rank smell of rotting flesh.

Across the cellar Torrey tried not to breathe, tried to hold the putrid foulness from his throat while one hand drew Kate close against him, the other holding tight to the lighted candle.

*'Listen to your heart . . . the words will come.'*

It seemed Martha's gentle old voice spoke outside himself. But the words wouldn't come . . . he didn't know any! Held in the crook of his arm Kate turned her head to the lovely god-like face and, reaching a hand to it, struggled to free herself.

He hadn't prayed since being a child, he had given all that up once his mother gave up sitting on his bed to listen. What good were prayers? Kate struggled again, crying out in the need that possessed her. Torrey looked at the glistening figure hovering at the brink of the circle. Maybe prayer would do no good, maybe it was too late for that . . . but what else did he have?

Staring straight into the vivid eyes he held the candle above his head, his voice strong and clear: 'Our Father, who are in Heaven, Hallowed by thy name . . .'

With the first words of the prayer the candle flared into

brilliant jets of white flame, a great aurora of light more brilliant than the light of day, a radiance so intense it wrapped them both like an iridescent cellophane, and with it came an elation that throbbed in Torrey like a living thing, singing along his nerves like high-voltage electricity. He didn't know the source of the power that surged in him, whether it was real or simply a reaction to over-stretched nerves and right now he didn't care, he could feel the effect of it lifting him, carrying him high and that was enough; questions, supposing he had any, and supposing he made it to another day, could come then.

Bathed in that wonderful light it seemed his mind was suddenly freed of the long-held repudiation of the power of prayer.

Softly now, no more than a whisper between God and himself, the words rose from the deepest reaches of his heart.

'Lord God, Creator of all things, may the light of thy mercy shine upon us, the strength of thy hand protect us, the power of thy love deliver us.'

With each murmur the light surrounding them expanded; ivory, alabaster, silver whirling together in a blinding intensity.

The smile faded from the golden face, replaced by a look radiant in its hatred.

'Hear me, Ashmedai, Highest of the Angels of Darkness, Destroyer of Life.' Crowley's laugh had died in his throat and now his voice trembled. 'I, the servant of the Great One, command you. Place the kiss of death upon him you were summoned to bring to the Master.'

Slowly the figure turned and as its glittering eyes fastened on Crowley the gold of it became grey as lead. One hand lifted and bolt after bolt of brilliant blue-black flame burst from snake-like fingers, splintering into a myriad serpents that flicked their fork-tipped tongues at the terrified magician.

'You have failed the Master—'

The voice that had been silken velvet was now hard and sharp as a rasp, seeming to slash with every word while flashes of forked light leapt from the extended hand, the flesh they touched beginning to burn.

'– for that you must pay—'

Caught in the dark gleam of the creature he had called forth, Crowley's features were a mask of terror, his hands and face scorched and blistered as if touched by a branding iron. Screaming now he stared at bubbling, carbonised flesh, bits cauterising together as they dropped from the bone.

The reek of burning flesh filling lungs forced to breathe, Torrey pressed a hand to Kate's head as she screamed, holding her face close into his shoulder so she would not see the horror, but his own eyes he could not turn away. Almost mesmerised, he watched wisps of smoke curl upwards from searing flesh, heard the terrible voice that rose over Crowley's screams as a finger of black light touched his brow, burning in the mark of the seal he had seen on Penny Smith's arm.

'– your powers are stripped from you, but the soul that was exchanged for them remains forfeit; you have tasted the vengeance of the Great Lord of Darkness, the vengeance of him to whom that soul belongs, a soul he will claim. But before he brings you to kneel at the Throne you will suffer the vengeance of man.'

'No . . . o . . . o . . .'

Crowley's scream rang from him but the figure turned away, its earlier brilliance now dark and vaporous, the flaming eyes glittering malevolence as it floated once more towards the circle of salt. A yard from the rim it paused.

Hovering just beyond the fall of that intense white light the vaporous mouth smiled and one mist-formed hand lifted.

'Katherine—'

It was a breath, a whisper on the silence but with its coming Kate lifted her head, turning her face to a figure that shimmered and changed, dark grey to silver, then pale lemon until finally it assumed its previous aureole burnished gold, and the silken velvet voice rang like a great bell.

'Katherine—'

The beautiful mouth smiled, the gleaming saffron-gold eyes burning into Kate's.

'I am Ashmedai, Keeper of the Great Seal, Highest of the High Angels of the Dark Throne and you, Katherine, are my chosen consort. Come to me.'

'Yes . . . yes . . .' It sobbed from her as she reached for that golden hand.

'Kate!' Torrey held on. 'Kate, it's not real, it's a trick, for God's sake, Kate . . .'

But Kate Mallory was beyond listening. Eyes flaming with the need to break free lifted momentarily to Torrey's face then her teeth sank into the hand that held her.

'Come to me, Katherine –' wonderful in its beauty the Messenger smiled at her '– be with me for all eternity.'

Shock of the bite releasing Torrey's fingers he saw her reach for the hand and the glow of triumph in the golden stare that reached for him. Crowley had won despite himself, this thing from hell would take him . . . but not Kate . . . it wouldn't take Kate, he wouldn't let it! Reaching out he caught the collar of her coat, snatching her hard off her feet. His own voice firm and steady, he faced the floating menace.

'In the name of God, I defy you and your Master, and in His name I place my trust.'

Across the circle the golden smile dropped away, virulent rage twisting the perfect features, snake-tipped fingers reaching out.

Torrey lifted his head in defiance, the rest of his words a soft echo of his prayer: 'Our Father in Heaven . . . deliver us from evil.'

Almost as the words left his lips a great swell of sound, a music that was no music, filled the room and the brilliant light that had surrounded them lifted, rising above their heads, the low ceiling no barrier to its ascent.

Steady again on her feet, Kate Mallory felt the hold on her mind snap away. 'Torrey.' She gripped tight to the arm she had bitten. 'Torrey . . . for God's sake, what's going on?'

Taking her in his arms he made no attempt to answer, how could he when he had no idea himself.

In the shadowed far corner of the room Julian Crowley sobbed openly then gasped as the great spinning vortex of white began to spread, wide . . . wider, going beyond walls that were no hindrance, past ceilings that might not have existed, its indescribable light enclosing everything beneath it. Then, as it seemed to encompass the earth itself, the outer edges contracted, coming together, taking on shape while its centre increased to a brilliance that stung the eyes.

Unable to look away Torrey felt his eyeballs burn as he stared at the great, shining silver-pearl figure, two great wings shimmering like frosted snow.

Slowly, like some wonderful pure white lily, a hand lifted, pointing at the devil's advocate, and in that same instant a voice rang out.

# Chapter Twenty-Eight

'I couldn't believe it . . . and I still don't.' Kate Mallory twisted the coffee mug in her hands.

'Believe it or not, it happened.' And you don't know how close you came to becoming the bride of Beelzebub! Torrey kept the last to himself.

'Thank God Daniels came when he did.'

Adding sugar to his coffee Torrey watched the creamy circles spin as he stirred. Thank God for a lot of things.

'Torrey –' her brown eyes reflecting her uncertainty, Kate looked across Annie's kitchen table '– did I see what I thought I saw? I mean the way Crowley burned yet there was no mark anywhere except on his brow . . . so how—'

'I told you, Kate, Crowley is an accomplished hypnotist.'

'Mmm.' She accepted the answer, only half believing it. 'But not a good enough one to hypnotise that judge, fifteen years . . . Lord, I almost pity him.'

'Not me!' The reply was sharp. 'To my way of thinking the key to his cell should be thrown away. When I think of what he tried to do . . .'

'Well thanks to Fred it didn't come off.'

'And thanks to you, Kate, let's not forget that. If it hadn't been for you bringing those plates to the works then Daniels could well have had no case.'

'But he has, and I've got the scoop of the year, do you think I might celebrate with a tab?'

'Why not?' Torrey grinned. 'You can always get a room at my doss when Annie throws you out for smoking in her kitchen.'

'No thanks.' Her tip-tilted mouth lifting, she returned the grin. Then suddenly serious, she added, 'It was a terrible thing Crowley was planning, and for what . . . what did he stand to gain . . . surely no amount of money was worth that!'

'It wasn't money, it was power, power on earth and a throne of his own in hell.'

'He's welcome to it,' Kate sipped the hot coffee, 'and I think he'll have plenty of experience of that place long before he arrives there, prisons are not the easiest places to live, and speaking of prisons what happened to that sheikh . . . why was he not prosecuted?'

'It's called diplomatic immunity but in reality it's a case of you scratch my back and I'll scratch yours. It's my guess the government might have had their eye on him for some time but with this country wanting their oil then it has to turn a blind eye to the luggage of its ambassadors.'

'I didn't know Sheikh Hamed el Wotsit was an ambassador!'

'He isn't as such,' Torrey answered, 'but he is a prince of the ruling house and that carries the same perks, if not more. He comes to Britain several times a year seemingly to buy gowns et cetera for the many women of his house. Many women equals a lot of boxes from the House of Jarreaux and with each one hiding several layers of counterfeit money, getting it out of the country was no problem, but as the National Security Team told Daniels when they took over, being who he is won't save Khadja's skin back in his own country. They won't be able to take the slightest risk of appearing involved in his capers whether they are or not; a breath of what they had planned reaching the ears of the rest of the Arab Emirates and their balloon would be popped but good!'

'That's something else bugs me.' Kate gathered the empty mugs, rinsing them briskly at the sink. 'The way those National Security bods just sail in and take everything out of Daniels's hands.'

'It was bigger than it looked, Kate.' He smiled, amused at the defensive fury in her eyes . . . was it only two days ago she was condemning Daniels for being so tight-lipped? 'That department had to be called in and even they had to join forces with International Security, there were too many countries threatened for us to go it alone.'

'And that, I suppose, is why I had to sit on my story until it almost choked me!'

The lady was brewing again. Torrey hid his grin. She had seethed every moment of those weeks it had taken to wipe out Khadja's little plan and to get the United Nations to 'accidentally' uncover the stacks of weapons of war, fretted that one of the nationals would get wind of what was going on and break with the story before she did. But true to his word the inspector had kept the lid hard down, somehow managing to arrange with the government departments they do the same.

'Why not have that tab?' He suggested the usual panacea to Kate's irascibility.

Placing the mugs on to their hooks on Annie's pine dresser she turned, leaning her slim hips against it.

'Frying Pan?'

'Unless you have some other place in mind.'

Kate's tilted grin returned. 'Throw in a lager and lime and I'll get my coat.'

* * *

*'Well done, Daniels, that is another one for the force.'*

Inspector Bruce Daniels brought his foot down on the accelerator of the blue Ford estate car his wife's legacy had paid for, the words of his superior drumming in his brain.

*'The boys from the Ministry might have done the mopping up but the kiss was ours.'*

Ours! He swallowed, grimacing as the sour taste of bile flooded past his throat. Where did the bloody 'ours' come in? What part had that swarmy git Quinto played, how many hours had his arse been glued to a chair sorting out that raid? What part had the Chief Detective Inspector deigned to play? What part did he have the brain to play . . . if wit was shit the man would be constipated!

Swinging the car around the traffic island, Daniels submerged the accusation beneath a welter of bitterness. True, he hadn't told Quinto all he could have told, but do that and the self-important prat would have been in faster than a ferret down a rabbit hole, and left just as much mess behind him; but what had all the effort brought Daniels? Turning into the forecourt of the Frying Pan he switched off the engine, staring at the shadowed building. The kill had been his . . . the credit was Martin Quinto's! It took no guessing to see whose shoulders the gold braid would land on!

Looks like the man has just been face-to-face with his own particular demon! Glancing up as Daniels entered the crowded lounge bar, Torrey felt a stab of sympathy. The inspector wasn't exactly top of the list of the world's most charming people but he deserved more than a kick in the teeth, which was what he'd got from the media; there was more to be milked from the top brass; only the *Star* had paid him full due.

'Do you mind, Kate, if I invite him over?'

'Not at all.' Sherry-brown curls gleamed as she shook her head. 'I'll even stand the man a pint.'

'Thanks.' Daniels nodded as the glass was set in front of him at their table. 'And thanks again for your tip-off, if it hadn't been for you, young woman, the world would soon have been in a sorrier state than it is now.'

Torrey shook his head slowly. 'I wonder if Fred knew the full extent of what was going on.'

'Of the counterfeiting maybe,' Daniels answered, 'but not the reason behind it. I can't see Baker being in agreement with that.'

'He wouldn't have been!' Kate answered dogmatically. 'That is why—' Catching the swift warning in Torrey's glance she broke off, they had both agreed to say nothing of the black magic and the events that took place in that cellar prior to the arrival of Daniels and his uniformed constables.

'Why what?' Daniels's keen gaze had missed nothing.

Her recovery admirable, Kate's tip-tilted mouth smiled, 'Why he sent those plates to the *Star*.'

They hadn't been sent to the *Star*. Daniels had seen the address on that parcel, but raking ashes never built a fire. He took a swallow from his glass. He wouldn't go over that now.

'We all have a lot to thank Fred Baker for,' Torrey said.

Including Martin Quinto! The thought bringing as much acid as the ale surging into his mouth, Daniels took a tablet from the carton nestled in his pocket.

'Just about all of the Middle East,' Torrey added even now finding it difficult to come to terms with the sheer magnitude of it all.

'The Middle East,' Daniels echoed. 'They fight with fanatical fury over land that's little more than stone and desert, bringing everything to ruin by years of war, Arab against Arab, Arab against Jew, and given Crowley's help it would have been the world. Khadja had worked secretly for years with Crowley and his associates, that last order for Emissary planes and missiles was only the cherry on a very large cake; his boss, Ibn Qasim, had been stockpiling, it seems. The United Nations reps found caves full of every kind of weapon including those for germ warfare. He wanted the whole of the Middle East and he was willing to pay for it.'

'And he found the perfect way to do it.'

'Khadja and Qasim,' Daniels nodded, 'together they made a pretty brainy pair.'

'Brainy, yes,' Kate smiled, 'as for the looks . . . I pass!'

'It was quite a scheme.' Daniels sucked hard on the tablet. 'Everything that benighted country needs apart from oil has to be purchased from others and that's where the truly clever part comes in. Apart from those Israeli shekel plates you brought in, Security unearthed Jordanian, Bahranian, Democratic Republic of Yemen, Iraqi and Kuwaiti dinar plates; Saudi Arabian, Qatar and Yemeni Arab Republic rial plates, as well as those for printing Syrian and Lebanese pounds. Qasim was having phony money produced ready to pass to each country. He knew Arabs are a naturally mistrustful breed, they like to have payment in the hand rather than in a bank; gold or paper money they can hold, cheques are something Westerners wipe their backsides on. Qasim counted on this. He would pay whatever was asked by those slipping goods past the embargo, but he would pay in dud money. By the time his little ruse came to light each country would have accused another of passing counterfeit money and with them at each other's throats he moves in with his planes and tanks and a third of the world fights itself into extinction, leaving one man with what he wanted.'

Not just one man. Torrey listened in silence, his own thoughts running ahead. The devil too would have had what he wanted.

'But thanks to Kate Mallory, Khadja's plan became unstuck.' Daniels lifted his glass to Kate. 'And not only his, but Crowley's as well. Once we found counterfeit notes *and* the rest of those plates at Whitefriars, there was no way he could work his way out. I hope your editor gives you the credit you deserve.'

'Scotty was delighted.'

So was Quinto! Daniels emptied his glass. Tomorrow he would suffer for drinking, but tomorrow was still a long way off. Fetching his round from the bar he settled again at the table.

'I suppose Crowley had come looking for the plates Fred Baker took but why the look on his face? It was the same as I saw on that old man's corpse; if I was a superstitious man I'd say something had frightened the sh—the wits out of Crowley. Just what did happen in that cellar?'

'We told you.'

'Yes, you told me.' Daniels looked from one to the other. 'But I'd lay a year's wages to a penny you didn't tell it all. Crowley was more than scared, he was terrified . . . why?'

'Beats me!' Torrey shrugged. 'P'raps the man is afraid of rats, maybe he saw one when he was rummaging about for those plates.'

'And maybe you think I be a mental tourist!' Daniels answered quickly. 'You think that following the lead you gave my mind will wander from the question; but it won't. I've seen two men with faces showing the kind of fear only a vision from hell could instil and I intend finding out its cause.'

'Well if anything scared him it didn't scare him in that cellar.' Torrey avoided looking at Kate who was now pretending her attention was on lighting another cigarette.

'No!' Daniels ran his sharp glance over both faces. 'Yet the two of you looked pretty shook up when we came in; why was that, Torrey? Crowley had no gun and there were no bully boys with him, so why did the two of you look so shook up?'

Don't let Kate answer, one word about that thing Crowley had conjured and Daniels was still likely to call in the white-coat brigade. A smile touching his mouth, Torrey answered, 'Not shook up, Inspector . . . cut up, we were both depressed at the death of a friend.'

'You need to practise, Torrey.' Daniels got to his feet. 'You don't yet have the knack of convincing me you're telling the whole truth and nothing but the truth. One thing, though. Whatever put the wind up Crowley, it wasn't a hiding. We had the quack give him a thorough going over and there wasn't a mark on his body, apart from what looked like a bruise on his forehead. Strange, that!' He tapped a hand to the pocket that held keys and tablets. 'I ain't seen a bruise like that before . . . funny shape . . . almost like a seal, as if he'd been branded.'

'Phew!' Kate breathed a noisy stream of smoke through her teeth as the inspector left. 'He never gives up does he?'

'He's a good cop.' Torrey watched the door close behind the other man. 'Pity he doesn't get the recognition.'

'That might be worth investigating.'

'You keep your nose out of the man's affairs unless you want it considerably re-shaped!'

Her brown eyes glinting with mischief, Kate grinned. 'You have to admit it would be much cheaper than cosmetic surgery, but then mebbe's I'll keep to the nose me mam gave me.'

Comfortable in each other's company, neither spoke again for some minutes, then screwing the end of her cigarette into the ashtray, Kate said thoughtfully, 'Do you think you will see any more of your girl in white?'

'No.' Torrey shook his head. 'No, I think Penny Smith achieved what she came for.'

'Help for herself?'

Torrey's glance turned again to the door that gave on to the forecourt of the pub and the hint of a smile curved his strong mouth as a faint, almost undiscernbile whiteness formed in its shadow.

'No, Kate, not for herself,' he said softly, 'I think what she asked was help in saving Fred; somehow or other she knew what was to happen.'

'That Crowley would kill him?'

Eyes still on the faint outline of white, Torrey shook his head.

'More than that. Don't ask me how but I feel she knew Crowley would try to terrify Fred into becoming tied to the devil, to fall in with more than printing counterfeit money, but she couldn't prevent it on her own.'

'And so she came to you and you didn't turn your back.'

'Huh!' He held the half-laugh in his throat. 'I certainly did my best to try.'

'That was because you didn't understand.'

Was it? Had he truly wanted to help Penny Smith? Lord, who would have thought he could ever ask himself such a question! Torrey, the man who didn't believe in ghosts, was now asking himself had he really helped one. Maybe he had, but not in the way he would have wished. Crowley had set that sign on the girl, only a transfer, yes, but she had died with it on her arm, the Seal of Ashmedai, and it marked her as the devil's own and he could not save her from that.

'Torrey . . .'

The word whispered over the buzz of conversation while in the shadowed alcove of the doorway the pale, almost translucent mist that hovered like a thin gauzy cloud suddenly shimmered into the radiant glistening figure of a girl.

'Torrey . . .'

The smiling mouth moved and a finger touched the arm where once a transfer had stained it, but now it was clear and bright as the rest.

'Thank you.'

Across from him the figure faded, leaving the alcove a shallow well of grey shadow.

'You didn't understand,' Kate repeated, reaching for his hand then withdrawing it as his dark eyes swung to her. 'Once it became clear to you then nothing – not even a certain Messenger – could turn you back. You know, Torrey,' she smiled, 'me mam would have called you a canny lad . . . and you know something else? I agree with her.'

LB